I'm Tracy Beaker.
This is a book
all about me.
I'd read it if
I were you.

Wow, three whole stories devoted to ME, Tracy Beaker Superstar. Read THE STORY OF TRACY BEAKER, STARRING TRACY BEAKER and THE DARE GAME to find out exactly why I'm destined to be a Great Inventor of Extremely Outrageous Dares, a Future Glamorous Hollywood Actress, Successful Writer and Star Football Player.

But that's not all! Before you read my incredible, dynamic, heart-rending story, marvel at a fact file totally devoted to yours truly! I've written down my thoughts on family, friends, school and food, given you my Top 10 Loves (mmm, Big Macs and french fries!) and Top 10 Horrible Hates, plus some tips and mottoes to use whenever life gets tough. Oh, and I've generously allowed the writer of the books, Jacqueline Wilson, and the illustrator, Nick Sharratt, to get in on the act too . . .

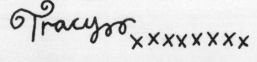

Tracy xxxxxxx

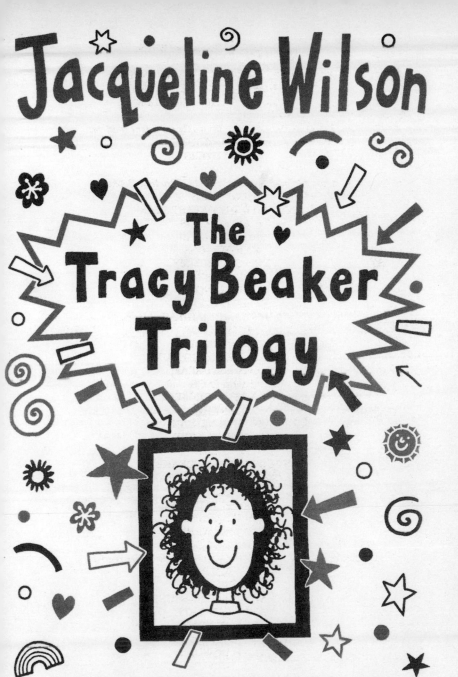

Jacqueline Wilson

The Tracy Beaker Trilogy

Incorporating THE STORY OF TRACY BEAKER,
STARRING TRACY BEAKER and THE DARE GAME

Illustrated by Nick Sharratt

DOUBLEDAY

THE TRACY BEAKER TRILOGY
A DOUBLEDAY BOOK 978 0 385 61611 9

This collection first published in Great Britain by Doubleday,
an imprint of Random House Children's Books
A Random House Group Company

This edition published 2008

1 3 5 7 9 10 8 6 4 2

Copyright in this edition © Jacqueline Wilson, 2008

THE STORY OF TRACY BEAKER
Copyright © Jacqueline Wilson, 1991
Illustrations copyright © Nick Sharratt, 1991

STARRING TRACY BEAKER
Copyright © Jacqueline Wilson, 2006
Illustrations copyright © Nick Sharratt, 2006

THE DARE GAME
Copyright © Jacqueline Wilson, 2000
Illustrations copyright © Nick Sharratt, 2000

The Random House Group Limited makes every effort to ensure that
the papers used in its books are made from trees that have been legally sourced
from well-managed and credibly certified forests. Our paper procurement
policy can be found at: www.randomhouse.co.uk/paper.htm

Mixed Sources
Product group from well-managed
forests and other controlled sources
www.fsc.org Cert no. TT-COC-2139
© 1996 Forest Stewardship Council

FSC

RANDOM HOUSE CHILDREN'S BOOKS
61–63 Uxbridge Road, London W5 5SA

www.kidsatrandomhouse.co.uk
www.rbooks.co.uk

Addresses for companies within The Random House Group Limited
can be found at: www.randomhouse.co.uk/offices.htm

THE RANDOM HOUSE GROUP Limited Reg. No. 954009

A CIP catalogue record for this book is available from the British Library.

Printed and bound in Great Britain by Clays Ltd, St Ives plc

Tracy's Thoughts on Friends

Obviously I'm incredibly popular and have had my pick of best friends, but since Justine Pain-in-the-Bum Littlewood stole Louise away, I haven't actually got one RIGHT NOW. Weedy Peter follows me around like a bad smell, but he doesn't count.

Here are all the people who I live with at the Dumping Ground, very artistically portrayed by me:

Tracy's Thoughts on School

My school in THE STORY OF TRACY BEAKER is called Kinglea Junior School and obviously I am a model pupil and top of every class. Er, well I think I'm good at story-writing. And art. I'm not so good at arithmetic and, according to Miss Brown, paying attention.

In STARRING TRACY BEAKER I have a special art and drama teacher called Miss Simpkins. She's evidently very clever and perceptive, as she called me 'a very lively and imaginative girl', and cast me in the school production of . . . you'll have to read the story to find out!

Tracy's Thoughts on Food

Birthday cake is my absolute favourite food.

But I also like (deep breath): other kinds of cake, Big Macs and french fries with strawberry milkshake, Smarties, Cornettos and all other sweets. Also Mike's spaghetti bolognese always cheers me up when I'm sad.

Here are my Top 10 Loves

1 Going to McDonald's.

2 Acting in the school play and having everyone applaud me.

HURRAY!

THE GREATEST PERFORMANCE EVER!

WELL DONE TRACY!

MAGNIFICENT!

A TRUE STAR IS BORN!

3 Playing with make-up! I'm particularly good at the natural look.

4 Horror films – the scarier the better!

5 The presents my mum sends me, like Bluebell the doll.

6 Playing football.

7 Dogs – especially Rottweilers!

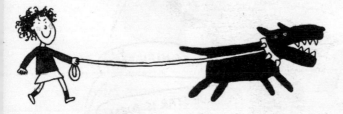

8 Story-writing. Cam gives me a few tips – not that I need them.

9 Getting a gold star at school. This is quite rare.

10 The colour red – BLOOD red, to be precise.

And here are my Top 10 Horrible Hates:

1 My mum's ex-boyfriend the Monster Gorilla. He's the reason I'm in care.

2 Justine Littlewood. She deserves a bop on the nose.

3 My mum not turning up when she's PROMISED she would. This happens a lot.

4 Getting into trouble at school when it's totally not my fault.

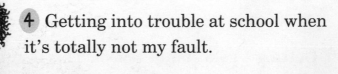

5 Being laughed at: it makes me angry and I explode like a firework.

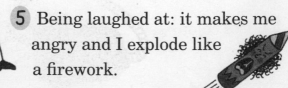

6 Not having enough money for designer clothes.

7 The lumpy stew like molten sick one of my foster mothers used to make me. YUCK.

8 My hair, which is not long and fair but instead is dark and difficult and sticks up in all the wrong places.

9 Having to clean the Dumping Ground as punishment.

10 Weedy Peter following me round all the time.

Jacky on Tracy

Tracy Beaker is by far the most popular of all the characters I've ever invented. [I KNEW it! – Tracy] She must be glorying in the fact that there are now three books about her, a very popular long-running television series, a magazine, a musical, and all sorts of merchandising, from pyjamas to pillow cases!

I got the idea for THE STORY OF TRACY BEAKER from seeing photos of children in care in my local paper, all longing to be fostered. I looked at those touching pictures and wondered what it would be like to be advertised in that way. It would be great if you found brilliant foster parents as a result, but how would you feel if no one at all came forward to meet you? I decided to write a story about a tough feisty little girl in a children's home who gets advertised like this.

I knew almost straight away that I was going to call her Tracy. It seemed a perfect modern street-wise bouncy sort of name. I had problems finding a suitable surname. I was thinking about it when I was lolling in my bath one morning. I peered all round the steamy room for some kind of inspiration. There aren't a lot of possibilities in the average bathroom! I wondered about Tracy Flannel, Tracy Soap, Tracy Tap, Tracy Toothbrush, Tracy Toilet – and decided I'd never ever find a sensible surname that way. I got on with washing my hair and then reached for the old plastic Snoopy beaker I kept on the side of the bath to rinse all the shampoo away. I stared at it. Tracy Beaker? Yes, I had the right name at last.

Jacqueline Wilson

x x x

The Story of Tracy Beaker

Jacqueline Wilson

Illustrated by Nick Sharratt

To Bryony, David, Miranda, Jason and Ryan

My Book About Me

ABOUT ME

My name is Tracy Beaker

I am 10 **years** 2 **months old**.

My birthday is on 8 May. It's not fair, because that dopey Peter Ingham has his birthday then too, so we just got the one cake between us. And we had to hold the knife to cut the cake together. Which meant we only had half a wish each. Wishing is for babies anyway. They don't come true.

I was born at some hospital somewhere. I looked cute when I was a little baby but I bet I yelled a lot.

I am   **cms tall**. I don't know. I've tried measuring with a ruler but it keeps wobbling about and I can't reach properly. I don't want to get any of the other children to help me. This is my private book.

I weigh   **kgs**. I don't know that either. Jenny has got scales in her bathroom but they're stones and pounds. I don't weigh many of them. I'm a little titch.

My eyes are   black and I can make them go all wicked and witchy. I quite fancy being a witch. I'd make up all these incredibly evil spells and wave my wand and ZAP Louise's golden curls would all fall out and ZAP Peter Ingham's silly squeaky voice would get sillier and squeakier and he'd grow whiskers and a long tail and ZAP . . . there's not room on this bit of the page, but I've still got all sorts of ZAPs inside my head.

My hair is fair and very long and curly. I am telling fibs. It's dark and difficult and it sticks up in all the wrong places.

My skin is spotty when I eat a lot of sweets.

Stick a photo of yourself here

I'm not really cross-eyed. I was just pulling a silly face.

I **started this book on** I don't know. Who cares what the date is? You always have to put the date at school. I got fed up with this and put 2091 in my Day Book and wrote about all these rockets and space ships and monsters legging it down from Mars to eat us all up, as if we'd all whizzed one hundred years into the future. Miss Brown didn't half get narked.

MORE THINGS ABOUT ME

Things I like

My lucky number is 7. So why didn't I get fostered by some fantastic rich family when I was seven then?

My favourite colour is blood red, so watch out, ha-ha.

My best friend is   Well, I've had heaps and heaps, but Louise has gone off with Justine and now I haven't got anyone just at the moment.

I like eating   everything. I like birthday cake best. And any other kind of cake. And Smarties and Mars Bars and big buckets of popcorn and jelly spiders and Cornettos and Big Macs with french fries and strawberry milk shakes.

My favourite name is   Camilla. There was a lovely little baby at this other home and that was her name. She was a really sweet kid with fantastic hair that I used to try to get into loads of little plaits and it must have hurt her sometimes but she never cried. She really liked me, little Camilla. She got fostered quick as a wink. I begged her foster mum and dad to bring her back to see me but they never did.

I like drinking pints of bitter. That's a joke. I *have* had a sip of lager once but I didn't like it.

My favourite game is playing with make-up. Louise and I once borrowed some from Adele who's got heaps. Louise was a bit boring and just tried to make herself look beautiful. I turned myself into an incredible vampire with evil shadowy eyes and blood dribbling down my chin. I didn't half scare the little ones.

My favourite animal is Well, there's a rabbit called Lettuce at this home but it's a bit limp, like its name. It doesn't sit up and give you a friendly lick like a dog. I think I'd like a Rottweiler – and then all my enemies had better WATCH OUT.

My favourite TV programme is horror films.

Best of all I like being with my mum.

Things I don't like

the name Justine. Louise. Peter. Oh there's heaps and heaps of names I can't stand.

eating stew. Especially when it's got great fatty lumps in it. I used to have this horrid foster mother called Aunty Peggy and she was an awful cook. She used to make this slimy stew like molten sick and we were supposed to eat it all up, every single bit. Yuck.

Most of all I hate Justine. That Monster Gorilla. And not seeing my mum.

MY OWN FAMILY

Stick a photo of you and your family here

This was when I was a baby. See, I was sweet then. And this is my mum. She's ever so pretty. I wish I looked more like her.

The people in my own family are My mum. I don't have a dad. I lived with my mum when I was little and we got on great but then she got this Monster Gorilla Boyfriend and I hated him and he hated me back and beat me up and so I had to be taken into care. No wonder my mum sent him packing.

My own family live at I'm not sure exactly where my mum lives now because she has to keep moving about because she gets fed up living in one place for long.

The phone number is Well, I don't know, do I? Funny though, I always used to bag this toy telephone in the playhouse at school and pretend I was phoning my mum. I used to have these long long conversations with her. They were just pretend of course, but I was only about five then and sometimes it got to be quite real.

Things about my family that I like I like my mum because she's pretty and good fun and she brings me lovely presents.

MY FOSTER FAMILY

There's no point filling this bit in. I haven't got a foster family at the moment.

I've had two. There was Aunty Peggy and Uncle Sid first of all. I didn't like them much and I didn't get on with the other kids so I didn't care when they got rid of me. I was in a children's home for a while and then I had this other couple. Julie and Ted. They were young and friendly and they bought me a bike and I thought it was all going to be great and I went to live with them and I was ever so good and did everything they said and I thought I'd be staying with them until my mum came to get me for good but then . . . I don't want to write about it. It ended up with me getting turfed out THROUGH NO FAULT OF MY OWN. I was so mad I smashed up the bike so I don't even have that any more. And now I'm in a new children's home and they've advertised me in the papers but there weren't many takers and now I think they're getting a bit desperate. I don't care though. I expect my mum will come soon anyway.

MY SCHOOL

My school is called It's Kinglea Junior School. I've been to three other schools already. This one's OK I suppose.

My teacher is called Miss Brown. She gets cross if we just call her Miss.

Subjects I do Story-writing. Arithmetic. Games. Art. All sorts of things. And we do Projects only I never have the right stuff at the Home so I can't do it properly and get a star.

I like Story-writing best. I've written heaps of stories, and I do pictures for them too. I make some of them into books. I made Camilla a special baby book with big printed words and pictures of all the things she liked best, things like TEDDY and ICE-CREAM and YOUR SPECIAL FRIEND TRACY.

I also like Art. We use poster paints. We've got them at the Home too but they get all gungy and mucked up and the brushes are useless. They've got good ones at school. This is a painting I did yesterday. If I was a teacher I'd give it a gold star. *Two* gold stars.

My class is 3a.

People in my class I can't list all their names, I'd be here all night. I don't know some of them yet. There's not much point making friends because I expect I'll be moving on soon.

Other teachers Oh, they're all boring. Who wants to write about them?

I get to school by going in the Minibus. That's how all the kids in the home get to school. I'd sooner go in a proper car or walk it by myself but you're not allowed.

It takes **hours** **mins** It varies. Sometimes it takes ages because the little kids can't find their pencil cases and the big ones try to bunk off and we just have to hang about waiting.

Things I don't like about school

They all wear grey things, that's the uniform, and I've only got navy things from my last school. The teachers know why and I don't get into trouble but the other kids stare.

BEING IN CARE

My social worker is called Elaine and sometimes she's a right pain, ha-ha.

We talk about all sorts of boring things.

But I don't like talking about my mum. Not to Elaine. What I think about my mum is private.

IF I WAS..

older, I would live in this really great modern house all on my own, and I'd have my own huge bedroom with all my own things, special bunk beds just for me so that I'd always get the top one and a Mickey Mouse alarm clock like Justine's and my own giant set of poster paints and I'd have some felt tips as well and no-one would ever get to borrow them and mess them up and I'd have my own television and choose exactly what programmes I want, and I'd stay up till gone twelve every night and I'd eat at McDonald's every single day and I'd have a big fast car so I could whizz off and visit my mum whenever I wanted.

a policeman, I would arrest the Monster Gorilla and I'd lock him up in prison for ever.

a kitten, I would grow very long claws and sharp teeth and scratch and bite everyone so they'd get really scared of me and do everything I say.

yelled at, I would yell back.

invisible, I would spy on people.

very tall, I would stamp on people with my great big feet.

very rich, I would buy my own house and then ... I've done all that bit. I'm getting fed up writing all this. What's on the next page?

MY OWN STORY

Use this space to write your story

THE STORY OF TRACY BEAKER

Once upon a time there was a little girl called Tracy Beaker. That sounds a bit stupid, like the start of a soppy fairy story. I can't stand fairy stories. They're all the same. If you're very good and very beautiful with long golden curls then, after sweeping up a few cinders or having a long kip in a cobwebby palace, this prince comes along and you live happily ever after. Which is fine if you happen to be a goodie-goodie and look gorgeous. But if you're bad and ugly then you've got no chance whatsoever. You get given a silly name like *Rumpelstiltskin* and nobody invites you to their party and no-one's ever grateful even when you do them a whopping great favour. So of course you get a bit cheesed off with this sort of treatment. You stamp your feet in a rage and fall right through the floorboards or you scream yourself into a frenzy and you get locked up in a tower and they throw away the key.

24

I've done a bit of stamping and screaming in my time.

And I've been locked up heaps of times. Once they locked me up all day long. And all night. That was at the first Home, when I wouldn't settle because I wanted my mum so much. I was just little then but they still locked me up. I'm not fibbing. Although I do have a tendency to tell a few fibs now and again. It's funny, Aunty Peggy used to call it Telling Fairy Stories.

I'd say something like — 'Guess what, Aunty Peggy, I just met my mum in the back garden and she gave me a ride in her flash new sports car and we went down the shopping arcade and she bought me my very own huge bottle of scent, that posh *Poison* one, just like the bottle Uncle Sid gave you for your birthday, and I was messing about

25

with it, playing Murderers, and the bottle sort of tipped and it's gone all over me as I expect you've noticed, but it's my scent not yours. I don't know what's happened to your. I think one of the other kids took it.'

You know the sort of thing. I'd make it dead convincing but Aunty Peggy wouldn't even listen properly. She'd just shake her head at me and get all cross and red and say, 'Oh Tracy, you naughty girl, you're Telling Fairy Stories again.' Then she'd give me a smack.

Foster mothers aren't supposed to smack you at all. I told Elaine that Aunty Peggy used to smack me and Elaine sighed and said, 'Well sometimes, Tracy, you really do ask for it.' Which is a lie in itself. I have never in my life said 'Aunty Peggy, please will you give me a great big smack.' And her smacks really hurt too, right on the back of your leg where it stings most. I didn't like that Aunty Peggy at all. If I was in a real fairy story I'd put a curse on her. A huge wart right on the end of her nose? Frogs and toads coming wriggling out of  her mouth every time she tries to speak? No, I can make up better than that. She can have permanent huge great bogeys hanging out of her nose that won't go away no matter how many times she blows it, and whenever she tries to speak she'll make this terribly loud Rude Noise. Great!

Oh dear. You can't win. Elaine, my stupid old social worker, was sitting beside me when I started writing THE STORY OF TRACY BEAKER and I got the giggles making up my brilliant curses for Aunty Peggy and Elaine looked surprised and said, 'What are you laughing at, Tracy?'

I said, 'Mind your own business' and she said, 'Now Tracy' and then she looked at what I'd written which is a bit of a cheek seeing as it's supposed to be very private. She sighed when she got to the Aunty Peggy part and said, 'Really Tracy!' and I said, 'Yes, really, Elaine.' And she sighed again and her lips moved for a moment or two. That's her taking a deep breath and counting up to ten. Social workers are supposed to do that when a child is being difficult. Elaine ends up doing an awful lot of counting when she's with me.

When she got to ten she gave me this big false smile. Like this.

'Now look, Tracy,' said Elaine. 'This is your own special book about you, something that you're going to keep for ever. You don't want to spoil it by writing all sorts of silly cheeky rude things in it, do you?'

I said, 'It's my life and it hasn't been very special so far, has it, so why shouldn't I write any old rubbish?'

Then she sighed again, but sympathetically this time, and she put her arm round me and said, 'Hey, I know you've had a hard time, but *you're* very special. You know that, don't you?'

I shook my head and tried to wriggle away.

'Yes, you are, Tracy. Very very special,' Elaine said, hanging on to me.

'Then if I'm so very very special how come no-one wants me?' I said.

'Oh dear, I know it must have been very disappointing for you when your second placement went wrong, love, but you mustn't let it depress you too much. Sooner or later you'll find the perfect placement.'

'A fantastic rich family?'

'Maybe a family. Or maybe a single person, if someone really suitable came along.'

I gave her this long look. 'You're single, Elaine. And I bet you're suitable. So why don't you foster me, eh?'

It was her turn to wriggle then.

'Well, Tracy. You know how it is. I mean, I've got my job. I have to deal with lots of children.'

'But if you fostered me you could stop bothering with all the others and just look after me. They give you money if you foster. I bet they'd give you lots extra because I'm difficult, and I've got behaviour problems and all that. How about it, Elaine? It would be fun, honest it would.'

'I'm sure it would be lots of fun, Tracy, but I'm sorry, it's just not on,' Elaine said.

She tried to give me a big hug but I pushed her hard.

'I was only joking,' I said. 'Yuck. I couldn't stand the thought of living with you. You're stupid and boring and you're all fat and wobbly, I'd absolutely hate the idea of you being my foster mum.'

'I can understand why you're angry with me, Tracy,' said Elaine, trying to look cool and calm, but sucking in her stomach all the same.

I told her I wasn't a bit angry, though I shouted as I said it. I told her I didn't care a bit, though I had these silly watery eyes. I didn't cry though. I don't *ever* cry. Sometimes people think I do, but it's my hay fever.

'I expect you're going to think up all sorts of revolting curses for me now,' said Elaine.

'I'm doing it right this minute,' I told her.

'OK,' she said.

'You always say OK,' I told her. 'You know: OK, that's fine with me, if that's what you want I'm not going to make a fuss; OK Tracy, yes I know you've got this socking great axe in your hand and you're about to chop off my head because you're feeling angry with me, but OK, if that's the way you feel, I'm not going to get worried about it because I'm this super-cool social worker.'

She burst out laughing then.

'No-one can stay super-cool when you're around, Tracy,' she said. 'Look kiddo, you write whatever you want in your life story. It's your own book, after all.'

So that's that. This is my own book and I can write whatever I want. Only I'm not quite sure what I do want, actually. Maybe Elaine *could* help after all. She's over the other side of the sitting-room, helping that wet Peter with his book. He hasn't got a clue. He's filling it all in *so* slowly and *so* seriously, not writing it but printing it with that silly blotchy biro of his, trying to do it ever so carefully but failing miserably, and now he's smudged some of it so it looks a mess anyway.

I've just called Elaine but she says she's got to help Peter for a bit. The poor little petal is getting all worried in case he puts the wrong answers, as if it's some dopey intelligence test. I've done heaps of them, intelligence tests. They're all ever so easy-peasy. I can do them quick as a wink. They always expect kids in care to be as thick as bricks, but I get a hundred out of a hundred nearly every time. Well, they don't tell you the answers, but I bet I do.

TRACY BEAKER IS A STUPID SHOW-OFF AND THIS IS THE SILLIEST LOAD OF RUBBISH I'VE EVER READ AND IF SHE'S SO SUPER-INTELLIGENT HOW COME SHE WETS HER BED LIKE A BABY?

Ignore the stupid scribble up above. It's all lies anyway. It's typical. You can't leave anything for two minutes in this rotten place without one of the other kids spoiling it. But I never thought anyone would stoop so low as to write in my own private life story. And I know who did it too. I know, Justine Littlewood, and you just wait. I'm going to get you.

I went over to rescue Elaine from that boring wimpy little Peter and I had a little peer into his book and I nearly fell over, because you'll never guess who he's put as his best friend. Me. *Me!*

31

'Is this some sort of joke?' I demanded.
He went all red and mumbly and tried to
hide what he'd put, but I'd already seen it.
My best friend is Tracy Beaker. It was down
there on the page in black and white. Well,
not your actual black and white, more your
smudgy blue biro, but you know what I mean.

'Go away and stop pestering poor Peter,'
Elaine said to me.

'Yes, but he's putting absolute rubbish in
his book, Elaine, and it's stupid. I'm not Peter
Ingham's best friend!'

'Well, I think it's very nice that Peter
wants you to be his friend,' said Elaine. She
pulled a funny face. 'There's no accounting for
taste.'

'Oh, ha-ha. Why did you put that, Peter?'

Peter did a little squeak about sharing birthdays and so that made us friends.

'It does *not* make us friends, dumbo,' I declared.

Elaine started getting on at me then, saying I was being nasty to poor little Peetie-Weetie and if I couldn't be friendly why didn't I just push off and get on with my own life story? Well, when people tell me to push off I generally try to stick to them like glue, just to be annoying, so that's what I did.

And then Jenny called me into the kitchen because she made out she wanted a hand getting the lunch ready, but that was just a *ploy*. Jenny doesn't smack. She doesn't even often tell you off. She just uses ploys and tries to distract you. It sometimes works with the thicker kids but it usually has no effect whatsoever on me. However, I quite like helping in the kitchen because you can generally nick a spoonful of jam or a handful of raisins when Jenny's back is turned. So I went along to the kitchen and helped her put an entire shoal of fish fingers under the double grill while she got the chip pan bubbling. Fish fingers don't taste so great when they're raw. I tried nibbling just to see. I don't know why they're called fish *fingers*. They don't have fingers, do they? They ought to be fish *fins*. That Aunty

Peggy used to make this awful milk pudding called tapioca which had these little slimy bubbly bits and I told the other kids that they were fish eyes. And I told the really little ones that marmalade is made out of goldfish and they believed that too.

When Jenny started serving out the fish fingers and chips, I went back into the sitting-room to tell everyone that lunch was ready. And I remember seeing Louise and Justine hunched up in a corner, giggling over something they'd got hidden. I don't know. I *am* highly intelligent, I truly wasn't making that up, and yet it was a bit thick of me not to twig what they were up to. Which was reading my own life story and then scribbling all over it.

A little twit like Peter Ingham would tell, but I'm no tell-tale tit. I shall simply get my own back. I shall think long and carefully for a suitable horrible revenge. I don't half hate that Justine. Before she came Louise and I were best friends and we did everything together and, even though I was still dumped in a rotten children's home, it really wasn't so bad. Louise and I made out we were sisters and we had all these secrets and—

One of these secrets was about a certain small problem that I have. A night-time problem. I've got my own room and so it was always a private problem that only Jenny and I knew about. Only to show Louise we were the bestest friends ever I told her about it. I knew it wasn't a sensible move right from the start because she giggled, and she used to tease me about it a bit even when we were still friends. And then she went off with Justine and I'd sometimes worry that she might tell on me, but I always convinced myself she'd never ever stoop that low. Not Louise.

But she has told.
She's told Justine, my
worst enemy. So what
am I going to do to
her? Any ideas ticking
away inside my head?

Well, I could beat her up.

Tick, tick, tick.
I could deliver a karate chop death blow.

Tick, tick, tick.
I could get my mum to come in her car and run her over, squashing her hedgehog-flat.

Tick, tick, tick. Hey! Tick tock. Tick tock. *I* know. And I also know I'm not leaving this book hanging about. From now on I shall carry it on my person. So, ha-ha, sucks boo to you, Justine Littlewood. Oh you're going to get it. Yes you are, yes you are, tee-hee.

I'm writing this at midnight. I can't put the light on because Jenny might still be prowling about and I don't want *another* ding-dong with her, thanks very much. I'm making do with a torch, only the battery's going, so there's just this dim little glow and I can hardly see what I'm doing. I wish I had something to eat. In all those Enid Blyton school stories they always have midnight feasts. The food sounds a bit weird, sardines and condensed milk, but I could murder a Mars Bar right this minute. Imagine a Mars Bar as big as this bed. Imagine licking it, gnawing away at a corner, scooping out the soft part with both fists. Imagine the wonderful chocolatey smell. I'm slavering at the thought. Yes, that's what those little marks are on the page. Slavers. I don't cry. I don't *ever* cry.

I acted as if I didn't care less when Jenny had a real go at me. And I don't.

'I think you really do care, Tracy,' she said, in that silly sorrowful voice. 'Deep down I think you're really very sorry.'

37

'That's just where you're wrong,' I insisted. 'Come off it now. You must know how you'd feel if your mother had bought you a special present and one of the other kids spoilt it.'

As she said that I couldn't help remembering being in the first Home, long before the dreaded Aunty Peggy or that mean hateful unfair Julie and Ted. My mum came to see me and she'd brought this doll, a doll almost as big as me, with long golden curls and a bright blue lacy dress to match her big blue eyes. I'd never liked dolls all that much but I thought this one was wonderful. I called her Bluebell and I undressed her right down to her frilly white knickers and dressed her up again and brushed her blonde curls and made her blink her big blue eyes, and at night she'd lie in my bed and we'd have these cosy little chats and she'd tell me that Mum was coming back really soon, probably tomorrow, and—

OK, that sort of thing makes me want to puke now but I was only little then and I didn't know any better. The housemother let me cart Bluebell all over the place but she tried to make me give the other kids a go at playing with her. Well, I wasn't going to let that lot maul her about, so of course I didn't let them hold her. But I came unstuck when I started school. You weren't allowed to take toys to school, only on Friday afternoons. I cried and fought but they wouldn't let me. So I had to start leaving Bluebell at home. I'd tuck her up in my bed with her eyes closed, pretending she was asleep, and then when I got home from school I'd charge upstairs into our crummy little dormitory and wake her up with a big hug. Only one day I woke her up and I got the shock of my life. Her eyelids snapped open but her blue eyes had vanished inside her head. Some rotten lousy pig had given them a good poke. I couldn't stand it, seeing those creepy empty sockets. She stopped being my friend. She just scared me.

The housemother took Bluebell off to this dolls' hospital and they gave her some new eyes. They were blue too, but not the same bright blue, and they didn't blink properly either. They either got stuck altogether or they flashed up and down all the time, making her look silly and fluttery. But I didn't really care then. She was spoilt. She wasn't the same Bluebell. She didn't talk to me any more.

I never found out which kid had done it. The housemother said it was A Mystery. Just One Of Those Things.

Jenny didn't call it a mystery when Justine went sobbing to her because her silly old Mickey Mouse alarm clock had got broken.

Clocks break all the time. It's not as if it's a really flash expensive clock. If I'd been Jenny I'd have told Justine to stop making such a silly fuss. I'd have stopped up my ears when that sneaky little twerp started going on about me. 'I bet I know who did it too, Jenny. *That Tracy Beaker.*'

Yes, she sneaked on me. And Jenny listened, because she came looking for me. She had to look quite a long time. I kind of suspected what was coming, so I cleared off. I didn't try to hide in the house or the garden like one of the little kids. I'm not that dumb. They can flush you out in five minutes no matter where you are. No, I skipped it out the back door and down the road and went for a wander round the town.

It was great. Yes, I had the most amazing time. First I went to McDonald's and had a Big Mac and french fries with a strawberry milk shake and then I went to the pictures

40

and saw this really funny film and I laughed so much I fell out of my seat and then I went off with this whole crowd of friends to an amusement arcade and I kept winning the jackpot on the fruit machines and then we all went off to this party and I drank a whole bottle of wine and it was great, it just tasted like lemonade, and this girl there, we made friends and she asked me if I'd like to stay the night, sharing her twin beds in this fantastic pink and white room, in fact she said I could stay there permanently if I really wanted and so I said . . .

I said: 'No thanks, I'd sooner go back to my crummy children's home.' ?

Of course I didn't say that. Well, she didn't say it either. I sort of made her up. And her party. I didn't go down the amusement arcade. Or to the pictures. Or McDonald's. I *would* have done, but I couldn't, on account of the fact I ran off with no cash whatsoever.

I said I tell fibs sometimes. It makes things more interesting. I mean, what's the point of writing what I really did? Which was loaf about the town feeling more and more fed up. The only thing I could think of to do was sit in the bus shelter. It got a bit boring. I pretended I was waiting for a bus and I tried to think of all the places I'd like to go to. But that began to depress me because I started thinking about Watford, where my mum said she lived. And last year I got all the right money together (which created a few problems afterwards as I sort of borrowed it without asking) and sussed out the journey and got all these trains and buses and all the rest of it, so that I could pay my mum a visit and give her a lovely surprise. Only it was me that got the surprise because she wasn't there, and the people who lived in that house said she'd moved on about six months ago and they didn't have a clue where she'd gone now.

So it's going to take a bit of organized searching to find her again. I could catch a different bus every day for the rest of my life and maybe not find her. It's hard when you haven't got a clue where to look.

I was still scrunched up in the bus shelter when a familiar white Minivan hoved into view. It was Mike, come looking for me. Mike looks after us with Jenny. He isn't half a bore. He doesn't often get cross but he whinges on about Rules and Responsibility and a whole lot of other rubbish.

So by the time I'd got back to the Home I was sick to death of the subject, but then Jenny came into my bedroom and *she* started. And she assumed it was me that broke Justine's clock though she had no proof whatsoever. I told her so, and said she just

liked picking on me, and it wasn't fair. She said I'd feel better if I owned up to breaking Justine's clock and then went to say sorry to her. I said she had to be joking. I wasn't the slightest bit sorry and anyway I didn't didn't *didn't* break Justine's rotten clock.

That isn't necessarily a fib. I don't absolutely one hundred percent *know* that I broke it. All right, I did go into her bedroom when she was in the bathroom, and I did pick up the clock to look at it. Well, she's always going on about it because she's got this boring thing about her dad. She makes out he's so flipping special when he hardly ever comes to see her. The only thing he's ever given her is that stupid tinny old alarm clock. I wanted to look at it to see if it was really so special. Well, it wasn't. I bet he just got it from Woolworth's. And it certainly wasn't made very carefully because when I twiddled the knobs to make the little Mickey on the end of the hands go whizzing round and round he couldn't keep it up for very long. There was this sudden whir and clunk and then the hand fell off altogether and Mickey fell too, with his little paws in the air, dead.

But he might have been about to take his last gasp anyway. That hand might well have fallen off the next time Justine touched the stupid clock to wind it up.

I'm not going to say sorry no matter what.
I wish I could get to sleep.
I'll try counting sheep . . .

I *still* can't get to sleep and it's the middle
of the night now and it's rotten and I keep
thinking about my mum. I wish she'd come
and get me. I wish anyone would come and
get me. Why can't I ever get a good foster
family? That Aunty Peggy and Uncle Sid were
lousy. But then I could suss them out and tell
they were lousy right from the start. Anyone
who smacks hard and serves up frogspawn for
your pudding is certainly not an ideal aunty.
But last time, when I got fostered by Julie
and Ted, I really thought it was all going to
work out happily ever after, and that it was
my turn to be the golden princess instead of
a *Rumpelstiltskin*.

They were great at first, Julie and Ted. That's what I called them right from the start. They didn't want to be a prissy aunty and uncle. And Julie said she didn't want me to call her Mum because I already had a mum. I thought such a lot of Julie when she said that. She wasn't exactly my idea of a glamorous foster mum – she had this long wispy brown hair and she wore sludge-coloured smocky things and sandals – and Ted looked a bit of a wimp too with his glasses and his beard and weirdo comfy walking shoes, not so much

Hush Puppy as Shut-your-face Hound-Dog —
but I thought they were the sort of couple you
could really trust. Ha!

Because I went to live with them and
I thought we were getting on really great,
though they were a bit boringly strict about
stuff like sweets and bedtimes and horror
videos, but then Julie started to wear bigger
smocks than ever and lolled about on the sofa
and Ted got all misty-eyed behind his glasses
and I started to realize that something was
up. And so I asked them what it was and
they hedged and pulled faces at each other
and then they looked shifty and told me that
everything was fine and I knew they were
lying. Things weren't fine at all.

They didn't even have the guts to tell me
themselves. They left it to Elaine. She'd only
just started to be my social worker then (I've
had heaps because they kept moving around
and leaving me behind and I got passed on
like a parcel). I wasn't that keen on Elaine
in those days. In fact I was really narked
with her, because I'd had this man social
worker Terry before her and he used to call
me Smartie and he used to give me the odd
tube of Smarties too, and I felt Elaine was a
very poor substitute.

I wish I hadn't thought of those Smarties.
I wish I had some now, I'm simply starving.

I'm sure Elaine marked me down as Sulky and Non-co-operative in her little notebook. The day she told me the Julie and Ted Bombshell I'm sure she scribbled TRACY TOTALLY GOB-SMACKED. Because Julie was having her own baby, after years of thinking she couldn't have any kids.

I didn't get it at first.

'So what's the problem, Elaine?' I said. 'We'll be a proper family then, four of us instead of three.'

Elaine was having difficulties finding the right words. She kept opening her mouth and closing it again, not saying a sausage.

'You look just like a fish when you do that, did you know?' I said cheekily, because my heart was starting to hammer hard against my chest and I knew that when Elaine eventually got the words out I wouldn't like the sound of them.

'The thing is, Tracy ... Well, Julie and Ted have loved fostering you, and they've got very fond of you, but ... you see, now they're having their own baby they feel that they're not really going to be able to cope.'

'Oh, I get it,' I said, in this jokey silly voice. 'So they're going to give the boring old baby away because they can't cope with it. And keep me. Because they had me first, didn't they?'

'Tracy—'

'They're not really going to dump me, are they?'

'They still very much want to keep in touch with you and—'

'So why can't I go on living with them? Look, I'll help all I can. Julie doesn't need to worry. I'll be just like a second mum to this baby. I know all what to do. I can give it its bottle and change its soggy old nappy and thump it on its back to bring up its wind. I'm dead experienced where babies are concerned.'

'Yes, I know, Tracy. But that's the trouble. You see, when Julie and Ted first fostered you, we did tell them a bit about your background, and the trouble you had in your first foster home. You know, when you shut the baby up in the cupboard—'

'That was Steve. And he wasn't a baby. He was a foul little toddler, and he kept mucking up our bedroom so I tidied him up into the cupboard just for a bit so I could get everything straightened out.'

'And there was the ghost game that got totally out of hand—'

'Oh that! All those little kids *loved* that game. I was ever so good at finding the right hiding places and then I'd start an eerie sort of moan and then I'd jump out at them, wearing this old white sheet.'

49

'And everyone got scared silly.'

'No they didn't. They just squealed because they were excited. *I* was the one who should have been scared, because they were all the ghost-busters you see, and I was the poor little ghost and—'

'OK, OK, but the point is, Tracy, it makes it plain in your records that you don't always get on well with little children.'

'That's a whopping great lie! What about Camilla? I looked after her at that children's home and she loved me, she really did.'

'Yes, I'm sure that's true, Tracy, but— Well, the thing is, Julie and Ted still feel they don't want to take any chances. They're worried you might feel a bit uncomfortable with a baby in the house.'

'So they're pushing me out?'

'But like I said, they still want to keep in touch with you and maybe take you out for tea sometimes.'

'No way,' I said. 'I don't want to see them ever again.'

'Oh Tracy, that's silly. That's just cutting off your own nose to spite your face,' said Elaine.

That's such a daft expression. How on earth would you go about it?

It wouldn't half hurt.

It hurt a lot leaving Julie and Ted's.

They wanted me to stay for a few months but I couldn't clear out of there quick enough. So here I am in this dump. They've tried to see me twice but I wasn't having any of it. I don't want any visitors, thanks very much. Apart from my mum.

I wonder where she is. And why didn't she leave a forwarding address at that last place? And how will she ever get to find me here? Yeah, that's the problem. I bet she's been trying and trying to get hold of me, but she doesn't know where to look. Last time I saw her I was at Aunty Peggy's. I bet Mum's been round to Aunty Peggy's and I bet that silly old smacking-machine wouldn't tell her where I'd gone. So I bet my mum got really mad with her. And if she found out just how many times that Aunty Peggy smacked me then wow, ker-pow, splat, bang, I bet my mum would really let her have it.

I don't half want my mum.

I know why I can't sleep. It's because I'm so starving hungry, that's why. Crying always makes me hungry. Not that I've been crying now. I don't *ever* cry.

I think maybe I'll try slipping down to the kitchen. Jenny's bound to be fast asleep by now. Yeah, that's what I'll do.

I'm back. I've had my very own midnight feast. And it was absolutely delicious too. Well, it wasn't bad. I couldn't find any chocolate, of course, and that was what I really fancied. But I found an opened packet of cornflakes and got stuck into them, and then I tried raiding the fridge. There weren't too many goodies. I didn't go a bundle on tomorrow's uncooked mince or yesterday's cold custard, but I poked my finger in the butter and then dabbled it in the sugar bowl and that tasted fine. I did quite a lot of poking and dabbling actually. I know Jenny might notice so I got my little finger nail and drew these weeny lines like teethmarks and then did some paw prints all over the butter, so she'd think it was a mouse. Mice do eat butter, don't they? They like cheese, which is the same sort of thing. Of course this is going to have to be a mountaineering mouse, armed with ice-pick and climbing boots, able to trek

up the grim north face of the Frigidaire. And then it's got to develop Mighty Mouse muscles to prise open the door of the fridge to get at the feast inside.

Maybe Jenny will still be a teensy bit suspicious. But I can't help that. At least she didn't catch me while I was noshing away at my midnight feast.

Someone else did though. Not in the kitchen. Afterwards, when I was sneaking up the stairs again. They're very dark, these stairs, and they take a bit of careful negotiating. One of the little kids is quite likely to leave a teddy or a rattle or a building brick halfway up and you can come an awful cropper and wake the entire household. So I was feeling my way very very cautiously when I heard this weird little moaning sound coming from up on the landing. So I looked up, sharpish, and I could just make out this pale little figure, all white and trailing, and it was so exactly like a ghost that I opened my mouth to scream.

But Tracy Beaker has a lot of bottle. I'm
not scared of anybody. Not even ghosts. So I
clapped my hand over my mouth to stop the
scream and pattered right on up the stairs to
confront this puny little piece of ectoplasm.
Only it wasn't a ghost after all. It was just
snivelling drivelling Peter Ingham, clutching
some sheets.

'Whatever are you up to, creep?' I whispered.

'Nothing,' Peter whispered back.

'Oh sure. You just thought you'd take your
sheets for a walk in the middle of the night,'
I said.

Peter flinched away from me.

'You've wet them, haven't you?' I said.

'No,' Peter mumbled. He's a useless liar.

'Of course you've wet them. And you've
been trying to wash them out in the bathroom,
I know. So that people won't guess.'

'Oh don't tell, Tracy, please,' Peter begged.

'What do you take me for? I'm no tell-tale,' I
said. 'And look, you don't have to fuss. Just get
Jenny on her own in the morning and whisper
to her. She'll sort it all out for you. She doesn't
get cross.'

'Really?'

'Truly. And what you do now, you get
yourself some dry sheets from the airing

54

cupboard, right? And some pyjamas. Goodness, you don't know anything, do you? How
long have you been in care?'

'Three months, one week, two days,' said
Peter.

'Is that all? I've been in and out of care
nearly all my life,' I said, getting the sheets
for him. 'So why are you here now then? Your
mum and dad get fed up with you? Can't say
as I blame them.'

'They died when I was little. So I lived with
my nan. But then she got old and then– then
she died too,' Peter mumbled. 'And I didn't
have anyone else so I had to come here. And
I don't like it.'

'Well, of course you don't like it. But this
is a lot better than most children's homes.
You ought to have tried some of the places
I've been in. They lock you up and they beat
you and they practically starve you to death
and then when they do give you meals it's
absolutely disgusting, they pretend it's meat
but it's really chopped up worms and dried
dog's muck and—'

'Shut up, Tracy,' Peter said, holding his
stomach.

'Who are you telling to shut up?' I said,
but not really fiercely. 'Go on, you'd better
shove off back to your room. And put your

55

dry pyjamas on. You're shivering.'

'OK, Tracy. Thanks.' He paused, fidgeting and fumbling with his sheets. 'I wish you would be my friend, Tracy.'

'I don't really bother making friends,' I said. 'There's not much point, because my mum's probably coming to get me soon and then I'll be living with her so I won't need any friends here.'

'Oh,' said Peter, and he sounded really disappointed.

'Still. I suppose you can be my friend just for now,' I said.

I don't know why I said it. Who wants to be lumbered with a silly little creep like that? I'm too kind-hearted, that's my trouble.

There wasn't much point in getting to sleep, because when I did eventually nod off I just had these stupid nightmares. It's as if there's a video inside my head and it switches itself on the minute my eyes close and I keep hoping it's going to be showing this great comedy that'll have me in stitches but then the creepy music starts and I know I'm in for it. Last night was the Great Horror Movie of all time. I was stuck in the dark somewhere and there was something really scary coming up quick behind me so I had to run like mad. Then I got to this big round pool and there were these stepping stones with people perching on them and I jumped on to the first one and there was no room at all because that fat Aunty Peggy was spread all over it. I tried to cling to her but she gave me a big smack and sent me flying. So then I jumped on to the next stepping stone and Julie and Ted were there and I tried to grab hold of them but they just turned their backs on me and didn't even try to catch me when I fell and so I had to try to reach the next stepping stone but I was in the water doing my doggy-paddle

and it was getting harder and harder, and
every time I swam to a stepping stone all
these people prodded at me with sticks and
pushed me away and I kept going under the
water and . . .

. . . and then I woke up and I know
that whenever I dream about water it spells
Trouble with a capital T. I had to make my
own dash to the airing cupboard and the
laundry basket. I was unfortunate enough
to bump into Justine too. She didn't look as
if she'd slept much either. Her eyes seemed
a bit on the red side. I couldn't help feeling
a bit mean then, in spite of everything. So I
gave her this big smile and I said, 'I'm sorry
about what happened to your alarm clock,
Justine.'

I didn't exactly tell her that *I* did it. Because
I still don't know that it really was me. And
anyway, I'd be a fool to admit it, wouldn't I?
But I told her that I was still sorry, just like
Jenny had suggested.

Only there's no point trying to be nice to
pigs like Justine Littlewood. She didn't smile
back and graciously accept my apologies.

'You'll be even sorrier when I've finished
with you, Tracy Beaker,' she hissed. 'And
what have you been doing, eh? Wet the
bed again? Baby!' She hissed a lot more
too. Stupid insulting things. I'm not going to

58

waste my time writing them all down. Words can't hurt me anyway. Only I can't help being just a bit worried about that threat. What's she going to do to get her own back for the clock? If only we had poxy locks on our bedroom doors. Still, at least we've got separate bedrooms in this Home, even though they're weeny like cupboards.

It's new policy. Children in care need their own space. And I want to stay in my own space, doing all this writing, but Jenny has just put her head round my door and told me to buzz out into the garden with the others. And I said No Fear. Being in a Home is lousy at the best of times, but I just can't stick it in the school holidays when you're all cooped up together and the big ones bully you and the little ones pester you and the ones your own age gang up on you and have secrets together and call you names.

'How's about trying to make it up with Justine?' Jenny suggested, coming to sit on my bed.

So I snorted and told her she was wasting her time, and more to the point, she was wasting *my* time, because I wanted to get on with my writing.

'You've done ever such a lot, Tracy,' said Jenny, looking at all these pages. 'We'll be running out of paper soon.'

'Then I'll use the backs of birthday cards. Or bog roll. Anything. I'm inspired, see. I can't stop.'

'Yes, you've really taken to this writing. Going to be a writer when you grow up, eh?'

'Maybe.' I hadn't thought about it before. I was always sure I was going to be on telly with my own chat show. THE TRACY BEAKER EXPERIENCE and I'd walk out on to this stage in a sparkly dress and all the studio audience would clap and cheer and all these really famous celebrities would fight tooth and nail to get on my show to speak to me. But I reckon I could write books too.

'Tell you what, Tracy. We've got a real writer coming round some time this afternoon. You could ask her for a few tips.'

'What's she coming for?'

'Oh, she's doing this article for a magazine about children in care.'

'Oh that boring old stuff,' I said, pretending to yawn but inside I start fizzing away.

I wouldn't mind my story being written up in some magazine. A book would be better of course, but maybe that could come later. I'd have to be careful what she said about me though. Elaine the Pain made a right mess of my newspaper advert. I was Child of the Week in the local paper. If she'd only let me write it I'd have been bowled over by people rushing to adopt dear little Tracy Beaker. I know just how to present myself in the right sort of way.

TRACY BEAKER

HAVE YOU A PLACE IN YOUR HEARTS FOR DEAR LITTLE TRACY? BRILLIANT AND BEAUTIFUL, THIS LITTLE GIRL NEEDS A LOVING HOME. VERY RICH PARENTS PREFERRED, AS LITTLE TRACY NEEDS LOTS OF TOYS, PRESENTS AND PETS TO MAKE UP FOR HER TRAGIC PAST.

Elaine is useless. Doesn't have a clue. She didn't even let me get specially kitted out for the photograph.

'We want you looking natural, Tracy,' she said.

Well I turned out looking too flipping natural. Hair all over the place and a scowl on my face because that stupid photographer kept treating me like a baby, telling me to Watch the Birdie. And the things Elaine wrote about me!

TRACY

Tracy is a lively, healthy, chatty, ten-year-old who has been in care for a number of years. Consequently she has a few behaviour problems and needs firm loving handling in a long-term foster home.

I ask you!

'How could you *do* this to me, Elaine?' I shrieked when I saw it. 'Is that the best thing you can say about me? That I'm *healthy*? And anyway I'm not. What about my hay fever?'

'I also say you're lively. And chatty.'

'Yeah. Well, we all know what that means. Cheeky. Difficult. Bossy.'

'You said it, Tracy,' Elaine murmured.

'And all this guff about behaviour problems! What do I do, eh? I don't go round beating people up? Well, not many. And I don't smash the furniture. Hardly ever.'

'Tracy, it's very understandable that you have a few problems—'

'I *don't*! And then how could you ask for someone to handle me *firmly*?'

'And lovingly,' said Elaine. 'I put loving too.'

'Oh yes, they'll tell me how much they love me as they lay into me with a cane. Honestly, Elaine, you're round the twist. You're just going to attract a bunch of creepy child-beaters with this crummy advert.'

But it didn't even attract them. No-one replied at all.

Elaine kept telling me not to worry, as if it was somehow my fault. I know if she'd only get her act together and do a really flash advert there'd be heaps of offers. I bet.

But maybe I'm wasting my time nagging Elaine. This woman who's coming this afternoon might be just the chance I've been waiting for. If she's a real writer then she'll know how to jazz it all up so that I sound really fantastic. Only I've got to present myself to her in a special way so that she'll pick me out from all the others and just do a feature on me. So what am I going to do, eh?

Aha!

Not aha. More like boo-hoo. Only I don't ever cry, of course.

I don't want to write down what happened. I don't think I want to be a writer any more.

I tried, I really did. I went flying up to my bedroom straight after lunch and I did my best to make myself look pretty. I know my hair is untidy so I tried scragging it back into these little sticky-out plaits. Camilla had little plaits and everyone cooed over them and said how cute she looked. I thought my face looked a bit bare when I'd done the plaits so I wetted some of the side bits with spit and tried to make them go into curls.

I still looked a bit boring so I decided to liven my face up a bit. So I sneaked round to Adele's room. She's sixteen and she's got a Saturday job in BHS and she's got a drawer absolutely chock-a-block with make-up. I borrowed a bit of blusher to give myself some colour in my cheeks. And then I thought I'd try out a pink glossy lipstick too. And mascara to make my eyelashes look long. I tried a bit on my eyebrows too, to make them stand out. And I put a lot of powder on to be

like the icing on a cake. I thought I looked
OK when I'd finished. Well, at least I looked
different.

I changed my clothes too. I didn't want this
writer to see me in a scrubby old T-shirt and
skirt. No way. It had to be posh frock time.
Only I don't really have a posh frock of my
own. I did try on a few of Adele's things but
somehow they didn't really suit me.

So then I started thinking about all the other girls. Louise had this really fantastic frock that she got a couple of years ago from some auntie. A real posh party frock with smocking and a flouncy skirt and its own sewn-in frilly white petticoat. It was a bit small for her now, of course, but she could just about squeeze into it for special days. And Louise and I are about the same size.

I knew Louise would go spare if she saw me parading around in her best party frock but I decided it might be worth it if I made a great impression on the writer woman first. So I beetled along the corridor towards her room, but I didn't have any luck. Louise was in her room. With Justine. I heard their voices.

They were discussing me, actually. And nappies. They were snorting with laughter and normally I'd have marched right in and punched their silly smirky faces but I knew if I got into a fight Jenny would send me to my room and make me stay there and I'd miss out on meeting the woman writer.

So with *extreme* self-control I walked away, still musing on what I was going to wear. I know it's summer, but I'd started to feel a bit shaky and shivery so I put on this mohair sweater that Julie knitted me for Christmas. When Julie and Ted dumped me I vowed not to have anything to do with them and I even thought about cutting up the mohair sweater into little woolly hankies but I couldn't quite do it. It's a pretty fantastic sweater actually, with the name Tracy in bright blue letters. That way it's obvious it's mine, specially made for me. Of course it's a bit tickly and prickly, but my mum once said you have to suffer if you want to look beautiful.

She's always looked beautiful. I don't half wish I took after her. I wasn't too bad as a baby. I was still quite cute as a toddler. But then I went off in a big way.

Still, I was trying my hardest to look OK. I only had my old skirt to wear with my mohair sweater, and there were dark blue stains all down one side where a biro exploded in my pocket, but I couldn't help that. The woman writer might just think it was a tie-and-dye effect. And at least the blue matched the lettering on my jumper.

I kept on prinking and preening in my room. I heard all the other kids go clattering downstairs. I heard Louise and Justine go giggle-snigger-titter along the corridor. My face started burning so that I didn't need my blusher. Then I heard Adele rampaging around because some rotten so-and-so had been in her room and rifled through all her make-up and mucked it all up. I decided to hang about in my room a bit longer.

I heard the front door bell. I heard Jenny talking to someone down in the hall. I heard them go into the sitting-room. I knew it was time to make my Entrance.

So I went running down the stairs and barging into the sitting-room with this great big smile on my face. It's no use looking sad or sulky if you want people to like you. Mum always tells me to give her a big smile. Even when she's saying goodbye to me. You can't look gloomy or it just upsets people and they don't want any more to do with you.

You've got to have this great big s-s-s-m-m-m-i-i-i-l-l-l-e-e-e.

Everyone looked up at me when I went
into the sitting-room. And they all smiled
too. Just for a moment I was daft enough
to think they were all smiling back at me.
But then I saw they were the wrong sort of
smiles. They were smirks. And Justine and
Louise nudged each other and giggled and
spluttered and whooped. And Adele glared
at me. Peter Ingham was the only one with
a proper smile. He came over to me. He was
blinking a bit rapidly.

'You look . . . nice, Tracy,' he said.

But I knew he was lying. It was no use
kidding myself. It was obvious I looked a
right prat. Jenny's pretty laid back about
appearances but even she looked shocked at
the sight of me. And it looked like all that
effort was for nothing, because she didn't
seem to have the woman writer person with
her after all.

I've seen women writers on chat shows
on the telly. They're quite glamorous, like
film stars, with glittery frocks and high heels
and lots of jewellery. They look a bit like my
mum, only nowhere near as pretty of course.

The woman with Jenny looked like some
boring social worker or teacher. Scruffy brown
hair. No make-up. Scrubby T-shirt and rumpled jeans. A bit like me on an off-day, grown
up.

69

I decided to slope off back to my bedroom. It seemed sensible to steer clear of Adele anyway. But Jenny caught hold of me by the back of my jumper.

'Hang about, Tracy. I thought you wanted to meet Cam Lawson.'

'Who?' I said.

'You know. The writer. I told you,' Jenny hissed. Then she lowered her voice even more. 'Why are you wearing your winter jumper when it's boiling hot today? And what on earth have you done to your face?'

'She thinks she looks pretty,' said Justine, and she clutched Louise and they both shrieked.

'Pipe down, you two,' said Jenny. 'Tracy. Tracy!' She hung on to me firmly, stopping me barging over to that stupid pair of titterers so as I could bang their heads together. 'Leave them, Tracy. Come and meet Cam.'

I wanted to meet this Cam (what sort of a silly name is that?) even though she didn't look a bit like a *proper* writer, but I sort of hung back. I'm usually the last person to feel shy, but somehow I suddenly didn't know what to say or what to do. So I growled something at Jenny and twisted away from her and stood in a corner by myself, just watching.

Peter came trotting after me. Justine and Louise were still having hysterics at my appearance. You could tell they'd actually got over the giggles by this time, but Justine kept going into further false whoops and Louise was almost as bad.

'Don't take any notice of them,' Peter whispered.

'I don't,' I said crossly.

'I like your jumper,' said Peter. 'And your make-up. And the new hairstyle.'

'Then you're mad. It looks a mess. I look a mess. I look a mess *on purpose*,' I said fiercely. 'So you needn't feel sorry for me, Peter Ingham. You just clear off and leave me alone, right?'

Peter fidgeted from one foot to the other, looking worried.

'Clear off, you stupid little creep,' I said.

So of course he did clear off then. I wondered why I'd said it. OK, he *is* a creep, but he's not really that bad. I'd said he could be my friend. And it was a lot better when he was with me than standing all by myself, watching everyone over the other side of the room clustered round this Cam person calling herself a writer.

She's a weird sort of woman if you ask me. She was chatting away and yet you could tell she was really nervous inside. She

kept fidgeting with her pen and notebook and
I was amazed to see she bites her nails! She's
a great big grown-up woman and yet she does
a dopey kid's thing like that. Well, she's not
great big, she's little and skinny, but even so!

My mum has the most beautiful fingernails, very long and pointy and polished. She
varnishes them every day. I just love that
smell of nail varnish, that sharp peardrop
niff that makes your nostrils twitch. Jenny
caught me happily sniffing nail varnish one
day, and do you know what she thought?
Only that I was inhaling it, like glue sniffing.
Did you ever? I let her think it too. *I* wasn't
going to tell her I just liked the smell because
it reminds me of Mum.

I'll tell you another weird thing about Cam Whatsit. She sat on one of our rickety old chairs, her legs all draped round the rungs, and she talked *to* the children. Most adults that come here talk *at* children.

They tell you what to do.

They go on and on about themselves.

They talk about you.

They ask endless stupid questions.

They make personal comments.

Even the social workers are at it. Or they strike this special nothing-you-can-say-would-shock-me-sweetie pose and they make stupid statements.

'I guess you're feeling really angry and upset today, Tracy,' they twitter, when I've wrecked my bedroom or got into a fight or shouted and sworn at someone, so that it's *obvious* I'm angry and upset.

They do this to show me that they understand. Only they don't understand peanuts. *They're* not the ones in care. I am.

I thought Cam Thing would ask questions and take down case histories in her notebook, all brisk and organized. But from what I could make out over in the corner she had a very different way of doing things.

She smiled a bit and fidgeted a lot and sort of weighed everybody up, and they all had a good stare at her. Two of the little kids

73

tried to climb up on to her lap because they do that to anyone who sits down. It's not because they *like* the person, it's just they like being cuddled. They'd cry to have a cuddle with a cross-eyed gorilla, I'm telling you.

Most strangers to children's homes get all flattered and make a great fuss of the littlies and come on like Mary Poppins. This Cam seemed a bit surprised, even a bit put out. I don't blame her. Little Wayne in particular has got the runniest nose of all time and he likes to bury his head affectionately into your chest, wiping it all down your front.

Cam held him at arm's length, and when he tried his burrowing trick she distracted him by giving him her pen. He liked flicking the catch up and down.

She let little Becky have a ride on her foot at the same time, so she didn't feel left out and bawl. Becky kept trying to climb up her leg, pulling her jeans up. Some of Cam's leg got exposed. It was a pretty ropey sort of leg if you ask me. A bit hairy for a start. My mum always shaves her legs, and she wears sheer see-through tights to show them off. This Cam had socks like a schoolgirl. Only they were quite funny brightly patterned socks. I thought the red and yellow bits were just squares at first, but then I got a bit closer and saw they were books. I wouldn't mind having

a pair of socks like that myself, if I'm going to write all these books.

She's written books. Old Cammy. Cammy-knicker, ha-ha. The other kids asked her and she told them. She said she wrote some stories but they didn't sell much so she also wrote some romantic stuff. She doesn't look the romantic type to me.

Adele got interested then because she loves all those soppy love books and Cam told her some titles and the boys all tittered and went yuck yuck and Jenny got a bit narked but Cam said she didn't mind, they were mostly yuck but she couldn't help it if that's what people liked to read.

Then they all started talking about reading. Maxy said he liked this book *Where the Wild Things Are* because the boy in that is called Max, and Cam said she knew that book and she made a Wild Thing face and then everyone else did too.

Except me. I mean, I didn't want to join in a dopey game like that. My face did twitch a bit but then I remembered all the make-up and I knew I'd look really stupid.

Besides, I'd got her sussed out. I could see what she was up to. She was finding out all sorts of things about all the kids without asking any nosy questions. Maxy went on about his dad being a Wild Thing. Adele went on about love, only of course real life wasn't like that, and love didn't ever last and people split up and sometimes didn't even go on loving their children.

Even little creepy Peter piped up about these Catherine Cookson books that his nan used to like, and he told Cam how he used to read them to her because her eyes had gone all blurry. And then *his* eyes went a bit blurry too, remembering his nan, and Cam's hand reached out sort of awkwardly. She didn't quite manage to hold his hand, she just sort of tapped his bony wrist sympathetically.

'My nan's dead too. And my mum. They're both together in heaven now. Angels, like,' said Louise, lisping a bit.

She always does that. Puts on this sweet little baby act when there are grown-ups about. Like she was a little angel herself. Ha. Our little Louise can be even worse than me when she wants. She's had three foster placements, no, was it four? Anyway, none of them worked out. But Louise always swore she didn't care. We used to have this pact that we'd do our best not to get fostered at all and we'd stay together at the Home till we got to be eighteen and then we'd get them to house us together. In our own modern flat. We'd got it all planned out. Louise even started thinking about our furniture, the ornaments, the posters on the walls.

And then Justine came and everything was spoilt. Oh how I hate that Justine Littlewood. I'm glad I broke her silly Mickey Mouse alarm clock. I'd like to break her into little bits and all.

Anyway, Louise lisped on about angels and I'll give that Cam her due, she didn't go all simpering and sentimental and pat Louise on her curly head and talk about the little darling. She stayed calm and matter-of-fact, and started talking about angels and wondering what they would look like.

'That's simple, Miss. They've got these big wings and long white nighties and those gold plate things stuck on the back of their heads,' said Justine.

'Draw one for me,' said Cam, offering her pen and notebook.

'OK,' said Justine, though she can't draw for toffee. Then she had a close look at the pen in her hand. 'Here, it's a Mickey Mouse pen. Look, Louise, see the little Mickey. Oh Miss, where did you get this pen? It's great! I love Mickey, I do. I've got this Mickey Mouse alarm clock, my dad gave it me, only some *pig* broke it deliberately.' Justine looked over her shoulder and glared at me.

I glared back, making out I couldn't care less. And I *couldn't*. My face started burning, but that was just because of my mohair sweater.

Justine drew her stupid angel and Cam nodded at it.

'Yes, that's the way people usually draw angels.' She looked at Louise. 'So is this the way you imagine your mum and your nan?'

'Well. Sort of,' said Louise.

'Is that the sort of nightie that your nan would wear? And what about the halo, the gold plate bit. Would that fit neatly on top of her hairstyle?'

Louise giggled uncertainly, not sure what she was getting at.

'You draw me what you think your mum and nan look like as angels,' said Cam.

Louise started, but she can't draw much either, and she kept scribbling over what she'd done.

'This is silly,' she said, giving up.

I knew what Cam was on about. I'd have

done a really great drawing of Louise's mum
and nan in natty angel outfits. Like this.

'I'll draw you an angel, Miss,' said Maxy,
grabbing at the pen. 'I'll draw me as an angel
and I'll have big wings so I can fly like an
aeroplane, y-e-e-e-o-o-o-w, y-e-e-e-o-o-o-w.' He
went on making his dopey aeroplane noises all
the time he was drawing.

Then the others had a go, even the big
ones. I got a bit nearer and craned my neck
to see what they'd all drawn. I didn't think
any of them very inspired.

I knew exactly what I'd draw if she asked
me. It wouldn't be a silly old angel.

Then Cam looked up. She caught my eye. She did ask me.

'Have a go?' she said, dead casual.

I gave this little shrug as if I couldn't care less. Then I sauntered forward, very slowly. I held out my hand for the pen.

'This is Tracy,' said Jenny, poking her big nose in. 'She's the one who wants to be a writer.'

I felt my face start burning again.

'What, her?' said Justine. 'You've got to be joking.'

'Now Justine,' said Jenny. 'Tracy's written heaps and heaps in her Life Book.'

'Yeah, but it's all rubbish,' said Justine, and her hand shot out and she made a grab

underneath my jumper, where I was keeping
this book for safety. I bashed out at her but I
wasn't quick enough. She snatched the book
from me before I could stop her.

'Give that here!' I shrieked.

'It's rubbish, I tell you, listen,' said Justine,
and she opened my book and started reading
in a silly high-pitched baby voice "Once upon
a time there was a little girl called Tracy
Beaker and that sounds stupid and no wonder
because I *am* stupid and I wet the bed and—
Ooooowwww!" '

Things got a bit hazy after that. But I got
my book back. And Justine's nose became a
wonderful scarlet fountain. I was glad glad
glad. I wanted her whole body to spout blood
but Jenny had hold of me by this time and
she was shouting for Mike and I got hauled
off to the Quiet Room. Only I wasn't quiet in
there. I yelled my head off. I went on yelling
when Jenny came to try and calm me down.
And then Jenny went away and someone else
came into the room. I wasn't sure who it was
at first because when I yell my eyes screw up
and I can't see properly. Then I made out the
jeans and the T-shirt and the shock of hair and
I knew it was Cam Whosit and that made me
burn all over until I felt like a junior Joan of
Arc.

There was me, throwing a hairy fit, and there was her standing there watching me. I don't care about people like Jenny or Elaine seeing me. They're used to it. Nearly all children in care have a roaring session once in a while. I have them more than once, actually. And I usually just let rip, but now I felt like a right raving loony in front of her.

But I didn't stop yelling all the same. There was no point. She'd already seen me at it. And heard me too. She didn't try to stop me. She wasn't saying a word. She was standing there. And she had this awful expression on her face. I couldn't stand it. She looked sorry for me.

I wasn't having that. So I told her to go away. That's putting it politely. I yelled some very rude words at her. And she just sort of shrugged and nodded and went off.

I was left screaming and swearing away, all by myself.

But I'm OK now. I'm not in the Quiet Room any more. I stayed in there ever such a long time and I even had my tea in there on a tray but now I'm in my bedroom and I've been writing and writing and writing away and it looks like I can't *help* being a writer. I've written so much I've got a big lump on the longest finger of my right hand. You look.

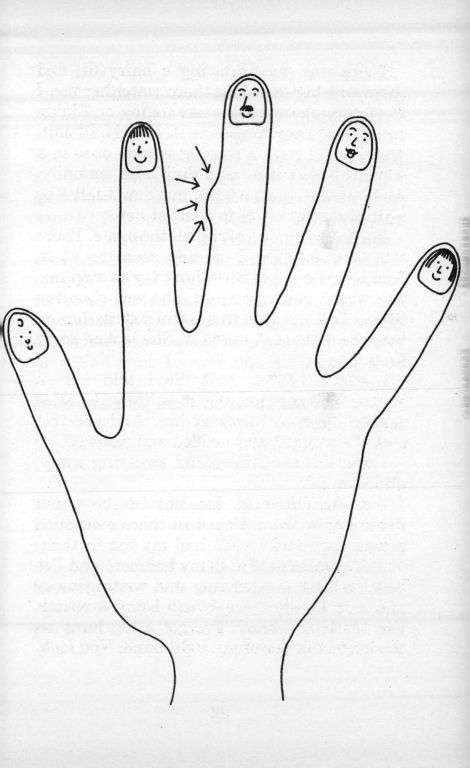

I used to play this daft game with my fingers. I'd make them into a family. There were Mummy Finger and Daddy Finger, big brother Freddy Finger, pretty little Pinkie Finger, and Baby Thumbkin. I'd give myself a little puppet show with them, making them jump about, and I'd take them for walks up and down the big hill of my leg and I'd tuck them up for the night in my hankie.

Baby Camilla used to like that game ever so much. I'd give the Finger family different squeaky voices and I'd make them talk to her and take it in turns to tap her tiny little nose and she'd always chuckle so much her whole body jumped up and down. I don't half miss Camilla.

Hey. Sudden thought. Cam. Is Cam short for *Camilla*?

I was delighted at breakfast to see that Justine has a swollen nose and a sticking plaster.

The swollen nose matches her swollen head. Justine Littlewood thinks she's really it. And she isn't. I truly don't get what Louise sees in her. If *I* were Louise I'd much sooner be Tracy Beaker's best friend.

What really gets me is that I was the one who palled up with Justine first. She turned up at the Home one evening, all down and droopy because her mum had cleared off with some bloke and left Justine and her two little brothers and her dad to get on with it. Only her dad couldn't get on with it, and the kids got taken into care. The brothers got into a short-term foster home because they were still nearly at the baby stage and not too much bother. But Justine didn't get taken on too, because they thought she'd be difficult.

I generally like kids who are difficult. And I thought I liked the look of Justine. And the sound of her. Because after the first droopy evening she suddenly found her tongue and she started sounding off at everyone, getting really stroppy and swearing. She knew even more swear words than I do.

She was like that all week but she shut up on Sunday. Her dad was supposed to see her on Sunday. She was sitting waiting for him right after breakfast, though he wasn't supposed to be coming till eleven o'clock. Eleven came and went. And twelve. And then it was dinnertime and Justine wouldn't eat her chicken. She sat at the window all afternoon, not budging.

My tummy went tight whenever I looked at her. I knew what it was like. I used to sit like that. Not just here. I used to wait at both my crummy foster homes. And the children's homes in between. Waiting for my mum to come.

But now I've got myself sorted out. No more dumb sitting about for me. Because my mum's probably too far away to come on a quick visit. Yeah, that's it, she's probably abroad somewhere, she's always fancied travelling.

She's maybe in France.

Or Spain, she likes sunshine.

What am I thinking of? She'll have gone to the States. Maybe Hollywood. My mum looks so great she'd easily get into the movies.

You can't hop on a bus and visit your daughter when you're hundreds and thousands of miles away in Hollywood, now can you?

All the same, even though I don't sit waiting, I always go a bit tingly when there's a knock at the door. I hold my breath, waiting to see who it is, just in case . . .

So I could understand what old Justine was going through. I didn't try to talk to her because I knew she'd snap my head off, but I sort of sidled up to her and dropped a lollipop on her lap and backed away. It wasn't exactly my lollipop. I'd snaffled several from little Wayne. His dopey mum is younger than Adele and she hasn't got a clue about babies. Whenever she comes she brings Wayne lollipops. Well, they've got sticks, haven't they? We don't want little Wayne giving himself a poke in the eye. And he's normally so drooly that if you add a lot of lolly-lick as well he gets stickier than Superglue. So it's really a kindness to nick his lollies when he's not looking.

'But why did you want to give one to that Justine?' Louise asked. 'She's horrible, Tracy. She barged right into me on the stairs yesterday and she didn't even say sorry, she just called me a very rude word indeed.' Louise whispered it primly.

'Um. Did she really say that?' I said, giggling. 'Oh she's not so bad really. And anyway, I didn't give her the *red* lollipop. I saved that for you.'

'Thanks, Trace,' said Louise, and she beamed at me.

Oh we were like *that* in those days.

I kept an eye on Justine. She didn't budge for a good half hour, letting the lollipop lie in her lap. And then I saw her hand creep out. She unwrapped it and gave it one small suspicious lick, as if I'd poisoned it. But it must have tasted OK because she took another lick, and then another, and then she settled down for a good long suck. Lollipops can be very soothing to the stomach.

She didn't say thank you or anything. And when she eventually had to give up waiting and go to bed she stalked off by herself. But the next day at breakfast she gave me this little nod. So I nodded back and flicked a cornflake in her direction and she flicked one back, and we ended up having this good game of tiddlyflakes and after that we were friends. Not best friends. Louise was my best friend. Ha.

She moaned at first.

'Why do we have to have that Justine hanging round us all the time?' she complained. 'I don't like her, Trace. She's dead tough.'

'Well, I want to be tough too. You've got to be tough. What do you mean, *I'm* tougher than Justine,' I said, sticking my chin out.

'Nutter,' said Louise.

It started to get to me though. I started swearing worse than Justine and Jenny got really mad at me because Maxy started copying me and even little Wayne would come out with a right mouthful when he felt like it.

So then I started the Dare Game. I've always won any dare. Until Justine came along.

I dared her to say the rudest word she could think of when the vicar came on a visit. And she did.

She dared me to go out in the garden stark naked. And I did.

I dared her to eat a worm. And she did.

She dared *me* to eat a worm.

I said that wasn't fair. She couldn't copy my dare. Louise opened her big mouth and said that I hated worms. 'Then I dare her to eat *two* worms,' said Justine. So I did.

I *did*. Sort of. It wasn't my fault they made me sick. I did swallow them first. Justine said I just spat them out straight away but I *didn't*.

I thought hard. I happen to be a crack hand at skateboarding. Justine's not much good at getting her balance and her steering's rotten. So I fixed up this skateboard assault course round the garden, with sloping benches and all sorts. And I dared Justine to have a go. So she did.

She fell over a lot. But she kept getting up and carrying on. So I said she was disqualified. But Louise said Justine should still win the bet if she completed the course. And she did.

Then Justine dared me
to climb the tree
at the end of the garden.
So I did.
It wasn't *my* fault
I didn't get right to
the top. I didn't ask
that stupid Mike to
interfere. But Justine said
I'd lost that dare,
and Louise backed her up.
I couldn't believe my ears.
Louise was *my* friend.

We couldn't do any more dares because Jenny PUT HER FOOT DOWN. You don't argue when she does that.

The next day Justine's famous dad put in an appearance at long last. Justine had gone on and on about how good-looking he was, just like a pop star, and he actually had an evening job singing in pubs, which was why he couldn't be at home to look after her and her brothers. Well, you should have seen him. Starting to go bald. Pot belly. Medallion. He wasn't *quite* wearing a frilly shirt and flares, but almost.

You wouldn't catch me wanting a dad like that. But Justine gave a weird little whoop when she saw him and jumped up into his arms like a great big baby. He took her on some dumb outing and when she got back she was all bubbly and bouncy and showing off this . . . this present he'd bought her.

← whoops!

I don't know why, but I felt really narked at Justine. It was all right when she didn't get a visit, like us lot. But now I kept picking on her and saying silly sniggery things about her dad. And then she burst into tears.

I was a bit shocked. I didn't say anything *that* bad. And I never thought a really tough girl like Justine would ever cry. *I* don't ever cry, no matter what. I mean, my mum hasn't managed to come and visit me for donkey's years and I don't even *have* a dad, but catch me crying.

And then I got another shock. Because Louise turned on me.

'You are horrid, Tracy,' she said. And then she put her arms right round Justine and gave her a big hug. 'Don't take any notice of her. She's just jealous.'

Me, jealous? Of Justine? Of Justine's dopey dumb dad? She had to be joking.

But it didn't look like she was joking. She and Justine went off together, their arms round each other.

I told myself I didn't care. Although I did care a little bit then. And I did wonder if I'd gone over the top with my remarks. I can have a very cutting tongue.

I thought I'd smooth things over at breakfast. Maybe even tell Justine I hadn't really meant any of it. Not actually apologize, of course, but show her that I was sorry. But it was too late. I was left on my own at breakfast. Louise didn't sit next to me in her usual seat. She went and sat at the table by the window – with Justine.

'Hey, Louise,' I called. And then I called again, louder. 'Have you gone deaf or something?' I yelled.

But she could hear me all right. She just wasn't talking to me. She wasn't my best friend any more. She was Justine's.

All I've got is silly squitty twitty Peter Ingham. Oh, maybe he's not so bad. I was writing all this down when there was this tiny tapping at my door. As if some timid little insect was scrabbling away out there. I told this beetle to buzz off because I was busy, but it went on scribble-scrabbling. So eventually I heaved myself off my bed and went to see what it wanted.

'Do you want to play, Tracy?' he said.

'Play?' I said witheringly. 'What do you think I am, Peter Ingham? Some kind of infant? I'm busy writing.' But I'd been writing so much my whole arm ached and my writing lump was all red and throbbing. Oh, how we writers suffer for our art! It's chronic, it really is.

So I did just wonder if it was time for a little diversion.

'What sort of games do *you* play then, little Peetle-Beetle?'

He blinked a bit and shuffled backwards as if I was about to squash him, but he managed to squeak out something about paper games.

'Paper games?' I said. 'Oh, I see. Do we make a football out of paper and then give it a kick so that it blows away? What fun. Or do we make a dear little teddy out of paper and give it a big hug and squash it flat? Even better.'

Peter giggled nervously. 'No, Tracy, pen and paper games. I always used to play noughts and crosses with my nan.'

'Oh gosh, how incredibly thrilling,' I said.

Beetles don't understand sarcasm.

'Good, *I* like noughts and crosses too,' he said, producing a pencil out of his pocket.

There was no deterring him. So we played paper games after that.

I suppose it passed the time a bit. And now I've just spotted something. Right at the bottom of the page, in teeny tiny beetle writing, there's a little message.

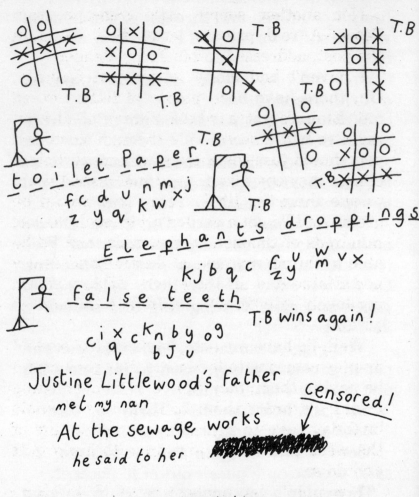

toilet Paper

Elephants droppings

false teeth

T.B wins again!

Justine Littlewood's father
met my nan
At the sewage works
he said to her

censored!

I don't half like
you, Tracy.
signed Peter Ingham.

Guess what! I've got a letter!

Not another soppy little message from Peter. A real private letter that came in the post, addressed to Ms Tracy Beaker.

I haven't had many letters just recently. Oh, there have been plenty of letters *about* me. Elaine's got a whole library of files on me. I've had a secret rifle through them and you should just see some of the mean horrid things they say about me. I had a good mind to sue them for libel. Yeah, that would be great. And I'd get awarded all these damages, hundreds of thousands of pounds, and I'd be able to thumb my nose at Justine and Jenny and Elaine and all the others. I'd just clutch my lovely lolly in my hot little hand and go off and . . .

Well, I'd have my own house, right? And I'd employ someone to foster me. But because I'd be paying them, *they'd* have to do everything *I* said. I'd order them to make me a whole birthday cake to myself every single day of the week and they'd just have to jump to it and do so.

I wouldn't let anybody else in to share it with me.

Not even Peter. I had to share my *real* birthday cake with him. And he gave me a nudge and said 'What's the matter, Tracy? Don't you feel well?' just when I'd closed my

eyes tight and was in the middle of making my birthday wish. So it got all muddled and I lost my thread and now if my mum doesn't come for me it's all that Peter Ingham's fault.

Well, maybe it is.

But I'd still let him come round to my house sometimes and we could play paper games. They're quite good fun really, because I always win.

Who else could I have in my house? I could try and get Camilla. I'd look after her. I could get a special playpen and lots of toys. I've always liked the look of all that baby junk. I don't suppose I had much of that sort of thing when I was a baby. Yeah, I could

have a proper nursery in my house and when
Camilla wasn't using it I could muck about in
there, just for a laugh.

I wonder if Camilla remembers me now?
That's the trouble with babies.
I wonder if Cam *is* short for Camilla?
That's who my letter was from.

I was a bit disappointed at first. I thought it was from my mum. I know she's never written to me before but still, when Jenny handed it to me at breakfast I just clutched at the envelope and held it tight and shut my eyes quick because they got suddenly hot and prickly and if I was a snivelly sort of person I might well have cried.

'What's up with Tracy?' the other kids mumbled.

I gave a great swallow and sniff and opened my eyes and said, 'Nothing's up! Look, I've got a letter! A letter from—'

'I think it's maybe from Cam Lawson,' Jenny said, very quickly indeed.

I caught my breath. 'Yeah. Cam Lawson. See that? She's written me my own personal letter. And she's not written to any of you lot. See! She's written to *me*.'

'So what does she say then?'

'Never you mind. It's *private*.'

I went off to read it all by myself. I didn't get around to it for a bit. I was thinking all these dopey things about my mum. And I had a bad attack of hay fever. And I didn't really want to read what Cam Lawson had to say anyway. She saw me having my hairy fit. I was scared she'd think me some sort of loony.

Only the letter was OK.

                                        10 Beech Road
                                        Kingtown

Dear Tracy

    We didn't really get together properly when
I came on my visit. It was a pity because Jenny
told me a bit about you and I liked the sound of
you. She said you're very naughty and you like
writing.

    I'm exactly the opposite. I've
always been very very good. Especially
when I was at school. You wouldn't half
have teased me.

    I'm not quite so good now, thank goodness.

    And I hate writing. Because it's what I do
for a living and every day I get up from my cornflakes
and go and sit at my typewriter and my hands clench
into fists and I go cross-eyed staring at the blank
paper - and I think - what a stupid way to earn a
living. Why don't I do something else? Only I'm
useless at everything else so I just have to carry
on with my writing.

    Are you carrying on with your writing? You're
telling your own story? An actual autobiography?
Most girls your age wouldn't have much
to write about, but you're lucky in that
respect because so many different things
have happened to you.

    Good luck with it.

            Yours,

                Cam

Dear Ms Lawson,
         Jenny says that's what I should

call you, Ms Lawson, although you wrote Cam
at the bottom of your letter. What sort of name is
Cam? If you're called Camilla then I think that's
a lovely name and don't see why you want to muck
it up. I had a friend in this other home called
Camilla and she liked her name. I had a special way
of saying it, Ca-miiii-lla, and she'd always
giggle. She was only a baby but very bright.
         Why don't you mind me being naughty?
Actually, its not always my fault that I get
into trouble. People just pick on me. Lots of
people, but I won't name names because I don't
tell tales, not like <u>some</u> people.

Do you like my drawing? I
liked yours, I thought they
were funny. What do you
mean, you hate writing?

I think that's weird when it's what you do. I like writing. I think it's ever so easy. I just start and it goes on and on. The only trouble is that it hurts your hand and you get a big lump on your finger. And ink all over your hand and clothes and paper if some clueless toddler has been chewing on your felt tip.

Are you having trouble writing your article about us? I could help you if you liked. I can tell you anything you need to know about me. And the others. How about it?

Yes I am still writing my autobiography. I like that word. I asked Jenny and she said it's a story about yourself, and that's right, that's exactly what I'm writing. I'd let you have a look at it but it's strictly personal. Don't take any notice of what that moron Justine read out. There are some really good bits, honest.

Yours
From your fellow writer

R.S.V.P
That means you've got to reply.

10 Beech Road.

Dear Tracy,

Thanks for your lovely letter. It made me laugh. Do you know what? I think you're a born writer.

I could do with some help on my feature.

Are you around next Saturday morning? Hope to see you then. Cam.

I hate Camilla. I used to get teased rotten at school for having such a soppy name.

The dumping Ground.

Dear Camilla,
          It's not a soppy name. You've got to be proud of it. You want to try having a name like Tracy Beaker. Excuse this crummy writing paper. Jenny lent me the first lot but she says I'm costing her a small fortune in paper and can't I give it a rest. So I borrowed this from one of the little ones. Isn't it yucky? I know.

← This is Goblinda the Goblin and she's going to gob all over these daft fairies.

Yes, I'll help you out on Saturday. If I'm there, of course. My Mum often comes to take me out. Although she may be abroad just now. I think she's going to take me on a trip abroad too. But it mightn't be for a while, so I'll see you on Saturday morning probably. About what time? We have breakfast at 8.30 on Saturdays and I always eat quickly so about 8.35?

Yours, from your fellow - hang on, I'm not a fellow

Yours, from another lady writer,

Tracy

R.S.V.P
So as I know what time to start waiting.

10 Beech Road

Dear Sister Writer,

See you Saturday morning. 8·35 impossible.

I look like this at 8·35.

zzzz

How about 10·35?

Cam. Sorry. Camilla. Ugh!

P.S. I love Goblinda. Put her in a story.

Imagine staying in your bed half the morning. She is lazy. And she was late even then. It was 10.41 before she turned up. I'd practically given her up. She's supposed to be a professional writer and yet she can't even keep an appointment on time.

She's pretty hopeless if you ask me. She didn't half muck up this morning. I'd got it all worked out. I was ready to fill her in on all the facts. Mostly about me, of course. But I thought maybe she might fancy interviewing Peter too, to balance things up. A girl's point of view, and a boy's. No need to bother with any of the others.

Cam's got this dinky little tape recorder and after just one minute of instruction I mastered all the mechanism and had great fun fast-forwarding and rewinding and playing back. I had a little go first, trying out all my different accents, doing my Australian G'day routine and my American gangster and my special Donald Duck, but then I decided we'd better get down to business and as I'm not the sort of girl to hog the limelight I said Peter could go first.

He backed away from the tape recorder as if it was a loaded gun.

'Don't be so silly, Peter. Just act normal and speak into it.'

'What shall I say?' Peter squeaked.

I sighed impatiently. 'Just tell Cam your life story.'

'But I haven't got a story. I couldn't think of anything to put when Elaine gave me that book,' said Peter. 'I lived with my nan. And she died. So I came here. That's all there is.'

'That's OK, Peter. Don't let Tracy bully you into it. You don't have to say anything,' said Cam.

'What a cheek! I'm not a bully. Huh, *I* was the kid who always *got* bullied. This other Home I was in, there was this huge great teenage bloke, and he was a really tough skinhead and he had these bovver boots and I filled them up with custard for a joke and he didn't see the funny side of it

and yet he didn't half look hilarious, all this frothy yellow liquid squishing up his trouser legs – so anyway, from then on my name was mud, and he really had it in for me. The things he used to do!'

I was about to launch into a long account but typical typical that Justine Littlewood came barging over.

'It's not fair, Miss. You're letting that stupid Tracy show off like mad, and you're not giving any of us a go.'

'You shut your face, blabbermouth,' I said. 'She's not come to see you lot. She's come to see *me*. A strictly private appointment. So clear off. Isn't that right, Cam?'

'Well. Yes, I've come to talk to you, Tracy. But we could all have a go on the tape recorder for a bit,' she said.

What a gutless creep she is. She was there just to see *me*. We had a proper business appointment. All she had to do was tell Justine and the others to buzz off. It wouldn't have mattered if Peter stayed, because he's not really any bother. But the others! It was useless. Practically the whole morning was wasted. She let them all muck around on the tape recorder and then some of the littlies wanted another go drawing with her Mickey Mouse pen, and then Jenny came in with coffee for Cam and coke for us and it was like some big party. Only I didn't feel like the birthday girl. I felt squeezed out to the edge again.

After a bit I stomped off. I kept looking back over my shoulder and I thought she didn't even notice. But then she sidled up. She still had baby Becky on one hip and little Wayne clinging to her leg like a limpet. She gave me a dig in the back with her Mickey Mouse pen.

'Hey,' she said softly. 'Shall we get started on your interview now, Tracy?'

115

'Well, you've got all these other kids. Why waste your time with me?' I said acidly. 'I mean, I'm only the one you were *supposed* to see.'

'Tell you what. Let's go up to your room. Just you and me. How about it?'

'OK,' I said, yawning and shrugging. 'If you really want. I've gone off the idea now. But if you insist. Just for a minute or two.'

It took her a while to dump the baby and prise Wayne away, and then all the others kept clustering around, saying it wasn't fair. So do you know what she did? She said they could do interviews on her tape recorder. And she put *Justine* in charge of it.

'You aren't half making a mistake there, Cam. You're crazy. They'll wreck it in two minutes,' I said.

'No they won't. Justine will work it. And everyone take a two-minute turn. Introduce yourselves first, and then say whatever you want. But don't worry, Peter, you don't have to.'

'You are stark staring mad,' I said. 'Look, if anyone's in charge of that tape recorder it's got to be me. I'm the only one who knows how to work it properly.'

'Well, show Justine,' said Cam. 'Then she'll be able to work it too.'

'I'm not showing *her*,' I said. But in the end I did. And of course Justine was clueless and didn't catch on and I kept sighing and groaning and she got narked and gave me a push and I clenched my fist ready to give her a thump but Cam got in between us and said, 'Look, I'll run through it. Here's the record button, Justine, right?' and *eventually* Justine got the hang of it. I don't know why she's called Littlewood. Little*brain* would be far more appropriate.

Then Cam and I went up to my room and left them to it.

'You thought you'd found a way of getting Justine and me to make friends,' I said. 'But, ha-ha, it didn't work, did it? Because we're always going to be deadly enemies.'

Cam laughed at me. She laughed at the notice taped on my bedroom door too.

'It's OK. You can come in. You're my guest,' I said, opening the door for her.

My room looked a bit of a tip actually. I hadn't got round to making the bed and the floor was littered with socks and pyjama tops and bits of biscuit and pencil sharpenings, so she had to pick her way through. She didn't make a big thing of it though. She looked at all the stuff I've got pinned to my noticeboard, and she nodded a bit and smiled.

'Is that your mum?' Cam asked.

'Isn't she lovely? You'd really think she was a film star, wouldn't you? I think she maybe *is* a film star now. In Hollywood. And she'll be jetting over to see me soon. Maybe she'll take me back with her, and I'll get to be a film star too. A child star. The marvellous movie moppet, Tracy Beaker. Yeah. That would be great, eh?'

I spun around with a great grin, doing a cutsie-pie curtsey – and Cam caught on straight away and started clapping and acting like an adoring fan.

'I hope you're still going to be a writer too,' she said. 'Have you done any more about Goblinda?'

'Give us a chance. I've been too busy doing my autobiography,' I said.

'I suppose this autobiography of yours is strictly private?' Cam asked, sounding a bit wistful.

'Of course it is,' I said. But then I hesitated. Elaine the Pain has seen bits of it. And Louise and Littlebrain. And I did show a bit to Peter actually, just to show him how much I'd done. So why shouldn't I show a bit to Cam too? As she's a sort of friend.

So I let her have a few peeps. I had to be a bit careful, because some of the stuff I've written about her isn't exactly flattering. She came across a description of her by accident, but she didn't take offence. She roared with laughter.

'You really should be the one writing this article about children in care, Tracy, not me. I think you'd make a far better job of it.'

'Yes, have you made a start on this article yet?'

She fidgeted a bit. 'Not really. It's difficult. You see, this magazine editor wants a very touching sentimental story about all these sad sweet vulnerable little children that will make her readers reach for a wad of Kleenex.'

'Yeah, that's the right approach.'

'Oh come off it, Tracy. None of you lot are at all *sweet*. You're all gutsy and stroppy and spirited. I want to write what you're really like but it won't be the sort of thing the editor wants.'

'And it won't be the sort of thing *I* want either. You've got to make me sound sweet, Cam! No-one will want me otherwise. I've gone past my sell-by date already. It gets hopeless when you get older than five or six. You've stopped being a cute little toddler and started to be difficult. And I'm not pretty either so people won't take one look at my photo and start cooing. And then it's not like I'm up for adoption so people can't ever make me their little girl, not properly.'

'You're not up for adoption because you've still got your mum?'

'Exactly. And like I said, she'll be coming for me soon, but meanwhile I'd like to live in a proper homey home instead of this old dump. Otherwise I'll get institutionalized.'

Cam's eyebrows go up.

'I know what it means and all. I've heard Elaine and some of the other social workers going on about it. It's when you get so used to living in an institution like this that you never learn how to live in a proper home. And when you get to eighteen you can't cope and you don't know how to do your own shopping or cooking or anything. Although I can't see me ever having that problem. I bet I could cope right this minute living on my own. They'd just have to bung me the lolly and I'd whizz off down the shops and have a whale of a time.'

'I bet you would,' said Cam.

Then Maxy started scratching at my door

and whining and complaining. I told him to push off, because Cam and I were In Conference, but he didn't take any notice.

'Miss, Miss, it's not fair, them big girls won't let me have a go on the tape, I want a go, Miss, you tell them to let me have a go, they're playing they're pop stars, Miss, and *I* want a go.'

Cam smiled and sighed, looking at her watch.

'I'd better go back downstairs. I've got to be going in a minute anyway.'

'Oh that's not fair! Aren't you staying? You can have lunch with us lot, Jenny won't mind, and it's hamburgers on Saturday.'

'No, I'm meeting someone for lunch in the town.'

'Oh. Where are you going then?'

'Well, we'll probably have a drink and then we'll have a salad or something. My friend fusses about her figure.'

'Who wants boring old salad? If I was having lunch out I'd go to McDonald's. I'd have a Big Mac and french fries and a strawberry milkshake. See, I'm not the slightest bit institutionalized, am I?'

'You've been to McDonald's then?'

'Oh, heaps of times,' I said. And then I paused. 'Well, not actually *inside*. I was

fostered with this boring family, Julie and
Ted, and I kept on at them to take me, but
they said it was junk food. And I said all their
boring brown beans and soggy veggy stews
were the *real* junk because they looked like
someone had already eaten them and sicked
them up and – well, anyway, they never took
me.'

'No wonder,' said Cam, grinning.

'I am allowed to go out to lunch from
here, you know.'

'Are you?'

'Yes. Any day. And tell you what, I really
will work on that article for you. I could
work on it this week and show you what I've
done. And we could discuss it. Over lunch. At
McDonald's. Hint, hint, hint.'

Cam smacked the side of her head as
if a great thought has just occurred to her.

'Hey, Tracy! Would you like to come out
with me to McDonald's next week?'

'Yes please!' I pause. 'Really? You're not
kidding?'

'Really. Next Saturday. I'll come and pick
you up about twelve, OK?'

'I'll be waiting.'

And so I shall. I'd better send her a letter
too, just in case she forgets.

The dumping ground.

Dear Camilla,
    I'm working hard on the article.
I'll show you on Saturday. Remember we have
a lunch-date. At 12. To go to McDonald's.
       From your co-writer Tracy Beaker.

P.S Goblinda says if you took her to
McDonald's she'd be ever so good and wouldn't
gob once.

I know she said twelve o'clock. And she's not exactly the most punctual of people. She mightn't get here till ten past. Even twenty or half past. So why am I sitting here staring out of the window when we've only just had breakfast?

I hate waiting. It really gets on my nerves. I can't concentrate on anything. Not even my writing. And I haven't done any writing in this book all week because I've been so busy with my article for Cam. I've got it all finished now and even though I say it myself I've done a really great job. She can just bung it at her editor and no-one will be any the wiser. I should really get the whole fee for it myself. But I'm very generous. I'll share fifty fifty with Cam, because she's my friend.

Old Pete's my friend too. We've been bumping into each other in the middle of the night this week, on a sheet sortie. Mostly we just had a little whisper but last night I found him all huddled up and soggy because he'd had a nightmare about his nan. Strangely enough, I'd had a nightmare about my mum and it had brought on a bad attack of my hay fever. Normally I like to keep to myself at such moments as some stupid ignorant twits think my red eyes and runny nose are because I've been crying. And I never *ever* cry, no matter what.

But I knew Peter wouldn't tease me so I huddled down beside him for a bit and when I felt him shivering I put my arm round him and told him he was quite possibly my best friend ever.

He's just come up to me now and asked if I want to play paper games. Yeah, it might pass the time.

_ A _ _ I L L A _ L A _ _ O N

B K U D E Y J P T R Y

Oh charming! Peter and I had just got started and I was about to win the first game when Elaine the Pain comes buzzing in. She's here dumping off some boring new kid and now she wants to have a little chat with Peter.

'Well, tough, Elaine, because *I'm* having a little chat with Peter right now,' I said.

'Now now Tracy,' said Elaine.

'Yes, *now*,' I said.

Elaine bared her teeth at me. That smile means she'd really like to give me a clip around the ear but she's going to make allowances for me.

'I expect you're feeling a bit het up this morning, Tracy, because of this writer coming to take you out. Jenny's told me all about it. It'll be a lovely treat for you.'

'You bet. And it'll be a lovely treat for her too because I've written this article for her.'

'Well, I might have a little treat up my sleeve for Peter here,' Elaine said, and she shuffled him off into a corner and started talking to him earnestly.

She's still talking to him. She's keeping her voice down. But I can have very large waggly ears when I want. Elaine's going on about these people she knows. An older couple whose children have all grown up. And now they're a bit lonely. They'd like to look after someone. A little boy. Maybe a little boy just like Peter.

So that's it. Little Peetie-Weetie is obviously going to get fostered and live Happily Ever After.

Well, that's good, isn't it? Because he's my best friend.

No, it's bad, because he won't be able to be my best friend any more if he goes off and gets himself fostered.

And it's not fair. He's hardly been here any time. I've been here ages and ages and no-one ever wants to foster me now.

Still, who wants to be fostered by some boring older couple anyway? Older might mean really ancient. And crabby. And strict. They'd never wear jeans or write funny letters or take Peter to McDonald's.

I wish Cam would hurry up and come for me. Although it's nowhere near time. It's daft me sitting here by the window like this. Waiting.

Justine is hovering behind me. I think she's waiting for her dad. I hope she won't tell him about the little accident to her Mickey Mouse clock. He might come and beat me up. Even though the clock's all mended now. Jenny took it in to this shop and they sorted it. I was glad to see old Mickey tick-tocking round and round again. Justine caught me looking and she gave me this great fierce push that nearly knocked me over and told me that if I so much as touched her clock again she'd duff me up good and proper. Honestly! My fists clenched and I was all set to have a real go at her because no-one talks to Tracy Beaker like that, but then I remembered my lunch date. Jenny isn't best pleased with me at the moment. If I got into a punch-up with Justine then she mightn't let me go out with Cam.

So I Kept Calm. I smiled at Justine in a superior sort of way.

'Really Justine, do you always have to resort to violence?' I said.

My superior willpower was wasted on Justine. She just thought I was chicken.

'Cowardy cowardy custard,' she's mumbling under her breath now. 'Tracy Beaker's got no bottle.'

I shan't take any notice of her. I shall just sit here writing. And waiting. It's not *that* long now. Only it seems like for ever.

I used to sit like this. When I waited for my mum. I wonder when she will come. I had that awful dream about her. I was out having lunch with Cam in McDonald's and it was really great and we were having a smashing time together when I looked up at the clock and saw it had gone one o'clock, and

it suddenly rang a terrible bell in my head, and I remembered that my mum was coming to take me to lunch at one o'clock, and I just went panic panic panic.

I charged off to try to get back to the Home in time and I got a bus but they chucked me off because I didn't have enough money and then I ran into Aunty Peggy and she chased after me to give me a good smacking and Julie and Ted tripped me up and Justine caught me and threw me in a river and I couldn't swim and I was drowning . . . and then I woke up. Wet.

So OK, I know it was only a dopey old nightmare. But what if it was some kind of *premonition*??? What if my mum really comes for me today and I miss her because I'm having lunch with Cam?

I'll have to talk to Elaine.

Well, I've talked. Sort of.

'Can I have a little chat, Elaine?' I said.

'Tracy. I'm still having a little chat with Peter.'

'You've *had* a little chat with Peter. Correction. You've had an extremely long and boring endless conversation with him. And you're my social worker just as much as his. So could you *please* come and have a little chat with me. It's sort of urgent.'

Elaine sighed. She ruffled Peter's hair and gave him a little chuck under the chin. Then she came over to me at long last.

'What is it then, Tracy?'

I swallowed, not sure how to put it.

'Tracy, are you just winding me up?' said Elaine.

'No! It's just ... Look, about my mum. She doesn't know I'm here, does she?'

'Well. No, I don't think so.'

'But if she wanted to find me she could, couldn't she?'

I said it in a whisper but Justine heard.

131

'Who'd ever want to come looking for you, Tracy Beaker?' she said.

'You shut your mouth!'

Justine pulled a hideous face and Louise giggled. Then she tugged at Justine's sleeve.

'Come on. Let's see what that new girl's doing. She's got two whole suitcases with her, so she must have heaps of clothes.'

But Justine wanted to stay at the window so Louise wandered off by herself. I knew Justine was still listening for all she was worth (honestly, some people have no decency whatsoever) but I had to keep on asking Elaine.

'If my mum wanted she could go round to that old children's home. And they could tell her where I am now, couldn't they?'

'Yes, of course they would,' said Elaine. 'Don't worry, Tracy. Each time you get moved on somewhere else, there's a special record kept. So if your mum wants to see you then it's easy. They look up your name and file number and find your present address.'

'Good,' I said.

'What's up, Tracy? You still look a bit worried.'

'I'm OK.'

Only I don't feel OK. What if my mum does come today? And I'm out having lunch with someone else? Will she wait for me? Or

132

will she get fidgety and fed up and zoom off again? And I'll get back here and Jenny will say, 'Oh, by the way, Tracy, your mum called when you were out, but she couldn't wait for you. She was all set to take you back to Hollywood with her but she had this plane to catch so she couldn't hang about.'

What am I going to do?

Maybe she won't come today. She hasn't ever come before. And yet, what if she did? I *wish* I hadn't had that dream. Dreams *can* come true.

I feel sick. Maybe I don't really want to go to McDonald's after all.

See that? It's real blood.

I'm not going to get to go to McDonald's now, whether I want to or not. I've had a fight. I'm in the Quiet Room.

This is how it happened. I went over to Peter. I whispered in his ear.

'Would you like to go to McDonald's with Cam?'

Peter scrunched up his neck because my whispers can be a bit tickly.

'You mean, go with you?'

133

'No. Go instead of me. I've kind of gone off the idea. It's OK, I'll tell Cam when she comes. She quite likes you, so she won't mind taking you instead.'

Peter looked worried.

'I can't, Tracy. I'm going out too. With these people.'

'What, with this boring older couple?' I said.

Elaine raised her eyebrows at me but I took no notice.

'I bet they won't take you to McDonald's,' I said.

'Why don't *you* want to go, Tracy?' Elaine asked. 'I thought you were so looking forward to it.'

'Yes, but ... I want to stay here. Just in case.'

Elaine is a pain but she's also quite quick at putting two and two together.

'Tracy, I don't think your mum will be coming today,' she said quietly.

'Oh. I know that. Only I had this dream. She did in the dream.'

'Yes, I'm sure she did. And I expect it was a lovely dream but— '

'No, it was a perfectly foul dream because I wasn't here to see her and— '

'And you woke up blubbing with a soaking wet bed, *baby*,' Justine muttered.

'I told you to shut *up*,' I said, getting really riled.

'I'd go out with your writer friend, Tracy,' said Elaine.

'Mm. Well. I'm not sure I really want to now, anyway.' I glare at Peter. 'Why do you have to be seeing this boring old couple today, eh? You could see them any old time. You go and have a Big Mac with Cam.'

Peter wriggled. Elaine put her hand on his shoulder. He looked up at her and then at me.

'Sorry, Tracy. I want to meet them. Aunty Vi and Uncle Stanley.'

'Of course you want to meet them, Peter. And Tracy is going to meet her writer,' said Elaine.

'No, I'm not.'

'*I'd* go,' said Justine. 'Only I can't, because of my dad. I'm going out to lunch with him.'

'You were supposed to be going out with him last Saturday. Only he never turned up,' I said.

'OK, but he does come *sometimes*. Not like your famous mum. She's never ever ever come for you,' said Justine.

'Oh yes she has!' I yelled. 'She's come for me lots of times. She's going to come and take me away for good, we're going to Hollywood together and — will you stop *laughing* at me, you great big pig.'

'You're so stupid,' Justine gasped. 'Your mum's not a film star. Louise told me about your mum. She's nothing. And she's never coming for you. She hasn't been near you since you were little. I bet she's forgotten all about you. Or she's had heaps of other kids and doesn't want to think about that boring ugly Tracy ever again.'

So I hit her. And I kept on hitting her. And I don't care. I've made her nose bleed again. She's hurt me a bit too, but I don't care. And now I'm stuck in the Quiet Room and it's gone twelve and one of the other kids will get to go out to lunch with Cam instead of me and I don't care. At least it won't be Justine.

Maybe my mum *will* come.

There's someone outside the door. It's opening. *Is it Mum???*

No. It wasn't Mum. It never is. It was Cam, of course.

I took one look at Cam and burst into tears. Well, I would have done, if I was a crying sort of person.

'Oh dear,' said Cam. 'I don't seem to have a very good effect on you, Tracy.'

She sat right down on the floor beside me, waiting for me to quieten down a bit. Then she dug in the pocket of her jeans and found a crumpled tissue. She passed it to me and I mopped up my hay fever.

'Now,' said Cam. 'What do you want to do?'

'I haven't got any choice, have I? I'm stuck here.'

'No you're not. You can still come out to lunch with me. I've asked Jenny. Elaine explained why you got upset.'

'She doesn't know! I hate the idea of you lot all blabbing away about me,' I said fiercely.

'Yes, it must get a bit annoying,' said Cam. 'Still, at least it means you're the centre of everyone's attention. Here, you've still got a runny nose. Good job you weren't wearing your make-up this time.'

'Are you laughing at me?'

'Just a little tease. Coming?'

'You bet.'

Only I *still* felt bothered about my mum, even though I knew it was silly. I knew she almost definitely wouldn't be coming. I knew deep deep down that Justine was maybe right about her. But I still worried.

'My mum,' I mumbled.

'You're scared she'll come and you won't be here?' said Cam. 'OK. Tell you what we'll do. You can phone home when we're out. To check she's not arrived. And if she *has* I'll whisk you straight back. How about that?'

'That sounds great,' I said.

So Cam and I went off together for our lunch appointment after all. She's got this ancient grass-green Citroën which made a bit of a change from the Minivan.

'My mum wouldn't be seen dead in this sort of naff car,' I said. 'She drives a Cadillac you know.'

'Mm,' said Cam.

138

I squinted at her. 'You're just nodding to
be nice to me, aren't you?' I said. 'You don't
really believe my mum's got her own Cadillac.'

Cam looked at me. 'Do you believe it,
Tracy?'

I thought for a bit. 'Sometimes.'

Cam nodded again.

'And sometimes I know I'm sort of making it
up,' I mumbled. 'Do you mind that? Me telling
lies?'

'I make things up all the time when I
write stories. I don't mind a bit,' said Cam.

'I've got that article with me. I've written
it all. You won't have to bother with a thing.
Shall I read a bit to you? You'll be really
impressed, I bet you will. I think I've done
a dead professional job.'

So I started reading it to her.

'You can see the signs of suffering on little Tracy Beaker's elfin face. This very very intelligent and extremely pretty little girl has been grievously treated when in so-called Care. Her lovely talented young mother had to put her in a home through no fault of her own, and in fact she might soon be coming for her lovely little daughter, but until then dear little Tracy Beaker needs a foster family. She is deprived and abused in the dump of a children's home— Why are you laughing, Cam?'

'Abused?' Cam spluttered.

'Look at my hand. My knuckles. That's blood, you know.'

'Yes, and you got it bouncing your fist up and down on poor Justine's nose,' said Cam. 'You're the one who deprives and abuses all the others in your Home.'

'Yes, but if I put that no-one will want me, will they?'

'I don't know,' said Cam. 'If I were choosing, I'd maybe go for a really naughty girl. It might be fun.'

I looked at her. And went on looking at her. And my brain started going tick tick tick.

I was mildly distracted when we got to
McDonald's. I ate a Big Mac and a large
portion of french fries, and washed it down
with a strawberry milkshake. So did Cam.
Then she had a coffee and I had another
milkshake. And then we sat back, stuffed.
We both had to undo our belts a bit.

I got out my article again and showed
her some more, but she got the giggles all
over again.

'I'll give myself hiccups,' she said weakly.
'It's no use, Tracy. I think it's great, but
they'll never print it. You can't say those
sort of things.'

'What, that Tracy Beaker is brilliant and
the best child ever? It's true!'

'Maybe! But you can't say all the other
things, about Justine and Louise and the rest.'

'But they're true too.'

'No, they're not true at all. I've met them. I like them. And you certainly can't say those things about Jenny and Mike and your social worker and all the others. You'd get sued for libel.'

'Well, you do better then,' I said huffily. 'What would you put?'

'I don't know. Maybe I don't want to do the article now anyway. I think I'd sooner stick to my stories, and blow the money.'

'That's not a very professional approach,' I said sternly. 'Maybe you ought to give up writing. Maybe you ought to do some job that gives you a whacking great allowance. Looking after someone. You get an allowance for that.'

Cam raised her eyebrows.

'I can barely look after myself,' she said.

'Well then. You need someone to look after you for a bit,' I said. 'Someone like me.'

'Tracy.' Cam looked me straight in the eye. 'No. Sorry. *I* can't foster you.'

'Yes, you can.'

'Stop it. We can't start this. I'm not in any position to foster you.'

'Yes you are. You don't need to be married, you know. Single women can foster kids easy-peasy.'

'I'm single and I want to stay single. No husband. And *no kids*.'

'Good. I hate other kids. Especially boring little babies. You won't ever get broody, will you, Cam?'

'No fear. Holding that little Wayne was enough to douse any maternal urges for ever,' said Cam.

'So it could be just you and me.'

'No!'

'Think about it.'

Cam laughed. 'You aren't half persistent, girl! OK, OK, I'll think about it. That's all. Right?'

'Right,' I say, and I tap her hand triumphantly. 'Can I phone home now? I sound like E.T., don't I? We've got through two videos of that already. So, can T.B. phone home? Only she doesn't have any change.'

Cam gave me ten pence and I went to the phone by the Ladies and gave Jenny a buzz. My heart did thump a bit when I was waiting for her to answer. I felt a little bit sad when she told me that Mum hadn't come. Even though that was the answer I was really expecting.

But I had other things to fuss about now. I whizzed back to Cam.

'Well? Have you had your think? Is it

OK? Will you take me on?' I asked eagerly.

'Hey, hey! I've got to think about this for ages and ages. And then I'm almost certain it's still going to be no.'

'*Almost* certain. But not absolutely one hundred percent.'

'Mm. What about you? Are you absolutely one hundred percent sure you'd like me to foster you?'

'Well. I'd sooner you were rich. And posh and that, so that I could get on in the world.'

'I think you'll get on in the world without my help, Tracy.'

'No, I need you, Cam.'

I looked straight at her. And she looked straight at me.

'We still hardly know each other,' she said.

'Well, if we lived together we would get to know each other, wouldn't we, Cam? Camilla. That sounds classier. I want my foster mum to sound dead classy.'

'Oh Tracy, give it a rest. Me, classy? And I told you, I can't stick Camilla. I used to get teased. And that's what my mum always called me.' She pulled a face.

I was shocked by her tone and her expression.

'Don't you ... don't you *like* your mum?' I said.

'Not much.'

'Why? Did she beat you up or something?'

'No! No, she just bossed me about. And my father too. They tried to make me just like them and when I wanted to be different they couldn't accept it.'

'So don't you see them any more?'

'Not really. Just at Christmas.'

'Good, so they'll give me Christmas presents, won't they, if I'm their foster grandchild?'

'Tracy! Look, it really wouldn't work. It wouldn't work for heaps of practical reasons, let alone anything else. I haven't got room for you. I live in this tiny flat.'

'I'm quite small. I don't take up much space.'

'But my flat's really minute, you should see it.'

'Oh great! Can we go there now?'

'I didn't mean— ' Cam began – but she laughed again. 'OK, we'll go round to my flat. Only I told Jenny I'd take you back to the Home after lunch.'

'T.B. can phone home again, can't she?'

'I suppose so. Tell Jenny I'll get you back by teatime.'

'Can't I come to tea with you too? Please?'

'Tell you what. We could pretend to be posh ladies just to please you and have afternoon tea. About four. Although I don't know how either of us could possibly eat another thing.

And then I'll take you back to the Home by five. Right?'

'What about supper? And look, I could stay the night, we're allowed to do that, and I don't need pyjamas, I could sleep in my underwear, and I needn't bother about washing things, I often don't wash back at the Home—'

'Great! Well, if you ever lived with me – and I said *if*, Tracy – then you'd wash all right. Now don't carry on. Five. Back at the Home. That'll be quite enough for today.'

I decided to give in. I sometimes sense I can only push so far.

I phoned, and Cam spoke to Jenny for a bit too.

'T.B.'s phoned home twice now. Like E.T. Do you know what E.T. got?' I said hopefully. 'Smarties.'

'You'll be in the Sunday papers tomorrow, Tracy. THE GIRL WHOSE STOMACH EXPLODED,' said Cam.

But she bought me Smarties all the same. Not a little tube, a great big packet.

'Wow! Thanks,' I said, tucking in.

'They're not just for you. Take them back and share them with all the others.'

'Oh! I don't want to waste them.'

'You're to share them, greedyguts.'

'I don't mind sharing them with Peter. Or Maxy. Or the babies.'

'Share them with everybody. Including Justine.'

'Hmm!'

She stopped off at another shop too. A baker's. She made me wait outside. She came out carrying a cardboard box.

'Is that cakes for our tea?'

'Maybe.'

'Yum yum. I'm going to like living with you, Cam.'

'Stop it now. Look Tracy, I seem to have got a bit carried away. I like seeing you and I hope we can go out some other Saturdays—'

'Great! To McDonald's? Is that a promise?'

'That really is a promise. But about fostering . . . I'd hate you to build your hopes up, Tracy. Let's drop the subject now and just be friends, OK?'

'You could be my friend *and* my foster mum.'

'You're like a little dog with a bone. You just won't let go, will you?'

'Woof woof!'

147

I'm getting good at making her laugh. I like her. Quite a lot. Not as much as my mum, of course. But she'll do, until my mum comes to get me.

Her flat came as a bit of a shock, mind you. It really is weeny. And ever so shabby. It's in far worse nick than the Home. And you should see her bedroom. She leaves her pyjamas on the floor too!

Still, once I get to live there I'll get her sorted out. Help her make a few improvements.

'Show me your books then,' I said, going over to the shelves. 'Did you write all this lot?'

'No, no! Just the ones on the bottom shelf. I don't think you'll find them very exciting, Tracy.'

She was dead right there. I flicked through one, but I couldn't find any pictures, or any funny bits, or even any rude bits. I'll have to get her to write some better books or she'll never make enough money to keep me in the style to which I want to become accustomed.

Maybe I'll have to hurry up and get my own writing published. I got Cam to give me a good long go on her typewriter.

It took me a while to get the hang of it. But eventually I managed to tap out a proper letter. I left it tucked away on Cam's desk for her to find later.

```
    DEAR CAM,  I WILL BE THE BESTEST FOSTER
CHILD EVER.  YOU'LL SEE.  WITH LOVE FROM
TRACY BEAKER, THE GIRL WHOSE STOMACH DIDN'T
EXPLODE.
```

It did nearly though. Guess what she bought for tea! A birthday cake, quite a big one, with jam and cream inside. The top

was just plain white, but she took some of my Smarties and spelt out T.B. on the top.

'So that it's all my cake,' I said happily.

'Aren't I going to get a slice?' asked Cam.

'Oh yes. Of course. But I don't have to share it with anyone else. I had to share my proper birthday cake with Peter, wasn't that *mean*!'

'I thought Peter's your friend.'

'Well. He is. But still. You don't want to share your birthday cake even with your bestest friend ever,' I said.

Only I started thinking about it all the time I was chomping my way through my first great big slice. And my second slice with extra jam and cream. And my third weeny slice. And my nibbles at a bit of icing.

'This is much better than that birthday cake at the Home, you know,' I said.

'Good.'

'Peter's gone out with this dumb sounding old auntie and uncle today,' I said.

'Has he?'

'But I bet they won't take him to Mc-Donald's. Or buy him his own special cake.'

'Maybe not.'

'Well, seeing as we are friends, Peter and me, and we share a birthday, and we shared that other birthday cake – maybe we *ought* to share this one too,' I said. 'Shall I take a slice back for my friend Peter?'

'I think that would be a good idea,' said Cam. 'I'll wrap up a slice for Peter. And another slice for you. Just so long as you promise me you won't throw up all night.'

'Of course I won't. Here, can I do the cutting this time? Because if this is like a birthday cake I get a wish, don't I?'

So Cam gave me the knife and I closed my eyes and wished really really hard.

'I bet you can't guess what I wished,' I said to Cam.

'I bet I can,' said Cam.

'I'll tell you if you like.'

'Oh no. You're supposed to keep birthday cake wishes secret,' said Cam.

I pulled a little face at her. Then I thought.

'Here, if this is a sort of birthday, then it's a pity there aren't any presents too.' I paused. 'Hint hint hint.'

'Do you know what you are, Tracy Beaker? Absolutely shameless.'

But it worked!

Cam looked all round her room and stared for a while at her bookshelves. I thought I was going to end up with a boring old book. But it was much much better. She went to her desk and picked up her Mickey Mouse pen.

'Here we are, Tracy. Happy Unbirthday,' she said, and she pressed the pen into my hand.

Just for a moment I was lost for words. And that doesn't happen very often to me. I was scared I might even get another attack of my hay fever. But I managed to grin and give her the thumbs up sign and show her that I was ever so pleased.

We got back to the Home at five. On the dot. Trust her to be punctual at the wrong time. I made a bit of a fuss on the doorstep. I sort of clung a bit. It was just that I was enjoying myself so much that I wanted to go *on* enjoying myself. That's not being difficult, is it?

But it's still OK. She's coming next Saturday. She's promised. Twelve o'clock. We have a date, me and my future foster mum. I'm going to make that wish come true.

It took me a bit of time to calm down after we'd said goodbye. I missed out on tea, but it didn't really matter, seeing as I'd had more than half my cake and the McDonald's lunch and the Smarties. There were still quite a few Smarties left. Just no red ones. Or pink or mauve or blue. They're my favourite colours. But there were plenty of the boring ones to share with the others.

When I came out of the Quiet Room I collected my Smarties and the two slices of cake. They'd got a bit squashed as I was saying goodbye to Cam, but Jenny helped me spruce them up a bit and put them on a plate.

I went to find Peter. He was up in his room, sitting on his bed, looking a bit quiet.

'Oh oh,' I said. 'This older couple. They didn't turn up?'

'Oh yes. They did,' said Peter.

'But they were pretty awful, yes? Never you mind, Pete, see what I've got for us? Look, really yummy cake.'

'Thank you, Tracy,' said Peter, and he took his slice absent-mindedly. 'No, they aren't awful, Auntie Vi and Uncle Stanley. They're nice, actually.'

'I bet they didn't take you to McDonald's.'

'No, we went and had fish and chips. My nan and I always used to go and have fish and chips. With bread and butter and a cup of tea.'

'Boring! I had a Big Mac and french fries and a strawberry milkshake, two actually, and then Cam bought me these Smarties and then she bought me this really incredible cake and even put my name on the top. It was my extra special cake and I could have eaten it all up myself but I asked her to save a big slice for

154

you. So I did. And you haven't even started on it yet. Don't you like it? It was meant to be your big treat.'

'Oh, it's lovely, Tracy,' said Peter, munching politely. 'It's ever so good of you. I told Auntie Vi and Uncle Stanley all about you and said that you were my best friend. They want to meet you very much.'

'Well, it's no use them getting interested in me. I'm going to be fostered by Cam, you wait and see.'

'Really? That's wonderful. You see, I think Auntie Vi and Uncle Stanley want to foster me, Tracy. That's what they said. They want to take me almost straight away.'

'So you're zooming off and leaving me in this dump, are you?' I said. 'Terrific!'

'Well. I don't *want* to leave you, Tracy. I told them that. But if you're going to be fostered too . . .'

'Yeah, yeah, well Cam's desperate to have me, but you shouldn't always rush into these things you know, Peter. You should think it over carefully.'

'I know. That's what I've been trying to do,' said Peter. 'Tracy. No matter who fosters me, who fosters you, we can still stay best friends, can't we? And visit each other lots? And write letters?'

'I'll write you letters with my very own

special Mickey Mouse pen. Want to see it?'

'Oh Tracy, you didn't nick it from Cam, did you?'

'Cheek! What do you take me for? She gave it to me, dumbo. I told you she's dotty about me. OK, we'll make a pact. We'll stay best friends no matter what. Here, you're leaving all the icing. Don't you like it?'

'Well, I was saving the best bit till last. But you have it, Tracy. I want you to have it, really.'

It's quite good, sharing a cake with your best friend.

Then I went round the whole Home with the packet of Smarties. I gave one each to everyone. I even gave one to Louise and the new girl. They were upstairs together, trying on the new girl's clothes.

Justine was downstairs. At the window. Her dad hadn't turned up. She had a new sticking plaster on her face. She was sniffling.

I looked at her. My heart started going thump thump thump. I went up to her. She turned round, looking all hopeful. She thought I was Louise. But it looks like Louise might have a new best friend now. Louise is like that.

Justine jumped a bit when she saw it was me.

'What do you want, Tracy Beaker?' she mumbled, wiping her eyes.

'I've got something for you, Justine,' I said.

I thought I was going to give her a Smartie. But you'll never guess what I did. I gave her my Mickey Mouse pen.

I must be stark staring bonkers. I hope Cam can get me another one. Next Saturday. When I see her. When she tells me that she's thought it all over and she wants to be my foster mum.

This started like a fairy story. And it's going to finish like one too. Happily Ever After.

JACQUELINE WILSON

Dumping Ground

STARRING
TRACY BEAKER

Illustrated by
Nick Sharratt

To the staff and pupils at
Charles Dickens Primary School

I'm Tracy Beaker. Mark the name. I'll be famous one day.

I live in a children's home. We all call it the Dumping Ground. We're dumped here because no one wants us.

No, that's total rubbish. My mum wants me. It's just she's this famous film star and she's way too busy making movies in Hollywood to look after me. But my mum's coming to see me at Christmas. She *is*. I just know she is.

'Your mum's not coming to see you in a month of Sundays,' said Justine Littlewood. 'Your mum's never ever coming back because she doesn't want anything to do with an ugly manky bad-mouthed stupid show-off who wets the bed every ni—'

7

She never managed to finish her sentence because I leaped across the room, seized hold of her hair and yanked hard, as if I was gardening and her hair was a particularly annoying weed.

I ended up in the Quiet Room. I didn't care. It gave me time to contemplate. That's a posh word for think. I have an extensive vocabulary. I am definitely destined to be a writer. A *successful* glossy rich and famous writer, not a struggling scruffy hack like Cam.

I mused (*another* posh word for think!) over the idea of a month of Sundays.

It would be seriously cool to have a lie-in every single day and watch telly all morning and have a special roast dinner and never have to go to school. But then I pondered (posh alternative number *three*) on the really bad thing about Sundays. Lots of the kids in the Dumping Ground get taken out by their mums or dads.

I don't. Well, I see Cam now, that's all. Cam's maybe going to be my foster mum. She's going to classes to see if she's suitable. It's mad. I don't trust my stupid social worker, Elaine the Pain. I don't want Cam to get cold feet. Though she keeps her toes cosy in her knitted stripy socks. She's not what you'd call a natty dresser. She's OK. But a foster mum isn't like a *real* mum. Especially not a famous glamorous movie star

Elaine the Pain

mum like mine. It isn't *her* fault she hasn't shown up recently. She's got such a punishing film schedule that, try as she might, she simply can't manage to jump on a plane and fly over here.

But she *is* going to come for Christmas, so there, Justine Now-Almost-Bald-And-It-Serves-You-Right Littlewood. My mum promised. She really really did.

She was going to see me in the summer. We were going to have this incredible holiday together on a tropical island, lying on golden sands in our bikinis, swimming with dolphins in an azure sea, sipping cocktails in our ten-star hotel . . .

Well, she was going to take me out for the day. It was all arranged. Elaine the Pain set it all up – but my poor mum couldn't make it. Right at the last minute she was needed for some live television interview – I'm sure that was it. Or maybe *Hello!* or *OK!* magazine wanted an exclusive photo shoot. Whatever.

So she never showed up, and instead of being understanding I heard Elaine ranting on to Jenny at the Dumping Ground, telling her all sorts of stupid stuff, like I was crying my eyes out. That was a downright lie. I would never cry. I sometimes get a little attack of hay fever, but I never cry.

I felt *mortified*. I wanted to cement Elaine's mouth shut. We had words. Quite a few of mine were bad words. I told Elaine that she had no business talking about one of her clients – i.e. me – and I had a good mind to report her. It was outrageous of her slandering my mum. She was a famous Hollywood movie actress, didn't she *understand*? Elaine should be more *deferential*, seeing as she's just a poxy social worker.

Elaine said a bad word then. She said she understood why I was so angry. It was easier for me to take my anger out on her when I was *really* angry at my mum for letting me down yet again. *WHAT???* I wasn't the slightest bit angry with my mum. It wasn't her fault she's so popular and famous and in demand.

'Yeah, so why haven't we ever seen her in a single film or telly show, and why are there never any photos of her in any of the magazines?' said Justine Why-Won't-She-Mind-Her-Own-Business Littlewood.

'Wash your ears out, Justine Littlewood. My mum's a famous *Hollywood* actress. Like, Hollywood in America. She isn't in films and mags over *here*, but in America she's incredibly well known. She can't set foot outside the door without the photographers snapping away and all her fans begging for autographs.'

'Yeah, yeah, she signs all these autographs, yet when does she ever bother to write to you?' said Justine Won't-Ever-Quit Littlewood.

But ha ha, sucks to you, J.L., because my mum *did* write, didn't she? She sent me a postcard.

She really did.

I keep it pinned on my wall, beside the photo of Mum and me when I was a baby and still looked sweet. The postcard had a picture of this cutesie-pie teddy with two teardrops falling out of his glass eyes and wetting his fur and the word *Sorry!* in sparkly lettering.

On the back my mum wrote:

So sorry I couldn't make it, Tracy. Chin up, chickie! See you soon. Christmas?
      Lots of love,
         Mum
           ×××

I know it off by heart. I've made up a
little tune and I sing it to myself
every morning when I wake up
and every night when I go
to bed. I sing it softly in
school. I sing it when I'm
watching television. I
sing it in the bath. I sing
it on the toilet. I sing the
punctuation and stuff too,

Chin up, comma, ♭ ♪ chickie, Full stop

like: '*Christ-mas, question mark. Lots of love,
comma, Mum, kiss kiss kiss.*' It's a very catchy
tune. I might well be a song writer when I grow
up as well as a famous novelist.

Of course I'm also going to be an actress just
like my mum. I am soon going to be acclaimed as
a brilliant child star. I have the ☆STAR☆ part
in a major production this Christmas. Truly.

I am in our school's play of *A Christmas Carol*.

I haven't done too well in casting sessions in
the past. At my other schools I never seemed to
get picked for any really juicy roles. I was a donkey
when we did a Nativity play. I was a little miffed
that I wasn't Mary or the Angel Gabriel at the
very least, but like a true little trooper I decided
to make the most of my part.

14

I worked hard on developing authentic eeyore donkey noises. I eeyored like an entire herd of donkeys during the performance. OK, I maybe drowned out Mary's speech, and the Angel Gabriel's too (to say nothing of Joseph, the Innkeeper, the Three Wise Men and Assorted Shepherds), but real donkeys don't wait politely till people have finished talking, they eeyore whenever they feel like it. I felt like eeyoring constantly, so I did.

I didn't get picked to be in any more plays at that stupid old school. But this school's not too bad. We have a special art and drama teacher, Miss Simpkins. She understands that if we do art we need to be dead artistic and if we do drama then we should aim at being dead *dramatic*. She admired my arty paintings of Justine Littlewood being devoured by lions and tigers and bears.

'You're a very imaginative and lively girl, Tracy,' said Miss Simpkins.

I wasn't totally bowled over by this. That's the way social workers talk when they're trying to boost your confidence or sell you to prospective foster carers. 'Imaginative and lively' means you get up to all sorts of irritating and annoying tricks. *Me?* Well, maybe.

My famous imagination ran away with me when we were auditioning for *A Christmas Carol*. I didn't really know the story that well. It's ever so l-o-n-g and I'm a very busy person, with no time to read dull old books. Miss Simpkins gave us a quick précis version and I had a little fidget and yawn because it seemed so old fashioned and boring, but my ears pricked up – right out of my curls – when she said there were ghosts.

'I'll be a ghost, Miss. I'm great at scaring people. Look, look, I'm a headless ghost!' I pulled my school jumper up over my head and held my arms like claws and went, 'Whooooo!'

Silly little Peter Ingham squealed in terror and ducked under his desk.

'See, I can be really convincing, Miss! And I can do you all sorts of *different* ghosts. I can do your standard white-sheet spooky job, or I can moan and clank chains, or I could paint myself grey all over and be this wafting spirit ghost creeping up on people, ready to leap out at them.'

I leaped out at Weedy Peter just as he emerged from under his desk. He shrieked and ducked, banging his head in the process.

'Well, you're certainly entering into the spirit

17

of things, Tracy,' said Miss Simpkins, bending down to rub Peter's head and give the little weed a cuddle. 'There now, Peter, don't look so scared. It isn't a real ghost, it's only Tracy Beaker.'

'I'm scared of Tracy Beaker,' said Peter. 'Even though she's my friend.'

I wish the little creep wouldn't go around telling everyone he's my friend. It's dead embarrassing. I don't want you to think he's my *only* friend. I've got heaps and heaps of friends. Well. Louise isn't my best friend any more. She's gone totally off her head because she now wants to be friends with Justine No-Fun-At-All Littlewood. There's no one in our class who actually quite measures up to my friendship requirements.

Hey, I *have* got a best friend. It's Cam! She comes to see me every Saturday. She's not like my mum, glamorous and beautiful and exciting. But she can sometimes be good fun. So she's my best friend. And Miss Simpkins can be my second best friend at school.

Peter's just my friend at the Dumping Ground. Especially at night time, when there's no one else around.

Peter seemed to be thinking about our night-time get-togethers too.

'Promise promise promise you won't
pretend to be a ghost tonight, Tracy?'
he whispered anxiously.

'Ah! I'm afraid I can't
possibly promise, Peter. I am
the child of a famous Hollywood
star. I take my acting seriously.
I might well have to stay in
character and act ghostly all
the time,' I said.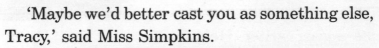

'Maybe we'd better cast you as something else,
Tracy,' said Miss Simpkins.

'Oh no, *please* let me be the ghost!' I begged.

It turned out there were four main ghosts in
A Christmas Carol and a motley crew of ghostly
extras too.

There was the Ghost of Christmas Past.

'Let *me* be the Ghost of Christmas Past, Miss
Simpkins,' I said.

'No, Tracy, I need a girl with
long fair hair to be the Ghost of
Christmas Past,' said Miss
Simpkins.

She chose *Louise*.

'Now there's the Ghost of

Christmas Present,' said Miss Simpkins.

'Let *me* be the Ghost of Christmas Present,' I said.

'No, Tracy. I need a big jolly boy to be the Ghost of Christmas Present,' said Miss Simpkins.

Freddy

She chose old Fatty Freddy.

'Now there's the Ghost of Christmas Yet to Come,' said Miss Simpkins.

'I thought Charles Dickens was meant to be a good writer. He's a bit repetitive when it comes to ghosts, isn't he?' I said. 'Still, let *me* be the Ghost of Christmas Yet to Come.'

Philip

'No, Tracy, I need a very tall boy to be the Ghost of Christmas Yet to Come,' said Miss Simpkins.

She chose this pea-brained boy called Philip who couldn't haunt so much as a graveyard.

'There's just one more main ghost and that's Marley's Ghost,' said Miss Simpkins. 'He wails and clanks his chains.'

'Oooh, I'm a totally terrific wailer and clanker, you know I am! Let *me* be Marley's Ghost,' I begged.

'I'm very tempted, Tracy, but perhaps you might indulge in a tad too much wailing and clanking,' said Miss Simpkins.

She chose *Justine Can't-Act-For-Toffee Littlewood*, who can't clank to save her life and can barely whimper, let alone give a good ghostly *wail*.

Justine!

I was Severely Irritated with Miss Simpkins. I decided she wasn't my friend any more. I didn't want to be in her stupid play if she wouldn't pick me for one of the main ghosts. I didn't want to be one of the no-name *extra* ghosts or any of the other people – these silly Fezziwigs and Cratchits.

I turned my back on Miss Simpkins and whistled a festive tune to myself . . . with new lyrics.

'Jingle Bells, Miss Simpkins smells,
Jingle all the day.
Oh what a fart it is to take part
In her stupid Christmas play.'

'And now there's only one part left,' said Miss Simpkins. 'Are you listening to me, Tracy?'

I gave the tiniest shrug, slumping down in my seat. I tried to make it crystal clear that I wasn't remotely interested.

'I'll take that as a yes,' said Miss Simpkins cheerfully. 'Yes, there's just the part of crusty old Ebenezer Scrooge himself to cast. Now, I'm going to have serious problems. This is the key part of the whole play. The *best* part, the *leading* part. I need a consummate actor, one who isn't phased by a really big juicy part, one who can act bad temper and meanness and lack of generosity, and yet one who can convincingly thaw and repent and behave wonderfully after all. I wonder . . .'

I sat up straight. I gazed at Miss Simpkins. She surely couldn't mean . . .

'You, Tracy Beaker! You will be my Scrooge!' she said.

'Yay!' I shrieked. I bounced up and down in my seat as if I had an india-rubber bottom.

'That's stupid, Miss!' said Justine Can't-Hold-Her-Tongue Littlewood. 'You can't let Tracy be Scrooge. Why should she get the best part? She just mucks around and doesn't take things seriously. You can't let her be in the play, she'll just mess it up for all of us.'

'I'll certainly mess *you* up,' I mumbled.

I rushed out of my seat, right up to Miss Simpkins.

'I'll take it all dead seriously, Miss Simpkins, I promise. You can count on me. And don't be surprised if I turn out to be unexpectedly brilliant at acting as my mum is a Hollywood movie star making one film after another.'

'As if!' said Louise.

'I know the only sort of movies Tracy Beaker's mum would star in. *Blue* movies!' said Justine Liar-Liar-Liar Littlewood.

My fists clenched, I so badly wanted to punch her straight in the nose, but I knew she was just trying to wind me up so Miss Simpkins would lose her temper with me and not let me be Scrooge after all. I simply raised my eyebrows and hissed a small rebuff along the lines that her dad belonged in a *horror* movie. Then I turned my back on her and smiled at Miss Simpkins.

'As I've got the biggest part you'd better give me a copy of the play straight away, Miss Simpkins, so I can get to be word perfect. In fact, maybe I ought to be excused all the boring lessons like literacy and maths just so I can concentrate on learning my part.'

'Nice try, Tracy, but I'm not that much of a pushover,' said Miss Simpkins. 'No, you'll have to learn your part in your own time.'

I was so anxious to play Scrooge I learned my lines in *other* people's time. Mostly Cam's. I used up two entire Saturday visits getting her to read out all the other parts while I Bah-Humbugged my way through Scrooge. Cam tried almost too hard at first, doing weird voices for all the Christmas ghosts and an extremely irritating little-boy lisp for Tiny Tim.

'Hey, *I'm* the one that's supposed to be acting, not you,' I said. 'Just *speak* the lines.'

'Look, I'm the adult. Aren't I the one supposed to tell *you* what  to do?' said Cam, swatting me with the script of the play. 'Oh no, sorry, I forgot. You're Tracy Beaker so you get to be Big Bossy-Knickers, right?'

'Absolutely right, Cam. You got it in one! Hey, all this saying lines about sucking pigs and sausages has made me simply starving. Any chance of us going out to McDonald's?'

Mike

Jenny

I didn't just pester Cam to hear my lines. I got Jenny and Mike at the Dumping Ground to help me out, though I got dead annoyed when they wanted Justine Utter-Rubbish Littlewood and Louise and weedy little Peter to attend our special rehearsals too.

'It's not fair! I can't concentrate with all that rabble around,' I declared. 'Let's send them packing.'

'They're all in *A Christmas Carol* too, Tracy. You're not the only one who needs help with your lines,' said Jenny.

'We can act it all out together,' said Mike. 'Trust you to behave like a prima donna, Tracy.'

'Yeah, trust me, because what is the definition of prima donna, Mike? Isn't she the star of the whole show? I rest my case!'

I even considered commandeering Elaine the Pain to help me with my part. She's always encouraging us looked-after kids to role-play and act out our angst so I wondered if she might have any useful tips.

I'd lost it a little there. As if Old Elaine could

26

ever be useful at anything! Especially Elaine in Christmas mode, decking our ropy Dumping Ground with tinsel and home-made paper chains, a pair of wacky rainbow antlers bobbing manically on her head and a Comic Relief nose pinching her own. She was wearing a holly-berry-red knitted jumper and an ivy-green skirt, way too tight, and was warbling the words of 'Rudolph the Red-nosed Reindeer'.

'Elaine my social worker
Had a very large fat bum,
And if you ever saw her
You would scream out loud and run,'
I sang under my breath.

Not quite under enough. Elaine heard and got quite aerated. She burbled on about Cheek and Attitude and Silly Offensive Personal Remarks that could be Really Hurtful. I started to feel a little bit mean. I was even considering saying sorry. Elaine can't *help* having a huge bum after all.

She said she understood I was feeling tense and anxious because she'd heard I'd taken on a huge part in our school play when I simply wasn't used to Applying Myself and Being Responsible.

I stopped feeling even the tiniest bit sorry. I was glad when I heard Elaine say to Jenny, 'Look, can I ask you for a really honest answer? Do you think my bu— behind looks a bit big in my new skirt?'

I decided I would simply rely on myself and learn my part properly and show them all. This was fine and dandy during the day but not quite so easy at night. I kept having these bizarre nightmares where I was all alone on stage and I kept opening my mouth like a goldfish but no sound at all came out. I couldn't so much as blow a bubble. The audience started getting restless, pelting me with rotten fruit. One maggoty old apple landed straight in my gaping mouth, so I looked exactly like the Ghost of Christmas Present's sucking pig.

Then they put me on a spit and roasted me. I screamed that I was burning so they threw water at me. Lots and lots of water . . . When I woke up my bed was unaccountably wet and I had to go on a dismal damp trek to the bathroom and the linen cupboard.

I met up with Weedy Peter on a similar mission. He was actually crying. Like I said, I never cry. I might occasionally have an attack of hay fever but that is a medical condition, not an emotional state.

'What are you blubbing for, silly?' I asked.

'I'm so scared I'll be rubbish in the school Christmas play,' Peter sobbed. 'I wish wish wish Miss Simpkins hadn't made me be Tiny Tim. I don't *want* to act. I can't remember the words and I can't figure out which leg to hop on, and it will all be so so so much worse with people watching us. It's all right for you, Tracy. You never get scared of anything and you're a terrible show-off so acting's right up your street.'

'Cheek! Don't you dare call me a terrible show-off!' I said.

'But you are.'

'Yes, I know, but you don't have to point it out.'

'I'd give *anything* to be a terrible show-off,' Peter said earnestly. 'Can't you show me how, Tracy? Is there a special trick?'

'It's just a natural gift, Peter,' I said. 'I was born showing off. I shot out of my mum and said, "Hi, folks!" to the doctor and the nurse, and then I turned a somersault, stood on my tiny feet and did a little tap dance on the delivery table.'

I felt for Peter's head in the dark. His mouth was hanging open. I closed it gently.

'Joke,' I said. 'OK, as an extra special favour to you, Peter, we'll act out all our scenes together.'

We started meeting up for midnight rehearsals on a regular basis. Peter was soon word perfect because he had hardly any lines to learn. I mean, how hard is it to remember 'God bless us, every one' for goodness sake? But though he could say the words he couldn't *act* them at all. He just mumbled them in a monotone.

'You certainly *are* rubbish at acting, Peter,' I said. 'Oh stop it, don't go all sniffly on me. I'm not being mean, I'm simply stating a fact. But don't worry, I'll help. You've got to feel your way into the part. You're this little weedy boy with a delicate constitution and a gammy leg. That's not hard, is it? Talk about type-casting.'

'I haven't got a gammy leg,' said Peter the Pedant.

'I'll kick it hard if you like,' I said. 'Now, even though you're down on your luck, you're a chirpy little soul, the favourite of your family. Your dad especially dotes on you.'

'I wish that bit was true,' said Peter mournfully.

'Yeah. Me too,' I said.

We huddled closer under our shared blanket.

'I wish I had a family to come and see me in the play,' said Peter. 'Well, maybe I don't – not if I'm rubbish.'

'You won't be rubbish, you'll be terrific with the

Totally Tremendous Tracy Beaker directing you. Yes, it's sad you haven't got anyone. Never mind, I'll ask my mum to give you a special wave.'

'Your mum's coming?' Peter asked, sounding astonished.

'You bet. She's coming for Christmas, she promised,' I said. 'She'll be desperate to watch me act to see if I've inherited her show-biz talents – which I *have*. I've written her a letter telling her all about the show.'

I'd written her several letters. In fact I wrote to her every single day and gave them to Jenny to post.

Dear Mum,

I can't wait to see you at Christmas, remember, you promised? Can you come a week early so you can come to my school play and see me in my ⭐STAR⭐ role as Scrooge? I am dead good at being a mean miserable old man.

Lots and lots and lots of love from your happy cheery little daughter

Tracy xxx

'I know just how much you want to see your mum, Tracy, but don't get *too* fixated on her coming to see you,' said Elaine.

'But she is, she wrote and said – she promised . . . practically.'

'I know how much you want her to come, but sometimes our wishes don't always come true,' said Elaine.

I wished I didn't have a social worker. I wished I had a fairy godmother who said, 'You want your mum to come and see you? Certainly, Tracy, no problem,' and she'd wave her wand and *wow! pow!* there would be my mum, all pink and powdery and perfect, her arms outstretched ready to give me a big hug.

I haven't got a fairy godmother. I have to work my own magic.

The next Saturday Cam came to see me at the Dumping Ground as usual. We had a quick run-through of the whole play – and I mean *quick*. I gabbled my way through my part like I was on fast forward. I possibly missed out whole chunks, but when Cam pointed this out I just said, 'Yeah, yeah, whatever, but I'm on *this* bit now,' and revved up into Thousand-Words-A-Minute Top Gear.

We finished the play in twenty minutes dead.

'Right! Done the rehearsal. Now let's go out,' I said.

'Ah! So McDonald's is calling?' said Cam.

'No. Well, *yes*, I'm starving actually, but I want to go round the shops. I want to do some Christmas shopping.'

Jenny gives all of us older kids a special Christmas shopping allowance. She goes shopping with the little kids and helps them choose – otherwise they just spend it on sweets for themselves. Us older kids usually snaffle a little for sweets too, but this time I wanted *all* my money for presents. One set of presents in particular.

'I might as well do my Christmas shopping too, Tracy,' said Cam.

'Ooh! What are you getting for me, Cam?' I asked, momentarily diverted. 'I could really do with some new jeans. Designer, natch. And one of those really cool furry jackets with a hood. And there's this seriously wicked motorized go-cart that would be fun for swooping all round the gardens of the Dumping Ground – *swoosh, swoosh* – Oh I'm *sorry*, Justine Littlewood, was that your foot?'

'Tracy, I can't afford to buy you so much as a motorized matchbox at the moment. I'm totally skint. You've got to adopt a new attitude. *It's the thought that counts.*'

'It strikes me *you* should be playing Scrooge, not me, if you're not giving proper Christmas presents,' I said. 'Honestly, Cam, why don't you get your act together and write a socking great bestseller? Something that would be snapped up by Hollywood in a million-dollar movie deal. Then me and my mum could star in it.'

'Dream on, sweetheart,' said Cam. 'I somehow don't think I'm bestseller material.'

'You've got to think positive, Cam. You've got to *make* your dreams come true,' I said.

I was intent on doing just that.

When we got to the shopping centre I got Cam to come to Boots with me to buy some really special make-up.

'So what's the *best* brand, Cam?' I asked.

'Don't ask me, Tracy, I hardly ever wear make-up. I just buy whatever's cheapest,' she said.

'Well, this is a present for my mum so I want the most glamorous gorgeous stuff possible.'

I fiddled around trying out different lipstick shades on my wrist until it looked like I had red-rose tattoos up both arms.

Then I finally selected the most perfect pearly pink.

Cam thought we were done.

'No, no! Hand lotion next!'

Cam sighed and fidgeted while I tried out all the lotions, sniffing them carefully and comparing them for creaminess. After a while my hands got very slippery and sticky and I had to wipe them on my skirt.

'I don't think Jenny's going to be very thrilled about those great greasy marks,' said Cam. 'Come *on*, Tracy, let's go to the bookshop now.'

'No, no, I've got to get my mum another present. I need a jewellery shop now.'

'But you've already got your mum the lipstick *and* the hand lotion.' Cam sneaked a peek in my purse. 'Don't forget you've got to buy Christmas presents for everyone.'

I wasn't interested in buying presents for everyone. I didn't want to buy a present for anyone but my *mum*.

I dragged Cam into a lovely sparkly jewellery shop, but when I saw the prices of even the weeniest rings I had to back away, sighing.

'That's real jewellery, Tracy. A little bit ostentatious, all that gold and diamonds. I think costume jewellery is much more tasteful,' Cam said quickly.

'OK. Where do you buy this costume jewellery then?'

She took me to the ground floor of this big department store and I walked round and round great glass cabinets of jewellery. I saw a pink heart on a crimson ribbon. It was utterly beautiful. I could just imagine it round my mum's neck. It was *very* expensive, even for costume jewellery, but I counted out every last penny in my purse and found I could just about manage it, keeping a fiver back for my last-of-all purchase.

'Are you *sure*, Tracy? I think maybe your mum would be happy with just the lipstick. Or the hand lotion.'

'My mum likes *lots* of presents,' I said. 'I know what I'm doing, Cam.'

I *didn't* really know what I was going to do about everyone else's presents. Still, I wasn't speaking to Louise any more on account of the fact she'd ganged up with Justine Ugly-Unscrupulous-Friend-Snatcher Littlewood so I didn't have to buy her anything.

There was Jenny and Mike, but they quite liked all that pathetic home-made calendar and dried-pasta-picture rubbish. Maybe Miss Simpkins at school would go for that sort of stuff too. Ditto Cam. She believed that it was the thought that counted, didn't she? She'd as good as indicated that I wasn't getting anything to speak of from her. It would only embarrass her if I gave her too lavish a gift.

That just left Weedy Peter. I was sure I could fob him off with something of mine I didn't want any more, like my leather wallet with the broken clasp or my leaky snowstorm or my wrinkly copy of *The Lion, the Witch and the Wardrobe* that got a little damp when I was reading it in the bath.

I heaved a sigh of relief. Christmas-present problem *sorted*. Now there was just one present left.

'Come on, Cam, I've got to go to a bookshop,' I said, tugging her.

She was peering at some very boring pearls in the jewellery cabinet.

'Bookshop! Now we're talking. But hang on. Look, what do you think of that little pearl necklace there – the one with the diamanté clasp? All the sparkly stuff's half price, special offer.'

'Cam, you are so *not* a pearl necklace person.'

'They're not for me, silly.'

I blinked at her. 'Look, Cam, it's very kind of you, but actually *I'm* not a pearl necklace person either.'

Cam snorted. 'You can say that again, Tracy. No no no, I'm thinking about my mum.'

'Ah. Yes. She's quite posh, isn't she, your mum?'

'Insufferably so. Very very much a pearl sort of person. But *real* pearls. These are fake so I expect she'd turn her nose up at them.'

'Well, get her real ones then.'

'Don't be a banana, Tracy. I couldn't possibly afford them. I can't actually afford the fake ones, even half price. You know, I'm like a fake daughter to my mum. She's *so* disappointed that I'm not all smart and glossy with a posh partner and a brilliant career.'

'Well, you could still try to get them,' I said doubtfully.

'I don't want to. I want to be *me*. It's so hard not to get wound up by my mum. I'm absolutely dreading going home for Christmas.'

'You're *dreading* going home for Christmas?' I said slowly.

Cam stopped gazing at the fake pearls and looked at me.

'Oh Tracy, I'm sorry. That was such a stupid tactless thing to say to you. I know just how much you want to see your mum this Christmas.'

'And I'm going to,' I said, very firmly and fiercely.

'Well, that would be truly great, but remember, your mum might just be busy or tied up or . . . or . . . abroad,' Cam said.

'No, she's going to be here. She's going to come and see me in my starring role in *A Christmas Carol*. And then she'll stay over. I dare say she'll take us to this top hotel and we'll have Christmas there. Yeah, it will be so great. We'll sleep in this big big queen-size bed and then we'll splash in our power shower and then we'll have the most immense breakfast. I'll be allowed to eat whatever I want. I can put six spoonfuls of sugar on my cereal and eat twenty sausages in one go and I'll have those puffy things with maple syrup—'

'Waffles?'
'Yeah, I'll scoffle a waffle,' I said as we walked out of the department store towards the

bookshop. 'I'll scoffle *six* waffles and I'll have hot chocolate with whipped cream, and *then* I'll open my presents and my mum will give me heaps and heaps and heaps of stuff – a whole wardrobe of designer clothes, enough new shoes and trainers and boots to shod a giant centipede—'

'And a motorized go-cart? Sorry, a whole *fleet* of them.'

'Yep, and bikes and scooters and my own trampoline, and I'll be able to bounce soooo high I'll swoop straight up to the sky and everyone will look up at me and go, *Is it a bird? Is it a plane? Is it Superman? Is it Santa? Noooo, it's the Truly Tremendous Tracy Beaker!'*

I bounced up and down to demonstrate. I accidentally landed on Cam's foot and she gave a little scream, but she was very nice about it.

We carried on playing the Christmas game until we got to the bookshop. Well, it wasn't exactly a game. I knew it was all going to come true, though perhaps I was embellishing things a little. I am occasionally prone to exaggeration. That means I can get carried away and tell socking great lies. They start to seem so real that I believe them too.

Cam was very happy to be in the bookshop. She ran her finger lovingly along the long lines of paperbacks.

'I'll have a little browse,' she said. 'The children's section is over in that corner, Tracy.'

'I don't want the children's books. I want the classics section,' I said loftily.

'Oh yes?' said Cam. 'You fancy a quick flick through *War and Peace*?'

'That's quite a good title. If I write my true life story about my Dumping Ground experiences I'll call my book *War and More War and Yet More War*. No, I'm going to peruse the collected works of Mr Charles Dickens.'

That showed her. I wasn't kidding either. I wanted to find a copy of *A Christmas Carol*. I found a very nice paperback for £4.99. I had just one penny left. I didn't put it back in my purse. I decided to throw it in the dinky wishing well by the shopping centre Christmas tree.

I could do with a good wishing session.

Cam was still browsing in the fiction, her nose in a book, her whole expression one of yearning. I knew she couldn't afford all the books she wanted. She said she often spent ten or twenty minutes in the shop reading a book before putting it back reluctantly. Once she'd even marked her place with a bus ticket so she could sidle back the next day – and the next and the next and the next – until she'd finished the whole story.

I suddenly wished I'd saved just a little bit of my Christmas money to buy Cam a paperback. I fidgeted uncomfortably with my wishing penny. I threw it up and caught it again and again, practising my wishing. Then I dropped it and it rolled off, right round the shelves. I ran after it and practically bumped my nose on the MIND BODY SPIRIT sign.

I picked up my penny, my eyes glazing over at all these dippy books about star signs and spiritual auras – and then I saw a title in sparkly silver lettering: *Make Your Wishes Come True*.

45

I reached for the book, my hand shaking. It was a slim little book, written by someone called Grizelda Moonbeam, White Witch. I considered calling myself Tracy Moonbeam, Very Black Witch. I'd learn magic spells and make frogs and toads spew out of Justine Get-Everyone-On-Her-Side Littlewood.

I opened the book and started flipping through the pages. It really was full of spells! I couldn't find a frog-and-toad curse for your worst enemy, but there were plenty of love potions and magic charms. I turned another page and then my heart started thumping.

'CHARM TO BE WITH YOUR LOVED ONE ON A FESTIVE OCCASION'.

My mum was my Very Much Loved One and you couldn't get a more Festive Occasion than Christmas. I so badly wanted her to come this Christmas and watch me act Scrooge on stage I was about ready to pop.

I read the charm carefully. Grizelda advised mixing one part mead to two parts dandelion wine, adding cinnamon for spice and ginger for warmth and sugar for  sweetness. She suggested stirring the mixture well while chanting the Loved One's name, then drinking from the wrong side of the glass without drawing breath.

I blinked. Easy-peasy! I gabbled the ingredients over and over again. I'd got so used to learning my Scrooge lines that the recipe tucked itself neatly inside my head without too much fussing. Then I reverently replaced Grizelda Moonbeam, danced seven times around the bookshelf because it seemed a magic thing to do, and then staggered giddily off to find Cam.

'Are you feeling OK, Tracy?' she asked, as I bumped right into her.

'I'm fine,' I said, carefully sorting out my carrier bags *and* my penny. 'Come on, Cam, let's get cracking. I've got all my Christmas presents now.'

'And I haven't got a sausage,' said Cam, sighing. 'Oh well, maybe I can make some of my presents this year.'

I shook my head at her. 'Look, Cam, making presents is for little kids. *I* can barely get away with it. You're way too old, believe me. And forget *all* about it on my behalf. I want a proper present!'

'You don't really work hard to get people to like you, Tracy,' said Cam, shutting her book with a snap.

'I don't have to. I'm bubbling over with natural charm,' I said.

However, I pondered her point as we left the bookshop. What *was* all this gubbins about getting people to like you? I didn't fancy sucking up to people all the time and saying they looked lovely when they looked rubbish and all that sick-making nonsense. Louise was a past master at that – and a present mistress too. She could flutter her long eyelashes, fix you with a

48

soulful glance with her big blue eyes and say softly that you were the funniest girl in all the world and she wanted to be your best friend for ever and you actually *believed* it, until she ganged up with Someone Else.

Still, I wouldn't want to be Louise's best friend any more. I don't *want* her to like me again. I definitely don't want Justine Dog-Breath-Snake-Tongue-Baboon-Bottom Littlewood to like me.

I don't need to work at getting people to like me. Heaps and heaps of people do. I go out of my way to *stop* Weedy Peter liking me. Elaine and Jenny and Mike like me too. They do heaps of things for me, don't they? Although they're paid to hang out with me. Maybe they simply can't stick me but don't tell me because it would be unprofessional.

It was silly thinking like this. I was starting to panic. It wasn't good for me to get so worked up, though of course all great actors were hypersensitive and temperamental. Miss Simpkins liked me or she wouldn't have offered me the starring part in her play. Unless . . . she was simply sorry for me because I was little Tracy No-Friends, the most unpopular girl in the whole school.

Maybe Cam didn't like me either. She just came to take me out every week as a duty. She was making a fuss of the Sad Ugly Kid with Mega Attitude Problems because it made her feel good. Maybe I was her Unpleasant Weekly Project, on a par with taking out the rubbish and cleaning the toilet.

'Tracy? Why are you breathing all funny?' said Cam, as we walked through the shopping centre.

'I'm hyperventilating on account of your hostile remarks,' I said, going extra gaspy to give her a fright.

'What do you mean?'

'You said no one likes me,' I said.

I suddenly couldn't *help* gasping I felt so horrible.

'I *didn't*!' Cam said.

'You did, you did, you did, and it's outrageous to say that to a looked-after child. You've probably traumatized me for life,' I said, giving her a shove.

I used my elbows and they're particularly sharp.

'Ouch! You've probably *punctured* me for life with your stiletto elbows.'

'Well, I'm fading away with hunger. It's no wonder I'm so skinny. You'd better whip me to McDonald's quick, what with my general anorexic state and my tragic realization that everyone totally hates me.'

'Oh Tracy, will you just *stop* it. I didn't say anyone hated you. I didn't say anyone didn't like you. I simply said you didn't try hard to make people like you.' Cam paused. She took hold of me by the shoulders, staring straight into my eyes. 'But even when you treat me like dirt *I* still like you.'

I relaxed.

'Mind you, I'd like you even more if you'd try being gentle and considerate and polite,' said Cam.

'*Me?*' I said. 'Dream on! Come on, I want my Big Mac and fries. Please. Dear kind pretty ever-so-nice-to-me Camilla.'

'Yuck! It was working till you said my name.

That's what my mum calls me. Oh God, I wish it wasn't nearly Christmas.'

I had my own wish to make. A real magic spell, *much* more powerful than throwing a penny in a polystyrene wishing well. I went over it in my head as I munched my burger and gobbled my chips and slurped my shake.

'Can we go back to your house for tea, Cam?' I asked. 'Hey, I've thought what I want for tea too.'

'You're only just having your lunch, girl.'

'Yeah, yeah, but I want something *special* for tea. Something Christmasy.'

'You know I'm pretty skint at the moment. I expect I can manage a sausage on a stick and a mince pie but that's about my limit.'

'Never mind that stuff. Well, yes to sausages and yes to mince pies too, and a chocolate log would be a good idea, come to think of it, but what I was really hoping for was Christmas punch.'

'What?'

'You know. A special festive drink. There's this amazing punch I've heard about. You mix one part mead to two parts dandelion wine, and then you add cinnamon and ginger and sugar, stir it all around, and Bob's your uncle, Fanny's your aunt, yummy yummy in your tummy.' I mimed being a cocktail barman for her and ended up with a flourish.

'Cheers!' I said, raising my imaginary glass.

Cam blinked at me. 'Well, personally I prefer a simple glass of wine as a festive drink, but each to their own. We can try and fix you something similar—'

'No, no, you can't muck about with the ingredients, it'll lose all its potency,' I said urgently.

Cam's eyes narrowed. 'Tracy, have you taken up witchcraft?'

She is so spooky at times. It's as if she can open a little flap in my head and peer straight into my mind.

'Watch out if I *am* a trainee witch, Cam. Think of the havoc I could wreak,' I said, contorting my face into a witchy grimace and making manic old-hag cackles.

'Help help help,' said Cam, raising her

eyebrows. 'OK, I'll see what we can do. Come on, let's have a trek round Sainsbury's and see what we can come up with.'

We couldn't find any mead at all *or* dandelion wine. I started to fuss considerably.

'It's OK, Tracy. Mead is a honey drink,' Cam told me. 'I've got a jar of honey at home so we'll put a spoonful of honey in a glass of wine, and pick a dandelion on the way home and chop it up and add it too, OK? I've got sugar and we'll buy a little pot of cinnamon and – what was the other thing? Oh, ginger. Well, I think I've got a packet of ginger biscuits somewhere. They might be a bit stale but I don't suppose that matters.'

I was still a bit doubtful. I wanted to do it all *properly* but it couldn't be helped. When we got back to Cam's I carefully washed the dandelion leaf. It had been very hard to find. Cam eventually reached through the slats of someone's gate and picked a plant from their front garden.

'Um!' I said. 'Isn't that stealing?'

'It's weeding,' said Cam firmly. 'Dandelions are weeds.'

'If that *is* a dandelion.'

'Of course it is, Tracy.'

'What do you know about plants, Cam?'

'Look, I might not be Alan Titchmarsh, but I know my dandelions from my dock leaves. That is a dandelion, OK? So get chopping.'

I chopped the dandelion into little green specks, I crumbled the biscuits and spooned out the honey and sugar. Cam poured some wine into her prettiest pink wine glass. She lifted it absent-mindedly to her lips.

'Hey, hey, it's *my* potion!' I said.

'OK, OK,' said Cam, sighing. 'Go on then, shove the rest of the stuff in – though it seems a shame to muck up a perfectly good glass of wine.'

'This isn't a *drink*, Cam. It's a potion. *My* potion,' I said. 'Now, let me sprinkle and stir. You keep quiet. I have to concentrate.'

I concentrated like crazy, sprinkling in every little green dandelion speck and the ginger

55

and the sugar and the honey, and then I stirred it vigorously with a spoon.

'Hey, gently with that glass!' said Cam.

'Shh! And don't listen to me, this is *private*,' I hissed. I took a deep breath. 'Please work, charm,' I muttered. 'Let me be with my Loved One on a Festive Occasion – i.e. this Christmas! I need her there to see me in *A Christmas Carol* and then I want her to stay so we have the best Christmas ever together.'

Then I raised the glass, stuck my chin in to reach the wrong side and took a gulp of wine without drawing breath. It tasted *disgusting*, but I swallowed it down determinedly, wishing and wishing to make it come true.

'Steady on, Tracy! Don't drink it all – you'll get drunk!' said Cam. I didn't want to break the spell so I ignored her. I took another gulp and then spluttered and choked. The potion went up my nose and then snorted back out of it in totally disgusting fashion. I gasped while Cam patted me on the back and mopped me with a tissue.

'Oh dear, have I mucked up the magic?' I wheezed.

'No, no, you absorbed the potion through extra orifices so I guess that makes it even more potent,' said Cam. 'Still, seriously, no more! Jenny would never forgive me if I took you back to the Home totally blotto.'

'Oh gosh, Cam, I think I *am* utterly totally sloshed out of my skull,' I slurred, reeling around, pretending to trip and stumble.

'Tracy!' said Cam, rushing to catch me.

'Only joking!' I giggled.

'Well, maybe I'd better have a swig too if it's as potent as that,' said Cam.

She took the spoon and stirred it around herself, and then she mouthed something before she took a sip, drinking from the wrong side of the glass without drawing breath. Then she choked too, dribbling all down her chin.

It was my turn to clap her on the back.

'Hey, gently, Tracy!' Cam spluttered. 'Oh God. It tastes revolting. What a waste of wine.

Let's hope it jolly well works for both of us.'

'So who is *your* Loved One?' I said.

I wasn't too happy about this. As far as I knew Cam didn't have any Loved Ones, and that suited me just fine. I didn't want some bloke commandeering her on Saturdays and mucking up our special days together.

I knew what blokes could be like. That's how I started off in Care. My mum got this awful Monster Gorilla Boyfriend and he was horrible to me so I had to be taken away. I'd just like to see him try now. I was only little then. Well, I'm still quite little now but I am Incredibly Fierce and a Ferocious Fighter. Just ask Justine Bashed-To-A-Pulp Littlewood. If I encountered Monster Gorilla Boyfriend *now* I'd karate-chop him and then I'd kick him downstairs, out of the door, out of my life.

If Cam's anonymous Loved One started any funny business then he'd definitely get treated the same way. Beware the Beaker Boyfriend Deterrent!

'You haven't got a boyfriend, have you, Cam?' I asked her, as she fixed me a fruit smoothie to take away the terrible taste of the potion.

'A boyfriend?' said Cam, looking re-assuringly surprised. 'Oh Tracy, don't *you* start. My mum always goes on at me whenever I see her.' She put on this piercing posh voice. *'Haven't you met any decent men yet, Camilla? Mind you, I'm not surprised no one's interested. Look at the state of you – that terrible short haircut and those wretched jeans!'*

Cam poured herself a glass of wine and took several sips. 'Oh dear. Shut me up whenever I get onto the subject of my mum.' She shuddered dramatically. 'OK, how's about trying a plateful of cinnamon toast?'

It was utterly yummy. I had six slices. I didn't get Cam's mum-phobia. I *love* talking about my mum. But then I've got the best and most beautiful movie-star actress for a mum. Maybe I wouldn't be anywhere near as keen if I had a snobby old bag for a mum like Cam.

I usually hate it when Cam takes me back to the Dumping Ground but I was quite cool about it this evening because I had Mega Things to Do. I raided Elaine's art therapy cupboard (I'm ace at picking locks) and helped myself to lots of bright pink tissue paper and the best thin white card and a set of halfway-decent felt-tip pens.

It wasn't really *stealing*. I was using them for dead artistic and extremely therapeutic purposes.

I shoved my art materials up my jumper and shuffled my way up to my room and then proceeded to be Creative. I was still actively Creating when Jenny knocked on my door. She tried to come in but she couldn't, on account of the fact that I'd shoved my chair hard against it to repel all intruders.

'What are you up to in there, Tracy? Let me in!'

'Do you mind, Jenny? I'm working on something dead secret.'

'That's what I was afraid of! What are you doing? I want to see.'

'No, you mustn't look. I'm making Christmas presents,' I hissed.

'Ah!' said Jenny. 'Oh, Tracy, how lovely. I'm sorry, sweetheart, I'll leave you alone. But it's getting late. Switch your light out soon, pet.'

She went off down the corridor humming 'Jingle Bells', obviously thinking I was making *her* Christmas present. I'd have to get cracking now and make her something. Ditto Mike. Ditto Elaine. And ditto Cam, of course, though I would have liked to give her a proper present. Still, I had to have my priorities. Mum came first.

I wrapped the lipstick in pink tissue. Then I cut out a rectangle from the cardboard, drew a pair of smiley pink lips and carefully printed in tiny neat letters:

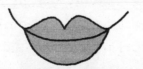

YOU WILL SMILE WITH SHINY LIPS
WHEN YOU SEE ME ACT SCROOGE
IN 'A CHRISTMAS CAROL',
7 PM WEDNESDAY 20 DECEMBER
AT KINGLEA JUNIOR SCHOOL!!!

I stuck the label on the first packet and then made three more. I drew two hands on the second label and printed:

YOU WILL CLAP TILL YOUR HANDS
ARE SORE WHEN YOU WATCH ME
AS SCROOGE IN 'A CHRISTMAS CAROL'
7 PM WEDNESDAY 20 DECEMBER
AT KINGLEA · JUNIOR SCHOOL !!!

I stuck this label on the wrapped hand lotion. On the *third* label I drew a big pulsing heart and printed:

YOUR HEART WILL THUMP WITH
PRIDE WHEN YOU SEE ME ACT SCROOGE
IN 'A CHRISTMAS CAROL'
7 PM WEDNESDAY 20 DECEMBER
AT KINGLEA JUNIOR SCHOOL !!!

Then I wrapped up the beautiful heart necklace, taking care not to twist the red ribbon, and stuck the label on the pink tissue parcel.

Three presents wrapped and labelled. Just one to go! It took the longest though, because I had to annotate the book of *A Christmas Carol*. I drew me dressed up as Scrooge inside the front cover, with a special bubble saying, '*Bah! Humbug!*' I drew me dressed up as Scrooge inside the back cover too, but this time I was taking a bow at the end of my performance. There were lots of clapping hands and speech bubbles saying HURRAY! and MAGNIFICENT! and WELL DONE, TRACY! and THE GREATEST PERFORMANCE EVER! and A TRUE STAR IS BORN!

BAH! HUMBUG!

I wrote on the title page:

You don't have to read all this book,
You just have to come and watch me act
Scrooge in 'A Christmas Carol', 7pm on
Wednesday 20 December at Kinglea
Junior School !!! I will dedicate my
performance to YOU, the best mum in
the whole world ever.

All my love

Tracy xxxxxxxx

Then I wrapped *A Christmas Carol* and worked on the last label. I drew the book, scrunching up the title really small so it would fit, and underneath I printed:

THIS IS A GREAT BOOK AND IT'S BEEN
TURNED INTO A GREAT PLAY AND THE
GREATEST PART IS SCROOGE AND I AM
PLAYING HIM (7PM ON WEDNESDAY
20 DECEMBER AT KINGLEA JUNIOR SCHOOL)
SO PLEASE PLEASE PLEASE COME AND
WATCH ME! ALL MY LOVE Tracy
                    XXXXXXXXX

Then I sat for a long time holding all four pink parcels on my lap, imagining my mum opening them and putting on her lipstick, rubbing in her hand lotion, fastening the heart necklace, looking at the messages in the book. I imagined her jumping in her car and driving directly to see her superstar daughter. She'd be so proud of me she'd never ever want to go away without me.

The next morning I cornered Jenny in her office and asked if she had a big Jiffy bag so I could send my presents to my mum.

'It's a little bit early to send your Christmas presents, isn't it, Tracy?' Jenny said.

'No, no, these are *before* Christmas presents,' I said. 'We have to send them off first thing on Monday morning. First class.'

'OK. First thing, first class. I suppose *I'm* paying the postage?' said Jenny.

'Yes, and can you write on the Jiffy bag *Urgent! Open Immediately!* Look, maybe *I'd* better do it,' I said.

'I think I can manage that, Tracy,' said Jenny.

'You are sure you've got my mum's right address?' I asked anxiously.

They don't let me have

it now on account of the fact that I tried to run away to find her. They won't let me have her phone number either. It is bitterly unfair, seeing as she's *my* mother. I have had major mega strops about it, but they won't give in.

'Don't worry, Tracy, I've got your mum's address,' said Jenny.

'It's just that it's ultra important. I need her to come and see me in the school play,' I said.

'I'm so glad you've been picked for the play, Tracy. You will take it seriously, won't you? No messing around or you'll spoil it for everyone.'

'Of course I'm taking it seriously, Jenny,' I said, insulted.

I was taking it very very very seriously – unlike *some* people. We had a play rehearsal every lunch time and half the kids mucked about and ate their sandwiches as they mumbled their lines. The carol singers sang off-key and the extra ghosts whimpered rather than wailed and the dancers kept bumping into each other and Weedy Peter kept forgetting his lines. He even forgot which was his lame leg, limping first on his left leg and then on his right.

'You are just so totally useless, Peter. How can you *possibly* keep forgetting "God bless us every

one"?' said Justine Big-Mouth
Littlewood. She seized hold of
him and made like she was
peering into his ear. 'Yes,
just as I thought. You've
not got any brain at all.
It's just empty space
inside your niddy-noddy
head.'

I was thinking on similar
lines myself, but when I saw
poor Peter's face crumple I felt furious with her.

'You leave Peter alone, Justine Great-Big-
Bully Littlewood. He's doing just fine – unlike
you! I've never seen such a pathetic ghost in all
my life. You're meant to be spooky but you
couldn't scare so much as a sausage.'

Miss Simpkins clapped her hands. 'Hey,
hey, girls! Calm down now. Concentrate on
the play,' she said. 'Justine, you could put
a little more *effort* into your Marley
portrayal. Tracy, maybe you could try
a little *less*. You're a splendid Scrooge
but you don't need to furrow your brow
and scowl *quite* so ferociously, and I
think spitting at people when you say

"Bah! Humbug!" is a little too emphatic, plus I don't think the caretaker would approve of you dribbling all over the stage.'

'I'm simply getting under the skin of my character, Miss Simpkins,' I said.

She wasn't listening. She was busy shepherding the spare ghosts into a haunting formation.

'Yeah, you get under everyone's skin, Tracy Beaker,' hissed Justine Make-No-Effort-At-All Littlewood. 'You're like a big pus-y pimple.'

Louise giggled. 'Watch out or we'll squeeze you!' she said.

I gave her a shove. She shoved me back. Justine shoved too, harder. I was a bit off balance, hunched up in crabbed Scrooge mode. I ended up on my bottom.

They laughed. I tried not to cry because it hurt so much. Not that I ever cry, of course.

But sudden shocks to my system occasionally bring on an attack of my hay fever. It wasn't just bumping my bum. It was the fact that Louise was being so horrible. I was used to Justine Mean-Mouth Littlewood being foul to me, but it was so unfair that Louise was ganging up with her against me.

Louise had always been *my* friend. Now I didn't have any friend at all apart from Weedy Peter, and he barely counted.

'She's *crying*! You baby!' said Justine Mockingbird-Big-Beak Littlewood.

'Why don't you fight back, Tracy?' said Louise, looking uncomfortable.

'She's lost her bottle,' said Justine Hateful-Pig Littlewood. 'Boo-hoo, boo-hoo, baby! Does little diddums wants her mumsy to kiss it better? Only dream on, diddums, cause Mumsy isn't ever ever ever going to come.'

'I'll show you if I've lost my bottle,' I said, struggling to my feet.

I went *push punch whack kick!* Justine reeled backwards, her big nose all bloody after intimate contact with my fist.

Mrs Darlow

At that precise moment Mrs Darlow the headteacher came through the swing doors to see how the Christmas play was progressing. For a split second we were all stopped in our tracks, as if we'd been Paused. Then we were Fast Forwarded into alarming and ear-splitting action.

Justine started screaming. Louise did too, though I didn't even touch her. Peter started wailing. Some of the little kid dancers and carol singers started whimpering. Miss Simpkins looked like she wanted to burst into tears too.

She rushed over to Justine and picked her up and peered at her bloody nose.

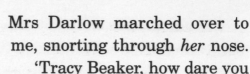

Mrs Darlow marched over to me, snorting through *her* nose.

'Tracy Beaker, how dare you attack another pupil! How many times have I got to tell you that I will *not* have fighting in my school?'

'But Mrs Darlow, it wasn't exactly my fault. I didn't start it,' I protested.

I wasn't going to tell tales on Justine Scarlet-Fountain-For-A-Nose Littlewood, but I felt I needed to indicate that I'd been Severely Provoked.

Mrs Darlow clapped her hands at me to shut me up. 'In my experience it's *always* your fault, Tracy Beaker,' she said.

This was profoundly unfair. I wished I had enough bottle left to *push punch whack kick* Mrs Darlow. I wanted to see her sprawling on her back, arms and legs flung out, skirts up, knickers showing.

It was such a bizarre image that I couldn't help sniggering. This was fatal.

'How *dare* you act as if this is a laughing matter! I'm tired of your temper tantrums. You're going to have to learn your lesson once and for all. You will not take part in the school play this Christmas!'

'But I have to be in the play, Mrs Darlow. I'm Scrooge. I'm the main part!'

'Not any more,' said Mrs Darlow.

'But my mum's coming to see me!' I said. 'I've written and told her all about it and she's coming specially.'

'I can't help that, Tracy Beaker. You're not taking part in the school play and that's that.'

I lost it then. Totally utterly out-of-it lost it. I opened my mouth and started yelling. Miss Simpkins put her arm round me but I shook her off. Peter clasped my hand but I wrenched it free. I lay down, shut my eyes and shrieked. And shrieked and shrieked and shrieked.

Eventually someone hoicked me up and carted me off to the sickroom. I opened my eyes momentarily. Justine Hate-Her-Guts Littlewood was sitting on a chair with her head back, a big wodge of tissues clutched to her bleeding nose. I closed my eyes and carried on shrieking.

I heard murmurings and mutterings. When I next opened my eyes I couldn't see Justine. I didn't know what had happened to her. I didn't care. I wished everyone in the whole world would disappear. Everyone except my mum.

I thought about Mum getting her Christmas presents, looking at her copy of *A Christmas Carol*, dressing up in her prettiest clothes and tying her heart necklace round her neck, rubbing her hand lotion on her slim fingers and applying her new lipstick into a shiny pink smile. I saw her arriving at the school on 20 December, sitting right at the front ready to watch me act. Only I wouldn't be in it. I wouldn't be in it. I wouldn't be in it.

I shrieked some more, even though my throat ached and my head thumped and I was burning hot and wet with sweat. I knew it was time to stop howling but I couldn't. I tried clamping my mouth shut but the shrieks built up inside and then came shouting out louder than ever. It was so scary that I started shaking. I couldn't stop. I was cursed like a creature in a fairy tale, condemned to scream for all eternity.

Then I felt new hands on my shoulders and Jenny's familiar firm voice.

'Easy, Tracy. It's OK. I'm here now. They sent for me. Now stop the noise.'

'I . . . can't!' I shrieked.

'Yes, you can. Take deep breaths. In. And now out. That's the ticket. Don't worry, I've got you. You're stopping now, see?'

I clung to Jenny like a little toddler. She knelt down and rocked me while I nuzzled into her shoulder.

'OK now?' she said eventually.

'No!' I paused. I opened my eyes and blinked hard, peering around the room.

'Justine?' I whispered.

'She's been taken to hospital,' said Jenny, sighing.

'Oh!'

I started shaking again. What had I *done*? I'd only bopped her on the nose. I'd done that several times before and she'd never been hurt enough to go to *hospital*. What if I'd hit her so hard her entire nose had burst and now she just had a big bloody blob in the middle of her face? What if her whole *head* had exploded and now they were trying to stitch all the bits back together again?

I hated Justine and I always would but I didn't want her to be seriously *hurt*. What if she didn't get better? What if she bled so much she died? I pictured her lying there limp and white in hospital, doctors and nurses and Louise and Justine's dad gathered round her bedside.

I saw her funeral, all the Dumping Ground kids trailing along in black behind her hearse. I saw Louise weeping, carrying a huge wreath.

I tried to tell her I was sorry, but she turned on me and told me I was a murderer. Everyone started murmuring the awful word – *Murderer, murderer, Tracy Beaker is a murderer* – and then I heard sirens and a whole squad of police cars arrived and the police leaped out and ran towards me brandishing their truncheons and I started to run in terror, screaming—

'Tracy! Don't start again,' said Jenny. 'I'm sure Justine is OK. Well, she's not, her poor nose bled horribly and you are going to be severely punished for it, my girl, but I don't think there's any long-term harm. Mrs Darlow is worried you might have broken Justine's nose, but I think she's over-reacting a little. Now, I'm going to take you back home. You need to calm down in the Quiet Room. Then we'll talk things over and see what we can do.'

I let her steer me out of the room and down the corridor. The bell had gone for play time and there were hordes of kids milling up and down, staring staring staring.

'Look at Tracy Beaker!'

'What's the matter with Tracy Beaker?'

'Hey, someone said she's had this ginormous tantrum and screamed her head off.'

'She screamed all sorts of bad words at Mrs Darlow!'

'She attacked Justine Littlewood and she's been rushed to hospital in an ambulance!'

'She punched Mrs Darlow right on the nose!'

'She's not allowed to be in the school play any more!'

I moaned and snorted and sniffled. Jenny gave me a gentle push past them all, out through the doors and across the playground. I started shivering and shaking, knuckling my eyes to try to dry them up.

I hated it that so many of them had seen me in a state. It's different at the Dumping Ground. Everyone understands that looked-after kids are a bit like fireworks with very short fuses. Beware matches! Some of us just do a little fizz and whizz when someone sets them off. Weedy Peter's mini-tantrums are like little kiddy sparklers. Some of us explode loudly like bangers, but it's all over quickly without too much show. And *some* of us are like mega rockets and we soar and swoop and explode into a million stars.No prizes for guessing which firework *I* fit.

They don't get it at school. They especially don't get me. I didn't mind them knowing I'd socked Justine. I rather liked it that they thought I'd punched Mrs Darlow. But I hated them all seeing me in such a state, all blood, sweat and tears. I didn't mind the blood, I didn't mind the sweat, but Tracy Beaker doesn't cry. Ever. Not publicly, anyway.

The minivan was a very private place. And so is the Quiet Room. And my bedroom. Jenny said I could come down to tea but I didn't fancy the idea.

Mike brought a tray upstairs to my room.

'Hey, Tracy. I know you're in disgrace, but I wouldn't want you to miss out on spag bol, and it's particularly tasty tonight.'

He thrust the tray under my nose. My nostrils prickled with the rich savoury smell, but I turned my head away.

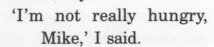

'I'm not really hungry, Mike,' I said.

'Miss Fussy-Gussy. I've slaved at the stove for hours so the least you can do is try a mouthful,' said Mike, balancing the tray on my lap and twisting spaghetti round and round the fork. 'Come on, sweetie. Here's an aeroplane – *wheee* through the air and *in* it swoops,' he said, guying the way he fed the very little kids in the Dumping Ground.

I kept my lips clamped. I didn't even smile at him. I didn't feel in the mood for jokes (even sweet ones) or food (though spag bol was a special favourite).

'Come on, Tracy. Even Justine hasn't lost her appetite, yet she's the girl with the poorly nose.'

'Is she back from the hospital?' I said.

'Yep. Poor, poor Justine,' said Mike.

'Is her nose really broken?' I whispered.

'Broken right *off*,' said Mike – but then he saw my expression. '*Joke*, Tracy. It's fine. You just gave her a little nosebleed. But Jenny and I have got to put our heads together and find some suitable means of punishment. You've got to learn to handle your temper, Tracy, especially at school. Jenny and I are sick of apologizing to old Dragon Darlow. She's always been a tad wary of all our kids – you in particular, Ms Biff and Bash Beaker. Every time you throw a wobbly at school you're confirming all her prejudices.'

'You can punish me any way you want,' I said wanly. 'You can beat me and starve me and lock me in the cupboard.'

'There's not much point,' said Mike. 'If I tried to beat you I'm sure you'd beat me right back. You're already starving yourself going without your spag bol. And there's no point shutting you in the art cupboard because I have a shrewd suspicion you know how to pick that lock already. No, I think we'll have to come up with something more to the point.'

'I told you, Mike, I don't care. Mrs Darlow's punished me already. She won't let me be Scrooge any more and my mum won't get to see me act,' I said.

Some drops of water dribbled down my face and splashed into the plate of spaghetti on my lap.

'I know how tough that is, Tracy,' Mike said, and he gave me a little hug. 'I know how hard you've worked on your part, and I'm sure you'd have been the Scroogiest Scrooge ever. I think we both know that we can't take it for granted that your mum can come to see you – but if she *did* just happen to be there she'd be so proud of you, sweetheart. All the kids think Mrs Darlow's being very unfair. They say the play won't be the same without you, Tracy.'

'Who are you trying to kid, Mike?' I said wearily, but I reached out and tried a very small forkful of spaghetti. It was still hot and surprisingly tasty.

'I mean it, Tracy. Little Peter's absolutely beside himself. He's thinking of starting up some petition.'

'Ah. Sweet,' I said, trying another forkful. 'Still, I bet Louise and

Justine are thrilled to bits that I'm out of the play.'

'Well, you're wrong then, chum. I know you three aren't the best of mates nowadays, but Louise seems quite uncomfortable about the situation. I think she feels she and Justine might just have provoked your sudden savage attack.'

'Really?' I said, starting to scoop up my spag bol enthusiastically. 'What about Justine? What does she say?'

'Well, she's probably the only one of the kids who isn't as yet a signed-up member of the Justice for Tracy Fan Club. That's hardly surprising as her poor nose is still swollen and sore.'

'Oh dear,' I said insincerely.

Mike ruffled my curls. 'You're a bad bad girl, little Beaker. We're going to have to channel all that aggression somehow.' That sounded ominous.

I was right to be suspicious. The next morning Jenny and Mike cornered me as I came downstairs, head held high, determined to show everyone I was absolutely fine now, so long as everyone kept their gob shut about mums and plays and headteachers.

I held my head a little too high, so I couldn't see where I was going. Some stupid little kid had set a small herd of plastic dinosaurs to graze on the carpet at the foot of the stairs. I skidded and very nearly went bonk on my bum again, but this time my natural grace and agility enabled me to keep my footing – just.

'Why don't you make the kids clear up all their little plastic whatsits?' I demanded.

'Good point, Tracy,' said Mike.

'Maybe you'll help us, Tracy,' said Jenny. 'It will make your job easier.'

I paused. I eyed them suspiciously. 'What job?'

'We've thought of an excellent way to channel your aggression,' said Mike.

'Don't think of this as a punishment, Tracy. It's a positive way to make this a happy, clean and tidy home,' said Jenny.

The words *clean* and *tidy* reverberated ominously, scouring my ears.

'Hey, you're not plotting that I'm going to be,

like, your *cleaning lady*?' I said.

'Quick off the mark as always, Tracy Beaker,' said Mike.

'We feel you'll do an excellent job,' said Jenny.

'You can't force me! There's a law against child labour!' I protested.

'We're not employing you, Tracy. We're simply helping you manage your anger in a practical fashion.'

'What sort of practical?'

'You just have to tidy and dust and vacuum and clean the bathrooms and give the kitchen floor a quick scrub.'

I thought quickly. 'So how much are you going to pay me?'

'Ah. Well, we thought you would want to do this first week as a trial run. If you want a permanent position after that I'm sure we could start financial negotiations,' said Jenny. 'Now, run and have your breakfast or you'll be late for school.'

'But—'

'No buts, Tracy,' said Mike firmly.

I know when it's a waste of Beaker breath pursuing a point. I stamped into the kitchen and sat down at the table. I shook cornflakes into a bowl so violently that they sprayed out onto the table. I poured milk so fiercely that it gushed like Niagara Falls and overflowed my bowl.

They were all staring at me warily. Even Justine looked a little anxious. She kept rubbing her nose.

'Are you OK, Tracy?' Peter squeaked.

'Do I *seem* OK?' I snapped, slamming my spoon down.

Peter jumped and the juice in his cup spilled onto the table.

'For heaven's sake, watch what you're doing!' I said, though I'd actually made much more mess myself. 'I'm the poor cleaning lady now. I've got to mop up after all you lot, so watch out, do you hear me?'

'I should think the people right at the end of the road can hear you,' said Louise. 'And don't pick on poor little Peter. He's started up a petition on your behalf: "Please let Tracy Beaker play Scrooge". He's going to get everyone to sign it.'

'Shh, Louise. It's a secret,' said Peter, blushing.

'Yes, like Mrs Darlow is going to be heavily influenced by Peter's pathetic petition,' I said.

Then I saw his little face. Crumple time again. I felt so mean I couldn't bear it, but I couldn't say anything in front of the others. I just gobbled down my breakfast and then cleared off back to my room to collect my school bag and stuff. I listened out for Peter. I caught him scuttling back from the bathroom, toothpaste round his mouth.

'Hey, Peter!' I hissed.

He jumped again, his tongue nervously licking the white foam off his lips.

'Come in my room a second,' I commanded.

Peter caught his breath. He backed into my bedroom obediently and stood with his back against my Vampire Bat poster, his fists clenched, as if he was facing a firing squad.

'It's OK, Peter,' I said. 'I'm not going to beat you up.'

'I'm sorry if I annoyed you with my petition idea. I know it's a bit silly and maybe pointless but I felt so bad about you not being in the play any more and I just wanted to do something.'

'I was just being a bad-tempered pig at breakfast. I didn't mean to get cross with you, Pete. I think your petition's a lovely idea. Nobody's ever put me in a petition before. I still don't see that it will *achieve* anything, but I think it's ever so sweet of you. You're a very special friend. Thank you. Ever so much.'

Peter still didn't move but he went raspberry-red and blinked at me rapidly.

'Oh, Tracy,' he said.

I gave him a little pat on the head. He tried to

give me a big hug but I wasn't prepared to go *that* far.

'Hey, watch out, you're wiping toothpaste all over me. Come on, we'll be late for school.'

'So can I carry on with my petition?'

'Feel free. Though I doubt you'll get many people to sign it on account of the fact that I'm not the most popular girl in the school. Um . . . have the kids here *really* signed it?'

'Yes, all of them. Well, Justine hasn't quite managed to get round to it yet, but I'll keep badgering her.'

'Oh, Peter, you couldn't badger anyone!'

'You wait and see, Tracy. I'll get the whole school to sign the petition. You *have* to be in the play. You're totally brilliant at acting Scrooge.'

'You're wasting your time, Pete, but thanks anyway,' I said. 'It's great that you've got such faith in my acting abilities. Tell you what, when I'm grown up and a famous movie star just like my mum, I'll let you be my agent, OK?'

This perked him up no end but it had the opposite effect on me. Just mentioning my mum made me want to start howling again. But I had to go to school and control all emotion. Yesterday I'd screamed and shrieked. Today I was going to be calm and in control to show everyone that Tracy Beaker is One Tough Cookie, able to cope with incredible public humiliation without turning a hair.

It wasn't as easy as that. I jumped out of the Dumping Ground minivan and walked into school as nonchalantly as possible, but everyone in the playground turned and stared and pointed at me. A group of little kids actually stood round me in a circle as if they could turn me on like a television and watch *The Tracy Beaker Freak Show*.

The kids staring at me wasn't the worse part. It was the teachers. They were crazily *kind* to me. Miss Brown actually hovered by my desk when she was collecting up maths homework and said softly, 'How are you doing, Tracy?'

Miss Brown

'Not too good, Miss Brown,' I muttered.

'I don't suppose you managed to do your maths homework last night?'

'I was kind of Otherwise Engaged,' I said.

'Oh well. Not to worry. You can do it in your lunch hour.'

'OK, I've got all the time in the world in my lunch hour now,' I said, sighing heavily.

The lunch hour was dreadful. Peter and Louise and Justine and all the other kids in *A Christmas Carol* rushed off to the hall to rehearse . . . without me.

I stayed in the classroom all by myself and did my maths homework. The inky numbers on my page kept blurring and blotching, as if they were being rained on. I used up two tissues and my sleeve mopping up.

I whizzed along to the cloakroom just before

91

the start of afternoon school to splash cold water on my face – and bumped into Miss Simpkins. She had Gloria Taylor, Emily Lawson and Amy Jellicoe with her. They were all looking up at her hopefully, eyes huge like puppies in Battersea Dogs Home, going, *Pick me, Miss Simpkins*.

'Oh, Tracy,' said Miss Simpkins. She waved her hand at Gloria and Emily and Amy. 'Run along, girls. I'll let you know tomorrow,' she said.

They each gave me a pitying glance and then ran off obediently.

'They've been auditioning for Scrooge, haven't they?' I said flatly.

'Yes, they have,' said Miss Simpkins. She lowered her voice to a whisper. 'And they all tried their best, but strictly between you and me, Tracy, they're rubbish compared to you.'

'So which one are you going to pick, Miss Simpkins?'

'I don't know,' she said, sighing. 'It's such a

big part and there's hardly any time left to learn it. Gloria's the only girl who could learn it all by heart, but she runs through it like a railway station announcer, with no expression whatsoever. Emily can at least act a little, but she can't remember two consecutive lines so she'd have to have the script in her hands the whole time and that would spoil things.'

'So are you going to choose Amy for Scrooge?'

'Amy is so sweet and soft and shy she can barely make herself heard and she can't act bad-tempered to save her life. She just doesn't *convince* as Scrooge.'

'Whereas I can act bad-tempered till the cows come home,' I said.

'Yes! You were my magnificent Scrooge,' she said, sighing.

'Until Mrs Darlow spoiled everything,' I said.

'No, Tracy. Until *you* spoiled everything,' said Miss Simpkins. 'Although I know you were severely provoked. I've tried explaining the circumstances to Mrs Darlow – in vain, I'm sorry to say.'

'Well. Thank you, Miss Simpkins,' I said. 'I'm sorry I mucked it all up.'

'It seems a shame you've got to pay so dearly

for it,' said Miss Simpkins.

'You don't know the half of it,' I said darkly. 'I'm paying for it with knobs on, even back at the Home. I'm acting as an unpaid skivvy clearing up after all the kids. Isn't that unbelievably unfair? I think you should report them to the NSPCC, OK?'

'I'll think about it,' said Miss Simpkins, but she was struggling hard not to laugh.

I *certainly* didn't feel like laughing when I came home utterly exhausted from school to have Jenny hand me the hoover and Mike thrust the mop and bucket at me.

I'd been secretly hoping that this was one big bluff. I was outraged to realize they really meant to go through with it.

'Let me have my tea first, for pity's sake,' I said.

I took my time munching my banana wholemeal sandwich and my handful of nuts and my orange and my apple juice. (Oh for the days of unhealthy eating when we wolfed down crisps and chocolate and cakes and Coke.) Then I stomped off to my room to change out of my school uniform and put on my oldest jeans and faded T-shirt.

I stopped to look at the postcard from Mum on my notice board. I suddenly felt so sad I had to lie on my bed with my head under my pillow just in case anyone overheard my sudden attack of hay fever. I was still feeling sniffly when I trailed down the stairs, sighing considerably. No one was around to hear me. The other kids all seemed to be whispering together in the kitchen. It was all right for *some* Ugly People. Poor little Cinderella Beaker had to stay home and tackle all the chores.

I picked up the hoover, switched it on and started shoving it backwards and forwards across the hall. It was so heavy, so clumsy, so awkward. My arms were aching and my back hurt from bending over already and yet I'd only done one weeny patch of carpet. I had the whole huge Dumping Ground to render spotless. I banged the hoover violently into the skirting board and gave it a kick. I was only wearing soft shoes. It hurt *horribly*. I switched the hateful hoover off and doubled up, nursing my poor stubbed toes.

I heard more whisperings and gigglings.

'Shut up, you lot!' I snarled.

Peter popped his head round the kitchen door.

'Tracy, are you *OK*?'

'I'm absolutely in the pink,' I said sarcastically. 'In the rose-pink, salmon-pink, petunia-pink – *not*. How do you think I feel, knowing I've got the tremendous task of cleaning up the Dumping Ground single-handed?'

'Not *quite* single-handed,' said Peter. 'Come on, gang!'

All the kids suddenly sprang out of the kitchen into the hall. Peter stood in front, jersey sleeves rolled up his puny little arms, a tea towel tied round his waist like a pinny. They were all clutching dusters and mops and brushes and pans. Louise was there, her long hair tied up in a scarf. Justine sloped out last, wearing Mike's stripy cooking apron and wielding a scrubbing brush.

'We're all going to do the cleaning,' said Peter. 'It seemed so horribly mean that you had to do it all, so we're helping out. It'll be fun!'

'Not *my* idea of fun, you little runt,' said Justine, juggling her scrubbing brush.

Louise caught it and held onto it. 'It was just as much our fault as yours, Tracy,' she said. 'We *all* got mad, so Peter's right, we should all channel our aggression into housework.'

'So OK, troops, let's get cracking!' Peter said. He looked at me. 'OK, Tracy?'

For once I was totally speechless. I just nodded very hard and blinked very hard and hoped very hard that I wouldn't utterly disgrace myself and howl. We let funny little Peter order us around, telling each of us what to do, because it was easier than us big ones arguing about it. We put radios playing the loudest rock and rap music in every corner of the Dumping Ground and then set to with a vengeance.

Elaine the Pain came calling halfway through. She cowered backwards, covering her ears, but when Jenny and Mike explained (having to bellow a bit), she clapped her hands excitedly and went prancing around congratulating everyone on their team spirit.

'It reflects the very essence of Christmas, loving and sharing and caring,' she said, jamming her reindeer antlers on her head and rushing around giving everyone a little pat on the back.

It's a wonder Elaine Ridiculous Reindeer Pain didn't make them think: *What on earth am I doing scrubbing away when I could be watching the telly or playing on my Xbox or simply lounging on my bed picking my nose because I definitely don't love Tracy Beaker and I don't care tuppence about her and I certainly don't want to share her stupid punishment.* But somehow they took no notice and carried on dusting and scrubbing and scouring and hoovering. I felt as if all the dirty grubby grimy greasy little bits of me were getting a clean and polish too. Maybe they did like me just a little bit after all.

I still had some stuff left over from my raid on the art cupboard. That night I laboured long and hard over a big card. I drew the Dumping Ground and all of us guys outside, armed with dusters and brushes and mops. I even drew Justine properly, though it was very tempting to cross her eyes and scribble little bogeys hanging from her nose. I put me in the centre with a big beaming smile. I drew little rays of sunshine all round my picture and

then I printed at the top in dead artistic rainbow
lettering:

THE TRACY BEAKER CLEANING SERVICE

THANKS FOR YOUR HELP EVERYONE!

I crept downstairs and stuck it on the table
so that everyone would see it at breakfast time.
I snaffled half a packet of cornflakes and an
orange so I could have breakfast in my room. I
didn't want to be hanging around when they
saw the card. It would be *way* too embarrassing.
I wasn't used to acting all mushy and saying
thank you. I'd have to watch it. I was used to

being the toughest kid on the block. It would be fatal to soften up now.

I tried hard to be my normal fierce and feisty self at school. I summoned up all my energy to cheek the teachers and argue with the kids but it was hard work. I found myself sharing my chocolate bar with Peter in the playground and picking up some little kid who'd fallen over and kicking someone's ball straight back to them, acting like Ms Goody-Goody Two Trainers instead of the Tough and Terrible Tracy Beaker,

When everyone went to rehearse *A Christmas Carol* I wondered which of the Three Stooges Miss Simpkins had picked as Scrooge. I couldn't help being glad that they were all pretty useless.

Halfway through the first lesson in the afternoon Mrs Darlow sent for me.

'Oh, Tracy,' said Miss Brown sorrowfully. 'What have you been up to *now*?'

'Nothing, Miss Brown!' I said. 'I've been a positive angel all day.'

Miss Brown didn't look as if she believed me. I couldn't really blame her. She wasn't to know I was this new squeaky-clean sweet-as-honey Beaker.

I plodded along to Mrs Darlow's study, wondering if she was going to blame me for someone else's misdemeanour. Maybe she'd think *I'd* written the very very rude rhyme in the girls' toilets. Maybe she'd think *I'd* superglued some teacher's chair. Maybe she'd think *I'd* climbed up the drainpipe after a lost ball and pulled the pipe right off the wall in the process. I *had* done all these things in the past, but not *recently*.

Still, I would doubtless be blamed. I sighed wearily and knocked on Mrs Darlow's door, deciding that there was no point protesting my total innocence to such a grim and unforgiving woman. She was doubtless preparing to Punish Tracy Beaker Severely. I saw her selecting her whippiest whip, her thumb crunchers, her nose tweakers, clearing her desk of superfluous paperwork so she could stretch me across it as if I was on a torture rack. I'd crawl out of school lashed into bloody stripes, thumbs mangled, nose pulled past my chin, stretched out and out and out like elastic.

Mrs Darlow was wearing her severest black trouser suit. She sat at her desk, her chin in her hands, frowning at me over the top of her glasses.

'Come and sit down, Tracy Beaker,' she said.

She always says my name in full, though there isn't another Tracy in the whole school.

'How are you today?' she enquired.

'Not especially happy, Mrs Darlow,' I said.

'Neither am I, Tracy Beaker, neither am I,' she said. She took hold of a large wad of paper scribbled all over with lots of names. 'Do you know what this is?'

I paused. I had a feeling that it wasn't the time to say 'pieces of paper'.

'I don't know, Mrs Darlow' seemed a safer bet. I truly didn't know. The handwriting wasn't mine. It was all different writing, some neat, some

104

scrawly, in black, blue, red – all the colours of the rainbow.

'This is a petition to reinstate you as Scrooge in the school play,' said Mrs Darlow.

'Oh goodness! Peter's petition!' I said.

'Are you sure you didn't put him up to it, Tracy Beaker?'

'Absolutely not!' I said. 'But he's got heaps and heaps of signatures!'

'Yes, he has. Though I've scrutinized every page, and some of the signatures are duplicated – and I'm not sure Mickey Mouse, Homer Simpson, Robbie Williams and Beyoncé are actually pupils at this school.'

My mouth twitched. I was scared I was going to get the giggles, and yet my eyes were pricking as if I had a bout of hay fever coming on. All those signatures! I thought of Peter going round and round and round the whole school with his petition and all those kids signing away, wanting *me* in the play.

'Peter's obviously a very kind friend,' said Mrs Darlow.

'Yes, he is,' I said humbly.

'I'm rather impressed by his initiative and perseverance. When he delivered the petition this morning he was trembling all over, but he still made his own personal impassioned plea. He stated – accurately – that there is no other girl remotely like you, Tracy Beaker.'

I smiled.

'He meant it as a compliment. I didn't,' said Mrs Darlow. 'I felt very sorry for poor Peter when I told him that it was highly unlikely I would change my mind, even though I was very impressed by his petition.'

'Oh,' I said, slumping in my chair.

'Then I had a visit from Miss Simpkins at lunch time. She's already tried to plead your cause, Tracy Beaker. She's told me that your appalling assault wasn't entirely unprovoked. However, I've explained to her that I can never condone violent behaviour, no matter what the circumstances.'

I sighed and slumped further down the chair.

'However . . .' said Mrs Darlow.

I stiffened.

'Miss Simpkins invited me along to rehearsals. The play itself is progressing perfectly. Everyone's worked very hard.

I watched Gloria and Emily and Amy play Scrooge, one after the other. They tried extremely hard. In fact I awarded them five team points each for endeavour. Unfortunately though, none of the girls is a born actress, and although they tried their best I could see that their performances were a little . . . lacking.'

I clenched my fists.

'Miss Simpkins stressed that *your* performance as Scrooge was extraordinary, Tracy Beaker. I am very aware that this is a *public* performance in front of all the parents.'

'My mum's coming,' I whispered.

'It is a showcase event, and therefore I want everything to be perfect. I don't want all that hard work and effort to be wasted. I've decided to reinstate you, Tracy Beaker. You may play Scrooge after all.'

'Oh, Mrs Darlow! You are a total *angel*!' I said, sitting bolt upright and clapping my hands.

'I'm not sure you're going to

think me so totally angelic by the time I've finished, Tracy Beaker. I said violent behaviour can never be condoned. You must still be severely punished in some other way.'

'*Any* way, Mrs Darlow. Be as inventive as you like. Whips, thumbscrews, nose tweakers, the rack. Whatever.'

'I think I'll select a more mundane punishment, Tracy Beaker, though the nose tweaker sounds tempting,' said Mrs Darlow. 'And appropriate in the circumstances, as you hit poor Justine on *her* nose. However, I'm not sure the school's petty cash can quite cover an instrument of torture. We are already well stocked with cleaning implements so we will stick with those.'

'Cleaning implements, Mrs Darlow?' I said. 'Oh no! I've already had to clean the entire Dumping Ground – I mean, the Home. You're not asking me to clean the whole *school*?'

'As if I'd ask you to do that!' said Mrs Darlow. 'I might not be angelic, but I am reasonable. I think I shall just ask you to clean the hall floor. If we're having all these guests then we can't have the setting looking downright scruffy. I'd like you to stay after school for half an hour every evening and polish up the parquet. It will not only enhance the look of the school, it will also act as a channel for your aggression.'

'My aggression's already been thoroughly channelled, Mrs Darlow,' I said. 'But all right, I will. I'll polish the whole hall until we can all see straight up our skirts, just so long as my mum will be able to see me act Scrooge.'

I don't know if you've ever done any serious polishing? Your hand hurts, your arms ache, your neck twinges, your back's all bent, your knees get rubbed raw, even your toes get scrunched up and sore. Think of the size of a school hall. Think of me.

Long long long did I labour. Dear old Peter and some of the other kids tried to sneak into the hall to help me out, but Mrs Darlow didn't appreciate this kind of caring and sharing teamwork.

'It's Tracy Beaker's punishment, not yours. I want her to labour on her own!' she said.

So labour I did, but I kept a copy of the play in front of me as I polished. I went over and over my lines in my head.

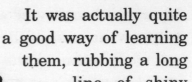

It was actually quite a good way of learning them, rubbing a long line of shiny wood while muttering a long line of Scrooge-speak. Every time I dipped my cloth into the polish I went, 'Bah! Humbug!' Whenever I finished a whole section I said Tiny Tim's 'God bless us, every one.' By the time I'd polished the entire hall floor I not only knew my lines, I knew everyone else's too.

I couldn't *wait* till Wednesday, the day of our performance. I was in a fever of impatience, positively burning up all over, so much so that Jenny caught hold of me at breakfast and felt my forehead.

'Are you feeling OK, Tracy? You're very flushed.'

'Oh, Tracy, you're not ill, are you?' said Peter. He shivered. '*I* feel ill. I hardly slept last night and when I did I kept dreaming I was standing on the stage all alone and people kept shouting rude things to me. I wish wish wish I didn't have to act. I'm simply dreading tonight. What if I forget what to say?'

'You'll be fine, Pete. You won't forget. And if you *do*, just look at me and I'll whisper them for you,' I said.

'Yeah, the one and only Big-mouth Beaker,' sneered Justine.

She didn't look too well herself. She was very pale, with dark circles under her eyes.

'You look like Marley's Ghost already, without bothering with make-up,' I said. 'Getting worried you'll be rubbish?'

'Absolutely *not*.' Justine paused. 'What about you, Tracy? Are you getting worried? Worried your mum might not turn up to watch you? Ha, that's a laugh. Your mum's as rarely sighted as the Abominable Snowman.'

There was a sudden silence. Everyone stopped chomping their cornflakes.

'Justine, button that lip!' said Mike.

'Tracy, don't start anything!' said Jenny.

I wasn't going to show Justine Spooky-Spectre Littlewood she could rattle me. I smiled at her, teeth clenched. I felt my tummy clenching too, into a tight little ball. Mum *would* come, wouldn't she?

111

She'd surely want to see me act the leading part in our school play. She'd want to sit right in the middle, surrounded by happy clapping parents, all of them saying, 'That Tracy Beaker's a great little actress. I wonder where she gets that from?' Then they'd look round and spot Mum, all glamorous and gorgeous, and go, '*She* must be Tracy's mum. Oh my goodness, of *course*! She's the movie star Carly Beaker!'

She'd be there tonight, clutching her copy of *A Christmas Carol*, wearing her lipstick and her hand cream and her heart necklace. She'd *have* to come when I'd tried so hard with her presents. She'd want to give me a big hug and kiss and clap till her hands smarted, and then she'd sweep me off for ever because she was so proud of me.

'Dream on, Tracy,' Justine Poison-Mouth Littlewood muttered.

The fist inside my tummy squeezed tighter. *Was* it all a daydream? Was I really just kidding myself?

'My mum *is* coming, just you wait and see,' I said.

'I'll be waiting – and we'll all be seeing,' said Justine About-To-Get-Her-Nose-Punched-Again Littlewood. 'We'll see my dad sitting there clapping away, but whoops, there'll be this *empty* seat right in the middle of the row where Mother Beaker's bottom should be, only she can't be bothered to come and see her only daughter – and who can blame her when she's as bonkers and batty and totally bananas as Tracy Beaker—'

I leaped up but Jenny caught hold of me and Mike hustled Justine out of the room.

'Cool it, Tracy,' said Jenny.

I couldn't cool it. I was burning up, about to erupt like a volcano. But then Peter clutched my hand.

'Take no notice of Justine. She's just jealous because you're such a brilliant actress and everyone signed my petition because they all know the play wouldn't work without you. And if you say your mum's coming, then of course she will. You always know everything, Tracy.'

I took a deep deep deep breath and then squeezed his hand.

'That's right, Peter,' I said. 'Thanks, pal. Don't fret. I wouldn't let a sad twisted girl like Justine wind me up.'

Jenny gave me a quick hug. 'Well done, girl.'

'Jenny?' I took another even deeper deeper deeper breath. 'I *know* my mum's coming, and I sent her all the details and all this stuff, but I don't suppose she's been on the phone just to *confirm* she's coming?'

'You know I'd have told you, Tracy.'

'Yeah, yeah, well . . . As if she *needs* to tell us. I mean, we can just take it as read, can't we?' I said.

'I'm coming,' said Jenny. 'And Mike. We're getting extra help here just so we can watch you. Elaine's coming. Don't pull that face, Tracy! Cam's coming. It will be wonderful if your mum comes too, but you'll still have lots of people in the audience absolutely rooting for you. OK?'

It wasn't OK at all. This was Careworker

Evasive-Speak. I *couldn't* take it as read that my mum was coming.

I knew that.

I didn't *want* to know.

I tried very very very hard indeed to take it as read. It was as if it was printed everywhere and I was literally reading it over and over again. I stared round the kitchen and saw it spelled out in spaghetti shapes all round the walls.

YOUR MUM'S COMING TO SEE YOU ACT SCROO

I went to the toilet and I saw it scribbled all over the door.

Your Mum's coming to see you act Scrooge.

I went to school in the minivan and I saw it flash up on the dashboard.

YOUR MUM'S COMING TO SEE YOU ACT SCROO

I looked out of the window and saw it on all the posters in town.

YOUR MUM'S COMING TO SEE YOU ACT SCROO

I got to school and it was chalked on the blackboard.

Your Mum's coming to see you act Scrooge.

I stood in assembly and it shone above the stage.

YOUR MUM'S COMING TO SEE YOU ACT SCROOGE.

The words flashed on and off in my mind all day long like little fairy lights.

OUR MUM'S COMING TO SEE YOU ACT SCROOGE.

I couldn't concentrate on a thing in class. I thought Henry the Sixth had eight wives, I couldn't even do short division, let alone long, I ran the wrong way in the obstacle race in PE, I coloured Santa's beard scarlet on my Christmas card. Luckily Miss Brown just laughed at me.

'I know you've got other things on your mind today, Tracy. Good luck with the play tonight. I'm so looking forward to it.'

But I *didn't* have the play on my mind. I couldn't get it *in* my mind. We had a last rehearsal

117

at lunch time, gabbling through our lines one last time. I stumbled and stuttered and couldn't remember a thing.

'I don't know what's gone wrong, Miss Simpkins!' I said frantically. 'I'm word perfect, I know I am. I could chant the whole play backwards yesterday, I swear I could.'

'I knew Tracy Beaker would mess up royally,' Justine whispered to Louise, though it was a loud enough whisper for me to hear.

'It's simply last-minute nerves, Tracy,' said Miss Simpkins. 'You'll be fine tonight. Don't worry about it.'

She was doing her best to be reassuring – but *she* looked worried. I could see her thinking, *Oh my Lord, I've gone out on a limb to keep problem kid Tracy in the play and now she can't even say a simple line! What have I done? I must keep smiling, stay calm. I'm not going to panic. I'll just tell the kid she'll be fine tonight.*

For the first and only time in my life I was in

total agreement with Justine Smug-Slug Littlewood. It looked like I was going to mess up royally.

We didn't go home for our tea. All the children in the cast had a packed picnic on my wondrously polished hall floor. If I'd been my usual self I'd have been incensed. They were spilling sandwich crumbs and scattering crisps all over the place. One of the kids even poured a carton of sticky squash all over my floor! But I was in such a state I barely noticed. I couldn't even eat my picnic. My egg sandwich tasted of old damp flannel, my crisps stuck in my throat, my yoghurt smelled sour.

'Eat up, Tracy. You're going to be burning up a lot of energy tonight,' said Peter. 'Here, do you want half my special banana sandwich? Hey, you can have all of it if you like.'

'Thanks, Pete – but no thanks,' I said.

I sat and brooded, snapping all my crisps into tiny golden splinters. I didn't know what to do.

I so so so wanted my mum to come and see me, but did I really want her to see me standing sweating on stage, mouth open, but no words whatsoever coming out?

I shut my eyes tight. 'Please, if there really is a Spirit of Christmas Past, a Spirit of Christmas Present and a Spirit of Christmas Yet to Come, help me now, and then I'll out-do Tiny Tim with my "God bless you"s,' I said inside my head.

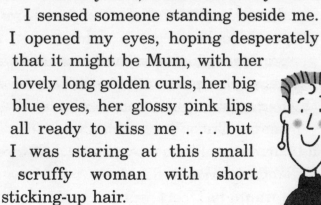

I sensed someone standing beside me. I opened my eyes, hoping desperately that it might be Mum, with her lovely long golden curls, her big blue eyes, her glossy pink lips all ready to kiss me . . . but I was staring at this small scruffy woman with short sticking-up hair.

'Oh, it's only you, Cam,' I said wearily.

'Happy Christmas to you too, Tracy,' said Cam, laughing.

'What are you doing here? The play's not for hours yet.'

'I know. I've come to help your Miss Simpkins do your make-up.'

120

'But you don't know anything about it! You never *wear* make-up.'

'I'm great at stage make-up, you wait and see.'

She sat down cross-legged beside me. She was wearing her usual jeans and jersey – but they were her newest not-frayed-at-the-hems jeans and she was wearing her best jumper with the knitted cats.

She thrust a big box of chocolates at me.

'Here. Have a nibble, then pass them round to all your pals.'

'Oh, Cam. Did you buy them specially for me?'

'Well, not exactly,' said Cam. 'They were going to be for my mum, when I went home for Christmas. Only I'm not actually *going* home as it turns out, so I thought we could have them now.'

'Well, it's very kind of you but I'm not a bit hungry. I feel kind of sick. Maybe I'm going to throw up on stage. If I do I hope it's when Justine's doing her Marley's Ghost bit,' I said.

I opened the box of chocolates all the same, simply out of curiosity. They were extra-special wonderful chocs, all sleek and shiny, some

121

wrapped in pink and silver and gold paper, others dotted with cherries and nuts and little crystallized roses.

'Oh, yum,' I said automatically. My fingers reached out for the biggest cherry chocolate of their own accord. I gave it one little lick and then popped it in my mouth quick.

I chewed, and the most beautiful cherry chocolate taste oozed all over my tongue and round my teeth.

'Mmm!' I said. My hand reached out again.

'I wouldn't have too many if you're feeling sick,' said Cam.

'Do you know something weird? I'm starting to feel just a tiny bit better. Hey, these are seriously scrumptious chocolates. Do I really have to hand them round? I'll have just *one* more, OK? Your mum's really missing out big-time. Why aren't you going to see her at Christmas then?'

'Oh. We had a row. We always have rows. I phoned her to ask if I could bring someone with me.'

'Who? Not a boyfriend!'

'I've *told* you, Tracy, I haven't got a boyfriend. This was someone else, but anyway, she didn't like that idea, and then she went on about this party she's giving, and saying stuff like will I please have my hair done and could I wear a decent skirt and proper heels.' Cam sighed. 'She's impossible.'

'No, she's not. You'd look *heaps* better with your hair done all fancy and a nice tight skirt, and why on earth *don't* you wear heels? My mum always does.'

I shouldn't have said the word *mum*. My tummy went tight all over again. I was on my fourth chocolate by this time. It didn't seem such a great idea.

Cam held my hand. 'Your mum's obviously a glamorous girly mum. I'm more your *casual* woman. Though *my* mum would say there's casual and there's downright ragbag.'

'Oh, Cam, do *you* think my mum will come to see me act Scrooge?'

Cam gripped my hand tightly. 'I'm sure she *wants* to come, badly. It's just . . . she could be tied up somewhere.'

'I'm going to let her down if she *does* come.'
I crept closer to Cam. I hissed in her ear so none
of the other kids could hear. 'I was totally rubbish
at the rehearsal at lunch time. I couldn't
remember a single word.'

'That's great, Tracy,' said Cam brightly.

'That's *great*?' I said. 'Oh thanks, Cam! I
thought you were supposed to be my *friend*? It's
great that Tracy Beaker is going to publicly
humiliate herself in front of the whole school,
all the parents, everyone from the Dumping
Ground and her own *mother*?'

'I *am* your friend and I'm talking sense.
Everyone knows that it's bad luck to have a dress
rehearsal that goes really well. The worse it is,
the better the actual performance.'

'You're kidding!'

'No, no, it's common knowledge in the acting
profession. I'm surprised your mum hasn't told
you. So you'll be great tonight, Tracy, you'll see.'

'But I can't remember a single line! What am
I meant to do? *Mime* it all?'

'Well, I'm sure you'd mime very expressively,
but I don't think that will be necessary. The
moment you get on stage I'm sure you'll be word
perfect again. The lines are all in there, Tracy.'

She swung our clasped hands upwards and gently tapped my head. 'You just need to press the right button and they'll come bursting out as easily as anything, believe me.'

I looked at her. I *didn't* believe her – but I was touched that she was trying so hard to convince me. I looked at Cam's best outfit. I looked at her earnest face and her funny scrubbing-brush haircut. I suddenly gave her a big hug right there in front of everyone.

Some skinny little kid playing Ignorance in the play piped up, 'Is that your mum, Tracy?'

'She's not my *real* mum,' I said. 'But she's kind of *like* a mum to me.'

Cam gave me a big hug back. 'That's the nicest thing you've ever said about me, Tracy,' she said.

'It's all this Christmas Peace and Goodwill stuff. It's getting to me,' I said.

I passed all the chocolates round. I *even* offered one to Justine, which was a waste of time.

'You've probably gobbed all over them, Tracy Beaker,' she said.

Mrs Darlow came trit-trotting out of her office,

in through the swing doors and over my beautifully shiny floor to wish us all luck.

Miss Simpkins came scurrying to my side, looking tense. I smiled at her reassuringly and offered Mrs Darlow a chocolate.

'Good luck, Tracy Beaker,' she said, popping a nut cluster in her mouth.

'Mind how you go in those little heels, Mrs Darlow. We don't want you slipping on the highly polished floor,' I said politely.

'Ah, yes. You've worked hard, Tracy. It's a little patchy here and there, but on the whole you've done a splendid job. Nothing beats a bit of elbow grease. I'm almost tempted to do away with the electric polisher and employ you on a permanent basis.'

'You have an electric polisher?' I said faintly. 'Yet you let me polish the entire floor by *hand*?'

'Tracy!' Cam hissed.

I took a deep breath. 'So the hall floor *could* have been polished in a matter of minutes, Mrs Darlow?'

'But that wouldn't have been such an excellent . . . what was the phrase? A channel for your aggression!' said Mrs Darlow, smiling at me. Triumphantly.

I looked at her. She looked at me. Cam was on one side of me, Miss Simpkins on the other. I knew both were holding their breath.

I suddenly burst out laughing. 'Nice one, Mrs Darlow,' I said. 'You win.'

'Thank you,' said Mrs Darlow. 'So you win tonight, Tracy Beaker. Act your little socks off.'

She zigzagged her way through the picnicking cast as if she was performing a complicated country dance and went out of the hall.

Cam and Miss Simpkins blew out their cheeks and sighed 'Pheeeeeew' simultaneously.

'You both thought I was going to blow it, didn't you?' I said.

'Well, the thought did just cross my mind,' said Miss Simpkins.

'It crossed and recrossed and danced up and down in *my* mind,' said Cam. She scrabbled in the chocolate box, found another great big cherry

cream and popped it in my mouth. 'Here, kiddo, you deserve it.'

'Now, I suppose we'd better start getting the show on the road,' said Miss Simpkins. 'OK, kids, clear up your picnic stuff as quick as you can. I want all the stagehands to go up on the stage and start sorting out the backdrops. I'll come and help in a minute. All the rest of you, come and find your costumes. Then, once you're dressed, go to Cam to get made up,' said Miss Simpkins.

'I wish we had *proper* costumes,' Justine complained.

'I do too, Justine, but we haven't had the time, money or indeed expertise to assemble proper Victorian costumes for a large cast. We've done our best with limited resources,' Miss Simpkins said crisply.

We all had to wear our ordinary school uniform, with coats on for everyone playing men. We had cardboard top hats and cardboard bonnets tied with ribbon. The children carol singers simply wound woolly scarves around their necks.

Carol Singer

Victorian Gentleman

Victorian Lady

Marley's Ghost

Miss Simpkins did her best to be inventive with the ghost costumes. Justine as Marley's Ghost had a big bandage round her head and a long dog chain with keys and purses and cash-boxes attached to it with Scoubidou strings.

As the Spirit of Christmas Past, Louise had a white frock and a white veil and her hair brushed out loose past her

Spirit of Christmas Past

shoulders. She danced round and round, pointing her toes.

'I'm glad I've got a pretty costume,' she said.

The Spirit of Christmas Present wore a Santa hat with a white cotton-wool beard and he had sprigs of holly pinned all over him. You couldn't get too near or he'd prick you.

The Spirit of Christmas Yet to Come wore a long black velvet gown (actually Miss Simpkins's dressing gown!) with a black scarf over his head.

Spirit of Christmas Present

Spirit of Christmas Yet to Come

Tiny Tim

That just left Peter and me. He didn't have a special costume as Tiny Tim, just a little cap and a crutch made out of an old broom handle.

I had *two* costumes. I wore my school shirt and grey trousers and an old grey raincoat cut at the back to make proper tails. I also had a white nightshirt with a white cap and slippers with pompoms for my night-time scenes.

Everyone laughed when I tried on the nightshirt, and started spreading rumours that it was *Mrs Darlow's* nightie. I started capering around doing a rude imitation of Mrs Darlow, sticking my bum right out and waggling it. Everyone laughed and I laughed too – though inside I felt so wound up I felt more like crying.

Was my mum going to come???

And if she did, would I let her down?

My capers got wilder. Cam collared me by the scruff of the nightshirt.

'Hey, hey, how about saving the acting for when you go on stage? Get into your Scrooge day outfit and then come to Classroom One. I'll do your make-up first, OK?'

'I don't want any experimenting! You're a total novice when it comes to make-up, Cam.'

'I tell you, I'm a dab hand at stage make-up, trust me. Come on, kiddo. You need to simmer down a little. There's no point being diplomatic with Mrs Darlow one minute and then sending her up rotten the next. If she walked in on your impersonation you'd be toast, Ms Beaker.'

We went to Classroom One together and she got out this huge case of make-up. She plonked me down on a chair and put a towel round my shoulders. She brushed my hair and yanked it into a tight topknot and then crammed a weird wig on my head, half pink rubber for a big bald patch, with straggly grey bits trailing to my shoulders.

'Now for your Scrooge face,' she said, starting to rub pale panstick into my skin.

'Hey, careful! You're getting it in my eyes!'

'Well close them, silly. Come on, Tracy, you want to look the part, don't you? Stop squirming round and act sensible.'

I sat still as a statue, eyes closed, while Cam dabbed and smeared at my face and then stuck stuff all over my eyebrows. She breathed heavily with concentration, tutting if I so much as twitched. Then she patted me lightly under the chin.

'There, Scrooge! You're done.'

I opened my eyes. Cam was holding a mirror in front of me. A mean whey-faced old man with whiskery eyebrows and grey frown lines peered back at me. I gasped – and the old man's thin lips gasped too.

It was me! I could hardly believe it I looked so different.

'I don't look like me any more!'

'Of course you don't. You're *not* you. You're Ebenezer Scrooge, the meanest man in the city.'

'I look *exactly* like the picture in the book I sent my mum . . .' My voice tailed away.

133

Cam put her face close to mine, her brown eyes big and pleading.

'Tracy. Listen to me. You know sometimes your mum hasn't been able to come to see you because she's making a movie somewhere? Well, that's because she knows how important it is to concentrate on her part. That's what you've got to do now. You're not Tracy Beaker any more, desperate to see her mum. You're Scrooge, and you haven't *got* a mum or a dad or anyone at all. You're a mean old misery-guts who hates everyone, and you especially hate this time of year, Christmas, the season of goodwill, because you don't wish anyone well and you think Christmas is total humbug. Think yourself into the character, Tracy. Don't go and mess around with the others. Stay centred on what you're doing.'

'Bah!' I said. 'Out of my way, Missy. Let me get back to my counting house. I need to give that varmint clerk of mine, Bob Cratchit, a severe talking to.'

Cam grinned and bobbed her head at me. 'Beg pardon, I'm sure, Mr Scrooge,' she said.

So I sloped off into Classroom Two and paced up and down the room telling myself I was Scrooge Scrooge Scrooge. Peter popped his head round the door and asked if I was OK.

'Bah! Humbug!' I growled.

He jumped back, looking upset. 'Sorry, Tracy!'

'I'm not Tracy, I'm Scrooge, you ignorant little lad. When I've been visited by Old Marley and the three Christmas Ghosts I shall have a change of heart and look on you kindly, almost as my own son, but for the moment, hop it!'

Peter hopped it. Literally, using his crutch.

I was fine all the time I was by myself. I thought myself into being Scrooge and acted some of the scenes, bending over like a gnarled old man. But then Miss Simpkins came to find me.

'Ah, Tracy, Cam said you were in here. You make an utterly splendid Scrooge – quite scary! OK, sweetheart, fifteen minutes to go till curtain up. Better whizz to the toilet and then come backstage with all the others.'

Suddenly I got so so so scared I stopped being

Scrooge. I didn't even feel like Tracy
Beaker any more. I felt like this tiny
trembly mini-mouse. My voice turned
into a squeak. I had to fight not to hang
onto Miss Simpkins's hand like some silly
little kid in the Infants. I wanted Cam but she
was still making people up in Classroom One.

I had to go and join Justine Hate-Her-Guts
Littlewood and Louise and Peter and all the
others. They were supposed to be sitting cross-
legged at the back of the stage, only speaking in
whispers. Of course they were all over the place,
giggling and gossiping, clowning around in their
costumes. The red velvet stage curtains
were pulled shut but Justine ran up to
them and had a little peep out.

'I can see him! There's my dad! My
dad's right at the front! Hey, Dad, Dad,
here I am!'

Then all the children rushed to the
gap in the curtains, sticking their heads
out and peering.

All the children except me.

I hung back. I thought of all those chairs, row
after row to the back of the hall. I thought of my
mum. I willed her to be sitting there right at the

front, but *not* next to Justine's dad. I wanted her to be there so much it was as if I had laser eyes that could bore right through the thick crimson velvet. There she was, sitting on the edge of her seat, smiling, waving, her pink heart gleaming round her neck . . .

I had to have one little look. Just to make sure.

I elbowed Justine Big-Bottom Littlewood out of the way and put one eye to the gap between the curtains. The hall was absolutely heaving, with almost every seat taken. I saw all the parents and the wriggly little brothers and sisters. I saw Jenny and Mike. I saw Elaine. She'd taken off her antlers but she had a sprig of mistletoe tied rakishly over one ear (who would want to kiss *Elaine*?). I saw Cam shunting along the front row, finished with her make-up session, every last member of the cast pansticked into character. I saw Justine's awful dad with his gold medallion and his tight leather jacket. I saw everyone . . . except my mum.

I looked right along every single row. She wasn't there. She wasn't in the front. She wasn't in the middle. She wasn't at the back.

Maybe she'd got held up. She'd be jumping out of her stretch limo right this minute, running precariously in her high heels, teeter-tottering up the school drive and now here she was . . .

Not yet.

Any second now.

I stared and stared and stared. Then I felt a hand on my shoulder.

'Get into place on stage, Tracy. We're about to start,' Miss Simpkins said softly.

'But my mum hasn't come yet! Can't we wait five minutes more? I don't want her to miss the beginning.'

'We'll wait one minute then. You go and settle yourself in your counting-house chair. I'll go and get the carol singers assembled. Then we'll *have* to start, sweetheart.'

'I can't. Not without my mum.'

'You're going to have to, Tracy. The show must

go on,' said Miss Simpkins.

I didn't care about the show now. There wasn't any point acting Scrooge if my mum couldn't see me. I clutched my chest. It really hurt. Maybe it was my heart breaking.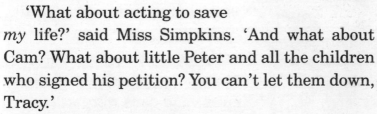

'I couldn't act to save my life,' I said.

'What about acting to save *my* life?' said Miss Simpkins. 'And what about Cam? What about little Peter and all the children who signed his petition? You can't let them down, Tracy.'

I knew she was right. I swallowed very very very hard to get rid of the lump in my throat. I blinked very very very hard to get rid of the water in my eyes. I took a deep deep deep breath.

'Bah!' I said. 'Humbug!'

Miss Simpkins gave me a thumbs-up and then beetled off to cue the carol singers. I sat in my chair, hunched up. They started singing 'Once in Royal David's City'. I started singing my own mournful little version:

'Once in poxy London city
Stood a lowly primary school
Where this girl waits for her mother
To come and see her act the fool.
Carly is that mother wild
Tracy Beaker is that child.'

Then the curtains parted with a swish, the lights went on dimly to show my candle-lit counting house, and I sat tensely in my chair, scowling.

I hated the noise of the chirpy carol singers. All *their* mums and dads were watching them, oohing and aahing and whispering, 'Ah, *bless*.'

My mum wasn't there. She couldn't be bothered to come, even though I'd bought her all those presents. She didn't care tuppence about me.

Well, I didn't care tuppence about her. I didn't care tuppence about *anyone*. I stomped to the side of the stage and shook my fist at the carol singers as they all cried, 'Happy Christmas!'

'Bah!' I said. 'Humbug. Be off with you!'

I felt as if I'd truly turned into Scrooge. My nephew came to wish me Merry Christmas and I sent him off with a flea in his ear. I didn't want to make merry with him. I bullied my stupid clerk Bob Cratchit, and then had a bite to eat. I ate my chicken drumstick like a finicky old man, and when one of the little kids played being a dog on all fours I snatched the bone away and shook my fist at him. He growled at me and I growled back. I heard the audience laugh. Someone whispered, 'Isn't that Tracy Beaker a proper caution!'

Then I went to bed and Justine Enemy-For-Ever Littlewood clanked on stage as Marley's Ghost, the coffin bandage round her head, her long chain trailing keys and padlocks and coinboxes.

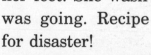

Justine's ridiculous dad started clapping wildly before she'd so much as opened her mouth and Justine Utterly-Unprofessional Littlewood totally forgot she was Marley's Ghost. She turned and waved excitedly at her father, just like a five-year-old in her first Nativity play.

I gave a gasp to remind Justine she was there to spook me out and give me a warning. Justine shuffled towards me unwillingly, still peering round at her dad. Her chain tangled around her feet. She wasn't looking where she was going. Recipe for disaster!

Justine tripped over her own padlock and went flying, landing flat on her face.

She lay there, looking a total idiot. Her face was all screwed up. She was trying not to cry.

My chest hurt. I knew just how she felt, falling over and making such a fool of herself in front of her dad. I reached out a shaking hand.

'Is it you, Jacob Marley, my old partner? It *can't* be you, because you're as dead as a doornail.' That was in Miss Simpkins's script. Now it was time for a spot of improvisation. 'Yet it must be you, Marley. You were unsteady on your feet in your last few years on earth – and you're unsteady now in your present spirit situation. Allow me to assist you, old chap.'

I took hold of Justine and hauled her up. The audience clapped delightedly because I'd saved the situation.

'Pray tell me why you're fettered,' I said, following the script again.

'I wear the chain I forged in life,' said Justine, pulling herself together. She sounded pretty miserable, but that was in character.

Then I was visited by Louise as the Spirit of Christmas Past. She'd put her own make-up on over Cam's so she looked more like she was going out clubbing than off haunting mean old men, but at least she didn't fall over.

We acted out the bit where little boy Scrooge was sent to a horrible boarding school and told he couldn't ever go home. It was a bit like me being sent off to the Dumping Ground.

I thought about Mum sending me there and not coming back to fetch me. Not even coming today, when I was starring as Scrooge. Tears rolled down my cheeks. I don't ever cry. But I wasn't being Tracy Beaker; I was acting Scrooge, and doing it so well I heard several snuffles in the audience. They were moved to tears too by my brilliant performance!

144

I had a chance to blow my nose on my nightshirt hem while everyone danced at the Fezziwigs' party. Then the curtains closed and the carol singers stood in front and sang 'Away in a Manger'.

I sang my own version to myself:

> *'Away in a schoolhouse*
> *No mum watched her daughter*
> *But Little Tracy Beaker*
> *Acted incredibly – she didn't falter!'*

Miss Simpkins and a host of little helpers rushed round the stage scattering real holly and ivy and mistletoe and fake painted plaster turkeys, ham, mince pies and clementines.

Then the curtains opened and I peered out, waving the carol singers away and going 'Ssh! Ssh!' to the audience. Fat Freddy waddled on stage in his Father Christmas outfit as the Spirit of Christmas Present and took me to see the Cratchit family.

Peter was shaking all over, scared out of his wits, but the moment he hopped across the stage using his crutch

145

everyone went 'Aaah! Doesn't he look *sweet*!' When he said, 'God bless us every one,' they all started clapping.

It looked as if weedy little Peter had stolen the show.

It was *my* show. I was Scrooge. I wanted them just to clap *me*. But Peter was my friend. He'd tried so hard for me. My chest hurt again. He liked me so much. And I liked him. I really did. Maybe I was a little bit glad he was being such a success. When the Spirit of Christmas Present told me Tiny Tim was going to die I cried straight from the heart, 'No, no! Oh no, kind Spirit! Say he will be spared!'

Then, as midnight struck, I spotted the two tiny children hiding under the Spirit's robes, the smallest skinniest kids Miss Simpkins could find, one playing Ignorance and one playing Want.

The last Spirit came creeping onto the stage,

draped in a long black robe, the scary Spirit of Christmas Yet to Come. The lights were very low so it looked as if we were wandering through the night together. We went to the Cratchit house, so melancholy without Tiny Tim. Then we went to the graveyard. Miss Simpkins shone a torch on the great cardboard tombstone. I saw my own name written there, Ebenezer Scrooge. I trembled and threw myself down on my knees.

'Oh, Spirit, have mercy!' I cried. 'Tell me I can sponge away the writing on this stone. I have learned my lesson. I will honour Christmas in my heart and try to keep it all the year.'

HERE
LIES
EBENEZER
SCROOGE

Then the lights went out and I jumped into my own bed quick as a wink and then acted waking up on Christmas Day. The carol signers sang 'We Wish You a Merry Christmas' outside my window. I sprang out of bed, did a little caper in my nightgown, and then went and called out to them.

147

'I wish you a Merry Christmas too, dear fellows. A Merry Christmas and a Happy New Year, and I, Ebenezer Scrooge, am going to lead a happy new life.'

Bells rang out and I danced up and down. Then I put my coat on over my nightshirt and rushed off stage, staggering back with the most comically enormous turkey, almost as big as me. I invited everyone to my house for Christmas. The whole cast crammed on stage and we 'ate' plastic mince pies and quaffed pretend wine – even Marley's Ghost and the three Christmas Spirits – and then we all sang 'God Rest Ye Merry Gentlemen'.

God rest ye merry gentlemen, let nothing you dismay...

I got Peter to shout out, 'God bless us every one!' right at the end.

Then the clapping started. It went on and on and on. We all stood holding hands and bowing. The four Ghosts got a special bow. Then Peter had to bow all by himself. He was so excited he did a little hoppy dance, waving his crutch, and the audience roared.

Then it was my turn. I stood in front of all the others. Cam and Jenny and Mike and Elaine stood up and started clapping and clapping. Miss Simpkins at the side of the stage was clapping and clapping. *Mrs Darlow* at the back of the hall was clapping and clapping. All the mums and dads were clapping and clapping.

But my mum wasn't clapping. She wasn't there.

HURRAH! Clap Clap BRAVO! Clap Clap Clap Clap BRAVO! MORE! Clap Clap Clap Clap Clap Clap MORE! Clap Clap Clap Clap Clap

It was the proudest moment of my life. I'd acted Scrooge and I'd been *good* at it. Glorious. Magnificent. The audience shouted '*Bravo!*' And '*Good for Tracy!*' And '*What a little star!*'

Mum didn't know. Mum didn't care.

I had a smile all over my face and yet my eyes were going blink blink blink. I was in serious danger of having an attack of hay fever in front of everyone.

Miss Simpkins came out onto the stage holding an enormous bunch of red roses and white lilies done up with a huge red satin ribbon.

'They've just arrived, Tracy. They're for you,'
she said, handing them over.

There was a card inside.

Congratulations, my little star.
Wish I could have seen you.
Lots of love, Mum xxx

'It's from my *mum*!' I said – but the note
proved *fatal* for my hay fever. Still, everyone
knows flowers trigger hay-fever attacks. I wasn't
crying. I don't *ever* cry.

Then we had a proper party in the hall with
real mince pies for everyone. Cam came and
hugged me hard and said she was so very proud
of me.

'You were totally brilliant, Tracy,' she said.
'And there's you saying you couldn't remember
a word!'

'Well, it didn't *feel* as if I was remembering it.

It wasn't like *acting*. It was as if I was really living it,' I said.

'Aha! That shows you're a *real* actor,' said Cam.

'Like Mum,' I said.

'Just like your mum.' Cam smiled at me. 'Aren't they gorgeous flowers? Wasn't it lovely of her to send them? Imagine, getting your own huge bouquet of flowers.'

'Yeah. With a lovely note. Did you see what my mum wrote?'

'Yes, Tracy.'

'The only thing is . . .' I swallowed. 'It's not my mum's handwriting.'

I looked hard at Cam. She didn't look away. She stared straight into my eyes.

'Of course it's not your mum's actual writing, Tracy. You order the flowers on the phone and say what you want on the card and then the local florist writes it down.'

'Oh!' I said. I swallowed again. The mince pie seemed made of very lumpy pastry. 'You wouldn't kid me, would you, Cam?'

'No one could ever kid you, Tracy Beaker,' said Cam.

'Well, I think it was lovely of my mum. But it would have been a lot lovelier if she'd actually come to see me,' I said.

'I'm sure she would have done if she possibly could,' said Cam.

'Do you think she's still coming to see me on Christmas Day?' I said.

'Well . . . maybe she is,' said Cam.

'And maybe she's not,' I said. 'So what am I going to do on Christmas Day, eh? I *hate* Christmas in the Dumping Ground. Jenny and Mike try hard but they've always got the little kids clinging to them and everyone tears open their presents too quickly and then fusses because they think the others have got better things, and there's never enough new batteries and often the stuff doesn't work anyway. We watch television but all the programmes are about families and we are all so *not* a family. We have turkey and Christmas pudding for dinner because Jenny wants it to be traditional so we don't miss out, but I don't really *like* turkey or Christmas pudding – though I eat too much anyway – and then we're supposed to play these

153

crazy games but the little kids are too dim to play and the big kids just want to slope off to their rooms and someone always throws a tantrum because they're so fed up and lonely and left out. That someone is quite often me, as a matter of fact.'

'Hmm,' said Cam. 'It sounds as if we both have crap Christmases. Tell you what, Tracy. Let's join up together. You come to me for Christmas. What do you think?'

'I think that sounds a brilliant idea,' I said.

So that's exactly what I did. I woke up very early on Christmas morning and opened all my presents peacefully, all by myself. Jenny gave me cool new jeans and a CD and Mike gave me new trainers and amazing black nail varnish. Elaine gave me a *little fluffy blue teddy bear* – yuck yuck yuck! Peter gave me a silver yo-yo. It was very sweet of him. I decided to give him the blue teddy.

My mum didn't give me anything.

I expect the roses and lilies cost a lot of money. Acting is a chancy profession. Maybe Mum was a bit strapped for cash at the moment.

Of course, Grizelda Moonbeam might work her magic and Mum might appear in person, weighed down with presents. But somehow it wasn't starting to seem very likely. It didn't look as if I was going to be spending this festive occasion with my Loved One. Unless . . . maybe *Cam* counted as a Loved One? Was I *her* Loved One?? Had the charm actually worked a double whammy???

I knew Cam was certainly short of money so I wasn't too hopeful about her present to me. She arrived astonishingly early. She was wearing a woolly hat and scarf and mittens, with a big woolly jumper over her jeans and woolly socks.

'Happy Christmas, Cam! Have you got woolly *knickers* on? Why are you all bundled up? And you're so *early*. We haven't even had breakfast yet. Do you want some?'

'Happy Christmas, Tracy. You need to pile on lots of woolly jumpers too. We're going for a walk. And we're having breakfast out, OK?'

She drove us for miles to this big park. It wasn't snowing but it was still early enough for there to be a frost so we could kid ourselves it was a real white Christmas.

'Come on!' said Cam, parking the car. She opened the door. It certainly *felt* frosty. I hadn't got quite enough woollies.

'It's freezing, Cam! Can't we stay in the car?'

'We're going for a walk, Tracy, to work up an appetite for our breakfast.'

'You go for a walk. I'll stay in the car and watch you,' I said.

She dragged me out, rammed her own woolly hat over my head, wound her scarf round and round and round me as if she was wrapping a mummy, and then took me by the hand.

'There! Cosy now? Off we go!'

'I'm not really *into* long country walks, Cam. I'm not built for it. Look at my spindly legs.' I made my knees knock together and walked with a Tiny Tim limp.

'Just come down this path with me,' said Cam, tugging me. 'Through the trees. You'll like what you see when you get to the end.'

I knew what I'd see. *Scenery*. A lot more trees and a hill or two. I didn't see the point. Still, it was Christmas after all. I didn't want to be too difficult. I sighed and staggered after Cam. I didn't get why she wanted to stay out in the cold, especially before breakfast.

'I don't want to moan, but my tummy's rumbling rather a lot. It's saying, *Tracy, Tracy, what's happened to my cornflakes?*'

'You'll have breakfast very soon, I promise,' said Cam, laughing.

'Are we having a picnic then?' I asked.

It seemed a mad time of year to have a picnic and I didn't see any signs of a hamper. Cam wasn't carrying so much as a lunch box. Perhaps she had a sandwich or two crammed in her pockets? It looked like it was going to be a very *little* picnic, yet I was totally *starving*.

Cam and I weren't the only ones embarking

157

on this mad early-morning Starve-In. There were lots of other cars in the car park and little bunches of bobble-hatted muffled weirdos trudged along too, all heading in the same direction. It was like we were all in *Doctor Who* and some alien force was messing with our heads, controlling our minds.

Then we rounded a bend. I saw a big pond in the distance. A lot of people were *in* the pond. No, no, they were *on* it, gliding across.

'They're skating!' I said.

'Yep.'

'Can *we* skate?'

'We'll have a go.'

'But we haven't got any skates.'

'You can hire them, Tracy, I checked. And they're serving a special Christmas breakfast.'

'Oh, wow! So you planned it all? Oh, Cam, you have some seriously cool ideas.'

I gave her a quick hug and then started running helter-skelter to the ice. There was a big van serving golden croissants and hot chocolate with whipped cream. We had breakfast first, just to fortify ourselves, and then we hired our skates, held hands and hobbled onto the ice.

I thought I'd glide off like a swan, swoop-swoop, swirl-swirl, the epitome of athletic grace. Ha! I staggered like a drunk, clonk-clunk, whizz, whoops, bonk on my bum. Cam pulled me up, trying not to laugh.

'Look, Tracy, point your boots out and do it like *this*,' she said, demonstrating.

Some kid hurtled past her, making her jump. She wavered, wobbled – and then went bonk on *her* bum.

I *did* laugh and Cam laughed too.

'I don't know about woolly knickers. I think we both need *padded* knickers,' she said as I pulled her up.

We held onto each other and tried again. This time we staggered all the way round the pond. I started to get more daring. I tried a little swoop.

159

It worked! I tried another – left, right, truly gliding – only I couldn't seem to stop. I went charging straight into a little cluster of kids in a line and mowed them all down.

'We're going to have to rename you Tracy Bulldozer,' said Cam, hauling us all up.

We skated for over an hour, losing count of the number of times we both fell over, but we could also both glide properly for a few seconds at a time, so considered ourselves champion skaters.

'I think we deserve another breakfast after all that effort,' said Cam, and we polished off *another* croissant and mug of hot chocolate.

Then Cam drove us back to her house. She had a little Christmas tree in her living room.

'I usually don't bother, but they were selling them half price in the market yesterday so I decided to go mad.'

'It looks a bit naked if you don't mind me saying so. Aren't you meant to have little glass balls and tinsel and fairy lights?' I said.

'Of course you are. I thought it would be fun if we decorated the tree together,' said Cam. 'Look in that big carrier bag. There's all the decorations.'

'Oh, fantastic! We don't have a proper tree at the Dumping Ground because the little kids are so dopey they might mistake the glass balls for apples and the big kids are so rowdy they might knock it all over. I've *always* wanted to decorate a tree!'

'Then be my guest. I'll go and sort out what we might be having for Christmas dinner. I know you don't go a bundle on turkey and I'm mostly veggie nowadays . . . I could do a sort of tofu and vegetable casserole?'

'That sounds absolutely temptingly delicious – *not*!' I said.

161

'I rather thought that would be your response. I don't fancy faffing around in the kitchen for hours anyway. How about egg and chips?'

'Now you're talking! With lots of tomato sauce?'

'You can dollop it all over your plate, Tracy. It's Christmas. Ah! What else do you get at Christmas? We've got a Christmas tree. We'll have our Christmas dinner. But there's something else you have at Christmas. Um. What could it be? Oh yes! Presents!'

She opened up a cupboard and pulled out three parcels in jolly Santa wrapping paper tied with red ribbon.

'Oh, Cam! Are they for me?'

'Well, they've all got Tracy Beaker on the labels, so if that's your name I'd say it was a safe bet they're all for you.'

I felt really really really great. Cam had bought me loads of lovely presents.

I felt really really really bad. I hadn't got Cam anything.

'Oh dear, why the saddo face? Did you hope there might be more?' Cam teased.

'*You* haven't got any presents, Cam!' I wailed.

'Yes I have. I've opened mine already. I got a silk *headscarf* from my mum – as if I'd ever wear it! Plus a posh credit-card holder when I'm so overdrawn I can't use my blooming cards anyway. I got lovely presents from my friends though. Jane gave me my woolly hat and scarf and mittens and Liz gave me a big box of chocs and a book token.'

'What's a book *token*?'

'It's a little card for a certain amount of money and when you take it to a shop you can change it for any book you fancy.'

'Oh, I get it.' I nodded. 'Good idea!'

'Come on then, open your presents from me.'

I opened the heaviest first. It was ten children's paperbacks. They were all a bit dog-eared and tattered.

'I'm afraid they're second-hand,' said Cam. 'I searched in all the charity shops. A lot of them were ten-pence bargains!'

163

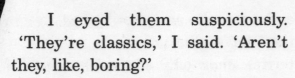

I eyed them suspiciously. 'They're classics,' I said. 'Aren't they, like, boring?'

'Is *A Christmas Carol* boring? No! These were all my favourites when I was your age. Cam Lawson's Top Ten Super Reads for kids your age. If you don't want them I'll have a great time re-reading them. *Little Women* is about this family of sisters and they like acting too, and reading Charles Dickens. You'll especially like Jo, who's a tomboy and wants to be a writer.

'Then there's *Black Beauty*. It's a wonderful story, and there's a very sad bit about a horse called Ginger which always makes me cry, but it's lovely all the same. *What Katy Did* is about a big family – Katy's the eldest, and she's always in heaps of trouble but then she falls off a swing and can't walk for ages. She's got a very saintly cousin who irritates a bit, but it's a great story, truly.

'*The Wind in the Willows* is about a mole

and a rat who are great chums and they have this pal Toad who's a terrible show-off, and there are some very funny bits. *Five Children and It* is also funny – it's about these kids who meet a sand fairy and all their wishes come true, but they always go wrong.'

'Chance would be a fine thing,' I said, sniffing.

'There's also *Mary Poppins*. The book's much better than the film. I loved *Tom Sawyer* because he's very badly behaved and always in trouble, and you might give *Anne of Green Gables* a go. It's all about this little orphan girl who won't ever stop talking. You'll identify big-time with those two.

'I'm sure you'll like *The Secret Garden* because Mary is wondrously grouchy and rude to everyone and has to live in a house with a hundred rooms on the Yorkshire Moors. And *Ballet Shoes* is a perfect book for you, because these three sisters go to a stage school and perform in lots

of plays, and I think that's maybe what you might end up doing, Tracy.'

'OK, OK. I'll give them a go,' I said. 'I can always share them with some of the other kids, eh? Peter might like the Mole and Rat and Toad book.'

I tried the next parcel, the biggest. It had a big drawing book, a big pail of felt tips and a giant tub of modelling clay, all different colours. These were all brand new!

'I thought it was about time you had your own art supplies instead of raiding poor Elaine's art cupboard,' said Cam.

'Oh wow! I'm *not* going to share these!'

Finally I picked up the tiniest parcel. I unwrapped it and found a little black box.

I opened it up – and there was a silver star pin badge.

'It's for you, Tracy Beaker Superstar,' said Cam, pinning it on me.

I gave her a big big big hug.

Then I decorated the tree, carefully dangling each glass ball and chocolate Santa and little bird and twirly glass icicle, while Cam wound the fairy lights round and round. When we switched them on the tree looked totally magical.

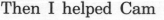

Then I helped Cam cook the lunch. She got me peeling potatoes. I had no idea that was the real way to make chips. Ours come in giant packets at the Dumping Ground, already peeled and sliced. I started peeling pounds of potatoes, whistling as I whittled.

'Steady on, girl. There's just the two of us,' said Cam.

'I never get quite *enough* chips at the Dumping Ground,' I said.

'OK. It's Christmas. Today you can eat until you burst,' said Cam.

She wouldn't let me fry them in the big

sizzling chip pan, but she *did* let me
fry our eggs and that was great fun.
We both had *enormous* piles
of golden chips on our
plates, with a fried egg
on top like snow on
a mountain peak.
I squirted mine
liberally with scarlet
sauce and then we
started eating. I ate
and ate and ate. My meal was delicious.

'I make the most excellent egg and chips ever,'
I said, licking my lips. 'Maybe I'm going to be a
famous chef as well as a brilliant writer and a
superstar actress.'

Cam ate her chips valiantly but had to give
up halfway through. We had clementines for
pudding, then Cam opened up her big box of
chocolates from Liz and we snaffled some of
those.

Then Cam undid her jeans and lay on the sofa,
groaning, while I got my new art stuff and started
creating. Cam rubbed her tummy, reached for a
book and started reading me the first Christmasy
chapter of *Little Women*. It was quite good in

an old-fashioned sort of way. Meg was a bit of a goody-goody and Beth was a bit wet and Amy was too pert and girly but I *loved* Jo.

Cam's voice tailed away after a while and she dozed off. I carried on and on and on creating. Then, when she started yawning and stretching and opening her eyes, I went and made her a cup of tea. No one has ever shown me how to do it but I'm not a total moron.

'Thank you, Tracy!' said Cam. She took a sip. 'Delicious!'

(I spotted her fishing several of the teabags out of her cup and spooning out a few of the still melting sugar lumps, but neither of us mentioned this.)

'I've got you some Christmas presents after all,' I said. 'Look on your coffee table.' I pointed proudly.

Cam nearly spilled her tea. 'Oh my lord! Multiple Tracy Beakers!' she said.

'Aren't they great!' I said. 'I made them with my modelling clay. The pink face was fine, and the red jumper and the blue skirt, but making my black curls all squiggly took *ages*.'

'Are all six for me?' said Cam.

'No, no. You have *this* one. She's the best, with the biggest smile. And I've got one for Peter and one for Jenny and one for Mike, and I suppose I ought to give one to Elaine and I thought I'd give one to Miss Simpkins when I go back to school.'

'That's a lovely idea. Well, I shall treasure my Tracy Beaker model. I'll put her on my desk. She can keep me company when I'm writing.'

'Don't crumple her up by mistake if you get stuck!' I said. 'Look, you've got another present.'

I handed her a folded piece of paper with a picture of me on the front.

'Oh, a card. How lovely!' said Cam.

'It's not a card. It's a Tracy token,' I said. 'You know, like a book token. But you don't get books with this token, you get *me*. Look inside.'

I'd written:

To Cam. Happy Christmas!

I, Tracy Beaker, promise to make you a plate of my famous egg and chips whenever I'm round at your place.  I will make you DOUBLE egg and chips on your birthday.

If I get to be a famous chef with my own swanky restaurant I will create a famous egg and chips dish and call it my <u>Cam Christmas Special.</u>

If I get to be a famous writer I will dedicate my second book to you. I hope that's okay, but I have to dedicate my first book to my mum.

If I get to be a famous superstar actress I will let you be my drama coach.

And if you finish your classes and go through wit fostering me I will be the best foster daughter ev

Love from
Tracy
xxx

Cam read it through, sniffling. 'Oh, Tracy,' she said. 'This is the best Christmas present I've ever had. And of course you'll be the best foster-daughter ever. You're *Tracy Beaker*.'

Yes I am. Tracy Beaker Superstar.

When I went to bed that night back at the Dumping Ground I gave Mum's photo a kiss.

'I hope you had a Happy Christmas, Mum,' I whispered. 'Maybe see you next year, yeah?'

Then I lay back in bed and sang a little Christmas carol to myself.

'Silent night, holy night,
Tracy is calm, Tracy is bright.
Mum didn't come but I had a good time,
I love Mum but I'm glad Cam is mine.
Now I'll sleep in heavenly peace,
S-l-e-e-p in heav-en-ly peeeace.'

The Dare Game

Jacqueline Wilson

Illustrated by Nick Sharratt

*To Jessie Atkinson
Francesca Oates
Zoe
Lee and Sarah
Emma Walker and all my friends at
Redriff School
and everyone else who ever wondered
what happened to Tracy Beaker*

No Home

You know that old film they always show on the telly at Christmas, *The Wizard of Oz*? I love it, especially the Wicked Witch of the West with her cackle and her green face and all her special flying monkeys. I'd give anything to have a wicked winged monkey as an evil little pet. It could whiz through the sky, flapping its wings and sniffing the air for that awful stale instant-coffee-and-talcum-powder *teacher* smell and then it would s-w-o-o-p straight onto Mrs Vomit Bagley and carry her away screaming.

That'll show her. I've always been absolutely Tip Top at writing stories, but since I've been at this stupid new school Mrs V.B. just puts *'Disgracefully untidy work, Tracy'* and *'Check your spellings!'* Last week we had to write a story about 'Night-time' and I thought it an unusually cool subject so I wrote eight and a half pages about this girl out late at night and it's seriously spooky and then this crazy guy jumps out at her and almost murders her but she escapes by jumping in the river and then she swims right into this bloated corpse and *then* when she staggers onto the bank there's this strange flickering light coming from the nearby graveyard and it's an evil occult sect wanting to sacrifice an innocent young girl and she's *just* what they're looking for . . .

It's a truly GREAT story, better than any that Cam could write. (I'll tell you about Cam in a minute.) I'm sure it's practically good enough to get published. I typed it out on Cam's computer so it looked ever so neat and the spellcheck took care of all the spellings so I was all prepared for Mrs V.B. to bust a gut and write: '*Very very very good indeed, Tracy. 10 out of 10 and Triple Gold Star and I'll buy you a tube of Smarties at playtime.*'

Do you know what she really wrote? '*You've tried hard, Tracy, but this is a very rambling story. You also have a very warped imagination!*'

I looked up 'warp' in the dictionary she's always recommending and it means 'to twist out of shape'. That's spot on. I'd like to warp Mrs Vomit Bagley, twisting and twisting, until her eyes pop and her arms and legs are wrapped right round her great big bum. That's another thing. Whenever I write the weeniest babiest little rude word Mrs V.B. goes bananas. I don't know what she'd do if I used *really* bad words like **** and **** and ****** (censored!!).

I looked up 'ramble' too. I liked what it said: 'To stroll about freely, as for relaxation, with no particular direction'. So that's *exactly* what I did today, instead of staying at boring old school. I bunked off and strolled round the town freely, as relaxed as anything. I had a little potter in Paperchase and bought this big

9

fat purple notebook with my pocket money. I'm going to write all my mega-manic ultra-scary stories in it, as warped and as rambly as I can make them. And I'll write *my* story too. I've written all about myself before in *The Story of Tracy Beaker*. So this can be *The Story of Tracy Beaker Two* or *Find Out What Happens Next to the Brave and Brilliant Tracy Beaker* or *Further Fabulous Adventures of the Tremendous Terrific Tracy Beaker* or *Read More About the Truly Terrible Tracy Beaker, Even More Wicked Than the Wicked Witch of the West*.

Yes. I was telling you about *The Wizard of Oz*. There's only one bit that I truly dread. I can't actually watch it. The first time I saw it I very nearly cried. (I *don't* cry, though. I'm tough. As old boots. New boots. The biggest fiercest reinforced Doc Martens . . .) It's the bit right at the end where Dorothy is getting fed up with being in Oz. Which is mad, if you ask me. Who'd want to go back to that boring black and white Kansas and be an ordinary kid where they take your dog away when you could dance round Oz in your ruby slippers? But Dorothy acts in an extremely dumb manner all the way through the film. You'd

10

think she'd have sussed out for herself that all she had to do was click those ruby slippers and she'd get back home. That's it. That's the bit. Where she says, 'There's no place like home.'

There's no place like home.

It gets to me. Because there's no place like home for me. No place at all. I haven't got a home.

Well. I didn't have up until recently. Unless you count the Home. If a home has a capital letter at the front you can be pretty sure it isn't like a *real* home. It's just a dumping ground for kids with problems. The ugly kids, the bad kids, the daft kids. The ones no-one wants to foster. The kids way past their sell-by date so they're all chucked on the rubbish heap. There were certainly some ultra-rubbishy kids at that Home. Especially a certain Justine Littlewood . . .

We were Deadly Enemies once, but then we made up. I even gave Justine my special Mickey Mouse pen. I rather regretted this actually and asked for it back the next day, pretending it had just been a loan, but Justine wasn't having any. There are no flies on Justine. No wasps, bees or any kind of bug.

It's weird, but I kind of miss Justine now. It was even fun when we were Deadly Enemies and we played the Dare Game. I've always been great at thinking up the silliest daftest rudest dares. I always dared everything and won until Justine came to the Children's Home. Then I *still* won. Most of the time. I *did*. But Justine could certainly invent some seriously wicked dares herself.

I miss her. I miss Louise too. And I especially miss Peter. This is even weirder. I couldn't stand weedy old Peter when he first came to the Home. But now it feels like he was my best ever friend. I wish I could see him. I especially wish I could see him right now. Because I'm all on my own and although it's great to be bunking off school and I've found the most brilliant hiding place in the whole world it is a little bit lonely.

I could do with a mate. When you're in care you need to make all the friends you can get because you don't have much family.

Well. I've got family.

I've got the loveliest prettiest best-ever mum in the whole world. She's this dead famous Hollywood movie star and she's in film after film, in so much demand that there isn't a minute of the day when she can see me so that's why I'm in care . . .

Who am I kidding??? Not you. Not even me. I used to carry on like that when I was little, and some kids took it all in and even acted like they were impressed. But now when I come out with all that movie guff they start to get this little curl of the lip and then the minute my back's turned I hear a splutter of laughter. And that's the *kinder* kids. The rest tell me straight to my face that I'm a nutter. They don't even believe my mum's an actress. I know for a fact she's been in *some* films. She sent me this big glossy photo of her in this negligée – but now kids nudge and giggle and say, 'What *kind* of film was your mum in, Tracy Beaker?'

13

So I duff them up. Sometimes literally. I'm very handy with my fists. Sometimes I just pretend it in my head. I should have pretended inside my head with Mrs Vomit Bagley. It isn't wise to tell teachers exactly what you think of them. She gave us this new piece of writing work this morning. About 'My Family'. It was supposed to be an exercise in autobiography. It's really a way for the teachers to be dead nosy and find out all sorts of secrets about the kids. Anyway, after she's told us all to start writing this 'My Family' stuff she squeezes her great hips in and out the desks till she gets to me. She leans over until her face is hovering a few inches from mine. I thought for one seriously scary second she was going to *kiss* me!

'Of course, *you* write about your foster mother, Tracy,' she whispers, her Tic-Tac minty breath tickling my ear.

She thought she was whispering discreetly, but every single kid in the room looked up and stared. So I stared straight back and edged as far away from Mrs V.B. as I could and said

14

firmly, 'I'm going to write about my *real* mother, Mrs Bagley.'

So I did. Page after page. My writing got a bit sprawly and I gave up on spelling and stopped bothering about full stops and capital letters because they're such a waste of time, but I wrote this *amazing* account of me and my mum. Only I never finished it. Because Mrs V.B. does another Grand Tour of the class, bending over and reading your work over your shoulder in the most off-putting way possible, and she gets to me and leans over, and then she sniffs inwards and sighs. I thought she was just going to have the usual old nag about Neatness and Spelling and Punctuation – but this time she was miffed about the content, not the presentation.

'You and your extraordinary imagination, Tracy,' she said, in this falsely sweet patronizing tone. She even went 'Tut tut', shaking her head, still with this silly smirk on her face.

'What do you mean?' I said, sharpish.

'Tracy! Don't take that rude tone with me, dear.' There was an edge to her voice and all. 'I did my best to explain about Autobiography. It means you tell a *true* story about yourself and your own life.'

'It *is* true. All of it,' I said indignantly.

'Really, Tracy!' she said, and she started reading bits out, not trying to keep her voice down now, revving up for public proclamation.

' "My mum is starring in a Hollywood movie with George Clooney and Tom Cruise and Brad Pitt and they all think she's wonderful and want to be her boyfriend. Her new movie is going to star Leonardo DiCaprio as her younger brother and she's got really matey with Leonardo at rehearsals and he's seen the photo of me she carries around in her wallet and he says I look real cute and wants to write to me," ' Mrs V.B. read out in this poisonous high-pitched imitation of my voice.

The entire class collapsed. Some of the kids practically wet themselves laughing. Mrs V.B. had this smirk puckering her lips. 'Do you really believe this, Tracy?' she asked.

So I said, 'I really believe that you're a stupid hideous old bag who could only get a part in a movie about bloodsucking vampire bats.'

I thought for a moment she was going to prove her bat-star qualities by flying at my neck and biting me with her fangs. She certainly wanted to. But she just marched me out of the room instead and told me to stand outside the door because she was sick of my insolence.

I said she made *me* sick and it was a happy chance that her name was Mrs V. Bagley. The other kids might wonder whether the V. stood for Vera or Violet or Vanessa, but I was certain her first name was Vomit, and dead appropriate too, given her last name, because she looked like the contents of a used vomit bag.

She went back into the classroom when I was only halfway through so I said it to myself, slumping against the wall and staring at my shoes. I said I was Thrilled to Bits to miss out on her lesson because she was boring boring boring and couldn't teach for toffee. She couldn't teach for fudge, nougat, licorice or Turkish delight. I declared I was utterly Ecstatic to be Outside.

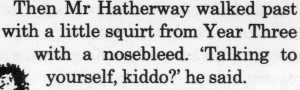

Then Mr Hatherway walked past with a little squirt from Year Three with a nosebleed. 'Talking to yourself, kiddo?' he said.

'No, I'm talking to my shoes,' I said crossly.

I expected him to have a go at me too but he just nodded and mopped the little spurting scarlet fountain. 'I have a quiet chat to *my* shoes when things are getting me down,' he said. 'Very understanding friends, shoes. I find my old Hush Puppies especially comforting.'

The little squirt gave a whimper and Mr Hatherway gave him another mop. 'Come on, pal, we'd better get you some first aid.'

He gave me a little nod and they walked on. Up until that moment I was convinced that this new school was 100% horrible. Now it was maybe 1% OK, because I quite liked Mr Hatherway. Not that I had any chance of having him as my teacher, not unless I was shoved out of Year Six right to the bottom of the Juniors. And the school was still 99% the pits, so I decided to clear off out of it.

It was easy-peasy. I waited till playtime

when Mrs V.B. waved me away, her nostrils pinched like I smelled bad. So I returned the compliment and held my own nose but she pretended not to notice. It was music in the hall with Miss Smith after playtime so I was someone else's responsibility then. Only I wasn't going to stick around for music because Miss Smith keeps picking on me too, just because of that one time I experimented with alternative uses of a drumstick. So I moseyed down the corridor like I was going to the toilets only I went right on walking, round the corner, extra sharpish past Reception (though Mrs Ludovic was busy mopping the little kid with the nosebleed. It looked like World War Three in her office) and then quick out the door and off across the yard. The main gate was locked but that presented no problem at all for SuperTracy. I was up that wall and over in a flash. I did fall over the other side and both my knees got a bit chewed up but that didn't bother me.

They hurt quite a lot now, even though they've stopped bleeding. They both look pretty dirty. I've probably introduced all sorts of dangerous germs into my bloodstream and any minute now I'll develop a high fever and start frothing at the mouth. I don't feel very well actually. And I'm *starving*. I wish I hadn't spent all my money on this notebook. I especially wish I hadn't picked one the exact purple of a giant bar of Cadbury's milk chocolate. I shall start slavering all over it soon.

I'd really like to call it a day and push off back to Cam's but the clock's just struck and it's only one o'clock. Lunchtime. Only I haven't any lunch. I can't go back till teatime or Cam will get suspicious. I *could* show her my savaged knees and say I had a Dire Accident and got sent home, but Cam would think I'd been fighting again. I got in enough trouble the last time. It wasn't *fair*. I didn't start the fight.

It was all that Roxanne Green's fault. She made this sneery remark to her friends about my T-shirt. She was showing off in her new DKNY T-shirt, zigzagging her shoulders this way and that, so I started imitating her and everyone laughed. So she goes, 'What label is *your* T-shirt, Tracy?'

Before I could make anything up she says, '*I* know. It's Oxfam!'

Everyone laughed again but this time it was awful so I got mad and called Roxanne various names and then she called *me* names and most of it was baby stuff but then she said the B word – and added that it was true in my case because I really didn't have a dad.

So I had to smack her one then, didn't I? It was only fair. Only Roxanne and all her little girly hangers-on didn't think it was fair and they told Mrs Vomit Bagley and she *certainly* didn't think it was fair and she told Mr Donne the headteacher and, guess what, he didn't think it was fair either. He rang Cam and asked her to come to the school for a Quiet Word. I was yanked along to the study too and I said lots of words not at *all* quietly, but Cam put her arm round me and hissed in my ear, 'Cool it, Trace.'

I tried. I thought c-o-o-l and imagined a beautiful blue lake of water and me swimming slowly along – but I was so sizzling mad the water started to bubble all around me and I ended up boiling over and telling the head what I thought of him and his poxy teachers and putrid pupils. (Get my vocabulary, Mrs V.B.!)

I very nearly ended up being excluded. Which is mad. I should have been even cheekier because I don't *want* to go to this terrible old school.

So I've excluded myself.

I'm here.

In my own secret place. Dead exclusive. My very own house.

Home!

Well, it's not exactly *homely* at the moment. It needs a good going over with a vacuum or two. Or three or four or five. And even though it's kind of empty it needs a spot of tidying. There are empty beer cans and McDonald's cartons chucked all over the place, and all kinds of freebie papers and advertising bumpf litter the hall so you're wading ankle-deep when you come in the front door. Only I didn't, seeing as it's locked and bolted and boarded over. I came in the back, through the broken window, ever so carefully.

I went in the back garden because I was mooching round and round the streets, dying for a wee. I came across this obviously empty house down at the end of a little cul-de-sac with big brambles all over the place giving lots of cover so I thought I'd nip over the wall quick and relieve myself. Which I did, though a black cat suddenly streaked past, which made me jump and lose concentration so I very nearly weed all over my trainers.

When I was relieved and decent I tried to catch the cat, pretending this was a jungle and the cat was a tiger and I was all set to train it but the cat went 'Purr-lease!' and stalked off with its tail in the air.

I explored the jungle by myself and spotted the broken window and decided to give the house a recce too.

It's a great house. It hasn't quite got all mod cons any more. The water's been turned off and the lights won't switch on and the radiators are cold. But there's still a sofa in the living room, quite a swish one, red velvet. Some plonker's put his muddy boots all over it, but I've been scratching at it with my fingernails and I think it'll clean up a treat.

I could bring a cushion. And a blanket. And some *food*. Yeah.

Next time.

But now it's time for me to go . . . back to Cam.

Cam's Home

Cam is fostering me. It was all my idea. When I was back in the Children's Home I was pretty desperate to be fostered. *Ugly* desperate. They'd even tried advertising me in the papers, this gungy little description of me outlining all my bad points together with a school photo where I was scowling – and so no-one came forward, which didn't exactly surprise me. Though it was still awful. Especially when one of the kids at school brought the newspaper into school and showed everyone. That was a different school. It wasn't much cop either. But it was marginally better than this one. This one is the worst ever.

It's Cam's fault. She said I had to go there. Because it's the nearest one. I *knew* I'd hate it from the very first day. It's an old school, all red brick and brown paint and smelly

25

cloakrooms and nearly all the teachers are old too. They sound like they've all been to this old-fashioned elocution school to get that horrid sarcastic tone to their voices.

You know: 'Oh, that's really *clever* of you, Tracy Beaker' when you spill your paint water (accidentally on purpose all over Roxanne's designer T-shirt!), and 'I'm amazed that *you're* the one who scribbled silly words all over the blackboard, Tracy Beaker' (wonderfully wicked words!), and 'Can you possibly speak up a bit, Tracy Beaker, I think there's a deaf old lady at the other end of the street who didn't quite catch that' (I *had* to raise my voice because how else can I get the other kids in my group to listen to me?).

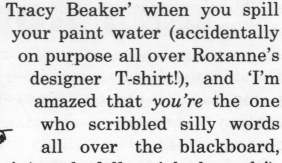

I hate it when we have to split up for group work. They all fit into these neat little groups: Roxanne and her gang, Almost-Alan-Shearer and the football crazies, Basher Dixon and his henchmen, Wimpy Lizzie and Dopey Dawn and that lot, Brainbox Hannah and Swotty Andrew – they're all divided up. And then there's me.

Mrs V.B. puts me in different groups each time. Sometimes I'm in a group all by myself. I don't care. I prefer it. I hate them all.

Cam says I should try to make friends. I don't *want* to be friends with that seriously sad bunch of losers. I keep moaning to Cam that it's a rubbish school and telling her to send me somewhere else. She's useless. Well, she did try going down to the Guildhall and seeing if they could swop me somewhere else but they said the other schools in the area are oversubscribed.

She just accepted it. Didn't make any kind of fuss. If you want anything in this world you've got to fight for it. I should know.

'You're on their waiting list,' Cam said, as if she thought I'd be pleased.

What use is that? I've been waiting half my life to *get* a life. I thought my big chance had come when Cam came to the Children's Home to research this boring old article about kids in care. (She only got £100 for it and I was barely mentioned!) I thought she might do as a foster mum as she's a writer and so am I.

She needed quite a lot of persuading.

27

But I can be pretty determined when I want. And I *did* want Cam. Badly.

So when she said, 'Right then, Tracy, let's give it a go. You and me. OK?' it was more than OK. I was over the moon. Soaring straight up into the solar system. I couldn't wait to get out of the Children's Home. I got dead impatient with Elaine the Pain my social worker because she seemed to be trying to slow things down instead of speed them up.

'No point in rushing things, Tracy,' she said.

I felt there was *every* point. I didn't want Cam to change her mind. She was having to go to all these interviews and meetings and courses and she's not really that sort of person. She doesn't like to be bossed around and told what to do. Like me. I was scared she might start to think it was all too much hassle.

But *eventually* we had a weekend together and that was great. Cam wanted it to be a very laid-back weekend – a walk in the park, a video or two, and a takeaway pizza. I said I did all that sort of stuff already at the Children's Home and couldn't we do something special to celebrate our first weekend together?

I told you I can be pretty persuasive. Cam took me to Chessington World of Adventures and it was truly great and she even bought me this huge python with beady green eyes and a black forked tongue. She dithered long and hard about it, saying she didn't want it to look like she was buying my affection, but I made the python wind round and round her beguilingly. He 'told' her he was desperate to be bought because the shopkeeper was really mean to him just because he'd got a teeny bit peckish and gobbled up a furry bunny and several toy mice as a little snack.

Cam bought him though she said she was mad and that she'd be eating bread and cheese for the rest of the week as the entry tickets and burger and chips for lunch had already cost a fortune.

I should have realized she can be a boring old meanie when it comes to money but I wanted Cam to foster me so much that I didn't focus on her bad points.

Maybe she didn't focus on *my* bad points???

Anyway, it was like we were both wearing our rose-coloured glasses and we smiled in our pink-as-petals perfect world and on Sunday evening when I had to go back to the Home Cam hugged me almost as tight as I hugged her and promised that she really wanted to go through with things and foster me.

So she did. And that's really where my story should have ended. Happily Ever After. Only I'm not always happy. And actually I'm not even sure Cam is either.

It was fine at first. Elaine says we went through this Honeymoon Period. Is it any wonder I call her a pain? She comes out with such yucky expressions. But I suppose Cam and I were a little bit like newly weds. We went everywhere together, sometimes even hand-in-hand, and whenever I wanted anything I could generally persuade her and I was careful not to get too stroppy because I didn't want her to go off me and send me back. But after a bit . . .

I don't know. Somehow it all changed. Cam wouldn't always take me out for treats and buy me stuff. Stuff I seriously *need*, like designer clothes, else I get picked on by poisonous girls like Roxanne. Cam says she can't afford it – which can't be true. I know for a fact she gets paid a fortune by the authorities for looking after me. It's a bit of a rip-off, if you ask me. And this is all on top of what she earns from being a writer.

Cam says she doesn't earn much as a writer. Peanuts, she says. Well, that's her fault. She doesn't write the right stuff. She's wasting her time writing these yawny articles for big boring papers that haven't got proper pictures. And her books are even worse. They're dreary paperbacks about poor women with problems. I mean, who wants to read that sort of rubbish? I wish she'd write more romantic stuff. I keep telling Cam she wants to get cracking on those great glossy books everyone reads on their holidays. Where all the women are beautiful with heaps of different designer outfits and all the men have

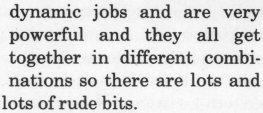

dynamic jobs and are very powerful and they all get together in different combinations so there are lots and lots of rude bits.

Cam just laughs at me and says she can't stick those sort of books. She says she doesn't mind not being a successful writer.

I mind. I want a foster mum I can show off about. I can't show off about Cam because no-one's ever heard of her. And she's not pretty or sexy or glamorous. She doesn't wear any make-up and her hair's too short to style so it just sticks straight up and her clothes are *awful* – T-shirts and jeans all the time and they're certainly *not* designer.

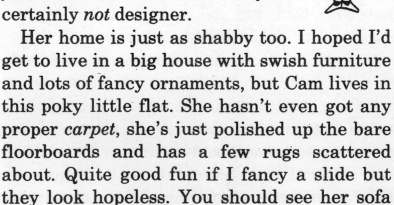

Her home is just as shabby too. I hoped I'd get to live in a big house with swish furniture and lots of fancy ornaments, but Cam lives in this poky little flat. She hasn't even got any proper *carpet*, she's just polished up the bare floorboards and has a few rugs scattered about. Quite good fun if I fancy a slide but they look hopeless. You should see her sofa too! It's leather but it's all cracked so she has to hide it with this old patchwork quilt and some lumpy tapestry cushions she cross-stitched herself. She tried to show me how to do cross-stitch. No wonder that's what it's called. The more I stitched the crosser I got, and I soon gave up in disgust.

I've got my own bedroom but it's not a patch on my room at the Children's Home. It's not much bigger than a *cupboard*. Cam's so mean too. She said I could choose to have my bedroom exactly the way I wanted. Well, I had some great ideas. I wanted a king-size bed with a white satin duvet and my own dressing

table with lights all round the mirror like a film star and white carpet as soft and thick as cat fur and my own computer to write my stories on and my own sound system and a giant white television and video and a trapeze hanging from the ceiling so I could practise circus tricks and my own ensuite bathroom so I could splash all day in my own private bubble bath.

Cam acted like I was *joking*. When she realized I wasn't joining in the general laughter she said, 'Come *on*, Trace, how could all that stuff ever fit in the box room?'

Yeah, quite. Why should I be stuck in the box room? Am I a box? Why can't I have Cam's room? I mean, she's got hardly any stuff, just a lot of books and a little bed. She could easily fit in the box room.

I did my best to persuade her. I wheedled and whined for all I was worth – but she didn't budge. So I ended up in this little rubbish room and I'm supposed to think it a huge big deal because I was allowed to choose the colour paint and pick a new duvet cover and curtains. I chose black to match my mood.

I didn't think Cam would take me seriously but she gave in on that one. Black walls. Black ceiling. She suggested luminous silver stars which are kind of a good idea. I'm not too keen on the dark. I'm not *scared*. I'm not scared of anything. But I like to look up from

my bed and see those stars glowing up above.

Cam hunted around and found some black sheets with silver stars and made curtains to match. She's pretty useless at sewing and the hems go up and down a bit but I suppose she was trying her best. She calls my black room the 'bat cave'. She's bought me several little black velvet toy bats to hang from the ceiling. They're quite cute really. And my python lies on the floor by the door and acts like a draught excluder and attacks anyone who dares try to barge in on us.

Like Jane and Liz. I can't stand Jane and Liz. They are Cam's friends. They keep coming over and sticking their noses in. I thought they were

OK at first. Jane is big (you should see the size of her bum!) and Liz is little and bouncy. Jane took me swimming once (she's not a pretty sight in her swimming costume) and it was quite good fun actually. There was a chute into the water and a wave machine and Jane let me ride on her shoulders and didn't get huffy when I pretended she was a whale. She even spouted water for me. But then she came over one day when Cam and I were having this little dispute – well, kind of mega-argument when I was letting rip yelling all sorts of stuff – and later when I was sulking in my bat cave I heard Jane telling Cam that she was daft to put up with all my nonsense and she knew I had had a hard time but that didn't give me licence to be such a Royal Pain in the Bottom. (A pain wouldn't have a chance attacking *her* bottom.)

I still thought Liz was OK. I was worried at first because she's a teacher but she's not a *bit* like Mrs V.B. She knows all these really rude jokes and she can be a great laugh. She's got her own rollerblades and she let me borrow them which was great. *I* was great too. I simply whizzed around and didn't fall over once and looked seriously cool – but then when I started getting on to Cam that it was time she bought me my *own* rollerblades seeing I was so super-skilled Liz got a bit edgy and told me that Cam wasn't made of money.

I wish!

Then Liz started off this boring old lecture about Caring not being the same as Spending Money and it was almost as if she'd morphed into Mrs Vomit Bagley before my very eyes!

I still thought Liz was kind of cool though but then one evening she came round late when I was in bed in the Bat Cave and I think maybe Cam was crying in the living room because we'd had some boring old set-to about something . . . I forget what. Well, I *don't* forget, I happened to have borrowed a tenner out of her purse – I didn't *steal* it – and anyway if she's my foster mum now she *should* fork out for me, and she's so mean she doesn't give me enough pocket money, and it was only a measly ten-pound note – I could have nicked a twenty – and why did she leave her purse lying around if she gets so fussed about cash going missing? – she's not part of the real world, old Cam, she wouldn't have lasted five minutes in the Children's Home.

Anyway, Liz came round and I slithered round my door like my python so I could hear what they were saying. I figured it would be about me. And it was.

Liz kept asking Cam what this latest crisis was all about and Cam kept quiet for a bit but then out it all came: naughty little Tracy is a thief. Cam started on about some other stuff too. OK, I borrowed one of her pens – well, several – and some silly old locket that her mum had given her. I didn't mean to buckle it. I was only trying to prise it open to see what she had inside.

I felt Cam was being a mean old tell-tale – and Liz was encouraging her for all she was worth, saying it was good for her to let it all out and have a moan and howl. Liz came out with all this s-t-u-p-i-d stuff that I was just nicking for affection and attention. All these teachers and social workers have got their heads full of this rubbish. I nicked the stuff because I was short of cash and needed a pen and . . . well, I just wanted the locket. I thought I could maybe put a picture of my mum in it. My real mum. I've got a photo, and she's looking dead glamorous, a true movie star, smiling and smiling. Guess what she's smiling at! This little baby in her arms  tugging at her gorgeous long blonde hair. It's me!

I wish Cam had long hair. I wish she looked glamorous. I wish she was something special like a film star. I wish she smiled more. She just slumps round all draggy and depressed. Over me.

She had a good cry to Liz and said she was  useless and that it wasn't working out the way she'd hoped.

I *knew* it. I *knew* she wouldn't want me. Well. See if I care.

Liz said that this was just a stage, and that I was acting out and testing my limits.

'She's testing *my* limits, I tell you,' said Cam.

'You mustn't let her get to you so,' said Liz. 'Lighten up a bit, Cam. Don't let your life revolve around Tracy all the time. You don't ever go out any more. You've even given up your classes.'

'Yes, well, I can't leave Tracy in the evening. I did bring up the idea of a babysitter but she was insulted.'

'What about your morning swimming then? You were getting really fit. Why don't you take Tracy too, before school? Jane says she loved it at the baths.'

'There just isn't time. We have enough hassle getting her ready for school at nine. And, oh God, that's another thing. She isn't settling and the head keeps ringing me up and I don't know what to do about it.'

'How about telling Tracy how you feel?'

'Tracy's not bothered about the way *I* feel. It's the way *she* feels that matters. And she's not feeling too great either at the moment. So she takes it out on me.'

'Try standing up to her for once. Put her in her place,' says horrible old Liz.

'That's just it. That's why she's so difficult. She doesn't know her place because she hasn't ever had one. A place of her own,' says Cam.

It made me feel good that she could suss that out and bad because I don't want her to pity me. I don't want her to foster me because she feels

40

sorry for me. I want her to foster me because she's dead lonely and it gives her life a purpose and she's crazy about me. She says she cares about me but she doesn't love me like a real mum. She doesn't want to buy me treats every single day and give me loads of money and keep me home from school because it's so horrible.

I'm not *ever* going back. I can bunk off every day, easy-peasy. I timed it to perfection, arriving back at Cam's dead on time. She was sitting on her squashy old sofa writing her sad old story in her notebook. I made her jump when I came barging in but she smiled. I suddenly felt weird, like I'd been missing her or something, so I ran over to her and bounced down beside her.

'Hey, Trace, watch the sofa!' she said, struggling back into the upright position. 'You'll break it. You'll break me!'

'Half the springs are broken already.'

'Look, I never pretended this was House Beautiful.'

'Hovel Hideous, more like,' I said, getting up and roaming round the shabby furniture, giving it a kick.

'Don't do that, Tracy,' Cam said sharply.

Aha! It was standing-up-to-Tracy time!
Well, I can stand up to her. And walk all over
her too.

Cam saw me squaring up and wilted. 'Don't
start, Tracy. I've had a hard day. You know
that article I wrote?'

'Rejected?'

'So I'm *de*jected. And I'm stuck halfway
through Chapter Four of my novel and—'

'And you want to write something that will *sell*. Something
action-packed!' I pretended to
karate chop her. I didn't touch
her but I made her
blink. 'Lively!' I jumped
up and down in front of
her. 'And sexy!' I waggled
my hips and batted my
eyelashes.

'Yeah yeah yeah,'
said Cam.

'I'm going to make my
fortune as a writer, you wait and
see,' I said. I looked at the little bits
Cam had scribbled in her notebook.
'I can write heaps more than that. I
wrote pages and pages and pages

today, practically a whole book.'

'Was that for English?'

'No, it was . . .' Oh-oh. Caution required. 'It was just something private I'm writing. At playtime and in the lunch hour.'

'Can I have a look?'

'No!' I don't want her to see this purple notebook. I keep it hidden in my school bag. Otherwise she might wonder when I bought it. And where I got the cash. She might start going through her purse again and we don't want another one of *those* rows.

'OK, OK, it's private, right. But couldn't I have one little peep?'

'You're getting as bad as old Vomit Bagley. She made us do this Exercise in Autobiography, the nosy old bag, all this stuff about "My Family".'

Cam stiffened and forgot about my private writing – as I intended!

'She says to me that I should write about my *foster* mum—'

'And did you?'

'No, I wrote about my mum. And how she's an actress in Hollywood and so busy she can't come and see me. You know.'

'Yeah. I know.'

'Only old Vomit Bag didn't believe me. She made fun of me.'

'That's horrible!'

'You believe me, don't you, Cam? About my mum?' I watched her very carefully.

'Well . . . I know just how much your mum means to you, Tracy.'

'Ha! You think it's all rubbish, don't you? A story I made up.'

'No! Not if . . . if you think it's true.'

'Well, it's not true.' I suddenly shouted it. 'None of it's true. I made it all up. It's dead babyish and pathetic. She's not an actress at all. She just can't be bothered to get in touch.'

'You don't know that, Tracy.' Cam tried to put her arm round me but I jerked free.

'I *do* know. I haven't seen her for *years*. I used to wait and wait and wait for her in the Children's Home. I must have been mad. She isn't ever going to come and get me. If someone said, "Do you remember anyone called Tracy Beaker?" she'd probably look vague and go, "Hang on – Tracy? Sounds familiar. Who *is* she, exactly?" Fat lot she cares. Well, I don't care either. I don't *want* her for my mum.'

I didn't know I was going to say all that. Cam

was staring at me. I stared back at her. My throat felt dry and my eyes prickled. I very nearly started crying, only of course I don't ever cry.

Cam was looking at me. My eyes blurred so that she went all fuzzy. I took a step forward, holding out my hands like I was feeling my way through fog.

Then the phone rang. We both jumped. I blinked. Cam said to leave it. But I can't stand leaving a phone ringing, so I answered it.

It was Elaine the Pain. She didn't want to talk to me. She wanted to speak to Cam. Typical. She's *my* social worker. And it was about *me*. But she had to tell Cam first. And then she told me.

You'll never ever ever guess.

It's my mum.

She's been in touch.

She wants to see me!

Elaine's Home

I haven't been to Elaine's *home* home. Just her office. She's done her best to turn it *into* a home. She's got all these photos of kids on the wall. I'm there somewhere. She's used the photo where I'm crossing my eyes and sticking out my tongue. She's got a similarly cross-eyed giant bear prowling the top of her filing cabinet, terrorizing a little droopy-eared mauve rabbit. There's an old Valentine propped on her desk which says inside (I had a quick nose), 'To my Little Bunny from Big Bear'. Y-U-C-K! She has a framed photo of this ultra-weedy guy with thick glasses who must be Big Bear. There are several framed mottoes too, like: 'You don't have to be mad to work here but it helps' and a poem about an old woman wearing purple and some long drivelly meditation about Listening to Your Inner Child.

Never mind Elaine's Inner Child. I am her Outer Child and it's mega-difficult to make contact with her, even when I bawl my head off.

'Now calm down, Tracy,' she said.

'I don't want to calm down!' I yelled. 'I want  to see my mum. I've waited long enough. Like, *years*! So I want to see my mum NOW!'

'You don't get anywhere by yelling, Tracy,' said Elaine. 'You should know how things work by now.'

'I know how they *don't* work! *Why* can't I see my mum right this minute?'

'Because we need to prepare for this meeting.'

'Prepare! I've been waiting half my life! I couldn't get more prepared if I tried.'

'That's just it, Tracy. We don't want you to get too worked up about things.'

'So you think telling me my mum wants to see me and *then* telling me I can't see her is going to calm me *down*????'

'I didn't say you can't see her. Of course you can see her.'

'When?'

'When we can all arrange an appropriate date.'

'Who's this "we"?'

'Well. I shall need to be there. And Cam.'

'Why? Why can't it just be my mum and me?'

It was just my mum and me once. I can remember it. I *can*. We had a great time, my mum and me. She's incredibly beautiful, my mum. Lovely long curly fair hair all round her shoulders, dead smart, with high heels. She looks amazing. Well, she did. Last time I saw her. Quite a while ago.

A long long time ago.

I *do* remember that last time. I was in the Home then but Mum visited me at first – she even gave me this doll, and she took me to McDonald's. It was a great day out. And she kissed me goodbye. I remember the way her blonde curls tickled my cheek and the sweet powdery way she smelled. I clung on tight round her neck, so tight that when she straightened up I was still clinging to her like a monkey, and that annoyed her because I got my muddy shoes over her smart black skirt and I was scared she was cross and wouldn't come back.

I said, 'You *will* come back, Mum, won't you? Next Saturday? You'll take me to McDonald's again? Promise?'

She promised.

But she didn't come back. I waited that Saturday. The Saturday after that. Saturday after Saturday after Saturday.

She didn't come back. She didn't come because she got this amazing offer from Hollywood and she starred in this incredible movie and—

And who am I kidding? Why am I spouting the same old babyish rubbish? She probably wasn't ever a proper actress. She certainly hasn't been in any Hollywood movies that I know of. She didn't come back because she couldn't be bothered. She left me in care. For years.

I was taken into care because she didn't look after me properly. She kept going off with this boyfriend and leaving me. And then she got this new scary guy who whacked me one whenever I yelled. I've had a little peep in my files. Though I can remember some of it too. Stuff that still gives me nightmares.

So why do I want to see my mum so much?

I don't want to see her.

I do.

Even after the way she's treated me?

She's still my mum.

I've got Cam now.

She's not my mum, she's just a foster parent. And she's sick of me anyway.

Is she?

I don't know.

I suppose I need to talk it over with Elaine.

So the next time I see her I'm all set. She's all smiles.

'Ah, Tracy, you'll be pleased to know it's all fixed now, this special meeting with your mum.' She beams at me, as happy as a bunny in a field of lettuce.

'I don't want to see her now,' I said.

Elaine's bunny nose went twitch-twitch-twitch. 'What?'

'You heard. I don't have to see her, not if I don't want. And I *don't* want.'

'Tracy, you are going to be the death of me,' she said, blowing upwards over her big bunny teeth. Then her eyes crossed a little with concentration and I knew she was counting up to ten, s-l-o-w-l-y. It's her little way of dealing with me. When she got to ten she gave me this big false smile. 'I understand, Tracy,' she said.

'No you don't.'

'It's only natural you feel anxious about this meeting. It obviously means a great deal to you. And you don't want to risk getting let down. But I've had several phone conversations with your mother and she seems as keen as you to meet. I'm sure she'll turn up this time, Tracy.'

'I *said*, I don't want to see her,' I declared, but I knew I wasn't kidding her.

She tried to kid me though. 'OK, Tracy, you don't want to see your mum – so I'll phone up right this minute and cancel everything,' she said, and she started dialling.

'Hey, hang about. No need to be quite so hasty,' I said.

Elaine giggled. 'Got you!'

'I don't think that's very professional of you, teasing like that,' I said, dead haughty.

'You would try the patience of a professional saint, Tracy,' said Elaine, and she ruffled my hair. 'Now, how are things with you and Cam?'

'OK. I suppose.'

'She's one hundred and one per cent supporting you over seeing your mum, you know, but it must be a little bit hard for her.'

'Well. That's what being a foster mum is all about, isn't it? Taking a back seat when necessary. Encouraging all contact with natural families. I've read the leaflets.'

'You're all heart, Tracy,' said Elaine, sighing.

'Not me, Elaine. Totally heart*less*,' I said.

So . . . I'm seeing my mum tomorrow! Which is maybe why I'm wide awake now at three o'clock in the morning. Scribbling away. And wondering what she'll be like. And if she'll really come.

Oh-oh. Stirrings from next door. Cam's spotted my light.

Later. I thought she might be a bit narked. But she made us both a cup of tea and then we sat at either end of my bed, sipping away. I don't usually like her ropy old herbal tea but she'd bought a special strawberry packet that doesn't taste too horrible.

I thought she might want a heart-to-heart (even though I haven't got one) but thank goodness she just started talking about this story she used to make up when she was a little kid and couldn't sleep. I said, 'Yeah, I do that, really scary bloodthirsty ghost stories,' and she said, 'No, little ghoul, this was supposed to be a *comfort* story,' and she started on about pretending her duvet was a big white bird and she'd be flying on its back in the starlight and then it would take her to a lake and they'd float on it in the dark and then they'd go to its great mossy nest . . .

'All slime and bird's muck, right?'

'Wrong! All soft and fresh and downy, and the big white bird would spread its wings and I'd huddle underneath in the quiet and

54

the warmth, hearing its heart beat under its snowy feathers.'

'Oh, I get it. This is the Get-you-back-to-sleep story,' I said – but after she'd taken my cup and tucked me up and ruffled my curls (why do they all do that, like I'm some unruly little puppy?) and I was left in the dark I tried out the story myself. Only I was in my black bat cave, and I'm Tracy Beaker, not a silly old softie like Cam, so I made up this big black vampire bat and we swooped through the night together. We'd zap straight through certain windows and nip

Mrs V.B. in the neck or nibble Roxanne right on the end of her nose and flap out again the second they started screaming. I think it took me to its real big black bat cave to hang by our toes with all our brother bats only I might have been asleep by then.

I'm awake now. Early. Waiting.

I wonder if she'll turn up?

She did, she did, she did!!!

Cam came with me to Elaine's. But she waited outside and, surprise surprise, Elaine did too. So the mega-meet of the century took place in private. Just me and my mum.

I was sitting in Elaine's room, swivelling round and round in her little chair on wheels, when this woman comes straight in and stands there blinking at me. A small woman with very bright blonde hair and a lot of lipstick, wearing a very short skirt and very high heels.

A beautiful woman with long fair hair and a lovely face in the most stylish sexy clothes.

My mum.

I knew her straight away.

She didn't know me. She went on blinking, like she'd just poked her mascara wand in her eye. 'Tracy?' she said, looking round, as if the room was full of kids.

'Hi,' I said, in this silly little squeak.

'You're not my Tracy!' said mum, shaking her head at me. 'You're too big!'

I'm quite small and skinny for my age so I

didn't get what she was on about.

'My Tracy's just a little kid. A funny little kid with weird sticky-out plaits. The tantrums when it was hair-brushing time!' She peered at me. 'Was that really you?'

I held out a strand of hair and mimed plaiting it.

'You had a filthy temper when you were a toddler,' said Mum. 'It *is* you, isn't it? My Tracy!'

'Mum.'

'Well!'

There was a bit of a pause. Mum half held her arms out but then changed her mind, acting like she was just stretching.

'Well,' she said again. 'How have you been then, darling? Did you miss me, eh?'

I did a rapid rewind through the years, remembering. I wanted to tell her what it was like. But I couldn't seem to get my act together at all. I'm the lippiest gabbiest kid ever, ask anyone – but now all I could do was nod.

Mum looked a bit disappointed by my response. '*I've* been driven crazy thinking about you!' she said. 'I kept making all these plans to get you back, but things kept going haywire. I was tied up with this and that . . .'

'Films?' I whispered.

'Mmm.'

'In Hollywood?'

'Not exactly.'

'But you *are* an actress, aren't you, Mum?'

'Yes, sweetie. And I do a lot of modelling too. All sorts. Anyway. I always planned for you and me to get back together, like I said. But I wanted it to be perfect, see.'

I didn't see. But I didn't say.

'I kept getting mixed up with the wrong kind of guy,' Mum confided, perching on the edge of Elaine's desk and rootling in her handbag.

'I remember,' I said cautiously. 'There was one . . . I hated him.'

'Yeah, well, like I said, there have been a few. And my latest! A total pig!' She shook her head and lit a cigarette, taking a long drag.

Elaine has a strict non-smoking policy in her room. In the whole building. If any of the staff or the clients want a quick fag they have to huddle outside the back entrance. I was sure the smoke alarm was going to go off any second.

'Mum,' I said, nodding at the crossed-out cigarette sign prominently displayed on the wall.

Mum tutted contemptuously and took another puff. 'I gave my heart to that man,' she said, tapping herself on her chest and scattering ash down her jumper. 'Do you know what he did with it?' She leant towards me. '*Stamped* on it!' Her high heel jerked as if she was doing the stamping.

'Men!' I said sympathetically, in the tone Cam and Liz and Jane frequently used.

Mum looked at me and then burst into peals of laughter. I felt daft and swivelled round and round on Elaine's chair.

'Hey, don't do that, you're making me feel giddy. Come here! Haven't you got a kiss for your mum after all this time?'

'Sure,' I said shyly, though I'm not really the kissy-kissy type.

Mum bent down, her head on one side. I pecked at her powdery cheek – and then the sweet smell of her made me suddenly clutch her tight.

'Hey, hey, careful, sweetie! Watch my cigarette! No need

to be so dramatic. Looks like *you're* the little actress!' She dabbed at my face. 'Real tears!'

'No they're not,' I said, sniffling. 'I don't ever cry. It's hayfever.'

'Where's the hay?' said Mum, peering round Elaine's office. Her ash was building up again. She tapped it into Elaine's special Bunnikins mug. I hoped Elaine would look inside before making herself a cup of coffee.

'I get allergic to all sorts,' I said, wiping my nose.

'Hey, hey, haven't you got a tissue?' said Mum, tutting at me. 'I hope you're not allergic to *me*.'

'Maybe it's your perfume – though it smells lovely.'

'Ah,' said Mum, dabbing at me with her own tissue. 'That's my Poison. That pig forked out for a huge bottle just before he cleared off. I'd like to poison him all right! The nerve! Left me for some silly little kid barely older than you.'

'Typical!' I said.

Mum chuckled again. 'Where do you get all your quaint ways, eh?'

'Cam says "typical" a lot,' I said, without really thinking.

'Who's Cam?' said Mum.

I felt a little *thunk* in my stomach. 'My . . . my foster mum.'

Mum straightened up and threw the damp tissue into Elaine's wastebin. Well, she missed, but she didn't seem to care. 'Ah!' she said, pinching the end of her cigarette so that she squeezed the light out of it. She threw it in the direction of the wastebin, missing again. 'She's the one who's taken a fancy to you. Your social worker –' Mum lowered her voice slightly, gesturing round the office – 'what's her name?'

'Elaine. The pain.'

Mum stopped looking stroppy and giggled again. 'She is, isn't she! Still, you watch your lip, Tracy.'

I stuck my lip right out and crossed my eyes, like I was watching it.

Mum sighed and shook her head at me. 'Cheeky! Anyway, she gets in touch with me – eventually – and tells me this woman has bobbed up out of the blue and has taken you out of the Children's Home. Right?'

I nodded.

Mum lit up another fag, getting dead irritated now. 'Why did you go along with it? You don't want to live with this woman, do you?'

I didn't know what to do. I just kind of shrugged my shoulders.

'She sounds a bit suspect, if you ask me. Single woman, no spare cash – obviously scruffy standards, judging by your little outfit. Where did she get your clothes, a jumble sale?'

'You got it.'

'No! You'd think they'd be a bit more picky with their foster parents. Couldn't they have found anyone better? Anyway, you don't need a foster mum. It's not like you're an orphan. You've *got* a mum. Me.'

I blinked at her.

She sighed again, dragging on her cigarette. 'I wanted you safe and sound in the Children's Home where everyone could keep an eye on you.'

'I don't want to go back!' I burst out.

Mum narrowed her eyes at me. 'What did they do to you there, then?'

'It was *awful*!' I launched in. 'They kept locking me in the quiet room if I did the slightest little thing and everyone kept picking on me. I got blamed for everything. And there was this big girl, Justine, she kept beating me up. Though I beat her up too. And we played this Dare Game and I was *heaps* more daring than she was. I ran all round the garden of the Children's Home without any clothes on and Justine only ate one worm but I ate two really wriggly ones—'

'Hey hey, you're a right little nutter, you are! They're not a good influence, children's homes. Still, don't worry, you're not going back.'

'So . . . am I going to stay with Cam?'

Mum put her head on one side. 'Don't you want to come and live with me?'

I stared at her. I stared and stared and stared. I wanted to rewind her so that I could hear her all over again. And again. I couldn't believe it. Or was she kidding? 'Really? With you, Mum?'

'That's what I said.'

'For how long? A whole week?' I asked.

'Never mind a week! How about for ever?'

'Wow!' She still had her fag so I didn't jump on her. I jumped on Elaine's swivel chair instead and whirled it round and round.

'Don't do that, you're doing my head in,' said Mum.

I stopped, sharpish.

'It's time we got together, darling,' she said softly. 'I've missed my little girl so much. We're going to make a go of it together, just you and me.'

It was like she'd taken me by the hand and we were climbing a golden staircase right up into the sky. And then I tripped on a step because I suddenly thought of something.

'But what about Cam?'

'What about her?' said Mum. She took a last drag and then squashed her cigarette fiercely inside the Bunnikins mug. I imagined all their powder-puff tails scorching. 'Never mind this Cam. She's not family. Oh, Tracy, we'll have such a great time together. First we'll kit you out with some new clothes, smarten you up a little—'

'I'll smarten up all you want, Mum, no

worries on that score. Designer clothes?'

'Only the best for my girl. None of this shabby chainstore stuff. You don't want to look the same as all the other kids. You want to look that bit *special*.'

'You bet!' I whirled round one more time. 'Genuine logos, not fake market stuff?'

'Who do you think I am?' said Mum, hands on hips.

'You're my *mum*,' I said.

S-o-o-o-o . . . I'm going to have my fairytale happy ending and more than half this notebook is still empty! I'm going to live with my mum. I am. I am. Just as soon as we've got it sorted out with Elaine.

'I'll sort her!' said Mum.

And of course there's Cam.

Cam.

Alexander's Home

I'm mad at Cam. I mean, I went through agonies telling her. I felt really bad. I was nearly crying. I thought it would be awful for her. But do you know something? She didn't seem to care at all! She didn't gasp and cry and cling to me. She just sat there, biting her nails, though she ticks me off something rotten if I do that. She didn't say anything. Not a single word. No 'Don't leave me, darling Tracy, you mean the whole world to me and I can't live without you.' Nothing.

So I got a bit mad then and told her that my mum thinks I look a right old scruffbag and she's going to get me kitted out in a full set

67

of designer clothes. I thought *that* might get her going. I thought she might say, 'Oh, Tracy, I feel so bad, I've never given you decent clothes, but tell you what, if you promise to stay with me we'll go into town right away and I'll wave my credit card like a wand and you can wear anything you want, money no object, just so long as you live with me.' But not a bit of it. She still said a big fat NOTHING.

So I got really *really* mad because she obviously couldn't care less so I went on about all this other stuff my mum was going to buy me, like a computer and rollerblades and a new bike and a trip to Disneyland and she didn't even flinch. Didn't try to compete. Simply couldn't be bothered. She just sat there, nibble nibble on her nails, like she was bored with the whole situation and couldn't wait to be shot of me.

So *then* I was so mega-mad I just wanted to don Doc Martens and jump up and down on her so I went on and on about my mum and how great she is and fantastically beautiful and wonderfully dressed and how we had these amazing cuddles and it was just like we'd never ever been parted.

And she *still* didn't say a word! Nibble

nibble on the nails till she was nearly down to her own knuckles.

'Say something!'

She just sat there and sat there and then she eventually took her hand out of her mouth and mumbled, 'I don't really know what to say.'

Call herself a *writer*!

'I thought you were meant to be good with words!'

'Just at the moment they're sticking in my throat,' she mumbled, like I'd just squirted Superglue round her tonsils.

I went and stood right in front of her. She was all huddled up, almost as if I *had* been jumping all over her. I had this sharp little pain in my chest. I suddenly felt like *I* was the mother and she was my little girl. 'You're sad, aren't you, Cam?' I said softly.

She made more mumbly noises and started nail-biting again.

I reached out and took hold of her nibbled hand. 'You're unhappy that my mum's come back, aren't you?' I said hopefully.

Cam didn't say anything for a few seconds. Then she gave me this weird smile, practically stretching from ear to ear. 'I'm happy for you, Tracy,' she said.

I dropped her hand like it was red hot and ran out of the room.

Happy! Smiling all over her face!

She obviously couldn't wait to be rid of me. She doesn't care about me at all. Well, *I* don't care. I don't need her. I've got my mum now.

I'll go and live with Mum and I shan't mind a bit if I never see Cam ever again. I'm not going to take any notice of her. I'm just going to put my life on hold until I can go and live with my mum. I'm not going to go to school either.

I'm in a bit of bother at school at the moment. I started up the Dare Game, quite by chance. Roxanne was calling me the B word again because she knows it really gets to me, so I dared her to say it in front of Mrs Bagley.

I thought she'd chicken out. But her eyes glittered and she said, 'Right!' She marched right up to Mrs V.B. and said, 'Tracy Beaker told me to say this weird word, Mrs Bagley,' and then she said it straight out and added, all Little Miss Innocence, 'Is it *rude*?'

So guess who got into trouble.

70

'And *I* won the dare,' said Roxanne.

I stuck my tongue out at her, waggling it as rudely as I could.

'It's my turn to dare you now,' said Roxanne. 'I dare you to stick your tongue out like that at Mrs Bagley!'

So I did. And guess who got into trouble again.

'But it's my turn now,' I said, catching up with Roxanne at break. I peered past the cloakrooms and had a sudden inspiration. 'OK, I dare you to run right into the boys' toilets!'

So she did. But she said I'd pushed her in. So I got into heaps more trouble.

And now it was her turn to dare me. She waited till lunchtime. It was spaghetti bolognaise. I don't like school spag bol. The cook makes it bright red like blood and the spaghetti seems extra wiggly like worms. I pushed my plateful away from me.

'Don't you want it, Tracy?' said Roxanne, her eyes going glitter glitter glitter. 'OK, I dare you to tip it over your head!'

So I did. And when Roxanne and all her

stupid friends started screaming with laughter I tipped Roxanne's spag bol over *her* head.

I ended up in BIG BIG BIG trouble. I had to stand outside the head's office for the rest of the day in Total Disgrace. Mr Hatherway went past and shook his head at me. 'Hair ribbon?' he said, picking a strand of spaghetti out of my curls. 'It looks like you've really hit the jackpot today, Tracy. What's poor Mrs Bagley going to do with you, eh?'

I was sure she was going to invent some serious form of torture.

I don't see why I should submit to serious Vomit Bag Aggro. I won't even go in for registration. What do I care if they phone up Cam and complain? I shan't be at that school much longer. My mum will send me to a brand-new super school where I'll be dead popular because of all my designer clothes and everyone will be in awe of me and be desperate to be my best friend and even the teachers will think I'm the greatest and I'll be top of the class and the best girl in the whole school.

You wait.

You just wait and see.

So when Cam took me to school this morning I waved goodbye and ran into the playground – and went on running, all round the kids and then back out again and down the road, running and running, and I kept it up for ages, acting like there were Tracy-catchers prowling with nets and hooks and manacles. I didn't know why I was running like crazy.

Then I realized where I was running to. My house.

I rounded the corner – and a football came whizzing straight through the air, about to knock my head clean off my shoulders. But I'm Tracy-SuperStar, the girl-goalie with nanosecond-quick reactions. I leapt, I clutched, I tucked the ball close to my chest – *saved*!

'Wow!' I yelled, congratulating myself.

This big burly kid came charging up, his

head as round as the football but with little prickles all over, a serious don't-mess-with-me haircut. Make that hair*shave*.

'Give us that ball,' he said.

'Did you see the way I caught it?' I said, leaping about. 'What a save, eh?'

'Sheer fluke,' said the Football guy. He knocked the ball out of my hand and started dribbling with it.

'Sheer *skill*!' I said indignantly. 'Come on, see if you can get another ball past me.'

'I don't play with girls.'

'Girls are great at footie,' I said. 'Well, *I* am. Let's play, yeah?'

'No! Get lost, little girly.'

I suddenly charged at him. He stiffened in surprise, expecting some kind of mad attack – and forgot about his ball. I gave it a nifty little hooking kick and whipped it right out of his reach.

'Superb tackle!' I yelled, nudging it along. 'The great Tracy Beaker and her brilliant footwork yet again. She's really come good, this girl – OUCH!'

Football did not tackle back with finesse.

74

He went whack. I went smack. On my back.

I lay there, groaning. Football stopped, bouncing the ball right by my head. 'You all right, kid?' he said.

'Oh yeah. Sure. Just having a little kip on the pavement,' I mumbled.

'I didn't mean to knock you flying like that. I didn't realize you're such a little kid.'

'I'm not!' I said, insulted.

'Here.' He reached out with his great pink hand and suddenly I was hauled upright. 'OK now? Mind you, it's your own fault. You shouldn't have messed around with my football.'

'I wasn't messing, I was tackling! You've got a totally useless defence. Here –' I gave a sudden lunge, all set to prove my point, but he was wise to me now and got the ball well away before I could get near it.

'Give over, kid!' he said, laughing – and then he dribbled the ball round the corner.

'Don't go! Hey, Football, come back. Play with me, eh? There isn't anyone else. Go on. Football?'

But he'd gone.

'See if I care. You're lousy at football anyway,' I yelled.

Then I sloped off. To the house. I decided it was definitely going to be *my* house. Until I go off and live with Mum and have my very own *real* house.

I'd not got the cushion and the blanket organized. Or any proper provisions. I searched my pockets for forgotten goodies. The best I could do was an ancient chewed piece of gum stuck in the corner of a tissue. Well, I *think* it was gum. Certainly it didn't look very appetizing, whatever. I didn't have any cash on me either. It looked like I was going to have to play skinny-starving-to-death-fashion-model in my house – not my most favourite game.

But the weirdest thing happened. I went up the scruffy path at the back, investigating an old Kentucky Chicken carton with my foot just in case. (No luck at all, totally licked clean to the bone.) I climbed in through the back window, negotiated the kitchen, and walked into the living room, my footsteps sounding oddly loud on the bare floorboards. The old curtains were drawn so it was quite dark in the room, but I could still see my red velvet sofa in the middle of the room . . . with

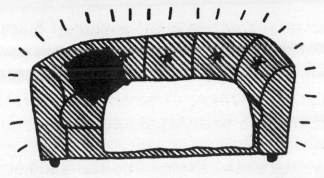

a big black velvet cushion at one end and a
blue blanket neatly covering the worst of the
muddy marks.

I stared at them as if I'd conjured them out
of thin air. It was like one of those old fairy-
tales. I squinted long and hard at the cushion
and the blanket to see if they were being toted
about by disembodied hands. I liked this idea
even if it was kind of spooky. Maybe the
hands were perched in a corner somewhere
ready to flap their flying fingers at my
command?

'OK, the cushion and the blanket are spot
on, but what about some *food*?' I said, snapping my own fingers.

Then I stopped mid-snap, my nails digging
into my thumbs. I'd spotted an upturned cardboard packing case over by the window, with
a checked dishcloth neatly laid over it like a
little tablecloth. There was a paper party

plate with an entire giant packet of Smarties carefully arranged on top in rings of colour – brown, green, blue, mauve, pink, red, orange, with yellow in the middle so that it looked like a flower.

I shivered from right up in the scalp down to the little taily bit at the end of my spine. My favourite food in all the world is Smarties. And here was a big plate of them beautifully laid out just for me.

'It *is* magic!' I whispered, and I circled the cardboard table.

I put out a hand and picked up a red Smartie. I licked it. It was real. I popped it in my mouth, and then hurriedly shoved another handful after it in case they suddenly disappeared. Then I went to draw the old dusty curtains so I could have a closer look and suss out how this magic was working.

AAAHHHH!!!

I yanked at the curtain – and screamed. Someone else screamed too!

A boy was sitting scrunched up on the window ledge, knees up under his little pointy chin, hands clasping a book, mouth gasping, eyes blink-blink-blinking.

'What are you *doing* here? Are you trying to frighten me?' I yelled.

He clasped his book so tightly it was in danger of buckling. His eyes were little slits because his face was so screwed up. 'You frightened *me*,' he whispered.

'What are you doing in my house?' I demanded.

He sat up a little straighter. 'It's my house, actually,' he said timidly.

'You don't live here.'

'Yes I do. Well, during the day I do. I'm making it my home. I brought the cushion. And the rug. And organized refreshments.'

'You what? Oh. The Smarties.'

He looked over at the plate. 'You spoilt my pattern,' he said.

'It's only babies who play with food. Well, that's what they said at the Children's Home when I made my peas climb up my mashed potato mountain.'

'Did you really think it was magic?' he asked.

'Of course not!' I said firmly.

'I thought by the sound of your footsteps

you were really big and scary,' he said, un-clenching and swinging his legs free. 'That's why I hid.'

'I *am* big and scary,' I said. 'Bigger than you, anyway, you little squirt.'

'Everyone's bigger than me,' he said humbly.

'How old are you then? Nine? Ten?'

'I'm nearly twelve!'

I stared. 'You don't look it!'

'I know.'

'So what are you doing here then?' I asked, helping myself to another handful of Smarties. I offered him the plate, seeing as they were his refresh-ments. He said thank you politely and ate one blue Smartie, nibbling at the edges first like it was a biscuit. He didn't answer me.

'Are you bunking off?' I asked.

He hesitated, then nodded. 'You won't tell, will you?' he said, swallowing his Smartie.

'I'm not a snitch.' I looked him up and down. 'Fancy you bunking off! You look too much of a goody-goody teacher's pet. Dead swotty!' I pointed to his big fat book, trying to work out the title. 'Alex-an-der the Great. The great what?'

'No, that was just what they called him.'

'As in Tracy the Great?' I rather liked the sound of it. 'That's me. Tracy.'

'I'm Alexander,' he said.

'Ah. Alexander the not-so-great. So. You're obviously dead brainy. Why do you need to bunk off? I bet you come top of everything.'

He nodded. 'Yep. Except for PE. I'm bottom at PE. I always bunk off on games days.'

'You're mad. PE's a bit of a laugh. Especially when it's football.'

I'm truly Tracy the Great at footie, famed for my nippy footwork and dirty tackles. Old Vomit Bagley goes bright red in the face blowing her whistle at me.

Alexander was whingeing on about them being even worse then.

'Them?'

'The other boys. They tease me.'

'What about?'

Alexander ducked his head. 'All sorts of stuff. Especially . . . when we're in the showers.'

'Aha!'

'They laugh at me because . . .'

'Because you're Alexander the not-so-great!' I said, giggling.

Alexander flinched as if I'd hit him. I suddenly felt mean. I hitched myself up on the window seat beside him. 'So you bunk off?' I said.

'Mmm.'

'Haven't they complained to your mum?'

'Yes.'

'So what did she say?'

'She never says anything much. It's Dad.' Alexander said the word 'Dad' as if it meant Rottweiler.

'What did *he* say?'

I could feel Alexander trembling. 'He said – he said – he said he'd send me away to boarding school if I didn't watch out, and then I couldn't play truant. And he said I'd *really* get bullied there.'

'He sounds dead caring, your dad,' I said, and I patted Alexander on his bony little shoulder.

'He says I have to learn to stand up for myself.'

I snorted and suddenly gave him the teeniest little push. He squealed in shock and nearly fell off the window seat. I hauled him back. 'You're not even very good at *sitting* up for yourself,'

I said, shaking my head at him.

'I know,' Alexander said dolefully.

'So come on then. Try fighting back.'

'I can't. I don't know how.'

'I'll show you.'

He was in luck. I'm the greatest fighter in the world. I'm especially good at getting a sly punch in first. And I don't just rely on fists. I'm great at kicking shins. If I'm really pushed I bare my killer choppers and bite.

I pulled Alexander off the window seat and tried to get him to put his fists up. His little hands drooped back down to his sides.

'I can't fight. And anyway, I can't hit a girl.'

'You won't get a chance, matey,' I said, putting my own fists up. I gave him one little gentle punch. Then another. He didn't react, apart from blinking rapidly.

'Come on! Try to hit me back.'

Alexander lunged at me feebly. His fist could have been cotton wool.

'Harder!'

He had one more go. I stepped sideways and he punched thin air, stumbled, and very nearly fell over.

'Oh well. I see what you mean,' I said,

realizing he was a totally hopeless case.

'I'm useless,' said Alexander, drooping all over.

'Only at fighting,' I said. I pondered. I looked at his funny little feet in their highly polished Clarks lace-ups. It didn't look like he'd be much of a kicker. His tiny teeth only seemed capable of a hamster nibble, not a vicious vampire bite. Other tactics might be required. I tried to think what I did those rare times when I was up against some huge gorilla guy who could jump up and down all over me. Easy. I got lippy (and then ran).

'See this,' I said to Alexander, and I stuck out my tongue. It is a very long pink tongue and I can waggle it till I almost touch my ears. Alexander backed away nervously. I replaced my tongue with pride. 'It's more cutting than the sharpest knife.'

Alexander nodded in agreement. I wondered if he got what I meant.

'You want to say something really cutting to those boys at your school.'

'Oh *sure*,' said Alexander. I detected a surprising spot of sarcasm. 'Then they'd beat me up even more.'

Maybe he had a point.

'So why don't you say something to make them laugh? Like when you're in the showers?'

'They laugh at me already.'

'Make them laugh *more*.' I thought hard, trying to imagine myself into the situation. I got the giggles. 'I know!' I snorted. 'You tell them they might all have zonking great cucumbers but you're very happy with your own little gherkin.'

Alexander blinked at me. 'I can't say that!'

'Yes you can.'

'I wouldn't dare.'

'Yes you would. *I* dare you. There. Now you've got to say it. If you want to be my friend.'

Alexander looked puzzled. 'Are we friends?'

The cheek of it!

'Don't you want to be friends?' I demanded.

Alexander nodded. Wisely.

'Right. So we're friends. And we'll meet up again tomorrow?' I said.

Same time. Same place. He'd better be there. I hope he organizes some more refreshments.

Football's Home

It was a little bit dodgy getting away. Cam came over all stroppy about school and the fact that I've been bunking off. Not that I *told* her. I'm not into that True Confession lark. But the head phoned her up to tell her little Tracy was conspicuously absent and Cam got seriously fussed.

She started giving me a l-o-n-g lecture and I just happened to give the teeniest little yawn. Cam caught hold of me by the shoulders so I had to look at her. 'Tracy, this is serious.'

'Yeah, yeah.'

'I mean it.' Her silly short hair was sticking up all over the place. I can't see why she can't grow her hair into a decent style. She'd look so much better if she wore make-up too. I don't know why she doesn't want to make herself look pretty. Like my mum.

I didn't really want to look at her. I blinked so that my eyes went blurry and I just mumbled 'Mmm.' Then I wriggled. 'You're digging into my shoulders, Cam.'

She looked like she really wanted to dig straight through my skin but she just nodded and let me go. 'It *is* serious, Trace. You keep on and you'll be excluded.'

'Wow! Really?'

That Football guy is excluded. It only happens to the really tough nuts. I rather fancy being the Toughest Nutter of all.

'Don't sound so hopeful!'

'It's mad – you bunk off school because you hate it and they get narked and threaten you with this huge punishment, No School At All, which is *precisely* what you want most in the world!'

'You don't really *hate* school, do you?'

'Oh per-lease!'

'I know you don't get on very well with Mrs Bagley.'

'Understatement of the century!'

'But you won't be stuck in her class for ever. You're bright; if you'd only give it a chance you could do really well, pass all your exams—'

'I don't need to pass exams to be an actress.'

'I thought you wanted to be a writer.'

'I've changed my mind. I'd much sooner be an actress.'

'Like your mum?'

'Yep.'

I went off into a little dream, thinking about Mum and how it was going to be. Maybe I  could get into acting straight away and we could be in films together, a real mother and daughter act: Mum could play my mum – not as a Mumsie type, naturally, more sexy and sassy – and I could be this cute kid with a sharp line in wisecracks. I could just see it.

'Tracy –' Cam's voice interfered with my imaginary reception. 'I know you love your mum very much. It's great you've been able to see her again. But maybe – maybe it might be better not to pin all your hopes on your mum.'

I knew what she was getting at. I didn't want to listen. I've got so many hopes pinned on my mum she's like a human pin-cushion.

It's going to be all right. We're going to be OK, Mum and me. We are we are we are. I'm going to stay with her next weekend and I can't *wait*.

Do you know something? Cam still doesn't seem to mind a bit. 'If it's what you want, Tracy,' she said.

'Of course it's what I want. But what do *you* want?'

'What I want is for you to stop playing truant. I want you to promise you won't bunk off school tomorrow. Or the next day. Or the next. Ever again. Promise, Tracy.'

I promised. With my fingers crossed behind my back. It doesn't matter. Cam doesn't keep promises herself. I mean, she was all set for it to be me and her together for ever. And yet now my mum's come back on the scene Cam acts like she can't wait to be rid of me. Well, see if I care.

My mum's *desperate* to get me back. She's FANTASTIC. Even better than I made up. The best mum in the world.

She is.

She IS.

Better than anyone else's. *Cam's* mum is this weird old posh lady who lives in the country somewhere and doesn't want to see Cam any more because she disapproves of her lifestyle.

Alexander's mum sounds like this little mouse who squeaks in a corner and shivers whenever his dad stalks past.

Football's mum is just the opposite, fiercer than fierce, and *foul*.

I saw her today when I bunked off school. I *had* to see if Alexander followed through with his dare. I went to the Spar on the corner first to fork out for a few refreshments with my school dinner money. I was wandering back up the road when I saw this woman coming out of her house yelling back into the hall, 'You can get out of your bed, you lazy great slummock, and get cracking with that vacuuming or you'll be for it when I get home. Did you hear me? I said, DID YOU HEAR ME?'

You could hear her all the way up and down the street. People were probably wincing and putting their hands over their ears the other side of town. She had a voice like a car alarm, going on and on and on, so loud and insistent it was like it was ringing inside your head as well as out.

'And if you dare get into one more spot of bother then I'm telling you straight, I'm having you put away. I'm sick to death of you, do you hear me? You're rubbish. No use to anyone. Just like your rotten father.'

She slammed the door and went slapping down the path in her grubby trainers, her huge thighs wobbling in her old leggings.

The upstairs window opened and the Football boy stuck his head out. He was in his vest, still all sleepy-eyed, straight from his bed, but he was still cradling his football.

'Don't you call my dad rotten!' he yelled.

'Don't get lippy with me, you lousy little whatsit!' she screamed. 'And don't you *dare* start sticking up for your lazy lying slug of a father!'

'Stop it! Don't call him names! He's worth ten of you!' Football shouted, going bright red in the face.

'You think you know it all, eh? Staying in your bed half the day, never helping out, mucking things up at school, in trouble with the old Bill – yeah, you've really got your life worked out, my son.'

'I wish I wasn't your son. I wish I lived with my dad.'

'Oh right. OK then. Off you go. Live with him, why don't you?'

Football's face got even redder. 'Yeah. Well. I would,' he mumbled.

'But he don't want you, right?' she yelled triumphantly. 'Face up to it, son. He's got his silly little lady friend – although by God she's no lady – and so he doesn't want me and he doesn't want you either, for all he goes on about you being best mates. He couldn't wait to turn his back on you – and he hasn't come back, has he?'

'He's taking me to the match on Saturday!'

'Oh yeah? Like he was a fortnight ago? He doesn't give a stuff about you.'

'He does, he does!' Football yelled, and there were tears dribbling down his bright red cheeks.

'You pathetic little cry-baby!' his mum jeered.

Football took aim. His football went flying through the air and landed wallop, right on her head. He cheered tearfully as she swore, words so bad they'd burn right through the page if I wrote them down.

Then she stopped rubbing her head and grabbed hold of his football. 'Right!' she said, and she kicked it way way way over the rooftops out of sight. I suppose she'd have made a seriously good footballer herself. Then *she* cheered.

'That's fixed *you*,' she said, and she marched off. She nearly bumped into me as she went. 'Had a good gawp, have you?' she said, pushing me out the way. 'Nosy little whatsit!'

I told her I wouldn't hurt my eyes gawping at something as ugly as her. Well, I whispered it. I didn't quite want to get into a shouting match with her myself.

Football was shouting too. At me. Telling me to clear off and mind my own business. Or words to that effect. Almost as bad as his mum.

He wiped his face very quickly so that I couldn't see the tears. Though I'd already seen them, of course. But I cleared off and ate most of my tube of Smarties to calm myself because I can't stick it if people start yelling and screaming – unless it's me. Then I made for the house and you'll never guess what! *There* was the football, in the garden, landed smack in a soggy carton of sweet and sour sauce. Now that had to be magic! I mean, fancy that football landing in *my* garden!

So I decided to be a good little fairy myself. I picked the football up gingerly and wiped all the orange goo off on the grass and bounced it all the way back to Football's house.

I banged at his door.

No answer.

I banged again.

Nothing. I stared at the peeling paint, wondering if I'd got the wrong house. No, I was pretty sure. I backed down the garden path and peered up at the window.

'Oi – you! Football guy!' I bellowed. 'Want

your ball back?' I bounced it hard to show I wasn't kidding.

It worked! The window went up and Football's head poked out. 'What are you doing with my ball?' he bellowed, as if *I'd* been the one to kick it over the rooftops.

'OK, pal, if you're not even *grateful* . . .' I said, and I turned my back and went bouncy-bouncy-bouncy to his gate.

'Wait!' he yelled.

I knew he would. He came charging out in two ticks in his vest and tracksuit bottoms and bare feet. Those little pink wiggly toes made him look much less fierce.

'Give us it then,' he said.

'Play a game of footie with me?'

'I told you before, I don't play with girls.'

'Then I'll take this ball and find some guy who *will* play with me,' I said.

He tried to tackle me then, but I was too quick for him.

'You little . . .' More *amazing* words.

'You haven't half got a mouth on you. You obviously take after your mum.'

That *really* got him going. Blank blank blankety blank, you blanking blanker.

'Hasn't anyone ever washed your mouth out with soap?' I said.

'Ha ha,' he said, not laughing. He was eyeing the ball, but I kept it out of his reach.

'They used to do it in the Children's Home. This careworker shoved a great cake of her Body Shop Dewberry soap right in my gob when I was just the weeniest bit lippy. It was *disgusting*. Still, I bit it into pieces so she couldn't use it any more. And then I was sick and she got scared in case I reported her for abuse. The sick was all foamy. It looked pretty impressive.'

Football was looking at me like he was a little impressed himself. 'You've been in care?' he said.

'Sure,' I said. 'Still am. Technically. Though any minute now I'm getting back with my mum. She's the most amazing actress and she's incredibly beautiful and she thinks I'll make it in the movies too and—'

And Football tackled me and got the ball back, laughing.

'You rotten . . .' My own language sparkled and hissed too.

I thought he'd go back indoors with his blooming ball and slam the door on me, but he hung around on his doorstep, heading the ball at the front wall, backwards and forwards.

'So, what's it like then?' he said, a little breathlessly because he was really whacking that ball. It made my eyes smart to watch him.

'What's what like? Hey, give me a go at heading it, eh?'

'You've got to be joking!'

'You're so mean! I got you your rotten ball back.'

'I don't think it's mine anyway.' Football caught it and swivelled it around. 'I had my name inked on it, plus a dire warning of what I'd do if anyone got their dirty mitts on it.'

'So it's really not yours?'

'Never mind. It's actually in better nick. I'd really hammered my last one.'

'Then it's just as much mine as yours – so give it here!'

'OK, OK, I'll play five minutes' footie with you – *after* you tell me what it's like to be in care.'

'What do you want to know for?'

'Because my mum keeps threatening stuff, see – and then I've got this social worker—'

'So have I. Elaine the Pain!' I pulled a face.

'What did you get up to then, a little kid like you?'

'I've been up to *all* sorts,' I boasted.

'But you haven't really been in trouble with the old Bill. I have. Lots,' said Football, swaggering.

'Yeah well. *I've* been too clever to get caught,' I said.

'So what *is* it like? Do they really beat you with wet towels so you don't get bruises? And do the older ones bash the little ones up and stick their heads down the toilets? And do the boys have to wear short trousers even in winter so they're a laughing stock? My mum says—'

Aha! I decided to wind him up just a tiny bit. 'That's right! Only it's far worse,' I said. 'The food's awful, all these meat loaves made of cow's nostrils and uddery bits, so you get mad cow disease as *well* as being sick. And *if* you're sick at a meal they pile it up on a plate and make you eat it.'

Football was staring at me, eyes popping, mouth open, like he was about to be sick himself. I could have nicked his ball – *my* ball – there and then, but this seemed like more fun. I went on elaborating and he carried on drinking it all in and it wasn't until I invented this torture chamber where they keep you handcuffed in the dark and let live rats run all over you and burrow down beneath your underwear that he suddenly twigged.

'You're having me on!' he said. He stared at me, his face scrunching up. I decided I might have to back off sharpish. But then this weird spluttery noise started up. Old Football was laughing!

'You're a weird little kid! OK, OK, I'll play footie with you. But just for five minutes, right?'

He went into his house to put on a T-shirt. He left the door ajar so I followed him in. It wasn't much cop at all. The carpet was all fraying at the edges and covered in bits. I could see why his mum had nagged on about the vacuuming. It looked like the whole house needed spring-cleaning. There were scuffs and marks all over the walls – obviously traces of Football's football.

He was in his living room, shoving his feet into his trainers. 'Here, you. I didn't ask you in.'

'I know. But I'm dead nosy. Seeing as I haven't got a real home.'

Football's certainly wasn't my idea of home sweet home. Yesterday's takeaways were congealing on trays by the sofa. The ashtray was so full it was spilling over and the whole room smelt stale. It was *empty* too. Well, there was a sofa and chairs and the telly, but that was about it. Cam's got all her cushions and patchwork and plants and pictures all over the walls and books in piles and little ornaments and vases of dried flowers and windchimes and notebooks and painted boxes and this daft old donkey she had when she was little. She said I could have Daisy if I wanted. I said I wasn't a silly little kid who played with toy animals. Cam said good, because she was a silly little woman who still liked cuddling up with Daisy when she was feeling dead depressed and she didn't really want to give her away.

I've tried hanging onto the old donkey once or twice, when Cam's not around. Daisy's got this old soft woolly smell, and the insides of her big ears are all velvety.

You can't cuddle up with anything at all in Football's house. Maybe Football doesn't mind. He's certainly not a cuddly kind of guy.

We played football out in the street. It was great for a bit.

But then these other guys came sloping past and Football acted like I was this little bee buzzing in his ear. He swotted me away and started playing football with these other guys.

'Hey, what about me?' I demanded indignantly.

'You push off now,' Football hissed out the side of his mouth, like he couldn't even bear to be seen talking to me.

'OK, OK. But you give me back my ball. I found it. And you said it wasn't yours.'

I got into a bit of an argument about it. Football and his new mates won.

I decided I didn't want to play footie with him if he were the last guy in the world. In fact, I'd gone off the game altogether so there was no point taking my ball with me. So I didn't insist.

I sloped off to the old house to see Alexander. I needed to see if he'd followed my advice and learned to stick up for himself.

Tracy and Alexander's Home

I let myself in the back window and noted straight away that someone had been making serious improvements in the kitchen. There was a big bottle of mineral water standing on the draining board, with a label saying THIS IS THE TAP. So I drank a little 'tap' water because Football (and the ensuing dispute) had been thirsty work. I slurped a little down my T-shirt but there was a clean towel hanging on a hook so I could mop myself up. A cardboard box was stacked in a corner with another label: THIS IS THE FRIDGE. I inspected the 'fridge' contents with interest. I discovered two rounds of tuna sandwiches, a packet of cheese and onion crisps, a Kit-Kat

and an apple. *Plus* a giant pack of Smarties!!!
I helped myself to a handful or two because
I'd already burnt up a lot of energy that
morning. I was all set to share my own refreshments – only I'd somehow or other eaten them
up. Still, I was sure Alexander would be happy
to share *his* refreshments with me.

'Alexander?' I called. It came out indis-
tinctly, because my mouth was full. I tried
again, louder. *'Alexander?'*

I heard a little mousy squeak from the living
room. Alexander was sitting cross-legged on a
little rug in front of another cardboard box.
There was a drawing of smiley *Blue Peter*
presenters on the front and another label:
THIS IS THE TELEVISION.

'It seems to be on permanent freeze-frame,'
I said wittily.

Alexander seemed unusually immobile too, hunched up with his chin on his chest.

'Are you OK?' I asked, sitting down beside him.

'Yes,' he said. Then, 'Well, no, not really.'

'Ah,' I said. 'What's up, then?'

Alexander sighed heavily. 'Everything,' he said sadly, and went back to watching the frozen TV programme.

'How did you get on at school?' I asked.

He didn't react, though his eyes flicked backwards and forwards as if the presenters were really doing something on the screen.

'You know, with the big bully boys in the showers?'

Alexander sighed again and slumped even further into his shoulders. 'The entire school calls me Gherkin now.'

I couldn't help spluttering. Alexander looked at me as if I'd kicked him.

'Sorry. *Sorry!* It just . . . sounded funny.'

'Everyone thinks it's very funny. Except me.'

'Oh dear. Well. Never mind.'

'I do mind. Dreadfully.'

'Still.' I struggled hard to say something optimistic. 'At least you won the dare. I dared you to do it, didn't I? And you did. So you get to win that dare.'

'Big deal,' said Alexander.

I thought hard. 'OK. You get to dare me now.'

'I don't really want to, thank you.'

I couldn't believe his attitude. Didn't he realize the potential of my offer??? 'Go *on*, Alexander,' I said impatiently, standing over him.

Alexander wriggled backwards on his bony bottom. 'I can't make up any dares,' he said meekly. 'You make one up, Tracy.'

'Don't be so wet! Come on. Dare me to do something really really wicked.'

Alexander thought hard. Then I saw light in his pale blue eyes. 'All right. I dare you to . . . I dare you to . . . stand on your head.'

He just didn't *get* it! But I decided to show willing. I spat on my hands and sprang forward. 'Easy-peasy,' I said, upside down.

'Gosh! You're really good at it.'

'Anyone can stand on their head.'

'I can't.'

I might have known. I tried hard to show him. He was useless. He just crumpled in a heap whenever he tried to kick his legs up.

'Watch *me*!' I said, doing headstands and handstands and then a cartwheel round the room.

'I can see your knickers,' said Alexander, giggling.

'Well, don't look,' I said breathlessly.

'I can't help it,' said Alexander. Then he started singing this weird song about leaping up and down and waving your knickers in the air.

'You what?' I said, right way up again.

'It's a song,' said Alexander. 'My dad sings it when he's in a good mood. Which isn't often when I'm around.' He sang it again.

'Is that another dare?' I said.

Alexander giggled.

'Right!' I said, and I whipped my knickers off and leapt up and down, waving them like a flag.

'Tracy! Um! You are *rude*!' Alexander spluttered, nearly keeling over sideways he was laughing so much.

I leapt right round the cardboard television, waving away, and pranced past the
window.

'Tracy! Get away from the window! Someone
will see,' Alexander screeched.

'I don't care,' I said, bouncing up and down
as if the bare floorboards were a trampoline.
'Look at me, everyone! Look at m-e-e-e!'

A football suddenly came flying
through the window and bounced
right across the floor. Alexander
must have seen it coming but he
didn't duck in time. It caught him bang
on the bonce.

'Ouch! A football!' he said, rubbing his head.

'*My* football,' I said, retrieving it
triumphantly.

'Who on earth threw it in here?' said
Alexander.

I didn't need three guesses. Football himself
came climbing through the window. It's a
harder window to negotiate than the one in the
kitchen at the back. He jumped down, lost his
balance, stumbled forward . . . and landed on
Alexander.

Alexander lay quivering, hands over his
head.

'You clumsy great oaf!' I said to Football. 'Are you all right, Alexander?'

'No,' said Alexander, whimpering.

Football picked him up and brushed him down. 'Yes you are,' he said firmly.

'Bully,' I said, bouncing the ball one-handed. 'First you beat me up. And I'm a girl and I'm younger than you. And then you pick on a total wimp like Alexander.'

I was *defending* Alexander but he crumpled again at the word wimp. I sighed. There's something about Alexander that kind of makes you *want* to bully him. Even though you know it's mean.

'Bully, bully, bully,' I said, bouncing the ball in time.

'Give me my ball back, kid,' said Football.

'It's *my* ball.'

'You gave it to me.'

'And then I took it back. It's my ball now. And this is *my* house and you're not invited so you can just clear off. What are you doing following me, anyway?'

'I didn't follow you. I was just checking up

on you. And it's not *your* house.'

'It is, it is, it is,' I said, bouncing.

'It's my house too,' said Alexander.

I smiled at him and bounced the ball to him. An easy-peasy bounce but he totally misjudged it. His hands closed on thin air and the ball bounced past. Football stuck out a paw and caught the ball.

'Alexander!' I said.

Alexander hung his head.

'*My* ball now,' said Football, smirking. He started bouncing so hard the cardboard furniture vibrated.

'You'll break the television,' said Alexander.

'You what?' said Football.

'You're interfering with the reception, look,' said Alexander.

I twigged that he was deliberately distracting him. I grinned – and as Football peered in disbelief at the cardboard box I whipped the ball from his arms. I used two hands – and Something fell on the floor. Football peered hard at the Something.

'I've got the ball, I've got the ball' I gabbled quickly, to distract him again.

This time it didn't work. Football bent over,

grinning, and picked up the
Something with his thumb and
forefinger. 'What's this, then?'
he said, grinning.

'Nothing,' I said. Though it obviously
wasn't Nothing. It was a pretty embarrassing
Something.

'It's your knickers!' Football chortled.
'She's been leaping up and down and
waving her knickers in the air.'

'Shut *up*, Alexander,' I said furiously.

I snatched my knickers back and stuffed
them in my pocket.

Football laughed loudly and made an
extremely coarse remark. I told him to watch
his mouth and he said I should watch his
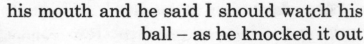 ball – as he knocked it out
of my arms. He
cheered himself
wildly and then
kicked the ball
all round the living
room, knocking the
television over and severely denting the table.

'Do you mind! This is my living room, not a
football pitch,' I said.

'It's my living room too,' said Alexander,

quickly dodging out of Football's way.

'I've got just as much right to be here as you have. And I say it's not a dopey old living room, it's a cracking indoor football pitch,' said Football, but this time he dribbled the ball carefully *round* the furniture, keeping up a running commentary all the time:

'Yeah, our boy's got the ball again, ready to save the day . . . *yes*, he intercepts the ball brilliantly, heading it s-t-r-a-i-g-h-t' (he took aim as he gabbled and suddenly kicked it hard against the wall) 'into the net! *Yes!*' (He punched the air.) 'I've never seen such a brilliant goal.'

'Sad,' I said to Alexander, shaking my head.

'You wait till I'm famous,' said Football, kicking the ball in my direction. Aiming *at* me, rather than to me.

But I'm no weedy Alexander. I stood my ground and kicked it straight back. 'Wow! Tracy's a gutsy little player!' I commentated. 'I bet I'm heaps more famous than you anyway.'

'Women footballers are rubbish,' said Football.

'I'm not going to be a footballer, you nutcase. I'm going to be a famous actress like my mum.'

'Now who's sad?' Football said to Alexander. He bounced the ball near him. Alexander blinked nervously. 'You going to be a famous actress too?' Football asked him unkindly.

'He could easily get to be famous,' I said. 'He's dead brainy. Top of everything at school. He could go on all the quiz shows on the telly and know every single answer. Only you'd better have a special telly name. Alexander isn't exactly catchy. How about . . . Brainbox?'

I was trying to be nice to him but I didn't seem to have the knack. Alexander winced at the word.

'They call me that at school,' he said mournfully. 'And other stuff. And my dad calls me Mr Clever Dick.'

'He sounds a right charmer, your dad,' I said.

'*My* dad's the best *ever*,' said Football, kicking his ball from one foot to the other.

'I haven't got a dad so I don't know whether he's the best or the worst,' I said. I've never really fussed about it. I never needed a dad, not when I had a mum. I needed her.

'My mum's going to take me to live at her

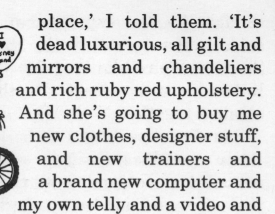

place,' I told them. 'It's dead luxurious, all gilt and mirrors and chandeliers and rich ruby red upholstery. And she's going to buy me new clothes, designer stuff, and new trainers and a brand new computer and my own telly and a video and a bike and pets and we're going on heaps of trips to Disneyland and I bet we won't even have to queue because my mum's such a famous actress.'

'What's her name then?' Football demanded.

'Carly. Carly Beaker,' I said proudly.

'Never heard of her,' said Football.

I thought quickly. I had to shut him up somehow. 'That's not her acting name.'

'Which is?'

'Sharon Stone.'

'If your mum's Sharon Stone then my dad's Alan Shearer,' said Football.

Alexander's head jerked. 'Your dad's Alan Shearer?' he piped up. 'No wonder he's good at football.'

Football shook his head pityingly. 'I

thought he was supposed to be bright?' he said. 'Anyway, my dad's *better* than Alan Shearer. We're like *that*, my dad and me.' He linked his stubby fingers to show us. 'We do all sorts together. Well. We did.'

Significant past tense.

'He's got this girlfriend,' said Football. 'My mum found out and now my dad's gone off with this girlfriend. I don't blame him. My mum just nags and moans and gives him a hard time. No wonder he cleared off. But he says it doesn't mean we're not still mates.'

'So your dad doesn't live with you any more?' said Alexander, sighing enviously.

'But we still do all sorts of stuff together,' said Football, kicking the ball about again. 'We always go to the match on Saturdays. Well, Dad couldn't make it this time. And last time. But that's because he's still, like, sorting out his new life – he's taking me *next* time, he's promised.' He stepped on the ball and patted his pockets, bringing out a cigarette-lighter. 'Look!'

I looked. He didn't produce the packet of fags to go with it.

'Let's have a smoke then,' I said. I like the way my mum holds her hand when she's got a fag lit – and the way her lips purse as she takes a long drag.

'I don't smoke, it's bad for my football, right?' said Football. 'No, this is my dad's lighter. See the make?' He held it out so we could admire it. 'It's not one of your tacky throw-away sort. It's *gold*.'

'Solid gold!' Alexander whispered.

'Well. Plated. Still cost a fortune. It's my dad's most precious possession. His mates gave it to him for his twenty-first birthday. He's never without it, my dad.'

'He seems to be without it now,' I chipped in.

'That's the *point*,' said Football. 'He's given it to *me*.' He flicked it on and off, on and off, on and off. It was like watching those flashing Christmas tree lights.

'You'll be waving it around at a rock concert next,' I said.

'You shut your face,' said Football, irritated that I wasn't acting dead impressed. 'You haven't even got a dad.' He kicked the ball hard. It bounced on the television set and ended up inside it.

'I wish I didn't have a dad,' said Alexander,

standing up and attempting repairs. 'Or I wish my dad would go off with a girlfriend. I wish wishes would come true. What would you wish for?' He looked shyly at Football. 'That you and your dad could be together?'

'Yeah,' said Football, looking amazed that Alexander could possibly have sussed this out. '*And* to play for United,' he added.

'What about you, Tracy?' asked Alexander.

'I don't want a dad,' I said quickly.

'What about your mum?' Alexander persisted. 'Would you wish you and your mum could be together?'

'That would be a totally wasted wish, wouldn't it, because I'm going to be with her *anyway*.'

But I'll still wish it even so. Let me be with my mum. Let me be with my mum. I'm wishing with all my heart. And my lungs and my liver and my bones and my brains. All the strings of my intestines are tied in knots I'm wishing so hard.

Mum's Home

Wishes come true. My fairy godmother has been working overtime! She made it come true. I spent the whole weekend with my mum and it was WONDERFUL and she says she wants me to go and live with her for ever and ever and ever, just as soon as Elaine gets it all sorted out officially.

Elaine didn't think my mum would turn up. She didn't say anything, but I'm not daft. I could tell. Cam dumped me off at Elaine's office. She said she would wait with me if I wanted but I didn't want. It's kind of weird being with Cam at the moment. She's *still* not making a big fuss and begging me not to go. Though I heard her crying last night.

I heard these little muffled under-the-duvet

sobs – and I suddenly couldn't stand it and stumbled out of bed and went running across the hall. I was all set to jump into bed with Cam and give her a big hug and tell her . . .

Tell her *what*? That was the trouble. I couldn't tell her I wouldn't go because I've *got* to go. My mum's my *mum*. Cam isn't anybody. Not really. And I've known my mum all my life while I've only known Cam six months. You can't compare it, can you?

So I didn't go and give her a cuddle. I made out I needed a wee and went to the bathroom. When I padded back the sobs had stopped. Maybe I'd imagined them anyway.

I don't know why I'm going on about all this sad stuff when I'm HAPPY HAPPY HAPPY. My mum didn't let me down. She came for me at Elaine's.

She was a little bit late, so that I had to keep going to the toilet and Elaine's bottom lip started bleeding because she'd nibbled it so hard with her big bunny teeth – but then suddenly this taxi drew up outside and my mum got out and she came running in on her high heels, her lovely blonde hair bouncing on her shoulders, her chest bouncing too in her tight jumper, and she clutched me tight in her arms so that I breathed her wonderful warm powdery smoky smell and then she said all this stuff about over-sleeping and missed trains and I didn't take any of it in, I was just so happy she was really there.

Though I didn't exactly *act* happy.

'Hey, hey, don't cry, kid, you're making my jumper all soggy,' Mum joked.

'I'm not crying. I never cry. I just get this hay fever sometimes, I told you,' I said, helping myself to Elaine's paper hankies.

Then Mum whisked me off and instead of bothering with boring old buses and trains we got into the taxi and drove all the way home. To Mum's house. Only it's going to be *my* house now.

It was miles and miles and miles and it cost a mega-fortune but do you know what my mum said? 'Never mind, darling, you're worth it!'

I very nearly had another attack of hay fever. And my mum didn't just fork out for the longest taxi ride in the world. Just wait till I write about all the presents! She's better than a fairy godmother! And her house is like a fairy palace too, even better than I ever imagined.

OK, it's not all that wonderful outside. Mum lives in this big block of flats on an estate and it's all car tyres and rubbish and scraggy kids outside. Mum's flat is right on the top floor and the lift swoops up faster than your stomach can cope. That's why I suddenly felt so weird – that and the pee smell in the lift. I got this feeling that the walls of the lift were pressing in on me, squashing me up so small I couldn't breathe. I wanted someone to come and hoick me out quick and tuck me up tight in my black bat cave. I didn't give so much as a squeak but Mum saw my face.

'Whatever's up with you, Tracy? You're not scared of a *lift*, are you? A big girl like you!'

She laughed at me and I tried to laugh too but it sounded more like I was crying. Only of course I don't ever cry. But it was all OK the minute I stepped *out* of the smelly old lift and *into* Mum's wonderful flat.

It's deep red – the carpet and the velvet curtains and the cushions, just as I'd hoped.

The sofa is white leather – s-o-o-o glamorous – and there's a white fur rug in front of it. The first thing Mum made me do was take my shoes off. I didn't notice the amazing twirly light fitting and the pictures of pretty ladies on the walls and the musical globe and the china figures at first because my eyes just got fixated on the sofa. Not because of the white leather. Because there was a pile of parcels in one corner, done up in pink paper with gold ribbon.

'Presents!' I breathed.

'That's right,' said Mum.

'Is it your birthday, Mum?'

'Of course it isn't, silly. They're for you!'

'It's not *my* birthday.'

'I know when your birthday is! I'm your *mum*. No, these are special presents for you because you're my own little girl.'

'Oh Mum!' I said – and I gave her this big hug. 'Oh Mum, oh Mum, oh Mum!'

'Come on then, don't you want to open them?'

'You bet I do!' I started tearing the paper off.

'Hey, hey, that cost ninety-nine pence a sheet. Careful!'

I went carefully, my hands trembling. I opened up the first parcel. It was a designer T-shirt, specially for me! I ripped off my own boring old one and squeezed into my BEAUTIFUL new status symbol.

'I could have got you a size or two bigger. I keep forgetting how big you are,' said Mum. 'Give it here, I'll change it for you.'

'No, no! It's wonderful! It's exactly the right size. Look, I can show my belly button and look dead sexy!' I did a little dance to demonstrate and Mum creased up laughing.

'You're a right little card, Tracy! Go on then, open the rest of your pressies.'

She gave me a fluffy pink rabbit. It's *lovely* if you like cuddly toys. Elaine would die for it. I decided to call it Marshmallow. I made it talk in a shy little lispy voice and Mum laughed again and said I was as good as any kid on the telly.

The next present was a H-U-G-E box of white chocolates. I ate two straight off, yum yum, slurp slurp. I wanted Mum to have one too but she said she was watching her figure, and they were all for me and I could eat as many as I liked. So I ate another two, yum yum, slurp slurp, same as before – but I started to feel a bit sickish again. They were WONDERFUL chocolates, and I bet they were mega-expensive, but somehow they weren't quite the same as Smarties. I know they'll be my favourites when I'm a bit older.

The last present wasn't for when I'm older. It was the biggest and Mum had left the price on the box so I knew it was most definitely the most expensive, amazingly so.

It was a doll. Not just any old doll, you understand. The most fantastic curly-haired Victorian doll in a flowery silk costume, with her own matching parasol clutched in her china hand.

I looked at her, holding the box.

'Well?' said Mum.

'Well. She's lovely. The loveliest doll in the whole world,' I said, trying to make my voice as bouncy as Football's ball, only it kind of rolled away from me and came out flat.

'You used to be such a dolly girl, even though you were a fierce little kid,' said Mum. 'Remember I bought you that wonderful big dolly with golden ringlets? You totally adored her. Wouldn't let her go. What did you call her? Rose, was it? Daffodil?'

'Bluebell.'

'So here's a sister for Bluebell.'

'That's great, Mum,' I said, my stomach squeezing.

'You've still got Bluebell, haven't you?' said Mum, squinting at me.

'Mmm,' I said. My tummy really hurt, as if this new doll had given it a hard poke with her pointy parasol.

'So did you bring her with you?' Mum persisted, lighting another cigarette.

'Give us a fag, Mum, go on, please,' I said, to try to divert her.

'Don't be so daft. You're not to start smoking, Tracy, it's a bad habit.' She started off this really Mumsie lecture and I dared breathe out. But my mum's not soft. 'So where

128

is she then? Bluebell?' she persisted.

'I . . . I don't know,' I said. 'You see, the thing *is*, Mum, I had to leave her in the Children's Home.'

'They wouldn't let you take your own dolly?'

'She got a bit . . . broken.'

'You broke your doll?'

'No! No, it wasn't me, Mum, I swear it. It was one of the other kids. They poked her eyes out and cut off all her ringlets and scribbled on her face.'

'I don't *believe* it! That place! Well, I'll get on to Elaine the Pain straight away. That doll cost a fortune.'

'It happened years ago, Mum.'

'Years ago?' Mum shook her head. It was like she couldn't get her time scales right. She kept acting like she'd only popped me in the Children's Home last Tuesday when I've actually been in and out of care since I was little. My folder's *this* thick.

'Oh well,' said Mum. 'Anyway. You've got a new dolly now. Even better than Bluebell. What are you going to call this one? Not a daft name like Marshmallow this time. She's a beautiful doll. She needs a proper name.'

'I'll call her . . .' I tried hard but I couldn't come up with anything.

'What's your favourite name? You must have one,' said Mum.

'Camilla,' I said without thinking.

Mum stood still.

BIG MISTAKE.

'That woman's called Camilla, isn't she?' said Mum, drawing hard on her cigarette.

'No, no!' I gabbled. 'She's Cam. She never gets called Camilla. No, Mum, I like the name *Camilla* because there was this little girl in the Children's Home, *she* was called Camilla.'

I was telling the truth. I used to love this little kid Camilla, and she liked me too, she really did. I could always make her laugh. I just had to pull a funny face and blow a raspberry and Camilla would gurgle with laughter and clap her pudgy little hands.

Camilla's been my favourite name for ages, long long before I met Cam. Cam never gets called Camilla anyway. She can't stand it. She thinks it sounds all posh and pretentious. I tried hard to get Mum to believe me.

'Camilla,' Mum said, like it was some particularly smelly disease. 'Your favourite name, eh? Do you like it better than Carly?'

'Of course not,' I said. 'Carly's the best ever name, obviously, because it's yours. But I can't call the doll Carly because *you're* Carly. Hey, maybe she should be called Curly?' I scooped the doll out of her box and shook her so that her ringlets wiggled. 'Yeah, Curly!'

'Careful! You'll muck those eyes up too!' Mum took the doll from me and smoothed her satin skirts.

'It wasn't me that poked her eyes out.'

'Even so, you must play with her *gently*.' Mum handed her back to me.

I held her at arm's length, not quite sure what to do with her. 'Hello, Curly. Little girly Curly. Curlybonce!'

'That's not a very nice name. She's a very special collector's doll, Tracy. Don't you like her ringlets?'

'Yes, they're lovely.'

'It's about time we tried to do something with *your* hair. Come here.' She fiddled in her handbag and brought out a little hairbrush. 'Right!' She suddenly attacked my head.

'O-w-w-w-w-w!'

'Keep still!' said Mum, giving me a little tap with the brush.

'You're pulling my head off!'

'Nonsense. It seems like it hasn't been brushed for weeks. It's like a bird's nest.'

'O-u-c-h!'

'Do you make this fuss when Cam does your hair?'

'She doesn't.'

Mum sighed, shaking her head. 'I don't know, she's being paid a fortune, and yet she lets you wander round like a ragamuffin.'

'Cam's not really into how you look,' I said, trying really hard to hold my head still though it felt like she was raking grooves in my scalp.

'Typical,' said Mum. 'Well, *I* care how you look.'

'I care too, Mum,' I said. 'Ouch! No, it's OK, don't stop. We women have to suffer for our beauty, eh?'

Mum creased up laughing though I hadn't meant it as a joke. 'You're a funny little thing,' she said. She paused, tapping the back of her hairbrush on her palm. 'You do love me, don't you, darling?'

'*Ever* so much,' I shouted.

It still didn't sound loud enough to Mum. 'More than anyone else?'

'Yes!' I insisted, though my throat ached as I

said it. 'Yes. You bet. You're my mum.'

She reached out and patted my face, cupping my chin. 'And you're my little girl,' she said. 'Though you're getting to be such a big girl now.' She fingered my lips. 'They're all chapped. You need a spot of lip balm. Half a tick.' She rooted in her handbag amongst her make-up.

'Oh, Mum, make me up properly, eh?'

Mum put her head on one side, looking amused. 'It might help give you a bit more colour, I suppose.'

'Yeah, I want to look all colourful like you, Mum.'

She laughed. 'We've got different skin tones, pet. But I can certainly liven you up a bit. You've got quite a nice little face, though you must watch it when you scowl. You don't want to be all wrinkly when you're my age. *Smile*, Tracy.'

I smiled until my ears waggled.

'Maybe you could get away with a pale pink lipstick and a spot of rouge on your cheeks.'

'I want bright red lipstick like yours!' I had a rootle in her bag myself.

'Get out of there!' said Mum, trying to snatch it back. 'Tracy! You're mucking up all my things.'

I'd found a red mock-crocodile wallet.

'You after my money?' said Mum.

'Is there a photo of me inside?' I said, opening it.

I peered. There *was* a photo but it certainly wasn't me. 'Who's he?' I asked.

'Give that wallet here,' said Mum, acting like she meant it now.

'Who's the guy?' I asked, handing it over.

'He's no-one,' said Mum. She took the photo out of the plastic frame. 'This is what I think of *him*,' she said, and she tore the photo into tiny little bits.

'Is it my dad?'

'No!' said Mum, sounding amazed, like she'd forgotten I'd ever had a dad. 'No, it's my boyfriend. My ex.'

'The one that went off with the young girl?'

'That's the one,' said Mum. 'The *slug*. Still, who needs him, that's what I say.'

I said he'd have to be crazy to go off with anyone else when he had someone as beautiful as Mum. She liked this a lot. We sat down on the sofa together, and I put Curly carefully on my lap and tucked Marshmallow under my arm. Mum fed me another white chocolate. I

134

didn't really fancy it but I ate it up anyway, licking her long pointy fingers so that she squealed.

'You and me will be all right, won't we, Tracy?' said Mum. It seemed like she was seriously asking me.

'We're going to be just great,' I said.

'We'll stay together, yes?'

'Yes, yes, yes!'

'It's what you want?' Mum persisted.

'More than anything in the world,' I said.

We had a huge hug, Mum and me (Curly and Marshmallow got a bit squashed but Mum didn't nag), and it was like we were spinning in our *own* little world, and it was whirling us all the way up into outer space.

The Tree Home

I got a bit miffed when I went back to my home. Football and Alexander were there already, playing football. Well, Football did the kicking. Maybe Alexander was meant to be the goalie. He seemed to be acting as a goalpost too.

I didn't think they had any right to be there. Well, not before me. I flounced back to the kitchen. Alexander had supplied the cardboard refrigerator with a packet of Jaffa Cakes. I felt this was extra mean as I'm not very keen on orange. I ate three even so, just to show him. I wanted a drink but there was just this silly cardboard cut-out kettle. I scrumpled it up. What sort of idiot was he?

'It took me a long time to get the sides equal and the spout right,' Alexander said reproachfully, standing in the kitchen doorway.

'Never mind your silly bits of cardboard!

Hey, you'll never ever guess what!'

'What?' said Alexander.

'I'm going to live with my mum.'

'Are you?' said Alexander, as if I'd said 'I'm going to help myself to another Jaffa Cake'.

'What do you *mean* "are you"? That's a bit of a limpy wimpy response. Why aren't you, like, "Wow, Tracy, you lucky thing, how fantastic, super-duper mega-whizzo brilliant"?'

Alexander stood to attention. 'Wow, Tracy. You lucky thing,' he said obediently. Then he paused. 'What else was it?' He was acting like he didn't think I was the luckiest kid in the whole world.

'Look, you haven't *seen* my mum.' I wished I had a photo to show him. 'She looks totally fantastic. She's really really beautiful, and she wears these wonderful clothes, and her hair and her make-up are perfect. She made me up too and styled my hair and I looked incredible.'

There was a very rude snort from the living room where Football was obviously flapping his ears, listening to every word.

I marched in to confront him, Alexander shuffling after me. Football dodged back and shielded his face, pretending to be dazzled. 'Here's Tracy the Incredible Beauty!' he said, fooling about.

I gave him an extra withering look. 'You can scoff all you like, but maybe I'll take after my mum and end up looking just like her,' I said.

'And maybe that's a little fat piggy flying through the air,' said Football.

Alexander's head turned, mouth open, looking for the flying pig.

'My mum's given me all these presents too,' I said. 'Heaps and heaps.'

'Whoops! There's a whole herd of piggies flying past,' said Football.

Alexander blinked and then got it at last and chortled loudly.

'It's true! She's spent a fortune on me. She's given me everything I could ever want.'

'What, the computer? And the rollerblades and the mountain bike?' said Football, starting to look impressed at long last.

I hesitated. 'She's giving me all those later, when I'm living with her.'

'Aha!' said Football.

'But she's already given me this new T-shirt. Look, it's designer, none of your market copy rubbish either, look at the label.'

'Cool,' said Football.

'*And* she gave me this enormous box of chocolates, so many I couldn't possibly eat them all.'

'Well, maybe you could pop them in our fridge,' said Alexander, still giggling weakly. 'We're a bit short on provisions at the moment.'

'Yeah, well, they're fresh cream, and when I got them back to Cam's they'd gone a bit funny-tasting so we had to throw them out. But I've still got the box. I'll show you it if you don't believe me, Football. And my mum gave me heaps of other stuff too, the most fantastic cuddly toys and a special collector's doll, an actual modern antique that costs hundreds of pounds.'

'A doll?' said Football.

'Well, it's more like a giant ornament. I tell you, it's simply beautiful. My mum's the greatest mum in all the world.'

Alexander was looking serious again, his eyes beady.

'What?' I said.

'She can't really be the best mum, not if she left you,' he said. 'I think if you leave your little girl it makes you a bad mum.'

'She couldn't help it,' I said quickly. 'It was just the way things were. She had things to do. And she had this really gross boyfriend. She didn't have any option. She thought I'd be fine in the Children's Home.'

'I thought you hated it,' said Alexander. He was really starting to get on my nerves.

'I got along OK,' I said fiercely.

'Not till Cam came along,' Alexander persisted. 'What about Cam, Tracy?'

'What about her?' I said, sticking my face into his and baring my teeth. I was very nearly tempted to bite. 'My mum says she can't really care about me. She's just fostering me for the money.'

'You can't be *easy* to foster, Tracy,' said Alexander, backing away from me. But he still wouldn't shut up. 'I think she's fostering you because she likes you. Don't you like her?'

'She's all right,' I said awkwardly. 'Anyway she can't like me all that much or she'd fight harder to keep me, wouldn't she?'

Alexander deliberated. 'Maybe she's just trying to fit in with what *you* want because she likes you lots and lots.'

'Maybe you should just shut up and mind your own business,' I said. 'What do you know anyway, Alexander-the-totally-teeny-tiny-gherkin.'

I gave him a push and waved at Football. 'Come on, let's play footie then. I'll give you a *real* game.'

Football stopped staring and sprang into action. He passed the ball to me and I kicked it so hard it bounced back off the opposite wall, hit the sofa, and then ricocheted straight into the television set.

'That's the second television gone for a burton – and it takes ages to make,' Alexander wailed.

'You and your stupid cardboard rubbish. Let's clear it all out the way,' I said, giving the crumpled cardboard another kick for good measure.

Alexander looked as if he was about to cry. I don't know why. I wasn't kicking *him*. But when Football caught on and got ready for a major WRECK-THE-JOINT I diverted him upstairs where it wouldn't matter so much. Alexander hadn't attempted any Interior Design – but there were old boxes to kick to bits and a filthy old mattress to jump on.

Alexander came trailing upstairs after us and stood anxiously in the doorway, not daring to join in. I felt mean, but I still couldn't forgive him for being so obstinate about my mum.

Football went into Major Demolition Mode for a minute or two and then decided to take a rest.

'You think it's great I'm going to live with my mum, don't you, Football?' I said. 'Hey, don't *lie* on the mattress, you'll get fleas.'

'Yuck!' said Football, leaping up again. 'Yeah, I think it's good about your mum, seeing as she's going to be giving you all them presents. You've got to look out for number one, Tracy. Go for what you can get and the one who'll give you the most.' He kicked his ball against the wall and then jumped up and headed it expertly back again. 'Wow! Did you see that?' He waved his arms in the air, showing off like mad.

'It's not just the presents and stuff,' I said. 'It's because she's my *mum*.'

'Mums are rubbish,' said Football.

'You wouldn't say that about dads!'

'Yes I would,' said Football, and this time he kicked the ball so dementedly it veered off the wall and smashed the opposite window. It disappeared out of sight.

'Whoops!' said Football.

'I think maybe that's enough wrecking,' I said.

'Watch that broken glass, Football,' said Alexander. 'You'll cut yourself.'

'What are you doing, you nutter?' I said, as Football opened the window, spraying more glass all over the place.

'We need a dustpan and brush,' said Alexander. 'Maybe I can devise something out of cardboard?'

'You and your daft bits of cardboard,' I said. 'Hey, Football, what are you doing *now*?'

Football was climbing out of the window!

'I'm getting my ball back,' said

Football, peering out. 'It hasn't come down. It's stuck up on the guttering, look!'

'Football, get back!'

'It's terribly dangerous, Football!'

'Not the drainpipe!'

'You're far too big. Don't!'

Football did. He reached for the drainpipe. It wobbled and then started to buckle. Football let go sharpish.

'Get back *in*, Football,' I said, clawing at his ankles.

He kicked my hands hard – and then leapt.

I screamed and shut my eyes. I waited for the crash and thump. But there wasn't one.

Alexander was making little gaspy noises beside me. 'Look at him!' he whispered.

I opened my eyes and stared in disbelief. Football had leapt across a sickening gap into the fir tree that grew up against the wall. He made loud triumphant Tarzan noises.

'You're *crazy!*'

'No, I'm not! Haven't you ever climbed a tree? And this one's a piece of cake, just like going up a ladder.'

Football climbed up steadily while we craned our necks, watching. Alexander gripped my hand tight, his sharp little nails digging into my palm.

Football very nearly reached the top, reached out – and clawed his ball back from the guttering. 'Yuck, it's got gunge all over it,' he said, wiping it on the tree branches.

'Just come back down, you nutter!' I yelled.

'I'll wash it for you, Football,' Alexander offered. 'Please, just come back!'

So Football climbed down again, threw the ball back in the broken window, leant over the dizzying drop, leapt for it, teetered on the window ledge, and then came crashing into the bedroom on top of us.

For a moment we were all too stunned to say anything. Football got up first. Alexander and I didn't have any option, seeing as he was on top of us.

'Dads *are* rubbish,' Football said, dusting himself down and wiping the gungy ball on Alexander's jersey. 'Smelly mouldering putrid rubbish.'

It was like there'd been no break in the conversation whatsoever.

'But you're nuts about your dad,' I said, getting up gingerly and waggling my arms and legs to make sure they weren't broken.

'That's what I was. Nuts,' said Football. 'That's your new nickname for me, isn't it? Nutter?'

Alexander sat up and looked at his stained jumper. 'It's my school one,' he said, in a very little voice. Then he swallowed hard. 'Still, it doesn't really matter, seeing as I hardly ever go to school now.'

'Oh dear, have I spoilt your school jersey?' said Football. 'I'm terribly sorry, Alexander, old chum.'

Alexander chose to take him seriously. 'That's quite all right, Football,' he said. He got up cautiously as if there was every chance he might be knocked down again. 'What happened with your dad, Football?'

I held my breath.

'You shut up, useless,' said Football, but he simply bounced his ball on Alexander's head.

'Didn't your dad take you to the match on Saturday?' I asked.

Football suddenly sat back down himself,

his back against the wall. He looked down at the bare floorboards. He didn't even bounce his ball. 'I waited. And waited. And waited,' he mumbled. 'But he never turned up.'

Football thought there was something wrong, like his dad was ill or in trouble, so he went round to his place, only there was no-one there. He sat on the steps outside his flat and waited for ages. Then when his dad eventually turned up he had his girlfriend with him, and he was slobbering all over her like she was an ice lolly. Football looked like he was going to be sick when he told us. And it got worse.

It turned out his dad had taken the girlfriend to the match instead of Football because she'd got this thing about the goalie's *legs*. They both laughed like it was really cute and funny and had no idea what they were doing to Football. He made out he didn't care. He said he was getting a bit sick of their football Saturdays anyway. And his dad got shirty then and said, Right, if that's your attitude . . .

So Football pushed off and then when he

got back home his mum saw he was upset but it just made her mad and she slagged off his dad all over again.

'So I called her all these names and said it was no wonder Dad left home because she's such a whining misery. Then she clumped me and cried and now she's not talking to me. So they both hate me, my mum and my dad. So they're rubbish, right? All mums and dads are rubbish.'

He stopped. We seemed to have stopped too. The house was very quiet. It was chilly with the window broken. I shivered.

'It doesn't necessarily follow that *all* mums and dads are rubbish,' said Alexander.

There are some silences that shouldn't be broken. Football bounced his ball at Alexander's head again. Hard.

'I don't really like it when you do that, Football,' Alexander said, blinking.

'Good,' said Football. He bounced his ball again. It was unfortunate for Alexander that Football has deadly accurate aim.

'Tracy?' Alexander said, a tear rolling down his cheek.

I felt like there were two Tracys.

One wanted to put her arm round him and wipe his eyes and yell at Football to go and pick on someone his own size. And the other wanted to bounce a ball on his brainy little bonce too.

The Tracy twins argued it out. Guess which one won.

'You're such a wimp, Alexander. Why can't you stick up for yourself? You daren't do anything.'

Alexander drooped. 'I *did* do that dare,' he said. 'Even though it meant the whole school called me names.'

'What dare?' said Football, still bouncing.

'I'm Tracy Beaker, the Great Inventor of Extremely Outrageous Dares,' I said proudly.

'Like?' said Football, catching the ball.

'Like anything,' I said.

'So dare me,' said Football, swaggering.

I let half a dozen ideas flicker in my head. None of them seemed quite suitable for Football. I squeezed my brain hard. I needed something suitably scary, rude and revolting.

Alexander seemed to think I needed help. 'Tracy dared wave her knickers in the air!' he announced.

'Shut *up*, Alexander!' I hissed.

Football grinned. 'OK, Tracy, I dare you wave your knickers. Go on!'

'Get lost,' I said. 'And anyway, you can't copy my dare.'

'All right. I'll think of a better one.' Football was grinning from ear to ear now. 'I dare you take your knickers off and hang them on the fir tree like a Christmas decoration!'

I stared at him. It wasn't fair. It was a BRILLIANT dare. Definitely Tracy Beaker standard. Oh how I wanted to zip his grin up!

'You can't ask Tracy to do that!' said Alexander. 'It's far too dangerous.'

'*I* climbed out into the tree,' said Football.

'Yes, but you're bigger and stronger than Tracy,' said Alexander. 'And madder,' he added softly.

'There isn't anyone madder than me,' I said. 'OK, I'll do your stupid old dare, Football, easy-peasy.'

'Tracy!' said Alexander. He looked at me, he looked at Football. 'Is this just a game?'

'It's *my* game, my Dare Game,' I said. 'Only it's way too daring for you, Little Gherkin.'

'Gherkin?' said Football. 'One of them

little wizened pickled things?'

'Alexander gets called Gherkin because everyone's seen what he looks like in the showers!'

Football cracked up laughing. 'Gherkin! That's a good one! *Gherkin!*'

Alexander looked at me, his eyes huge in his pinched face. 'Why are you being so mean to me today, Tracy?'

'*You're* mean to me, trying to stop me living happily ever after with my mum, when it's what I've always wanted more than anything in the whole world,' I said, and I marched to the window, kicking the broken glass out the way, and hitched myself up onto the window ledge.

'Tracy! Don't! What if you fall?' Alexander shrieked.

I hooked one leg out.

'Tracy! I wasn't serious. You're too little,' Football shouted.

'I'm not little! I'm Tracy the Great and I always win every single dare,' I yelled, getting the other leg out and standing up straight. Straightish. My legs were a bit wobbly.

I looked down – and then wished I hadn't.

'Come back, Tracy!' said Alexander.

But I couldn't go back. I had to go forward. 'This is the Dare Game, and I'm going to win it, just you wait and see.'

I looked at the tree – and jumped. One second I was in the air and there were screams – some mine – and then I had twigs up my nose and scratching my face and I was clinging there, in the tree, hands hanging onto branches, feet curled against the trunk.

I'd made it! I hadn't fallen! I had managed a thrilling death-defying l-e-a-p! Football gave his Tarzan cry behind me and I joined in too, long and loud.

'Now come back in, Tracy,' Alexander pleaded.

'I haven't started yet!' I said. 'Shut your eyes. And you, Football.'

They both blinked at me like they'd forgotten the whole point of the dare.

'I've got to take my knickers off now, so *no* peeping,' I commanded.

They shut their eyes obediently. Well, one of them did.

'Football! Think I'm daft? Stop squinting at me!' I yelled.

Football's eyes shut properly this time. I gingerly let go of the branch and started  fidgeting under my skirt. It was a lot more scary only holding on with one hand. It would have been much more sensible to take my knickers off *before* I was in the tree, but it was too late now. I got them around my knees, and then reached down. The garden wavered way down below me and I felt sick.

'Don't, Tracy! You'll fall!' Football shouted.

'Shut your ******* eyes!' I was so peeved he was peering right up my short skirt I forgot to be frightened, eased my knickers over my foot and then straightened up in a flash.

'They're off!' I yelled, waving them like a flag.

Football cheered. 'Shove them on a branch for a second and then get back in,' he shouted. 'You've won the bet, Trace. Good for you.'

'Yes, come back *now*, Tracy,' said Alexander.

I didn't want to come back right that instant.

I was starting to get used to it in the tree. I looked up instead of down. It was a great feeling to be up so high. I reached for the next branch and the next and the next.

The boys yelled at me but I took no notice. I'd turned into Monkey Girl, leaping about the treetops without a worry in the world.

The tree swayed a little more as I got nearer the top, but I didn't mind a bit. It felt soothing, not scary. If I was Monkey Girl I could swing in my tree all day long and at night I could fashion myself a leafy hammock and rock myself to sleep.

I started to think seriously about a treehouse. I could get Alexander to design it – *not* one of his cardboard concoctions, a proper planks of wood job. Football and I could knock it together and somehow secure it to the tree. Yes, a treehouse would be absolutely amazing. I could furnish it with blankets and cushions and have heaps of provisions and I could live up there all the time and spy on all my enemies and everyone would talk in awed tones about Tracy of the Treetops.

I decided to make a start on the treehouse idea for real, but then I remembered I was going to live with my mum any minute now so there wasn't any point and I got a bit distracted – and slipped. I scrabbled and grabbed the next branch down, hanging on for dear life. Or lousy life. Any kind of life.

'Watch out, Tracy!'

'Tracy! Come back! *You're* the nutter now!'

My heart was hammering and my hands were slippy with sweat but I thought I'd wind them up just a little bit more. I climbed higher, up and up, branch after branch, hand over hand, foot after foot, concentrating fiercely now.

I climbed until I was fast running out of tree, the branches becoming so delicate and spindly that some broke right off when I took hold of them – but I dared go even higher so that I could just about reach up up up to the very top. I hooked my knickers round and attached them to the tip like a big white star.

I saw stars too, a whole galaxy of constellations shining and sparkling in celebration. I'd done it! The most Daring Dare ever and *I'd done it*.

Then I climbed all the way down, feeling my way with my feet, down and down and down until at long last I came level with the window, and there were Football and Alexander gazing out at me open-mouthed as if I was an angel swooping straight down from heaven.

'Out the way then, you gawpers,' I commanded, and they drew apart like curtains.

I got ready to spring.

I made it right through the window. I didn't even fall over. I landed on my feet. Tracy the Fabulous Cat Girl with all her nine lives still in front of her.

'How about *that*!' I said, and I did this crazy dance around the room.

Football danced with me, leaping about, clapping me on the back. 'You're the greatest, kid. Knickers off and all!'

'Yeah, I'm the greatest, aren't I? Aren't I, Alexander?'

'You're the maddest!' said Alexander. 'I'm a total jelly with watching you. Look, I'm still shaking.'

'Gherkin jelly! Yuck,' I said.

'You're mad. You're both mad,' said Alexander. 'Can't you see? You could have been killed. It *doesn't* make you the greatest.'

'No, *you're* the greatest! The greatest meanest bore ever,' I said, poking him. How dare he try to spoil my Stupendous Achievement?

'She *is* the greatest. And so am I,' said Football, poking him too.

'Stop poking me,' said Alexander, hunching up small. 'You're not not not great, not just because you take stupid risks and nearly kill yourselves.'

I was starting to feel like killing Alexander. He was acting like this irritating little gnat nipping away at my ankles. Any second now I'd stick out my hand and go SWAT.

'Don't make me really mad, Alexander,' I warned him, giving him another poke.

'You're already mad at me for saying all that stuff about your mum. That's why you keep picking on me.'

'That's got nothing to do with it,' I said fiercely. I'm mad at you because you're *maddening*!'

'No wonder they all pick on you at your school,' Football jeered. 'No wonder even your own dad can't stand you.' He didn't touch him this time but somehow it was worse than a poke.

I wavered just a weeny bit. 'Well, he must like him really.'

'No he doesn't,' said Alexander. Big tears were rolling down his cheeks. 'He can't stand me.'

I felt so mean that it made me even angrier with him. 'That's rubbish! Don't be so stupid.' I gave him a sudden push. 'You're *really* starting to irritate me now.'

'You've always irritated me, Gherkin,' said Football.

'Don't call me that,' Alexander said, sniffling.

'Gherkin, Gherkin, Gherkin!' Football chanted. 'Wizened little Gherkin who can't play the Dare Game.'

'I *did* play it! I did do a dare, didn't I, Tracy?'

'Yeah, you were mad enough to tell the whole school to call you Gherkin!'

'Stop it!'

'Gherkin, Gherkin, Gherkin!' I yelled, right in his face.

Football was right beside me. 'You clear off, Gherkin, this is *our* house,' he said.

'I was here first,' Alexander wept.

'But we're here now,' I said.

'And we don't want you, do we, Trace?'

I couldn't be quite that mean. There was still a bit of me that wanted to put my arms round Alexander and give him a hug.

Alexander saw me wavering. He gave a giant sniff. 'I'll do another dare if you let me stay!'

'OK then, climb up the tree and fetch

Tracy's knickers back,' said Football, quick as a wink.

'No!' I said.

'Yes!' said Football.

'All right,' said Alexander.

'Don't be crazy,' I said, suddenly scared. It was like everything was spinning too fast and I couldn't stop it. 'Football, please. You can't dare him to do that.'

'*I* did it,' said Football. 'And you did it too, even though you're little and only a girl.'

'*I'll* do it,' said Alexander. 'I still think it's mad and I'll probably get killed but I don't care. I'll still do it. I'll show you.' He ran to the window.

'You mustn't, Alexander!' I ran after him, but he was surprisingly fast. 'You can't climb, you can't balance, you can't do anything! You'll fall!'

'I told you, I don't care,' said Alexander, and he tried to jump up on the window ledge. He mistimed it completely and banged his nose hard on the window frame.

'See, Alexander! Now you're the one who's being stupid,' I said, rushing to him.

He shook his head, stunned, his nose crimson.

'Football, take the dare back quick,' I said.

'OK, OK, I take the dare back, Gherkin,' said Football.

'I'll still do the dare if you promise never ever to call me Gherkin again,' said Alexander, his voice muffled because his hands were cupping his sore nose.

'You're not doing any dare. You're right, we were all crazy.'

'You told me to go away,' said Alexander, turning to the window.

'I didn't mean it,' I said. 'You're my friend, Alexander. I like you. Football likes you too.'

'No I don't,' said Football.

'You *do!*' I insisted.

'No-one likes me, not really,' said Alexander, and he made another dash for the

window, a sudden quick dart that took us by surprise.

He jumped high enough this time. He made the window ledge. But he didn't stop. He swooped right out into space, like a little cartoon animal running in mid-air. But

Alexander was real. He didn't hang, give a yelp, and pedal backwards. He plummeted down . : . down down down into the dark garden below.

The Garden Home

We thought he was dead. He was still lying
motionless when we hurtled downstairs and
out the back window into the
overgrown garden, his skinny
arms and legs spread wide.

'Alexander!' I cried.

'He's copped it,' said Football
– and he started to snuffle. 'I've
murdered poor little Gherkin.'

'You're never to call me
Gherkin again,' Alexander squeaked
in a little mouse voice.

We fell on him, hugging him
like he was our dearest friend.

'Careful!' said Alexander. 'I've
probably broken my neck. And my
arms and legs. And all my ribs.'

'Does it hurt terribly?' I said, taking his little
claw hand in mine.

'I'm not sure,' said Alexander. 'I feel weird, like I can't feel anything properly yet. But I think it might hurt a lot when I can.'

'What do you mean, you can't feel anything? Oh no, he's paralysed!' said Football.

I tickled the backs of Alexander's knees and he squealed and kicked. 'No he's not,' I said.

Do you know the most amazing thing ever????

Alexander wasn't hurt at all. He didn't break so much as a fingernail! We stared at him in awe, wondering how he could possibly have survived that great drop unscathed. I'd always thought there was something not quite human about Alexander. Perhaps he was really an alien from another planet? That would explain a lot.

But the real reason for Alexander's remarkable survival only became apparent when he very gingerly got onto all fours and then stood up. He had fallen onto an old discarded mattress!

'You must be the luckiest kid ever!' I said.

'Though you might have a fleabite or two,' said Football.

'I think I *might* have hurt myself somewhere,' said Alexander, sounding wistful. 'This leg feels a bit odd. It's throbbing. I think I could have broken it. Definitely.'

'You couldn't possibly have broken your leg,' said Football. 'You'd be, like . . .' He mimed a footballer writhing on his back. 'You'd have to be stretchered off.'

'Maybe . . . maybe I'm just better at putting up with the pain,' said Alexander, experimenting with a limp.

'It was your *other* leg you were rubbing a minute ago.'

'Perhaps I've broken both,' Alexander persisted.

'You haven't broken anything at all and I'm so *glad*, Alexander,' I said, giving him another hug.

'Yeah, me too,' Football said gruffly.

'And you won't call me the G word ever again?'

'Right.'

'Because I did almost do the dare, didn't I?' said Alexander. 'Maybe I *am* Alexander the Great.'

'You're Alexander the Small,' said Football, patting him.

'You're Football the ever so Tall,' said Alexander. He turned to me. 'And you're Trace who wins every race. OK?'

'OK.'

'And we're all friends now?' said Alexander.

'Yes, of course we are,' I said. 'Alexander, stop limping. There's nothing the matter with your leg.'

'There is,' said Alexander. 'If I've got a broken leg I won't have to do PE at school.'

'You're never at school anyway,' I said.

'No, but I might have to be soon,' said Alexander, sighing. 'They wrote a letter to my mum and dad and they went nuts. My dad says he's going to escort me to school himself.'

'You're going to enjoy that!' I said.

'So it's just going to be you and me hanging out at the house, Tracy?' said Football.

'Well. I can't, can I? Not if I'm at my mum's. I'll be moving right away. Hey, my mum's flat is incredible, you should see all the stuff she's got!'

They didn't seem that interested. 'You'll just muck it all up anyway,' said Football.

'No I won't!'

I've got it all sussed out. I'm going to dust all her dinky little ornaments and vacuum the carpets and Mum will think I'm s-o-o-o useful she'll never ever get fed up with me and send me away again.

'I'm going to be my mum's little treasure,' I declared.

'I don't know why you want to go and stay with her,' said Football. 'You must be mad. She *is* mad, isn't she, Gherkin?'

'You're not to call me that!' Alexander said, stamping his foot. 'Ouch! That was my bad leg.'

'Sorry, sorry! But she *is* mad, isn't she?' said Football.

Alexander glanced at me nervously – but nodded.

'Who cares what you two think?' I said fiercely.

They were wrong. I wasn't mad. Any girl would want to live with her mum. Even a girl who already had a sort-of mum.

I haven't written much about Cam recently. There have been lots and lots of Cam bits. I just haven't felt like writing them. I mean, writers can't put *everything* down. If you started writing everything exactly as it happened you'd end up with page after page about opening your eyes and snuggling down in bed for another five minutes and then getting up and going to the loo and brushing your teeth and playing games squeezing your name out in paste and seeing what you'd look like with a toothbrush moustache . . . well, you'd need a whole new chapter before you'd even got started on breakfast.

Writers have to be selective. That's what Mrs Vomit Bagley says. Did I put that she's got wondrously unfortunate teeth? She spits a little bit whenever she says an 's' word. If she's standing too near you then you're *not* wondrously fortunate because you get a little spray of V.B. saliva all over your face. Not that this has happened to me recently as I've hardly been to school, I've just been bunking off to go to the house.

They'll be getting in touch with Cam any minute. Maybe it's just as well I'm going off to my mum's. No, it's weller than well. I can't wait. I wish it wasn't being done in all these daft stages. Elaine says I can go for a week. I can't see why I can't go for ever right away. All this packing and unpacking is starting to get on my nerves.

Cam said she'd help me pack, but then she kept saying I didn't need this and I didn't need that – and *I* said it would be sensible to take nearly all my stuff seeing as I'd be staying there permanently soon.

Permanently was a very dramatic sort of word. It was like it bounced backwards and forwards between us long after I'd said it. As if it was knocking us both on the head.

Then Cam blinked hard and said, 'Right, yes, of course, OK,' in a quick gabble, shoving all my stuff in a suitcase, while *I* said, 'Perhaps it's a bit daft, and anyway, my mum will probably buy me all sorts of new stuff. Designer. Calvin Klein, Tommy Hilfiger—'

'NYDK, yes, yes, you keep saying.'

'DKNY! Honestly, you don't know anything, Cam,' I said, exasperated.

'I know one thing,' said Cam quietly. 'I'm going to miss you, kid.'

I swallowed hard. 'Well, I'll miss you too. I expect.' I hated the way she was looking at me. It wasn't *fair*. 'Fostering isn't, like, permanent,' I said. 'They told you that right at the beginning, didn't they?'

'They told me,' said Cam. She picked up one of my old T-shirts and hung onto it like it was a cuddle blanket. 'But I didn't get what it would feel like.'

'I'm sorry, Cam,' I said. 'I am. Really. But I've got to be with my mum.'

'I know,' said Cam. She hesitated. She looked down at the T-shirt as if I was inside it. 'But Tracy . . . don't get too upset if it doesn't quite work out the way you want.'

'It *is* working out!'

'I know, I know. And it's great that you're being reunited with your mum, but maybe you'll find it won't end up like a fairy story, happy ever after, for ever and ever.'

It will, it will. She just doesn't want it to.

'It *will* end happily ever after, you wait and see,' I said, pulling my T-shirt away from her and stuffing it in my suitcase with all the others.

'Tracy, I know—'

'You don't know anything!' I interrupted. 'You don't know my mum. You don't even know *me* properly. It's not like we've been together ages and ages. I don't see why you have to be so . . . so . . . so shaking your head and giving me all these little warnings about it not working out. You obviously think I'm so horrible and bad and difficult that my mum will get sick of me in two seconds.'

'I don't think that at *all*. And you're *not* horrible and bad and difficult. Well, you *are* – but you can be great too. It's just that even if you're the greatest kid in the whole world and behave beautifully with your mum it *still* might not work out. Your mum isn't used to kids.'

'Neither were you, but you took me on.' Ah! I had a sudden idea. 'You can take some other kid now.'

'I don't want some other kid,' said Cam. She put her arm round me. 'I want you.'

I could hardly breathe. I wanted to cuddle close and hang onto her and tell her . . . tell her all sorts of stupid things. But I *also* wanted to shove her hard and shout at her for spoiling my big chance to get back to my mum.

I wriggled away from her and went on packing my suitcase. 'If you *really* wanted me you'd have made far more fuss in the first place,' I said, tucking my scrubby old trainers

173

under my gungy chainstore denims. 'You'd have bought me decent clothes. And proper presents.'

'Oh Tracy, don't start,' said Cam, suddenly cross. She got up and started marching round my bat cave in an agitated fashion like she was a dog with fleas.

'You've hardly given me anything,' I said, cross too. 'I've never known anyone so stingy. And yet look at all the stuff my mum's given me.'

'A doll,' said Cam, picking it up. She held it at arm's length.

'Yes, but it's not like it's any old doll. It cost a fortune. It's not a little kid's doll, it's a collector's item. She gave it me like an ornament. Lots of grown-up ladies have doll collections. You wouldn't understand.' I sneered at Cam in her worn old plaid shirt and baggy jeans. 'You're not that sort of lady.'

'Thank God,' said Cam.

'I don't fit in here, Cam. Not with you. Or Jane and Liz and all your other stupid friends. I fit with my mum. Her and me. We're relatives. You're just my foster mum. You just get paid to look after me, that's all. I bet that's why you're making all the fuss, because you'll miss the cash when I'm gone.'

'Think that if you want, Tracy,' said Cam in this irritating martyr voice.

'It's true!'

'OK, OK,' said Cam, folding her arms.

'It *isn't* OK!' I said, stamping my foot. 'I don't know what you do with the money. It isn't like you spend it on me.'

'That's right,' said Cam, in this maddening there-there-I'll-agree-with-whatever-you-say-you-stupid-fool voice.

'It's *wrong* – and I'm sick of it,' I shouted. 'Do you know something? Even if it doesn't work out with my mum I still don't want to come back here. I'm sick of this boring old dump. I'm sick of you.'

'Well clear off then, you ungrateful little beast. I'm sick of you too!' Cam yelled, and she banged out of the bat cave in tears.

There. That's what she thinks of me. Well, see if I care. UNGRATEFUL. Why do I always have to be *grateful* to people?

Kids are always expected to be grateful grateful grateful. It's hateful being grateful. It's not fair. I'm supposed to be grateful to Cam for looking after me but I'm not allowed to look after myself. Though I could, easy-peasy. I'm supposed to be grateful for my yucky veggie meals (she hardly *ever* takes me to McDonald's) and my unstylish chainstore clothes (no wonder they pick on me at school) and my boring old books (honestly, have you *tried* reading *Little Women*? – who cares if Jo was Cam's all-time favourite book character?) and trips to museums (OK, I liked seeing the mummies and the little hunched-up dead man but all those pictures and pots were the *pits*).

If I could only earn my own money I could buy all the stuff I really need. It's not fair that kids aren't allowed to work. I'd be great flogging stuff down the market or selling ice creams or working in a nursery. If I could only get a job I could eat Big Macs and french fries every day and wear designer from top to toe, yeah, especially my footware, and buy all the videos and computer games I want and take a trip to Disneyland.

Yeah! I bet my mum will take me to Disneyland if I ask her.

It *is* going to end up like a fairy story. I'm going to live happily ever after.

I am.

Even if Football doesn't think so. I hate him.

No I don't. I quite like him in a weird sort of way. I'm worried about him. *He's* not going to live happily ever after.

I went to our house to say goodbye to Football and Alexander, seeing as I'm going to my mum's.

Alexander wasn't there. I didn't think Football was either. I went into the house and there was no sign of anyone – and no provisions in the cardboard fridge either. I checked upstairs and looked out of the window at the tree. My knickers were still up there. The tree seemed a long way from the window. We were all crazy. I looked down, my heart thudding when I thought of Alexander. And then I screamed.

Someone was lying spread-eagled on the mattress. Someone bigger than Alexander. Someone wearing last year's football strip.

'Football!' I yelled, and hurtled back inside the house and out the back window and down the overgrown garden to the mattress. 'Football, Football, Football!' I cried, standing over his still sprawled body.

He opened his eyes and peered at me. 'Tracy?'

'Oh, Football, you're alive!' I cried, going down on my knees beside him.

'Ooh Tracy, I didn't know you cared,' he said, giggling.

I gave him a quick flick round the face. 'Quit that, idiot! Did you fall?'

'I'm just having a little lie down.'

I touched his arm. He was icy cold and his shirt was damp. 'Have you been here all *night*? You're crazy.'

'Yeah. That's me. Mad. Nuts. Totally out of it.'

'You are,' I said. 'You'll make yourself ill.'

'So what?'

'You won't be able to play football.'

'Sure I will.' He reached for his football at the edge of the mattress and threw it in the air. He tried to catch it but it bounced off his fingertips into the undergrowth.

Football swore, but didn't bother to get up. He lay where he was, flicking his dad's lighter on and off, on and off above his head. His co-ordination was lousy.

'You'll drop it and set yourself alight, you nutter. Stop it!'

'I'm warming myself up.'

'*I'll* warm you up.' I rubbed his icy arms and blue fingers. He held onto my hands, pulling me down beside him.

'What are you playing at?'

'Keep me company, eh, Tracy?'

'Can't we go in the warm?'

'I like it cold. Kind of numb.'

'Yeah – you're a numskull,' I said, but I lay down properly on the smelly old mattress.

It was so damp it seemed to be seeping  right through my back. 'I feel as if I'm being pulled down down down into the earth,' I said, wriggling.

'Yeah, let's stay down here together, eh? You and me in our own little world.'

I wondered about staying in this garden home for ever. Football and I would lie on our backs on the mattress like marble statues on a tomb and ivy would grow over us and squirrels would scamper past and birds nest in our hair and we wouldn't move a muscle, totally out of it.

But I want to be *in* it. I've got to the fairytale ending of my story. I'm all set to live happily ever after.

'Come on! Getting-up time! Let's play football.' I found the ball and bounced it at Football's head to bring him to his senses.

Football scrambled to his feet, swearing. He tried to grab the ball but I was too quick for him.

'I'm Tracy Beaker the Great and I'm running like the wind, and wow, look, *I've* got the ball!'

'Get out of it, *I'm* the greatest,' Football said. He tried to tackle me. His great boot kicked me instead of the ball.

'Ooowww! My ankle! You're the greatest biggest booted bully!'

'I'm sorry.' Football peered at my leg. 'Red,' he said, sounding puzzled.

'It's blood!'

'I didn't mean to,' Football mumbled.

'Oh yes,' I said, busy dabbing and mopping. 'Like you had no control whatsoever over your foot, it just developed this wicked will of its own and gouged a huge lump out of my flesh. It *hurts*!'

'I'm really really sorry, Tracy.' Football looked like he was nearly in tears. 'I'd never try to hurt you. You mean a lot to me, kid. Tracy?' He tried to put his arm round me.

I dodged underneath. 'Get off me!'

'Go on, you know you like me too.'

'Not when you're all damp and smelly. Yuck, you don't half need a bath, Football.'

'Don't nag at me. You sound like my mum. You're all the same. Nag moan whine whinge. Think I really care about you? You're mad. I don't want you one little bit. No-one wants you, Tracy Beaker.'

'My *mum* wants me!' I yelled.

I roared it so loudly the birds flew into the air in terror and people stopped dead in their tracks all over town and cars ran into each other and aeroplanes stalled in the sky.

'MY MUM WANTS ME!'

Mum's Home (Again)

Mum's home was a little bit different this time. Mum was a little bit different too. She was very pale underneath her make-up and she wore dark glasses and when we had our big hug hello she smelt stale underneath her lovely powdery scent. Her home smelt too, of cigarettes and a lot of booze. The curtains were still drawn.

I went to open them but Mum stopped me. 'Not too much daylight, sweetie,' she said, holding her forehead.

'Have you got a hangover, Mum?'

'What? No, of course not. Don't be silly, darling. No, I have this nasty migraine. I get them a lot. I'm bothered with my nerves.' She lit a cigarette and drew on it desperately.

'I don't make you nervous, do I, Mum?' I asked.

'Don't be so silly, sweetie,' said Mum. 'Now, see what your mum's got for you.'

'Another present!'

I hoped it wasn't chocolates again because I was feeling a bit sick. I was bothered with my nerves too. I take after my mum.

The present was a big parcel, but soft and floppy. *Not* chocolates.

'Is it a rag doll or a teddy?' I asked cautiously, feeling for heads or paws under the wrapping paper.

'Have a look.'

So I carefully undid the wrapping paper, Ultra-neatly this time, and discovered an amazing pair of combat trousers – with a label to die for!

'Oh wow! Great!' I said, whirling around, clutching the trousers, making each leg dance up and down.

'You like them?' said Mum.

'I *love* them. They're seriously cool. Shame I haven't got a really great jacket to go with them.'

'You're not hinting, by any chance?' said Mum, smiling.

I decided to hint for all I was worth. 'Of

course, my old trainers are going to spoil the whole sharp look,' I said. 'I need a pair of Nikes to kind of complete the outfit.'

'I'm not made of money,' said Mum. 'I think it's a bit rich – ha, a bit *poor* – that Cam gets paid a fortune to look after you, while I won't get a penny.'

'Still, I'm worth it, aren't I, Mum?' I said, whirling closer.

'Of course you are, sweetheart,' she said. 'Do give over thumping about though, you're doing my head in.'

I made her a strong black coffee and she sat on her sofa and sipped. Then she lay back on the cushion and stayed very still, not answering when I spoke to her. It looked like she'd fallen asleep, though I couldn't see her eyes for the dark glasses.

I circled the sofa slowly, looking at her, still not quite able to believe she was really my mum and we were with each other and we were going to be together for ever and ever. I'd made it up so many times that it was hard to believe it was real now. I kept staring and staring until my eyes went blurry but Mum didn't vanish: she stretched out in her sparkly sweater and leopardskin pants, so splendid, so special, so sweet to me. So sleepy too.

She wouldn't wake up. I loved to look at her but it started to get just a weeny bit boring. I went for a wander round the room, emptying the ashtrays into the wastebin and taking the glass and empty bottle out into the kitchen like a real Mummy's Little Helper. I had a peer in all her kitchen cupboards and the fridge but there weren't many snacks to nibble on, just frozen packets and diet stuff and booze.

I played hopscotch across the kitchen tiles for a bit and then I took off my trainers and played ice skating and then I shuffled back to the living room hopefully because I heard Mum sigh, but she'd just turned over and was still playing Sleeping Beauty. One of her black suede high heels had fallen off. I tried it on, and then carefully eased the other one off her foot too. I had my very own pair of high heels. I clonked about the living room for a bit to get my balance and then staggered off to her bedroom to admire myself in her wardrobe mirror.

I had a little peep in her wardrobe – and

before I could stop myself I was
dressing up in her mohair sweater and
her leather skirt. I looked almost like
my mum! I pretended to be her. I
promised my little Tracy I would always
love her and be with her for ever no
matter what.

Then *my* mum came into the bedroom,
rubbing her eyes and lighting her fag. 'So
that's where you've got to. Did I doze off for
five minutes? Hey, you cheeky baggage,
you're all togged up in my clothes! Take them
off! And watch that skirt, it cost a fortune.'

'Oh Mum, please, let me keep them on, just
for a second. I look so beautiful. Just like you,'
I begged. I rootled through her wardrobe. 'Oh
wow! I love your red dress. Can I try that on
too? And the purply thing? And what's
this black dress? Oh, it's dead sexy.'

'Tracy!' said Mum, giggling. 'OK
then. Come here, we'll play dressing up.'

It was MAGIC. Mum got me all
beautifully dressed up – though we
both fell about laughing when I tried
the black dress on because it came right
down to my belly button and I wasn't
just topless, I was very nearly bottomless too.

I ended up back in the mohair sweater and the leather skirt and Mum's suede high heels, and she made me up like a real grown-up lady and did my hair too. I strutted about like a fashion model and Mum joined in too, showing me how to do the walk properly, and I did my best to copy her. Then we played being rock stars and Mum was incredible – she could do all the bouncy bits and the little dances and everything, and she could really sing too. She has this amazing voice. She said she was queen of the karaoke night down the pub and everyone always begged her to sing.

'It's karaoke night tonight, actually,' she said.

'Oh great! Can we go? I'd love to see you being the star singer.'

'You can't go to the pub, Tracy, you're just a little kid.'

'I went with Cam and Jane and Liz once. We sat in the garden and I had a cocktail called a St Clement's and three packets of salt and vinegar crisps.'

'Yes, well, my pub hasn't got a garden and you can't sit out in the evening anyway. No, I was wondering about *me* going.'

'But . . . what about me?'

'Well, you can go to bed. I'll make you up a bed on the sofa and then you can watch telly for a bit as a treat.'

'You're going to leave me on my own?' I said, my heart thumping.

'Oh come on, Tracy, you're not a baby,' said Mum.

'I don't really like being left on my own,' I said. 'Mum, can't you stay and play with me?'

'For goodness' sake, Tracy. I've been playing daft games with you for hours! You can't begrudge me an hour or two with my friends down the pub. A couple of drinks, that's all. I'll be home long before closing time, I swear. Anyway, you'll be asleep by then.'

'What if I can't get to sleep?'

'Then watch the telly, like I said.'

'I don't think there's anything good on tonight.'

'Well, watch a video! Honestly – kids! You can tell you've been spoilt. You're going to have to learn to do as you're told if we're going to get along.'

'You're not supposed to leave me.'

'I'll do what I like, young lady. Don't take that tone with me! Do you want me to send you back to the Children's Home?'

I shook my head. I couldn't speak.

'Well then. Don't you get stroppy with me. Out of my clothes and into your jim-jams, right?'

She started treating me like I was a sulky little toddler. She even washed all the make-up off my face herself and then she played silly games with the flannel, pretending it was a bird pecking off my nose. I laughed a lot and went along with the whole charade because I hoped if I was really really good and sweet and cute she'd change her mind and stay home.

But she didn't.

She left me.

She gave me a kiss and tucked me up on the sofa and waved her fingers at me and then she put on her coat and walked off in her black suede high heels.

I called after her. I said she didn't have to play with me, I'd lie watching telly as quiet as a mouse, I'd do anything she wanted, just so long as she stayed with me.

I don't know whether she heard or not. She still went anyway. So I was left. All on my own.

I got angry at first. She wasn't supposed to leave me. If I phoned Elaine and told tales Mum would be in serious trouble. But I didn't want to phone Elaine. I knew who I wanted to phone – but I couldn't. I couldn't let on to Cam that it had all gone wrong so quickly.

Then I got angry with myself. Had it really gone wrong? I didn't know why I was getting in such a state. So what if my mum had slipped out for a drink or two? Lots and lots and lots of mums went down the pub, for goodness' sake. And my mum had been wonderful to me. She'd bought me fantastic new trousers and she'd played games with me for ages. She was the best mum in the world and so why couldn't I just lie back on her lovely comfy sofa and watch telly and have a good time till she came back?

I knew why. I was scared. It reminded me of all those other times when I was little and she left me then. I couldn't remember them properly. I just remembered crying in the dark and no-one coming. The dark seemed to stretch out for ever into space and I was all by myself and Mum was never ever coming back for me.

I felt that way now, even though I knew it was stupid. I scrunched up in a tiny ball on the sofa and I thought about Cam and I wanted her so badly. No, I wanted my mum so badly. I was all muddled. I just felt so lonely, and after a long while I slept but when I woke up Mum still wasn't back even though the pubs had been shut for ages. I switched on the telly but it jabbered away too loudly in the silent flat so I shut it off quick and lay on the sofa, listening and listening, wondering what I would do if Mum never came back. And then when I'd very nearly given up altogether I heard footsteps and giggling and the key turning in the front door.

The light went on in the living room. I kept hunched down, my eyes squeezed shut.

'Whoops! I'd forgotten I'd tucked her up on the sofa!' Mum hissed. 'Funny little thing. Doesn't look a bit like me, does she? Oh dear. Come on, out we go. You'd better go home, sweetie. Yes, I know, but it can't be helped.'

There was a horrible male mumbling, a slurping sound, and more giggles from Mum.

'You naughty thing! No! Shh now, we'll wake the kid.'

I breathed as slowly and evenly as I could. The man was mumbling again.

'Oooh!' said Mum. 'Yes, I'd love to go to the races on Saturday. Great idea! Though ... well, my little Tracy will still be here. She can come too, can't she? She won't be any trouble, I swear.'

Mumble mumble, fumble fumble.

'I know it wouldn't be so much fun. What? I *see*. So we'd be staying the whole weekend? It does sound tempting. Go on, then, you've twisted my arm. I'll fix it.'

My eyes were still tight shut but I couldn't stop them leaking. It was OK. They didn't see. They weren't looking at me.

I was awake long before Mum in the morning. I had my bag all packed, ready. I wondered how she was going to break it to me, whether she'd tell me it straight or spin me some story.

It was the story. With a lot of spin on it. She came out with it at breakfast. I was amazed. It was the sort of stuff I made up when I was about six, the most pathetic never-ever tale about bumping into a film producer down the pub and how he was bowled over by her and he was giving her this big acting chance and he needed her to meet up with all his big-film-guy cronies at the weekend, *this* weekend, and she knew this weekend was the most special ever because we were supposed to be together but on the other hand we could spend every other weekend of our lives together but this weekend was her one chance of finding fame and fortune and I did understand, didn't I, sweetie?

I understood. I looked at my mum – really really looked at her – and I understood everything. I didn't have it out with her. I just made my lips turn up and said that of course I understood and I wished her luck. She went a bit  watery-eyed then, so that her last-night's mascara smudged, and she reached across the table so that her black nylon nightie dripped in my cornflakes and she gave me a big hug. I breathed in her warm powdery smell one last time. Then she gave me a little pat, ran her fingers through her rumpled hair, plucked at her soggy nightie, and said she'd better go and have a bath and get herself all prettied up and what did I want to do today, darling?

I knew what I was going to do. As soon as Mum was in the bath I went to her handbag, nicked some money, picked up my bag and scarpered.

I left her a note.

The note got a bit smeared and blotchy but there wasn't time to write it out again. I needed to leave her a message so she'd know I wasn't a thief.

It's OK, Mum. I know you don't really want me. I'll be fine. I've taken ten pounds for travelling but I'll save up and send it you back, honest. Thanks for everything.
With lots of love
from Tracy
xxx

Then I walked out, closing her front door ever so slowly so she wouldn't hear. Then I ran. And ran and ran and ran.

I didn't know where I was going. I didn't really have any place to go.

I could go back to Cam but she probably wouldn't want me back now. Not after all the things I said. I came out with all sorts of stuff. Things that I didn't want to write in this book. Things to hurt her. It was so hard choosing between Cam and my mum so I made it easy by doing such dreadful things to Cam that she'd never ever want me back.

Only I made the wrong choice. Now I haven't got anywhere to go.

Yes I have.

I know where I'm going.

The Smashed Home

I found my way, easy-peasy. I got a train and then a bus and I had lunch in McDonald's. It was great.

I don't need ANYONE to look after me. I don't need my mum. I don't need Cam. I can look after myself, no bother at all. And it isn't as if I haven't got a roof over my head. I've got a whole house. All to myself.

Well. Sometimes I share it. Someone had been doing some serious housekeeping. There were cans of Coke and Kit-kats in the 'fridge' in the kitchen, and a cardboard dustpan and brush that really worked – sort of. But the living room was the real picture. A brand new television, with a video recorder too. A table with a permanent embroidered tablecloth and place settings. Three chairs, all different sizes, like the Three Bears story – a big one for

Football, a medium size for me and the littlest for Alexander. Alexander himself, sitting on a special rug, was making yet more Ideal Home delights.

'Tracy!' he said, his eyes lighting up.

It felt so good that someone was pleased to see me that I gave his bony little shoulder a squeeze. 'Hi, Chippendale,' I said.

Alexander peered at me. 'Chip . . . ?' he said. 'Aren't they those big oily men who take off all their clothes? Are you teasing me?'

'Hey, Alexander, you're the one who's supposed to be the brainbox. I mean Chippendale as in *furniture*. He was some old guy in history who made posh chairs, right?'

'Oh, I *see*,' said Alexander, busily slotting one piece of cardboard into two grooves.

'Another chair, maestro?'

'No, I'm making a bookcase this time. I thought it would be great to have a bookcase. So we could keep our books in it. I could keep my *Alexander the Great* book here. And you could keep your diary in it.'

'*What* diary?'

'Well, whatever you write in your big fat purple book.'

'If you've been peeking in my big fat purple book I'll poke your eyes out!'

'I wouldn't dare, Tracy. Oops!' Alexander rolled his eyes. 'No more dares, eh?'

'Not for the moment, anyway. So. What are you doing here, Alexander? I thought you weren't going to come any more.'

'I know. My dad will kill me when he finds out I've been bunking off again. But when I went back to school I limped for all I was worth but Mr Cochran, he's the games master, he said I was a pathetic little weed and I had to play anyway. So I tried. And I got pushed over. And it hurt a lot so my eyes watered. And then everyone said I was crying and that just proved how weedy and wet I am and someone said "Gherkin is a jerkin" and they all started chanting it and—'

'I get the general picture,' I said. 'Still. It's not like it's the end of the world.'

'It kind of feels that way to me.'

'Some silly stuck-up kids call you names. And one of the teachers picks on you. Oh boo hoo! That's *nothing*. You want to hear what some of the kids at my school call me. And Miss Vomit Bagley has *really* got it in for me. She picks on me all the time – when I'm there. I bet some of your teachers think you're the bee's knees because you're a right old swotty brainbox.'

'Well . . .' Alexander considered. 'Yes, Mr Bernstein and Mr Rogers like me, and Mrs Betterstall says I'm—'

'Yeah yeah yeah. See? And I bet your horrible old dad really cares about you or he wouldn't go on so. I haven't even *got* a dad, have I?'

'You've got a mum though,' said Alexander, slotting the last cardboard shelf into place. He stood the bookcase up for me to admire – and then saw my face. He suddenly remembered. 'Oh! Your mum!'

'What about her?' I said fiercely.

'You were meant to be staying with her.'

'Yeah. Well. I got a bit fed up, if you must know.'

'Didn't she buy you all that stuff you wanted?'

'Yes, she did. She bought me heaps and heaps. Look!' I did a twirl in my new combat trousers.

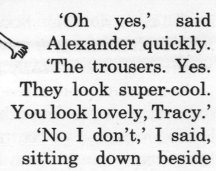

'Oh yes,' said Alexander quickly. 'The trousers. Yes. They look super-cool. You look lovely, Tracy.'

'No I don't,' I said, sitting down beside him. 'I look funny. My mum says.'

'Well, you *are* funny,' said Alexander. 'That's good, isn't it? Tracy . . . what went wrong with you and your mum?' He patted my knee timidly. 'Didn't she like you?'

I jerked away from him. 'Nothing went wrong. I told you. My mum's crazy about me. She can't make enough of a fuss of me. But after a bit I just thought, hey, who needs this? I don't need *her*.'

'Ah! You need *Cam*, don't you?' said Alexander, looking immensely pleased. 'I'm right, aren't I?'

'No!' I folded my arms. 'You're wrong wrong wrong. I don't need her.'

Alexander still wouldn't be squashed. 'Well, you need me. And Football. We're your friends.'

'I don't need you either. I don't need no-one.'

'That's a double negative. If you don't need *no*-one it means you need *some*one, don't you see?'

'I see that you're the most annoying little Smartypants and it's no wonder everyone picks on you. You really get on my nerves.' I gave him a push. Then I gave his bookcase a push too.

'Watch my bookcase!' said Alexander.

'It's a rubbish bookcase,' I said, and my fist went thump thump thump.

'My bookcase!' Alexander wailed.

'It's *my* house and I don't want your stupid bookcase in it, see?'

'I'll make one specially for you,' Alexander offered, trying to slot his shelves back into place.

'I don't want you to make anything for me. I don't need *anything*. It's my house and I don't want a single rubbish thing in it. I'm sick of homes, I'm sick of stuff. I want it to be *empty*.' I smashed his stupid bookcase flat and then I whirled round the living room, breaking up all Alexander's furniture.

'Don't, Tracy! Don't! Don't!' Alexander shouted.

I smashed. Alexander screamed. Football

suddenly came haring into the house.

'What is it? What's going on? You two all right?' he said. He looked about him. 'Who's turned the place over?'

'Oh Football, thank goodness!' said Alexander, clinging to him. 'Stop Tracy. She's wrecking everything. Even my new bookcase.'

'Sounds a good idea to me,' said Football, shaking Alexander off. 'Yeah, let's have a bit of fun, right, Tracy? What you doing here anyway? Didn't your mum want you after all?'

'You shut up, Football.' I glared at him. 'Your mum doesn't want you. And neither does your precious dad.'

I had to hurt everyone to show I didn't need any of them. So they couldn't hurt me. 'How's your dad, Football? How's your dad, Alexander?' I said.

'Quit it,' said Football.

'Why don't we *all* quit it?' Alexander begged. 'Let's make friends and . . . and mend the furniture.'

203

'Shut up, Gherkin,' said Football. 'Who cares about your boring old furniture?' He flicked his dad's lighter, waving it at the crumpled bookcase.

'Stop it!' Alexander shouted.

'Don't tell *me* to stop anything!' said Football, flicking again.

The flame leapt at the cardboard, singeing it for a second and then suddenly flaming.

'You're *crazy*!' said Alexander.

'Shut up,' said Football, stamping just in time.

'You'll set yourself alight! You'll set the whole place on fire,' Alexander cried. 'You mustn't ever ever ever play with fire.'

'Oooh, aren't I *naughty*!' said Football, imitating Alexander's high-pitched voice.

I giggled and Football grinned at me.

'Let's liven this dump up, eh, Tracy?' he said. He threw the lighter to me. 'Your turn.'

'Don't, Tracy. Don't be so *stupid*,' Alexander begged.

'I dare you, Tracy,' said Football.

I swallowed, the lighter hot in my hand.

'You mustn't, Tracy. You can't start that

awful Dare Game again. *Please* don't dare. You know it's crazy!'

Of course I knew it was crazy. But I *felt* crazy.

I suddenly flicked the lighter and held it to my small cardboard-box chair. A sudden flame leapt in the air. I went to stamp it out – but I wasn't big enough.

'Don't! You'll burn yourself!' Alexander screamed.

Football tried to elbow me out the way but I was determined to win this dare. I seized the flattened bookcase and beat hard at the flame – and it went out.

'There! I did it! I won the dare!' I yelled, leaping around and punching the air.

'That's great, kid. You and me, we're the greatest,' yelled Football.

'You're the greatest *idiots*,' said Alexander tearfully.

'You always try to spoil everything, Alexander,' I said. 'Go on. It's your turn now. I dare you.'

'No!'

'Come on, you've got to, if I dare you.' I

tried to pass him the lighter but he put his fists behind his back.

'I'm not going to. It's mad and dangerous,' said Alexander.

'He hasn't got the bottle,' said Football, sneering.

'Go on, Alexander,' I said. 'You felt great last time after you jumped out the window.'

Alexander shook his head violently. 'I was mad then. What if the mattress hadn't been there? I'd have been killed. I'm not taking any more chances.'

'Coward! Chicken!'

'Cluck cluck cluck!'

'You can cluck and call me all the names you like,' said Alexander. 'I'm still not going to do it.'

'Because you're too scared,' I said.

'You're only doing it because *you're* scared,' said Alexander. 'Scared Football won't think you as tough as he is. Only he's scared too.'

'*I'm* scared?' said Football, outraged. 'Who am I scared of, Gherkin?' He took the lighter from me and stood in front of Alexander, flicking it on and off, on and off. 'Am I scared of you, is that it? Or scared of skinny little

Tracy? I'm not scared of anyone, you stupid jerk.'

Alexander still didn't give up. 'You're scared your dad doesn't care about you any more, that's what you're scared of.'

I couldn't help nodding. 'Ah! He's got you there, Football.'

'No he hasn't. I'm not scared. I don't give a toss about my dad any more,' said Football.

'Yes you do,' said Alexander relentlessly. 'That's why you act crazy – because it's *driving* you crazy.'

'You think you know it all but you don't know anything,' Football shouted. 'Now button that lippy little mouth of yours or I'll set light to *you*.'

'You wouldn't dare!' Alexander squealed.

'Shut *up*, Alexander,' I said.

'I'll dare anything,' Football declared, waving his lighter round wildly.

Alexander snatched a cardboard shelf and held it up like a shield. Football lunged forward, expecting Alexander to dodge backwards. Alexander stood still – and there was a sudden flare of flame. Alexander stared, open-mouthed, unable to move.

I snatched the sizzling cardboard, threw it to the floor, and stamped on it.

'*Stop* it, Football!' I shouted. 'This is getting too scary now.'

'You can't stop me. No-one can stop me,' said Football. 'I'll show you, Tracy Beaker. I'll show you, Gherkin.'

'Why do you have to bully us? We're your *friends*,' Alexander said desperately.

'I don't need no friends,' said Football.

'No, Football, you can't say "no" friends because it's a double neg— aaaaah!' Alexander was cut off in mid-grammatical quibble because Football grabbed him by the front of his shirt with one hand. His *other* hand was still waving in the air, clutching the lighter. Alexander suddenly made a grab for it – snatched it – and then threw it wildly. It sailed right across the room and out the window.

'My lighter! My dad's lighter!' Football yelled, letting go of Alexander in his shock.

'Oh help! I didn't mean it to go out the window. I didn't know I could throw that far!' said Alexander.

'I'll kill you, Gherkin!' said Football, his eyes popping, his face purple.

'Run!' I yelled to Alexander. 'Get out the house, quick!'

Alexander ran – but he wasn't quick enough. Football caught him before he was even out the door. He raised his big fist ready to give him a punch – but I got there first. I shoved Alexander as hard as I could out the way and grabbed Football from behind.

'Don't you dare, you big bully!' I yelled.

Alexander collapsed in a heap and started whimpering. Football and I took no notice, too busy fighting.

'Get *off*, Tracy! Ouch! Don't you dare kick me!'

'I'll dare anything, same as you! You think you're so big and tough but I'll show you!' I kicked him again, wishing my trainers were socking great Doc Martens.

'You little whatsit!' said Football, nearly knocking me over.

I hit out hard, catching him right where it hurts most.

'Oooooomph!' said Football, doubling up. 'No wonder your mum doesn't want you. No-one could ever want you, Tracy Beaker.'

'No-one wants you either! Especially not your precious dad. He doesn't give a toss about you. It's obvious.'

'You shut up!' He wrestled me to the floor.

'*You* shut up, you stupid snot-nosed bully,' I gasped, kicking out from under him. 'That's all you can do, isn't it? Hit out at people. You think you're so great but you're useless. You're even useless at football.'

'Shut up or I'll bang your head on the floor!'

'You try!'

Football tried. It hurt like hell. So I spat hard. Upwards, right in his face.

Football stared down at me, wondrously spattered. 'You wouldn't dare do that again!'

I did.

'You dirty little monkey!' he said, banging my head again.

'It'll be right in your eye next!' I warned.

'I'll spit right back, *I'm* warning *you*!'

'Go on, then. I dare you!'

He dared all right. It was totally disgusting. I went to spit back but my mouth was too dry. 'I've run out of spit! It's not fair. Wait!' I tried but only managed the merest dribble.

'That was a bit pathetic!' said Football.

'You just wait. Oooh! I keep blowing raspberries instead of spitting.'

'Can't even spit!' Football jeered.

'Just give me a few seconds.'

'So I'm going to hang around waiting?' said Football, leaning back.

'Come *here*, Football!' I commanded, trying to summon up more spit by smacking my lips and sucking in my cheeks.

'You look like you're about to give me a great big kiss with your lips like that!' Football grinned.

'Yuck!' I couldn't help giggling at the very idea.

'You watch out or I'll kiss you!' said Football.

'No you don't!' I said, trying to wriggle free. 'Hey, come on, get off me, you big lump.'

Football did as he was told this time. The fight was over.

'I didn't hurt you, did I?' Football asked, picking me up and brushing me down.

'Oh *no*, whacking great kicks on the shin and bashes on the bonce don't hurt a *bit*!'

'You twit,' said Football. 'Hey, we made a poem!' He looked at Alexander. 'And you're a nit! There. You're in the poem too. Hey, Gherkin, we've stopped fighting. You can get up now.'

'It's OK, Alexander. Alexander? Are you all right?'

'N-o-o-o!' said Alexander, still lying on the floor, his leg stuck out at an odd angle.

'I didn't hurt *you*, did I?' said Football, looking stricken.

'It was – when – Tracy – knocked me – over. My *leg*!' Alexander gasped.

'Oh help!' I said. 'Stand up, Alexander, and let me have a look.'

'I can't. I really can't.'

I bent over him. I saw his leg. 'Oh no, Alexander! I've really hurt your leg! It's all bendy. How terrible! What am I going to do?'

'I think – better – get me – to hospital,' Alexander mumbled.

I tried to help him up. Alexander groaned with the pain.

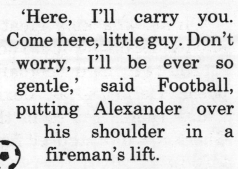

'Here, I'll carry you. Come here, little guy. Don't worry, I'll be ever so gentle,' said Football, putting Alexander over his shoulder in a fireman's lift.

'Oh Alexander,' I said, holding his hand. '*Please* be all right. I can't stand it if I've hurt you. You're my best friend in all the world. Please please please get better!'

Alexander's Real Home

We took Alexander to hospital. Football was willing to carry him the whole way but I still had some money from Mum's wallet so we took a taxi.

The taxi driver sighed when he saw Alexander. 'You kids been rough-housing?' he said, shaking his head.

Alexander looked delighted to be thought capable of roughing up a house. He was very brave. He was obviously in terrible pain, his face greeny-white, his fringe sticking to his sweaty forehead, but he didn't cry at all.

We waited with him at the hospital until he was whisked away in a wheelchair to the X-ray department.

'We'd better get going then,' said Football. 'They've phoned for his parents. I don't fancy meeting up with them. Especially the dad.'

'But we've got to wait to see if Alexander's all right!'

'Of course he'll be all right. He's in hospital,' said Football. He looked round the bleak orange waiting room and shuddered. 'I hate hospitals. They give me the creeps. I'm off.' He stood up. 'Come on, Tracy.'

'No. I'm waiting.'

'He'll be all right. It's just a broken leg. The nurse said.'

'How would you feel if you'd "just" broken your leg, Football?' I asked.

'Well. It would be tragic for me, seeing as it would affect my game. But Alexander's hardly going to bother, is he?' Football sat down again, sighing. 'I hate hospitals.'

'So you keep saying.'

'The way they look. All them long corridors and lots of doors with scary things going on behind them.'

'So close your eyes.'

'I can still smell I'm in hospital.' He sniffed and pulled a terrible face. 'It's making me feel sick.'

'How do you think Alexander feels *behind* one of the scary doors?' I said severely.

Football hunched down lower on his plastic chair. 'He's a weird little chap,' he said. 'He breaks his leg – well, you break it for him – and he hardly makes a sound. I've seen really tough nuts in agony on the football pitch, effing and blinding, even sobbing. Not old Alexander. He's really . . . brave?'

'I didn't *mean* to break his leg!'

'Yeah, I know, but I still think it's mad to hang around here. His mum and dad aren't going to be too pleased with you.'

'It was just one little push. I wasn't trying to hurt him, I was simply trying to get him out the way. I can't bear it that it's all my fault.' I started crying, snivelling and snorting like a baby – even though I never ever cry.

Football looked all round, embarrassed. 'Don't, Tracy, people are staring,' he hissed, giving me a nudge.

I went on crying noisily.

'Here, haven't you got a hankie?'

I shook my head, past caring that I had tears dripping down my face and a very runny nose.

Football darted across the room. I thought it had got too much and he was running away – but he dashed into the toilet and came back with a wad of loo-roll.

'Here,' he said, dabbing at my face. 'Don't cry so, Tracy. It wasn't really your fault at all. It was mine. I was the one who really lost it back at the house. I was out my mind setting all that stuff on fire.' He paused. 'Do you think I'm really crazy, Tracy?'

'Yes!' I said, blowing my nose. Then I relented. 'No, not really. Just a little bit bonkers.'

'Do you think I should get some kind of treatment?'

'You're fine, Football. It's Alexander we've got to worry about right now. I just don't get it. One little push, he falls over and breaks his leg. Yet when he falls off the roof he doesn't so much as break his big toe. He bobs up again as right as rain. He's a marvel, little Alexander.' I gave my face another mop. 'He *is* going to be all right, isn't he, Football?'

'Of course he is. It's only a broken leg.'

'Yes, but it might have been *badly* broken. It looked all funny and sticky-out in the wrong place. What if they can't set it properly? What if *infection* sets in? And his leg goes all mouldy and maggoty and has to be cut off?'

'Shut *up*, Tracy. That couldn't happen. Could it?'

'We didn't even notice. We were too busy fighting,' I wailed.

'You're a fierce little fighter, Tracy,' said Football.

'I'm going to give up fighting now. I hate it that Alexander got hurt.'

I sighed, wondering exactly what they were doing to Alexander. Football sighed too. We took it in turns. I fidgeted. Football fidgeted.

I stood up to stretch my legs – and nearly bumped into a couple who came rushing into the waiting room. The man was very big and bossy-looking with a briefcase. The lady was small and timid with a little twitchy mouse face. I didn't need three guesses to work out who they were. I whizzed back to my seat sharpish.

'I believe our son Alexander has been brought into Casualty,' the man said to a nurse.

'Please can we see him? Is he really all right?' the woman said, nearly in tears.

They were led along the corridor. Football let out a huge sigh. So did I.

'Time to get going, Tracy,' said Football.

I knew it was the wisest option. But I *had* to wait to see if Alexander was all right, even if it meant being beaten up by Briefcase Guy for injuring his son. Maybe I almost wanted to get into serious trouble with Alexander's parents. I felt I deserved it.

Football thought this was crazy – but he stayed too.

We waited and we waited and we waited. And waited some more. And then suddenly we heard Alexander's little piping voice nattering nineteen to the dozen and there he was in the wheelchair being pushed by his dad, with his mum running along beside him. His leg was propped up and covered in plaster.

'Alexander! How *are* you?' I said, charging up to him.

'Tracy! And Football! You waited for me all this time!' Alexander said excitedly. 'Mum, Dad, these are my friends.'

'Alexander's been telling us all about you,' said his mum.

'Yes, we should really give all of you a severe telling-off,' said his dad ominously.

'I *told* you we should have scarpered,' Football muttered.

'It was my fault,' I said. I meant to sound bold and brave but my voice went all high and squeaky so they didn't hear me properly.

'It's very silly to play truant. I'm sure you'll be in as much trouble with your schools as Alexander is with his,' said his dad, wagging his finger at Football and me. 'But I suppose I'm pleased you've all made friends. Alexander's always found it so hard to make friends because he's so shy.'

'You've been such good friends too,' said his mum. 'Alexander's told us all about his accident – how you were so kind and sensible when he tripped over. Other children might have run away and left him but you picked him up and looked after him and got him to the hospital. We're so grateful to you.'

Football and I shifted from one foot to the

other. We looked at Alexander. He grinned back at us.

'Alexander's our best ever friend,' I said.

'Yeah. He's our mate,' said Football. 'So – you're OK now, right?'

'Does he *look* all right?' I said, elbowing Football impatiently.

Football shrugged. 'I suppose that sounded a bit dumb,' he admitted. 'Seeing as he's in plaster almost up to his bum. Hey, poetry again!'

'You didn't sound at *all* dumb, Football,' said Alexander. 'Well, you couldn't literally *sound* dumb, but anyway. I *am* OK now. I've just fractured my tibia.'

'But you've hurt your leg!' said Football.

'Ultra-dumb!' I said. 'The tibia's a bone in his leg. And you've got a bone in your head, Football.'

'But you won't have to stay in a wheelchair for ever?' said Football.

'Oh no, dear,' said Alexander's mum. 'This is just while we're in the hospital. Alexander should be able to hobble about, using a crutch.'

'But I won't be able to walk properly for six whole weeks until the plaster comes off,' said Alexander.

'Six whole weeks! That's awful,' said Football.

'No, it's not, it's brilliant,' said Alexander, eyes shining. 'I won't be able to play games.'

'Really, Alexander,' said his dad, sighing impatiently.

'I'd die if I couldn't play football for six weeks!' said Football. 'I've been doing my nut stuck here for hours and hours not being able to kick my ball about.'

Alexander's dad nodded approvingly. 'How on earth did you two boys become chums?' he said.

'Do you go to Alexander's school?' his mum asked.

'They don't *go* to school, that's the point,' said Alexander's dad. 'What do your parents say?'

Football stuck out his lip. 'They don't care. Not my mum.' He paused. 'Nor my dad.'

Alexander leaned forward. 'I'm sorry I threw your precious lighter away, Football. Maybe you'll be able to find it in the garden.'

'Maybe. Still. It don't really matter. My dad's thrown *me* away, hasn't he?'

'What about you, Curly?' said Alexander's dad to me. 'Surely your mother and father

223

worry themselves sick about a little girl like you roaming the streets?'

'I haven't got a dad. And . . . and I don't expect I'll see much of my mum now,' I mumbled.

'Tracy's fostered,' Alexander explained.

They all stared at me. It's a wonder they didn't try to pat me on the head. I glared back.

'How about coming home with us for tea?' said Alexander's mum. 'You too, dear,' she added, nodding at Football a little warily.

'Yes, do come,' Alexander begged. 'My mum's mega-good at baking. Can we have chocolate cake, Mum?'

Football seemed keen on the idea. His own tea was usually just a trip down to the chippie. I was equally happy to go along with things seeing as I was starving hungry (it seemed months since I'd munched my Big Mac) and I didn't have any home of my own to go to.

We helped Alexander out onto the hospital steps. His dad went to get the car and his mum returned the wheelchair to the ward. Football and I supported Alexander, one on either side.

'You're a real gem for not telling your mum and dad it was all my fault,' I whispered, and I gave him a quick kiss on the cheek.

'It was my fault really,' said Football. 'I kept picking on you. But I won't any more, I swear.'

I could feel Alexander trembling. His face was peony red. 'You're both *really* my friends? You're not kidding me? This is so great!'

'*You're* great. Alexander the Great. Though you're also crazy, because your so-called friends have broken your leg,' I said.

'Yeah, you've had to spend hours and hours in hospital,' said Football.

'I like it in hospital,' said Alexander. 'It's been ever so interesting. The doctor showed me the X-ray and explained all about bones and it was fascinating. I think I might be a doctor when I grow up. So I suppose I'd really better stop bunking off school or I won't pass my exams. You have to get top grades to do Medicine. And school won't be anywhere near as bad if I'm off games for six whole weeks. Then you'll just have to push me hard again, Tracy, so I can break my other leg.'

'It was only a *little* push!'

'I know. I fell awkwardly. I *am* awkward.

That's why I'm so useless at football. My legs don't work the right way.'

'Your head's fine though,' said Football. 'Here, maybe I'll train you to do my famous Bonce-Buster so you can head the ball into the back of the net, easy-peasy.'

'That would be great,' said Alexander.

'That would be a blooming miracle,' I said.

Alexander and Football seemed to be bonding like Superglue. They chatted together in the car all the way to Alexander's home.

It was a *huge* house, one of those big black and white ones with criss-cross windows and neat little trees in tubs on either side of the front door. We hadn't realized quite how posh Alexander is. Things got even ritzier inside, with polished wood everywhere and matching sofas and chairs so vigorously tidied with cushions at exact angles that I only dared perch on the end of a hard chair with red and white stripes like toothpaste. Football stayed in the middle of the carpet standing on the outside edge of his trainers, his ball clasped close to his chest.

Alexander's mum got Alexander tucked up on an armchair with his bad leg propped on a footstool, and then she went away to make us all tea.

Alexander's dad gave us another one of his lectures about bunking off school and it all got seriously *heavy* and Alexander's face was as white and stiff as his plaster and Football rested his chin on his ball and I slid down the red and white stripes till my bottom was off the seat altogether. But then Alexander's mum came darting back with juice and home-made chocolate chip cookies which livened things up a little. I thought this was tea but it turned out this was just to keep us going until she'd cooked the *real* tea. She wanted Football and me to ring home to explain we were out for tea so no-one would worry. Football said his mum was at work so she wouldn't know – and added under his breath that she couldn't care less anyway.

'And what about your foster mother, Tracy, dear?' said Alexander's mum.

'She won't worry either, honestly,' I said firmly, though Alexander frowned at me.

Football had to drop his football to cope with his juice and cookie. His ball started rolling away so he gave it a nifty little kick up onto his trainer and back again.

'That was neat footwork, lad,' said Alexander's dad.

'Football's brilliant at football, Dad,' said Alexander proudly.

'I'm not bad,' Football mumbled, surprisingly bashful.

Alexander's dad started talking soccerspeak and after a few sentences Football joined in, and even demonstrated a few of his party tricks.

'Ooh dear, you will watch the ornaments, won't you?' said Alexander's mum, rushing back with bowls of crisps and saucers of Smarties.

'How about if we nip out into the garden, lad?' said Alexander's dad.

They went out through the French windows and almost immediately they were kicking the ball backwards and forwards like old pals.

Alexander peered at them a little wistfully. 'My dad likes Football,' he said.

'He likes you too, Alexander. Underneath.'

Alexander frowned and shook his head.

'Well, your mum definitely likes you.'

Alexander gave a little nod.

'And Football likes you. And *I* like you lots and lots. You do know that, don't you, Alexander?'

He seemed to. His head was bobbing about like he was little Noddy. 'I like you too, Tracy,' he said. 'And Football likes you ever so. He wants you to be his girlfriend.'

'Well. I'm not so sure about that,' I said. 'I *might* be his girlfriend. But I'll be your girlfriend too. If you want.'

'I do want! And – and your mum maybe can't always like you, but Cam does. It sounds like she really really cares about you.'

'No she doesn't. Anyway. I've blown it with her.'

I let myself think properly about Cam. All the stuff we did together. Daft things – like we'd dance to *Top of the Pops* and we'd shout out silly answers to the quizzes and we'd invent all sorts of new rude funny things to happen in all the soaps. And at night Cam would always tuck me up and ruffle my hair. And if I got scared at night – a bad dream or something – I could always go and climb into her bed. She'd moan and go, 'Oh Tracy Fidget

Bottom,' but she'd still cuddle me close. And though her food was so boring and healthy she took me to McDonald's too. And when I didn't get invited to Roxanne's party at school Cam said we could have our own private party just us two instead and we even had birthday cake.

It wasn't all Party Time of course. She could get dead narked sometimes and do a real moody on me – but then I suppose I could get a bit stroppy at times too. She didn't ever leave me alone at home. She didn't go off with any men. And one time when she was going to this very special concert with Jane and Liz and another friend was looking after me, Cam cancelled because I had this stomach upset. Imagine, she gave up going to a concert to mop up all my sick.

We got on OK, Cam and me. Like real friends. Sisters. Almost . . . almost like she was my mum.

It was weird. Alexander's mum fixed us this most magnificent tea ever, with pizza triangles and quiche fingers and little sausages and amazing chocolate cake and a sponge with pink icing too and ice cream with  special strawberry sauce – but when it was in my mouth it all tasted like Alexander's cardboard.

I couldn't chew properly because I had this big lump in my throat.

I wanted to go *home*.

Home Sweet Home

So I did go home. Alexander's dad insisted on driving me back to Cam's. He took Football too and they were still so busy nattering about football that they didn't notice I was getting quieter and quieter until I said nothing at all for the last five minutes.

I jumped out the car and waved goodbye to them and then I stared at the door and put my finger on the bell like I was actually pressing it. I heard the car drive off behind me. I stayed standing still with my finger hovering above the bell until my entire arm went numb. I rehearsed again and again in my head the things I was going to say. They all sounded stupid. I decided I couldn't say anything. I couldn't face seeing Cam because I was sure she'd push me away and tell me to clear off.

I would if she'd treated me the way I'd treated her.

I couldn't go back to my own mum. But I didn't have to wander the streets or crouch on cardboard furniture in our empty house. I knew the social services emergency number. I could summon Elaine within the hour and she'd be able to find me a bed for the night and get cracking on my case in the morning. Social workers don't ever give up on you. She'd grit her bunny teeth and do her level best to find me a new home.

But I didn't want a new home. I knew what I wanted even though it was too late. My finger suddenly stabbed all by itself and the bell rang and rang and rang. Then I heard footsteps running and the door flew open and there was Cam, her hair sticking up and her eyes red and her cardie on all the wrong buttons and yet she suddenly looked the most wonderful woman in the whole world.

'Cam!'

'Tracy!'

I leapt up at her and threw my arms round her neck and she hugged me tighter than tight and we held each other as if we could

never ever bear to let go. I was dimly aware
that Jane and Liz came out into the hall
and joined in the hug for a moment and then
they patted Cam on the back and ruffled my
hair and then let themselves out the door,
leaving Cam and me on our own. Hugging
and sniffing and snuggling. There was a little
damp patch seeping through my curls.

'Your tears are dripping on my head!' I
mumbled.

'Yours are making my shoulder all soggy,'
Cam sniffed.

'I'm not crying. It's hay fever,' I insisted.

'Idiot!' said Cam, hugging me harder.

'I thought you'd be really really cross with
me.'

'I *am* really really cross,' Cam said fondly.
'Where have you *been*? Elaine and I have
been going frantic ever since your mum rang
to say you'd done a bunk. The police are out
looking for you, I hope you realize.'

'Wow! What about telling the telly people?
I hope I'm on the news. Can we video it?'

'I'd better phone everyone in a minute to
say you're safe. So what happened, Tracy?
Your mum said she thought everything was
fine. She's very upset.'

'She couldn't wait to get shot of me!'

'That's not true. She really cares about you. You know she does. Look at all the presents.'

'Yeah. The presents. The doll and the chocolates and all that other stuff I didn't want.'

'It looks like you got some seriously cool combat trousers from her,' said Cam, holding me at arm's length and admiring my legs.

'I know. I like the clothes OK. And she was fun some of the time. She dressed me up in her stuff and it was great. But then she got fed up. She got fed up with *me*. She left me on my own while she went out drinking.'

'She shouldn't have done that,' said Cam, cuddling me close again. 'Was that when you ran away?'

'No, I cleared off this morning. She couldn't wait to get rid of me, Cam, really. So I thought I'd do her a favour and push off out of it.'

'And worry us all silly. Where did you *go*?'

'I got the train back.'

'Yes, OK, but where have you been all day? I've been round and round the town looking for you in the shops and McDonald's and everywhere I could think of. I even went to the school.'

'Are you crazy? As if I'd ever go there!'

236

'Well, where did you go then?' Cam put her hand under my chin so that I had to look up at her. 'Tell me, Tracy.'

I suddenly *wanted* to tell her. 'There's this house I go to. I've been there lots of times. When I should be at school, only don't get mad at me. I see some people there.'

All sorts of expressions were flickering across Cam's face as if she was a human kaleidoscope. 'Which house? Which people?' she said, struggling to sound casual, though her fingers were digging right into my shoulders.

'It's an empty house. No-one lives there. But these boys sometimes go there too. Alexander and Football. They're OK. They're my mates. Hey, they both want to be my boyfriend!'

'You're a bit young for boyfriends, aren't you, Tracy?'

'If you could see Alexander you wouldn't worry about him! And I can manage Football OK. Easy-peasy.'

'Do they go to your school?'

'Nope. Football's older – and Alexander goes to this posh all-boys place.'

'But they bunk off too?'

'Well, Football's excluded, so he can't go to school even if he wants. And Alexander's going to go back to his school now because he's decided he needs to do well in his exams.'

'Good for Alexander! So what are you going to do, Tracy? Get yourself excluded from school altogether or go back and try hard?'

'It's not like I've got a real choice. Alexander's an old brainy box, top of everything.'

'You've got a brainbox inside here too, you know,' said Cam, gently tapping me on the top of my head with her fist.

'Oh *sure* – and Mrs Vomit Bagley's going to make me her little teacher's pet and all the kids will want me to be their best friend?' I said sarcastically.

'You won't be in Mrs Bagley's class for ever. And it sounds as if you've got the knack of making friends now. But if you really hate this school we'll try again to get you in somewhere else. Liz says she might be able to get you into her school.'

'I bet she wouldn't half boss me about if she was my teacher.'

'You *need* bossing about. You're the naughtiest kid I know.'

'But you still want me back?'

'You know I do.'

'Even after all the stuff I said?'

'I said stuff too. But that's OK. People who love each other are allowed to have quarrels.'

'Love?' I said, my heart going thump thump thump.

'I love you,' said Cam.

My heart shone scarlet like a Valentine. 'No-one's ever loved me before.'

'Your mum loves you too,' said Cam. 'Maybe she's changed her mind about having you back on a permanent basis, but I'm sure she'll want to keep in touch.'

'Or maybe she'll wait another five years,' I said. 'We'll see. I don't care. I'll be OK with you, Cam. If that's what you really want.'

'Is it what you want, Tracy?'

'You know it is.'

I looked all round me. We were still in the hall. I looked down at the dingy bare floorboards and up at the grubby ceiling and around at the tattered posters on the walls. 'Though we could get this old dump smartened up a bit,' I said. 'Seeing as it's my home too. We could get a proper carpet for a start.'

'Maybe a rug,' said Cam. 'We could make one together, you and me.'

'And paint the walls something bright. Red!'

'Something subtle. Claret? Burgundy? Let's have a drink to celebrate your homecoming. Red wine for me, Coke for you, right?' Cam put her arm round my shoulders and we walked towards the kitchen.

'We could have new posters. You could choose. *Bright* ones,' Cam offered, resticking a tattered corner to the wall with a blutack blob.

I concentrated on the picture. There was a great big beach with a piano stuck on the sand with a little girl sitting on top, and a woman in a long dress and bonnet by her side.

'Why have they got a piano on the sand?'

'It's from a film. My favourite. About this mother and daughter. I've got it on video. Do you want to watch it?'

So we watch it together.

And the next day we got to watch *my* favourite film together.

There's no place like home. Well, most of the time. Cam and I still have mega-arguments sometimes. Lots of times.

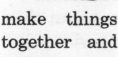

But then we make up.

We have great times together. Cam cooks me special treats.

Sometimes I cook her special treats too.

We work together and go out together and

make things together and

muck about together and chat together.

241

Of course we can't do everything together. I have to go to school, worse luck, worse luck, worse luck. I *might* be able to switch to Liz's school at the end of this term but till then I'm stuck with Mrs Vomit Bagley and Roxanne and all her putrid pals and even though this is a Happy Ever After ending Mrs V.B. is still the Wicked Witch and Roxanne is that weirdo princess that spews up toads and frogs every time she talks.

Mr Hatherway is all right though.

I've made a new friend at school too. He's called Trevor and he's the smallest boy in Year Three and everyone picks on him. (He's the one who had the nosebleed, remember?) Mr Hatherway asked if I'd keep an eye on him in the playground. So I do. Nobody dares go near little Trev when *I'm* around.

I think Trevor likes me, though he doesn't say much.

I know Alexander likes me – and he says lots and lots. I've been to his house again. I ate all my tea this time, and had a second and then a third helping of cake. Alexander's been to my house too. Alexander had a great time. He and Cam had this long long long discussion about books.

Alexander likes Cam a lot. But he likes me more.

I think Football likes me the most though. I don't go round to his house much but he comes round to my house lots. We play football, surprise surprise. Out in the yard. Sometimes Cam plays too. And Jane and Liz. You'll never guess what. Jane is brilliant at football, even though she's so big. She's better than Alexander's dad. Even better than Football himself. Though he won't admit it. He's working on his game. Alexander's dad has got him into this club. I'm not sure how long this will last. Football hasn't got the knack of getting on with people. He's had a few arguments already. He might find he gets excluded. But I'm never going to exclude him. He can stay my friend no matter what.

I think he still sometimes hangs out at the empty house. Alexander doesn't go there any more. I don't either. Though I took Cam there once.

I made out it was *my* home and I showed her all round. Most of Alexander's cardboard furniture got broken up and so the house looked a bit sad and empty and dirty.

'But I could make it look really great,' I said, taking Cam by the hand and leading her around the living room. 'Maybe I could live in this house when I'm grown up, right? I'll have a chandelier and a ruby-red carpet and a big squashy sofa and a telly as big as the wall. I'll stay up half the night watching telly and then sleep really late and then I'll do a bit of work. I'll write these best-selling books, OK? And then I'll stop writing around five and have tea. I'll have a big birthday cake every single day.'

'You'll get pretty tubby then,' said Cam, poking me in the tummy.

'I won't eat it all by myself. I'll share it. I'll invite Alexander round. He can pop in between his brain surgery operations. And I want Football to come too, though he'd better not eat too much birthday cake if he's in

244

serious training. And guess who else I'll invite?' I paused.

'Mrs Vomit Bagley?' said Cam.

'*No* chance!'

'Elaine?'

'Maybe. Once in a while, for old time's sake. No, someone else. Someone important.'

'Your mum?'

'If she'd come. I wouldn't bank on it though. Come on, Cam, *guess*!'

'I haven't a clue,' said Cam, but she was looking hopeful.

'YOU!' I said, and we had a big hug.

TOTALLY JACQUELINE WILSON

The essential Jacqueline Wilson experience!

This lavish, colourful Jacqueline Wilson extravaganza is an ideal gift for any Jacqueline Wilson fan. There are four brilliant new Jacqueline Wilson stories, with brand new pictures from Nick Sharratt. And that's not all!

You can also test your knowledge with the themed quizzes and get some top recommendations from Jacqueline's favourite books, art and films.

Find out how to make Jacqueline's favourite cake, how to have a Jacqueline-themed party, how to dress like her or decorate your room like one of her characters!

There's even a fantastic piece on What Happened Next in her stories, with suggested endings from fan club competition winners and Jacqueline's own thoughts about what happened after the last page was turned.

Dive in to find out more about Jacqueline's world!

Everybody knows Tracy Beaker, Jacqueline Wilson's best-loved character. But what do they know about Jacqueline herself? In this fascinating book, discover . . .

. . . how Jacky played with paper dolls like April in *Dustbin Baby*

. . . how she dealt with an unpredictable father like Prue in *Love Lessons*

. . . how she chose new toys in Hamleys like Dolphin in *The Illustrated Mum*

. . . how she enjoyed Christmas like Em in *Clean Break*

. . . how she sat entrance exams like Ruby in *Double Act*

But most of all how Jacky loved reading and writing stories. Losing herself in a new world was the best possible she could spend time. From the very first story she wrote, *Meet the Maggots*, it was clear that this little girl had a very vivid imagination. But who would've guessed she would grow up to be the mega-bestselling, award-winning Jacqueline Wilson!

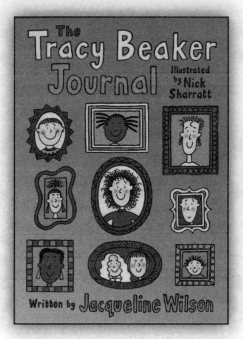

 THE TRACY BEAKER JOURNAL

Welcome to Tracy Beaker's top secret, totally cool, completely brilliant journal!

I'm Tracy Beaker. Mark the name, I'll be famous one day. Although this journal is all about ME, I've generously allowed you some space to write down your own thoughts, ideas and dreams. There are quizzes, games and loads of extra info about me – and pages for you to fill in about your family, friends, likes, dislikes and loads more!

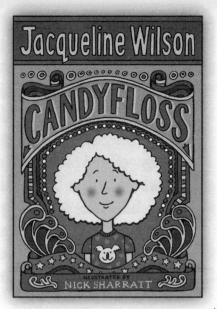

 CANDYFLOSS

Floss loves spending weekends with her dad in his greasy spoon café, even if it isn't the smartest place in town and only has three regular customers. Even Floss's best friend Rhiannon turns her nose up at it. When Floss's mum and her new husband Steve move to Australia, Floss faces a difficult choice – but decides to stay at home with Dad. He's not much good at ironing school clothes or putting up garden swings, but they muddle along happily on a diet of chip butties and candyfloss from the local funfair. But then disaster strikes and they find themselves homeless. Will their new fairground friends help out? Could Dad and Floss be destined for a life on the road?

A wonderfully moving and brilliantly entertaining story of family life from Jacqueline Wilson.

★ COOKIE ★

A wonderful new tale of family life,
friendship and cookies.

Beauty Cookson is really not very beautiful. She's plain and timid, and all the girls at school are super-confident and snooty. They think her name is ridiculous and have come up with a new one for her: Ugly!

Worse than the teasing in the playground, though, is the hurtful criticism from her father. Beauty and her mum live in fear of Dad's rages – sparked off when they break one of his fussy house rules, suggest something 'silly' like getting a pet, or if Beauty refuses to wear an outfit he's bought her. But Beauty's mum adores her and finds ways to keep Beauty happy despite all the shouting. Together they discover a new hobby – baking cookies – and a much better nickname is born.

After Beauty's disastrous birthday party, Dad's temper seems to be out of control. Can Mum and Beauty bear it any longer? Or can they find a way to start a sweet new life?

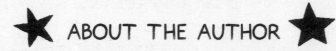

ABOUT THE AUTHOR

JACQUELINE WILSON is one of Britain's most outstanding writers for young readers. She is the most borrowed author from British libraries and has sold over 20 million books in this country. As a child, she always wanted to be a writer and wrote her first 'novel' when she was nine, filling countless exercise books as she grew up. She started work at a publishing company and then went on to work as a journalist on *Jackie* magazine (which was named after her) before turning to writing fiction full-time.

Jacqueline has been honoured with many of the UK's top awards for children's books, including the Guardian Children's Fiction Award, the Smarties Prize and the Children's Book of the Year. She was the Children's Laureate for 2005-2007, was awarded an OBE in 2002 and made a Dame in 2008.